D1530270

A SKY PAINTED GOLD

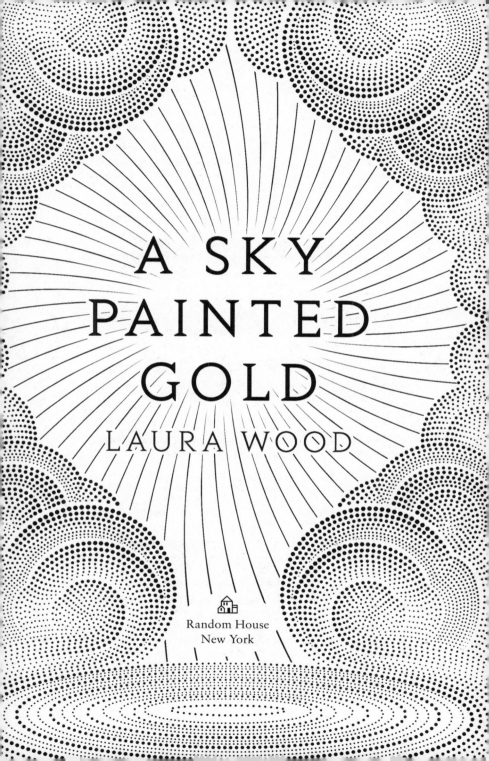

A SKY
PAINTED
GOLD

LAURA WOOD

Random House
New York

This is a work of fiction. Names, characters, places, and incidents either are the product of the author's imagination or are used fictitiously. Any resemblance to actual persons, living or dead, events, or locales is entirely coincidental.

Text copyright © 2018 by Laura Wood
Jacket art copyright © 2018 by Yehrin Tong

All rights reserved. Published in the United States by Random House Children's Books, a division of Penguin Random House LLC, New York. Originally published in paperback by Scholastic Ltd, London, in 2018.

Random House and the colophon are registered trademarks of Penguin Random House LLC.

Visit us on the Web! GetUnderlined.com

Educators and librarians, for a variety of teaching tools, visit us at
RHTeachersLibrarians.com

Library of Congress Cataloging-in-Publication Data
Name: Wood, Laura (Laura Clare), author.
Title: A sky painted gold / Laura Wood.
Description: First edition. | New York : Random House Children's Books, [2020] |
Originally published: London : Scholastic Ltd., 2018. | Audience: Ages 12 and up. |
Summary: In 1929 in a sleepy Cornish village, aspiring writer Lou Trevelyan,
age seventeen, is introduced to the glamour and secrets of high society
by summer neighbors Caitlin and Robert Cardew.
Identifiers: LCCN 2019032808 (print) | LCCN 2019032809 (ebook) |
ISBN 978-0-593-12722-3 (hardcover) | ISBN 978-0-593-12723-0 (library binding) |
ISBN 978-0-593-12724-7 (ebook)
Subjects: CYAC: Coming of age—Fiction. | Family life—England—Cornwall (County)—
Fiction. | Wealth—Fiction. | Brothers and sisters—Fiction. | Cornwall (England : County)—
History—20th century—Fiction. | Great Britain—History—George V, 1910–1936—Fiction.
Classification: LCC PZ7.1.W652 Sky 2020 (print) | LCC PZ7.1.W652 (ebook) |
DDC [Fic]—dc23

The text of this book is set in 11.5-point Sabon MT Pro.

Printed in the United States of America
10 9 8 7 6 5 4 3 2 1
First American Edition 2020

Random House Children's Books supports the First Amendment
and celebrates the right to read.

Penguin Random House LLC supports copyright. Copyright fuels creativity, encourages diverse voices, promotes free speech, and creates a vibrant culture. Thank you for buying an authorized edition of this book and for complying with copyright laws by not reproducing, scanning, or distributing any part in any form without permission. You are supporting writers and allowing Penguin Random House to publish books for every reader.

FOR MY BRILLIANT MUM,
who taught me that the clotted cream
always goes on top of the jam

PROLOGUE

It all started with an apple. Trouble often does, I suppose, and this particular apple was a real troublemaker—a Pendragon, red-fleshed and sweet, that I stole from someone else's orchard.

I don't know why I chose that particular day to make my way over to the island. After years of staring longingly across the water, it seemed suddenly urgent that I make it there, that I put my feet on the shore. When I arrived I practically fell into the orchard, plucking the shining red apple from its branch without a second thought. With the first bite of that apple I was lost.

By then the Cardew House in all its sprawling, faded beauty had not seen a single friendly face (or an unfriendly one, for that matter) in over five years. The walled orchard, like the house, had been abandoned, growing tangled and wild until I crept in and started helping myself. After that first taste I didn't even try to stay away. I came back the next day, and the next, always exploring a tiny bit further, pushing deeper into the secret island, making each part of it my own.

The house itself was on top of the island, a grand old Georgian building with far-reaching views. The front, facing toward the village on the mainland, was long and low with tall windows cut into the honey-colored stone and tangled ivy. Rough steps reached down through overgrown gardens to a sloping gravel driveway that stretched to meet the causeway. At the back, a huge lawn overlooked the changeable sea—at times a dazzling turquoise, at others a murky, mysterious gray-green. The orchard that first drew me to the island curled around one side of the house, groaning with apples, or ruby-skinned cherries, or heavy, velvet plums depending on the time of year. On the other side of the building, more crumbling steps wound their way down to a small hidden cove of golden sand where the sheltered waters were still and warm. It was a jewel, this island, a treasure left alone and unloved for too long.

A restless feeling hung over my visits, and I knew that it was only a matter of time before my curiosity moved beyond the grounds to the building itself. I began by skirting around the house, as though afraid of antagonizing it. When I discovered a broken window latch on the ground floor, it felt as though the decision had been made for me.

The old building should have been unwelcoming in its emptiness, with the furniture draped in sheets and the shutters closed up tight, but to me it felt calm and friendly. Odd shafts of light cut through the gloom here and there, illuminating clouds of dancing dust particles and giving the place an air of drowsy sadness. It seemed like the sleeping princess in a fairy tale just waiting to be brought back to life.

For almost a year after that first apple I escaped to the house at any opportunity—to raid the neglected library and to curl up comfortably on a faded oriental rug, enjoying the quiet. My own home was never quiet, but all that noise didn't stop me from feeling lonely at times. Somehow, despite being more alone than ever, I never felt lonely when I came here. Slowly, I began to feel that the sleeping house and I were getting to know one another. I daydreamed about what it would be like if it was full of people—about the conversations they would have, about the parties they might throw and the way the rooms would come to life, full of blazing light. I wrote pages of nonsense, scribbling furiously in my notebook, or I read detective novels and ate stolen apples, throwing the cores into the fire that I lit to warm the huge, empty sitting room.

In the end it was that fire that gave me away.

It was a cold, wet Friday when I first saw them.

Gray sheets of rain pounded outside while waves hammered against the rocks to the back of the house. I was oblivious to the noise, quite happily lost in an Agatha Christie novel, making myself sick on too much fruit. I had been there for a couple of hours, maybe more, when I heard a sound: something new, something more than the usual groans of the old house settling. I froze, the book dangling from my fingers, and strained my ears, listening carefully.

Voices.

Someone was here.

Someone had finally come.

And more than one someone: I heard the low rumble of a man's voice and the higher melody of a woman as well. Already I could tell that these voices belonged, that they fit into the house like missing puzzle pieces. Footsteps clipped along the floors, echoing through the empty hallways, growing louder as they came closer and closer to where I sat, still frozen.

My heart thundered, as though someone had broken in—although the only intruder here was me. I dropped the book and slipped over to the window as quickly and as quietly as I could, though my legs trembled at this abrupt breaking open of a space I had come to consider completely my own. I threw one shaking leg over the sill, and my bare foot burrowed into the long, wet grass below. There, half in and half out of the house, I realized that the voices were almost on top of me. I scrambled out of the window and stood safely on the other side, holding my breath and pressing myself flat against the wall. Then I heard the door to the sitting room open and the footsteps stopped.

"Robert! Who on earth has lit the fire?" The girl's voice was clear and precise, ringing through the air like a knife against a glass. "I didn't think we were expected?"

I didn't wait to hear any more. As fast as my legs would carry me I darted around the side of the house and down the crumbling steps, across the crunching gravel drive that led to the causeway. Luckily, the tide was out and, as I sped past it, I saw that the strangers had arrived in a dazzling blue car. With a glance over my shoulder and a small whoop of exhilaration at finding no one chasing after me, I plunged along the cobbled path, running until my chest ached, filling my lungs with jagged gulps of salty air.

I was laughing now, the runaway laugh of the thief who knew that she was getting away with it. I dared myself to turn around, to look back at the house.

A silhouette appeared in the front doorway—a man, tall and silent and too late to catch me. The wind whipped my hair around my face, stinging my flushed cheeks, and the rain had finally stopped.

I looked down, and I was still holding a shining red apple in my hand.

PART ONE

"And so with the sunshine and
the great bursts of leaves growing
on the trees, just as things grow
in fast movies, I had that familiar
conviction that life was beginning
over again with the summer."

—F. Scott Fitzgerald, *The Great Gatsby*

CHAPTER ONE

JUNE 1929

The morning of Alice's wedding dawns bright and clear. It is, naturally, the perfect summer morning: nothing but birdsong and pastel-blue skies and the whisper of a breeze rolling in from the sea. Anything less would be completely unacceptable for Alice's big day. When I wake, Alice is already up, her bed rumpled and empty. Aside from the imprint of her head on the pillow, there is no other sign of her. Pulling on a pair of shorts and one of Pa's old shirts, I slip my feet into my battered old shoes and make a beeline for the kitchen. It is early, but delicious smells are drifting up the stairs to meet me.

"Lou! Lou!" I am greeted by a trio of rowdy little boys in overalls, barefoot, with mouths full of bread and butter. The triplets are three years old, and until the recent birth of

Anthea (usually known simply as "the baby"), they were the youngest members of my ramshackle family. I am the second oldest, after Alice, who is nineteen, then after me comes Freya, who is fifteen, Tom, who is eleven, then the triplets and Anthea. Eight children in all, and Pa says that who knows but there might have been more if it hadn't been for the war, and we should thank God for small mercies. I'm fairly sure he's only joking, but he does sometimes look surprised by the number of children that tumble in and out of our small farmhouse, as if we are the result of an absurd magic trick rather than his own flesh and blood.

In the kitchen, the triplets, Joe, Max and Davy, are finishing their breakfast at the long table while Midge bustles about preparing the wedding feast that the village will enjoy later, the baby squawking cheerfully on her hip. Midge has a smudge of flour on the end of her nose, and a look of determined concentration in her eyes as she wrestles, one-handed, with enormous pats of golden butter and the collection of old tea tins that contain sugar and spices. I know better than to ask if she needs help.

"Where's Alice?" I ask over the noise instead, helping myself to a piece of bread and smearing it with Midge's famous ginger jam.

"Skipped out of the house an hour ago on the hunt for flowers," Midge says, in her gruff little voice. Midge is my mother, and even though her real name is Mary, everyone calls her Midge, including her husband and her children. At a dab over five foot tall, she is a reassuring, if tiny, force of nature. When I stand beside her I feel gangly and oversized. While she answers my question, Midge is stirring something together in a bowl with a burnished silver knife.

Midge always uses this knife to bake, and once, when our aunt Irene witnessed this, her face took on an expression of horror and she cried, "Ah, Midge! But you're never supposed to stir with a knife . . . stirring with a knife, that's stirring up trouble!"

Midge looked wholly unconcerned, replying placidly, "Well, then, I've been stirring up trouble so long it's hardly worth worrying about now, is it?" before carrying on just as before.

I don't know if it is because of the knife or not, but no one can cook like Midge; she's famous for it. Pa says he proposed to Midge over her Stargazy pie, which sounds quite romantic, I suppose, if you don't know that Stargazy pie is made with sardines whose heads stick through the pastry and stare up at you with mournful eyes. I don't think I would like a mournful sardine to be in attendance at *my* engagement, but then I am, as yet, fairly inexperienced in the art of romance. Apart from in books, of course. You can learn an *awful* lot from books . . . but it has always seemed highly unlikely that I'd stumble across any of the dashing heroes I read about on the streets of Penlyn, so what do I know? Perhaps with the right man a sardine pie can be sheer poetry. Midge certainly seems to think so, and she laughs a pleased, pink laugh whenever Pa tells the story.

I cut myself another piece of bread and munch on the

crust. A wail from the triplets alerts me to their own breadless state, and I prepare slices for each of them, although they're more interested in the bread as a jam delivery system than anything else. With three sticky faces enjoying their second breakfast of the day, a hush falls over the kitchen. In this moment of relative calm my thoughts turn—as they often seem to these days—to what is going on at the Cardew House.

For as long as I can remember that place has held me firmly under its spell. The island it stands on is separated from the mainland by a cobbled causeway. The road vanishes and rematerializes as the tide rushes in and out, submerging it entirely as if it were never there at all, or leaving it exposed and shockingly solid. There is something magical about this process, I think, the disappearance and reappearance of the ancient road—it comes and goes with the tide, but each time it emerges from the water it feels like a surprise. Its peculiar magic means that half of the time the house is cut off, a world of its own, remote and separate from the bustling life of our tiny fishing village.

When I had returned home, bedraggled and elated from my near-escape several months earlier, it was to the news that the owner of the Cardew House, Robert Cardew, was planning to holiday there for the whole summer, and so had come to look the place over for repairs.

Even in deepest, darkest rural Cornwall, we've heard all about Robert Cardew. Perhaps it is his connection to the village that sends whispers of his wild lifestyle and his fashionable friends snaking furiously from door to door through the winding lanes of Penlyn, but I think that even if it wasn't for the Cardew House, Alice and I would still be fascinated by the exploits of this man and his glittering band of bright young things. We devour the society pages, giddy on the glimpse they give us into a world so different from our own. It seems outrageous that a boy of twenty-three—not so much older than us—should have so much, that his life could be so completely unlike ours. When Lord Cardew died a couple of years ago the village was agog to see if the young heir would turn up, but there was no sign of him, no hint that he even remembered the old house lying empty and unloved. Until now. I lick the jam from my fingers thoughtfully. We have seen the photographs of him, of course, of the outlandish clothes, the outrageous parties, and we know that Robert will bring his fiancée, the *deeply* glamorous American heiress Laurie Miller, along with a menagerie of other exotic creatures, when he comes to stay.

According to the papers the couple have been engaged for about six months now. They've been positively splashed about on the pages. They've attended every party, every fashionable event, and they've looked *spectacular* while doing it. Alice and I have followed their romance closely. To us, they are paper dolls, characters in a story, and each week we eagerly await the next installment.

And soon, I remind myself with a delicious thrill, the subject of all this juicy gossip will be right here in Penlyn. It's hard to imagine a less likely place for such birds of paradise to roost. Our village is a world away from the bustling metropolis of nightclubs and dazzling parties that Robert Cardew usually inhabits.

But they *are* coming. Builders and decorators have been in and out of the house with increasing frequency over the last couple of weeks. Unfortunately, they all seem to be coming down from London, so no one in the village knows a thing about what is going on inside. This has been the subject of much ire because local workmen feel snubbed, and there has been some dark muttering that the "young people" who own the house now aren't behaving properly by bringing in outsiders. We're all also very nosy and, truthfully, the whole village is fizzing like so many overeager bottles of ginger beer to know what the place looks like and exactly when the new arrivals are due. Of course I haven't been able to visit the house again, not since my escape on that rainy afternoon. I did try once, but already the place was teeming with people and I was lucky to get away unseen.

My thoughts are interrupted by the triplets, who are being rackety, and the baby, whose squawks appear to be building up to a wail. Chaos seems inevitable, but this is the moment that Alice drifts in looking like an actual Greek goddess, and everything stops as she enters the room.

A halo of blue cornflowers crowns her golden head and her arms are full of trailing honeysuckle and delicate pink roses. "Give me a hand, Lou!" she huffs, rather spoiling the picture she's created by unceremoniously dumping the fragrant bundle into my arms and pinching the bread from between my fingers in one swift move.

"Where did you get all these roses?" I ask, admiring the fat, perfect blooms as I lay them gently on the kitchen table.

"From Mrs. Penrith's garden," Alice mumbles through a mouthful of bread and jam, and a dimple appears in her left cheek.

I raise my eyebrows.

"Alice Trevelyan." Midge stops her stirring and waves the knife rather menacingly in Alice's direction. "Tell me that you didn't steal those flowers from Susan Penrith's rose garden! You know she's so particular about them."

"I didn't *steal* them," says Alice, and she sounds as if she's offended by the very idea, even though it wouldn't exactly be out of character. "I *asked* for them, perfectly nicely, and Mrs. Penrith *gave* them to me." She pops the last mouthful of bread into her mouth and chews slowly. "It is my wedding day, after all," she finishes, and the expression on her face is one Midge would describe as "butter wouldn't melt."

It should really come as no surprise that Mrs. Penrith parted with her prizewinning roses at Alice's request. It's difficult to refuse my sister anything when she decides to be charming. One reason for this is that Alice is a beauty, plain and simple. People sometimes say we look a little alike when they're trying to be kind, but where Alice's hair shines smooth and golden blond, mine is curly and more of a muddy brown with just a touch of red. (Though sadly not enough to be described as auburn, let alone the longed-for and deeply romantic "titian.") Alice's eyes are as blue as the cornflowers she is wearing on her head, and mine are a murky, troubled gray. Alice's skin maintains a peaches-and-cream complexion no matter how much time she spends outdoors, while mine tans unfashionably and freckles scatter themselves across my nose with great abandon, despite my liberal and frequent application of lemon juice. We are the same height and we share similar features, but there is no question that I am my sister's shadow—a distorted, much less brilliant reflection of her perfect beauty. Alice through the looking glass.

And now, today, Alice, *my* Alice, is getting married! The thought rattles through me once more, as shocking as ever. She, on the other hand, seems unfazed. I watch her gathering flowers together and tying them with string, her movements deft and certain, and I think about the ways her life is about to change—the way all of our lives are about to change. No more Alice in the house. No one to chatter with while seeing to the chores, no older sister in the bed next to mine to whisper secrets to. The thought is strange and unnerving. Alice is humming, and she looks up and catches my eye. "Don't mope, Lou," she says with a laugh. "It's a wedding, not a funeral." She winds an arm around my waist and squeezes gently. And of course she's right, plus Alice is only moving a few minutes away, into the tiny cottage that Jack found for them in the middle of the village. Still, it feels as though it may as well be on the moon. It isn't the physical distance that I can't wrap my mind around, it is that Alice will be leaving us—me—behind, and becoming someone else. A grown-up. A wife.

And—I hardly want to think of it—if Alice leaves, becomes someone else, then I suppose I have to as well. Everything will change. I touch my finger to one of the creamy rose petals, and the morning dew is still clinging to it, quivering like a tear about to fall. I sigh deeply, wallowing quite happily in the beautiful melancholy of it all and thinking that it would make a pretty line in a story.

Alice snorts with knowing laughter. "Lou's writing melodramas again." She rolls her eyes, and I can't help laughing back, caught in the act.

"I was thinking about the wedding in *Lady Amelia's Revenge,*" I offer, "and the way I can foreshadow the death of . . ."

Alice clamps her hands over her ears. "Don't tell me!" she shrieks, and then her hands drop to her sides and her eyes widen. "It's Rudolpho, isn't it?" she asks in tragic accents. "You can't kill him, Lou, you *can't.*"

I keep my face as bland as possible, and mime locking my lips shut and throwing away the key. *Lady Amelia's Revenge* is a story that I've been working on for months, and Alice demands new pages all the time. Usually, I'm more than happy to provide them, but I lost one of my notebooks recently so things have been a bit slower, and Alice's questions and guesses about what's to come have become increasingly frantic. She's quite invested in the grisly adventures of my feisty heroine, and I have to admit that I love it. Although I suppose Alice won't have much time for silly stories when she's a married lady.

We are interrupted by Midge, who seems, as always, to

be wholly unmoved by the crashing waves of my emotional turmoil. "Well, you two had better go and get ready," she says. "Take these boys out from under my feet, and try and mop them up a bit, will you? I've got a million and one things left to do here, and your father's still not back from seeing to the top field."

The triplets groan and weep and protest as though they are deathly allergic to clean water and cotton face flannels, while Alice and I herd them up the higgledy-piggledy stairs. Finally, after a tense and rather soggy standoff, we send them off with a stern warning to stay away from anything sticky, and Alice and I make our way up another flight of stairs to our room.

CHAPTER TWO

The room I share with Alice is right at the top of the house, tucked away in the eaves. The ceiling slopes at both sides so that you can only really stand up properly in the middle, in the space between our two beds. On my side of the room is a small window, and if I kneel on the bed, stick my head through it and turn my neck slightly to the left, I can just see down the hill to the sea and the curve of golden sand cut into the cliffs. Tiny white houses are dotted about here and there, balanced precariously on the steep precipice and looking as though they might, at any moment, tumble into the water below. I can't see the island from here, but I know that it is there and my awareness of it is constant, inescapable. Over the weeks my desire to run off and hide there has only increased. With Alice preparing to leave our house, questions about my own future have started creeping up on me, and I'm not ready to start thinking about them yet.

Alice flops down onto her bed, almost crushing the flowers that still sit on top of her head. "Careful!" I exclaim, removing them and setting them on her bedside table. "Don't mess up your hair. That isn't very bride-like behavior."

"What is bride-like behavior, then?" Alice asks, unfussed. She rubs her nose and stares at the ceiling, her golden hair fanned out around her on the worn bedsheets. Like most properly beautiful people, Alice worries very little about her looks.

"I don't know," I say, almost able to ignore the familiar pang of jealousy over her effortless appearance. "Shouldn't you be all pale and trembling and a bit more . . . you know . . . *swoony*?"

Alice props herself up on her elbow and grins. "You've been reading too many romance novels. I'm hardly throwing myself at the mercy of some dark, brooding stranger."

I snort at this, because she's right, the words "dark, brooding stranger" are as far from those you would use to describe Jack Treglowen as possible. He's two years older than Alice; we've known him all our lives and he's been in love with my sister for as long as any of us can remember. Sweet Jack, with his coppery curls, strong arms and frank, open face. At one time or another every girl in the village has thought herself deeply in love with him—myself included—but he's only ever had eyes for Alice. Although for the longest time she didn't really seem to notice. Alice simply accepted his quiet adoration without comment; Jack's love was just a part of the fabric of her life, something comfortable— familiar and unchanging.

Until it wasn't anymore.

It was just over two years ago, when Alice was sixteen, that I finally felt something shift between them. The way they spoke to each other was different, their voices softer and yet full of something crackling and impatient. One night Alice came home bright-eyed and changed forever. She told me that Jack had kissed her and I pressed her for every detail.

Alice had been kissed before, of course—in fact, we both had (though Alice much more regularly—I, then fifteen, had been kissed only once by a boy called Martin, the butcher's son, and it was nothing like it had looked in the films, because for one thing he smelled like sausages, and for another the whole kiss was quite sweaty and awkward), but this was different. This wasn't the inexperienced fumbling of some boy who had taken her to the pictures in the hope of a quick feel, this was *Jack,* and when she said his name now it was in breathless italics.

Alice's eyes were starry and she kept touching her fingers to her lips as if she couldn't quite believe that the feeling of his mouth on hers was real. She said it was perfect, and suddenly my sister, who had never held anything back from me, who I had never had any secrets from, seemed to know something I didn't. It didn't matter how many questions I asked, I simply *couldn't* get at this secret thing, this changed, grown-up thing that Alice had experienced. Eventually, I stopped trying. I watched her humming and brushing her hair in front of the mirror and I felt a gap open up between us.

Not long after that Jack asked Alice to marry him, and no one was surprised except for me. It just seemed so fast, so sudden, so . . . *final*. It wasn't that I wasn't happy for them: it was absolutely impossible to be in Alice's radiant presence without absorbing some of the happiness that came off her in violent waves. No, selfishly, it was a feeling that I had lost something, that somehow I had come untethered.

I had been one half of Alice-and-Lou for so long that I wasn't sure what it meant to be *and-Lou* alone. I knew I looked like Alice's shadow, but as I felt my sister pulling away from me I realized that this description was true in more ways than I had first thought. Where Alice went, I followed. That was how it had always been. Only now Alice was leaving me behind, and I was going to have to find my own way, somehow. After all, a girl without a shadow was one thing, but a shadow without a girl . . . what became of her?

I spent more time alone, I began to write more, and then—of course—I found the Cardew House, a house full of shadows, and I knew, with a huge sense of relief, that I belonged there. It was no small thing, that sense of belonging, and I clung to it. It was almost a year since I had finished school and I felt as if I was treading water. Apart from my jobs on the farm I had nothing to do, no purpose that I could see. It had never been like that for Alice. Alice and Jack were already engaged when she was my age, and her future was laid out before her like a perfect, clear road map. When *I* looked ahead, all I saw was a terrible blank. The thing that made it worse was that no one else seemed worried. As far as I could see I was the only one who thought a giant question mark hung over my future, and although they didn't say it I felt the weight of expectation—not just from Midge and Pa, but from the whole village—that sooner or later I would follow Alice's nice neat road map as well. After all, what else was out there for me? The thought of leaving, of somehow making my own path, seemed a daunting impossibility. I was the follower, not the leader, and I truly had no idea where to go next. The Cardew House—even in its dilapidated state— felt like an answer. It wasn't really the grandeur of it that tugged at me, but the restless feeling of it, the feeling that was a bit like magic . . . the feeling that *something* exciting was bound to happen, that the shadows would come to life somehow. It was *different,* and different was precisely what I wanted.

I give my head a shake. It's silly to dwell on these feelings on such a happy day. Midge would laugh and scold me for being too dramatic, *as usual,* although I think that Freya is well on her way to usurping me as the family drama queen.

"Come on, then, Mrs. Treglowen," I say, pulling myself firmly back to this moment, to this day. "Let's get you ready."

Alice sits up at that, her mouth pulled down, her face a comical mask of disbelief. "Mrs. Treglowen," she murmurs. "Doesn't it sound . . ."

"Strange?" I ask.

"I was going to say grown-up," she replies, "but strange is right too." She lifts her chin, and her voice rings through the small room. "Mrs. Treglowen." She says it again, shaking her head. "I can't believe it's really happening!" and then the dimple peeps out and Alice is laughing and she reaches out and pulls me onto the bed with her. We lie there side by side, cackling at the joyful absurdity of it all. My heart lifts. Perhaps, after all, things won't be so different. It is hard to imagine my sister as anyone other than the giggling golden girl lying beside me.

"Are you two getting a move on?" Midge's voice drifts up the stairs. "We've got to be at the church in an hour!"

"Yes, Midge!" we sing out together, as we have a million times before, and again I am struck by the feeling that some things will never change. Then, in a haze of breathless excitement, we begin the process of getting ready.

Alice's wedding dress is a beauty. It is a delicate sheath of very, very pale yellow georgette with long sleeves and a scalloped hem that falls just below the knee. (This has been a hard-fought battle, but Alice's fashionable hemline was eventually approved by Midge and Aunt Cath after we showered them with pictures and patterns clipped from countless magazines. These, we felt, demonstrated that there is nothing risqué anymore in showing off your calves, because, after all, it *is* 1929.) A matching real lace sash is tied loosely around the dropped waist, and a dainty trail of flowers has been embroidered around the square neckline in ivory thread.

Midge and Aunt Cath have been hard at work on the

dress for months, and Alice and I—both obsessed with fashion magazines but completely hopeless at sewing—have been on hand to critique and offer plenty of impractical suggestions. These have been met, for the most part, with surprising patience from Midge and our aunt. There have been only two minor arguments and one major one in which scissors were brandished menacingly, but everything came out all right in the end, and you can hardly see where Alice kicked the kitchen table, so all in all I have marked the dressmaking process down as a very successful undertaking.

With a slightly shaky hand I lay the crown of cornflowers back on top of Alice's head, and pick up the long lace veil that is draped over the back of a chair. The veil was Midge's, and her mother's before her, and the froth of ivory lace feels as light as air in my hands. I know that the veil is meant for me one day, although I find such a day difficult to imagine.

"Oh, Alice," I whisper, and I can feel tears rushing to my eyes. "You look . . . absolutely *hideous*," I say. "Really, truly awful," I sniffle.

Alice dimples appreciatively, and drapes the veil over one arm, tilting her head to the side like an inquisitive bird as she gives herself a good stare in the mirror. "Do you think Jack will like it?" she asks in a voice that lacks her usual confidence. I think that even she is intimidated by the perfect image reflected back at her.

"I think he'll fall in a dead faint when he sees you coming down the aisle," I say with perfect honesty. "He won't believe his luck."

"Alice! Alice!" Voices are calling now from downstairs and, after giving me a gentle hug, being careful not to squash any of her finery, Alice begins to make her stately way down to show herself off, leaving me to change quickly into my bridesmaid's outfit.

I feel a shiver of excitement as my fingers stroke the dusty-pink chiffon. It is my first real, grown-up dress made just for me. It's a simple design, with soft pleats in the skirt and a V-shaped neckline (although nothing too scandalously plunging, more's the pity). Midge has made me a long, narrow scarf in the same material that I knot carefully around my neck, the ends trailing at the front. I pin my unruly curls up as neatly as possible and slip my feet into the little shoes that we have dyed pink to match the dress. I look in the mirror and see none of Alice's splendor. Despite my attempts at neatening up, I still look ruffled, unpolished. I try again to smooth my hair, but the curls spring out at disobedient angles.

"Lou." Pa's gentle voice reaches my ears, and I turn and scamper downstairs to meet him on the landing. He looks smart in his suit, with his father's old watch hanging from a well-polished chain in his pocket—a far cry from his usual overalls. Pa returns my look of admiration and I can't help but feel pleased. "Very nice," he says as I do a little twirl, trying not to trip over my own heels.

"Not exactly a fashion plate," I say ruefully.

"You'll do," Pa replies.

People always say that Pa is a man of few words, but the

funny thing is that they couldn't be more wrong. I inherited my own love of language from him. He may not be a big talker, but my father loves words. He reads anything he can lay his hands on and he saves up words that he knows I will like, words like "incarnadine" and "mellifluous," leaving them for me around the house, written on scraps of paper in his slightly shaky handwriting. He still keeps the first short story I ever wrote for him in a box with all his treasures. It is about a cat who learns how to sing.

Pa is a writer too. He writes poetry in small blue notebooks that he buys in bulk and he shares his writing with no one anymore—not even me. I have dim memories of him making up funny poems for me when I was three or four, poems about zoo animals, and about me and my sisters, that would make us howl with laughter. I even have faded, fragile copies of a couple that Pa sent to us just after he left to fight . . . but by the time the war had ended, so had the poems. Pa came back the same but different, a bit faded and fragile, just like the letters—quieter, and somehow further away.

"Midge is waiting," he says now. "Don't want to be late. You're to walk down with the others, and Alice and I will be behind." I briefly press him into a hug, surprised as always by how thin he feels, shocked that someone so strong can feel so breakable. Midge is constantly trying to feed him up, but no matter how many generously buttered scones he puts away, Pa remains spare and angular. "All elbows and knees," Midge says.

Midge stands outside now, tapping her foot and trying to

restrain the triplets from flinging themselves onto the ground and tussling like puppies. She looks pretty in a lilac suit that she made for our cousin Arla's wedding last year. Freya, as usual, looks a million miles away, staring shortsightedly into the distance, oblivious to the racket issuing from our noisy brothers. She is squeezed into a floral dress that is too tight for her, one of Alice's castoffs, I think, and her pale blond hair has been braided and pinned into a crown. Tom scuffs his shoes, looking uncomfortable and running a finger around his shirt collar as though it is trying to strangle him. He is leaning on the handlebar of the oversized pram in which the baby seems, thankfully, to be asleep.

"Here she is!" Midge exclaims. Her face softens. "And looking pretty as a picture too." I bask in her admiration for a moment, but Midge's appreciation is swiftly put to one side. "Now, we've got to take the flowers over, but the lads will be coming back later for the food," she says, and once again I find my arms full of delicious-smelling blooms as we begin to make our way along the path toward the village. The church bells are already ringing in the distance, filling the air with their joyful peals, and I turn my face toward the sky, feeling the sun spreading in golden waves across my skin.

"Alice looks like something in a story." Freya's voice is muffled as it drifts toward me from behind the bundle of honeysuckle she is carrying.

"Alice always looks like something from a story," I say.

There is a silence then as Freya thinks this over. "Yes," she replies. "But today she looks like something else too." Her eyes take on a misty, faraway quality and her lips are pursed as she weighs the words she wants to use. "She looks exactly like a bride," she says finally.

I suppose it's not the most profound statement to make about someone on their wedding day, but I know just what Freya means, and she's absolutely right. Alice looks more like a bride than any bride has ever looked before.

Tom, who is slightly ahead of us, pushing the rattling pram with much vim and vigor, gives a whoop then as he spots several of his friends running up from the church to meet us. There is no more time for reflection as we descend into the village and are bundled into the pretty church with roses around the door. Here we are caught up, shaking hands and sharing hugs with people and distributing the flowers that Alice has collected, although our neighbors have arrived before us and the place is already positively bursting with blooms.

Jack is there in a dark gray three-piece suit, looking lean and handsome. He doesn't look nervous at all, and a smile splits his face as he wraps me in his long arms. I take a deep sniff of his lovely clean smell and allow myself one last pretend that I really am in love with him and that my heart is breaking as I have to watch him marry my very own sister.

(If you live in a sleepy little village, I have found that you have to be adept at creating your own drama, and I had a good run on the unrequited love scenario, developing a short-lived but hulking great crush on Jack when I was around fourteen. After Alice and Jack announced their engagement, this crush was briefly reignited and I drifted sadly about the house for a couple of days, draping myself in black scarves and sighing forlornly, while writing searingly tragic love poems about doomed lovers and beautiful but lonely young spinsters—but I kept forgetting all about Jack in my efforts to keep my face interestingly pale with Alice's face powder, so ultimately I gave up the enterprise. Alice, very politely, ignored the whole thing.)

"Ready?" I ask Jack now.

"Can't wait," he answers with a wink.

And then we both realize that he doesn't have to, as the unmistakable roar and splutter of Pa's car can be heard approaching the church.

"Here they are," Jack says, and he puffs his cheeks out before releasing a long, slow breath. Perhaps he is a little nervous, after all. I grin up at him in what I hope is a reassuring manner.

"See you in a minute, then," I say, already tottering back up the aisle on my unfamiliar heels. The pews are filling up as I reach the back of the church and a low hum of chatter fills the air. I burst out into the sunshine.

Pa is helping Alice out of the car. Pa drives an old ABC, a small gray two-seater with a folding canvas hood and a dickie seat—an extra seat for two (very slim) passengers that folds out from the boot. The car is called Gerald and it is next to useless, but Pa loves it despite the fact it is temperamental and has to be dealt with very soothingly. Gerald is actually looking rather jaunty today, having been festooned in ribbons and flowers by a resourceful Freya. The sound of Mrs. Bastion hammering enthusiastically on the church's wheezy old organ drifts through the open door, and just like that it hits me. This is really happening. I think it hits Alice too.

"Oh!" She exhales the sound. I fling my arms around her and both of us show very little regard for our lovely frocks as we squeeze each other tightly. Finally, I break away, dabbing at my eyes and making a noise that is somewhere between a laugh and a sob. Alice is doing the same, and she carefully smooths the front of her dress and then adjusts her sash. Pa looks on with an air of befuddled pride.

I pick up my little bouquet of roses from Gerald's back seat and stand in front of Alice.

"Well, go on, then!" she says, and her voice is still a bit wobbly. "What are you waiting for?"

"Oh, right!" I have forgotten that I am going to have to kick this shindig off by drifting gracefully down the aisle. That *is* what bridesmaids do, after all, though I am not sure that the unfamiliar high heels are going to lend themselves too readily to much graceful drifting. Suddenly I feel nervous about it, but Alice gives me a nudge in the back.

"Go on," she repeats quietly, laughter rippling through her words. "Before Mrs. Bastion pulls a muscle." In fact, the music *is* reaching a rather vigorous crescendo and the organist *has* been known to overdo it in the past. (Mrs. Bastion claims to have Italian blood and that it is impossible for her to live without *great passion*. I admire that in a woman.) The time has come. I take a deep breath and step through the door.

CHAPTER THREE

The ceremony is over in next to no time. More than one person cries, and Alice and Jack stand just glowing at each other the whole way through. I have never seen two people so lit up in real life; it is as if we are all in a dark theater watching a film where two radiant actors shine out from the screen. Afterward, we spill out of the church, flinging confetti over the happy couple and making our way to the village green for a great big party. A long makeshift table has been set up, and it groans under the weight of the feast provided by Midge and other women in the village.

As I pile a plate full of food I bump into Mrs. Bastion, who is wearing a very tight-fitting floral dress and a lot of rouge.

"Oh, Lou!" she exclaims, tears in her eyes as she looks at Jack and Alice. "Don't they look wonderful together?"

"Yes, they do," I agree, watching Jack pull my sister's hand to his lips and say something that makes her laugh.

"It reminds me of how I was with my second husband," Mrs. Bastion sighs. "That was before I married Mr. Bastion, of course, may he rest in peace."

I am not too sure what to say about this. It is widely believed that Mr. Bastion's heart attack may have been down to his wife's more *passionate* behavior. (In the end, the Italian blood did him in, or so says the village gossip.) Luckily, before I can dwell too much on the unfortunate Mr. Bastion and the finer details of his untimely demise, Mrs. Bastion interrupts me. "And it will be you next, Louise!" She digs an elbow into my ribs and flutters her eyelashes coquettishly.

I try to keep myself from grimacing, although the thought of getting married and settling down, of following behind Alice as I always do, makes me feel panicky and short of breath. "Oh, I don't know . . . ," I say, but it turns out that she isn't terribly interested in my opinion.

"Of course it will! You'll be down the aisle in no time," she exclaims. "No need to be downhearted."

"I'm not—" I begin, but Mrs. Bastion has already sailed away to talk to someone else.

I secure myself a glass of ginger wine. I don't usually drink it as a rule, but I know that Mrs. Bastion isn't going to be the only one who wants to talk to me about my marital prospects and how I'd better be getting on with it. Besides,

how often does your older sister get married? I take a furtive sip, and choke a little over its strength. Then a pleasing
warmth begins to spread through my body and my limbs feel
looser. I take another sip and decide that I am ready to get
back to the party.

And what a party it is. The eating and drinking lasts
all afternoon, and then the music begins. A group of lads
from the village set up a rackety band, and someone rolls an
old upright piano out into the sunshine. The music is a bit
wheezy, a little out of tune, but it jangles cheerily through the
air. I kick off my shoes and dance in my stockinged feet, tipsy
and pink-cheeked. Alice and Jack are beside me and I am full
of love for them, full of love for everyone.

Then, all of a sudden, the festivities are interrupted by
a roaring sound that fills the air, humming and throbbing
louder and louder. I turn to see a convoy of four sleek automobiles rumbling through the village toward us at a terrific
pace. The music clatters to a halt and we all stop and stand,
our mouths hanging open as we watch the cars tear along the
road. Each vehicle has the roof pulled down, and men and
women wearing gorgeous evening clothes seem to be spilling out of them as they holler and cheer and wave on their
way past us. As the final car drives past, a girl hangs out of
the back with an open champagne bottle in one hand. She
is dazzling, clad in a dress of silver fringe, a jeweled headband wrapped tightly around her perfectly shingled hair. Her
eyes meet mine, and her crimson mouth curves into a wicked
smile. "Cheers, darling!" she calls, raising the bottle to her

lips. The cars disappear as quickly as they arrived, the only clue that they were ever here a cloud of dust, and the faint roar as they make their way down to the causeway.

I feel something leap inside me.

The appearance of the convoy of automobiles is like gasoline on a flame. Gossip and speculation fill the air, and it is as if a little bit of the glitter and glamour has rubbed off on us all, adding a frenzied feeling to the festivities that only grows as the ginger wine flows faster and faster. A cry goes up—is it, possibly, my own?—that we will show those Cardews a thing or two about throwing a party. Cheers ring out, and the night will be one that Penlyn talks about for years to come.

Alice and Jack's wedding celebrations last well into the early hours of the morning, and the sun is beginning to burn up the edges of the sky as I wind my way home, carrying my impractical shoes in one hand. Walking along the coastal path in the smudgy light of dawn, I can see the Cardew House blazing with light. A flutter of excitement dances in my stomach and I stand on the edge of the cliff, looking out over the water and straining my eyes to make out any details I can. After spending so much time imagining what the house *could* be, I am itching to know what is going on inside. Is it all I hoped for?

Except for the lights and the cars crammed onto the gravel drive I can see no immediate signs of life. "I know you're there," I whisper. Unfortunately, the silent house remains aloof, no longer quite my friend but not exactly a stranger.

I stand for a moment longer, my arms wrapped around my chest, watching and listening as hard as I can.

An enormous yawn that seems to reach up from my toes takes me by surprise, interrupting my reverie and leaving me swaying on tired legs. Bright young things will have to wait—I need my bed. I stagger the rest of the way home, and to my foggy brain the walk seems to take at least three times as long as it usually does. When I reach the farm, all is still and quiet, and I drag myself upstairs before collapsing fully dressed on my bed and promptly falling into a dead sleep.

When I wake up several hours later—though how many exactly, I have no idea—I think that my head is going to explode. My mouth is dry and the bright afternoon sunlight that filters in through the window makes me hiss like an unhappy vampire. There is a knock at the door and Midge sticks her head in. My eyes are bleary, but there is no missing the grin on her face. It's the same gleeful look that the triplets get when they think they are getting away with some mischief.

"Oho!" she exclaims with something that sounds suspiciously like a laugh. "I thought you might be needing this." And she hands me a large glass of water.

Gingerly, I sit up. The room swirls a little and then rights itself. I reach out gratefully for the water, taking a long, cold draft. I feel like a dry sponge. "What happened?" I wheeze.

"Well," Midge begins, perching on the end of the bed, "I think what happened is a good deal of Cath's ginger wine."

"Oooooooh," I moan, clutching my head. "Yes, I think you're right. I'm sorry."

Midge gives me a long look. "I should be cross, I suppose," she muses, "but you *are* almost eighteen now. Besides which, seeing the state of you, I think you'll be staying off the ginger wine for a while."

My stomach lurches at the mere mention of that devil brew. I whimper, burying my face in my pillow.

"When I left you were . . . singing," Midge continues gleefully, and I can't help but think that she's enjoying this all a bit too much for a responsible parent figure.

"No!" I groan, though it is all coming back to me. Someone had been plonking away at the piano and I stood on a chair and, "Oooooh!" I moan again.

Midge starts humming then, the melody to "Building a Nest for Mary," the song that I now realize I performed with some enthusiasm the night before. I have been singing it to Alice for weeks, teasing her with its lyrics about a man who wants to build a little bungalow and a little nursery for his sweetheart, Mary. At one point I think I tried swapping out the word "Mary" for "Alice" and the crowd cheered. My head crashes back into the pillow, and I understand, wincingly, that sudden movements are not my friend.

"What . . . what is in that stuff?" I ask weakly.

"It's your aunt Cath's secret recipe," Midge says, and she

pats my arm. "And it's taken down stronger folk than you. Absolutely lethal."

"Thanks for the warning," I mutter. The pounding in my head is relentless. "I think I'm dying," I croak, snuggling toward her.

"I don't think so," Midge says without a pinch of sympathy. "You'd better wash up and come and eat something. That'll sort you out." With that, she stands and makes her way out of the room, leaving me alone to deal with what feels like waves of rolling seasickness.

Summoning all of my effort, I struggle to my feet. Squinting back at me from the mirror is a very sorry-looking individual. My hair is sticking out in every direction, my dress is crumpled, my stockings are torn to shreds and there is lipstick smeared around my mouth. It is then, staring at my own terrible reflection, that I remember that the Cardew party have finally turned up. I remember the beautiful girl hanging out of the back of the car, and I wonder if she ever looks this bad in the morning after spending the night partying. *No,* a voice in my brain says very firmly. *Absolutely, definitely not.*

It takes a lot longer than it should, thanks to many rest breaks along the way, but eventually I end up in the kitchen, washed and dressed and looking almost presentable.

Midge makes me a steaming mug of tea and some thickly buttered toast, which, much to my surprise, I manage to eat and keep down. I have to admit that I am feeling much better. Perhaps things aren't so bad, after all.

Freya drifts in, a book in her hands. She appears to be

dressed as Queen Elizabeth, and she has a stiff paper ruff tied around her neck. "Gosh, you look terrible," she says, peering closely at my face. "You're all . . . green."

"Yes, thank you, there's no need to shriek like that, Freya," I whisper, resting my forehead against the cool, cool tabletop.

"Are you remembering when you fell over trying to show everyone how to do the Charleston on top of that table?" Freya's voice rings out. I groan again. That explains the bruise on my leg.

"I think I'll go for a walk," I say, pressing a hand to my forehead.

"Good idea." Midge nods. "Some fresh air will do you good. Go and get blown about on the beach a bit. Freya won't mind taking over your chores this morning."

I think I hear Freya muttering something to the contrary under her breath, but I don't have the energy to argue. I shove my seat back, wincing at the noise it makes, and stumble outside. The sun is blazing as I scramble along the coastal path as fast as I can, taking great gulps of the salty breeze blowing in from the sea. It's as if I can feel the cool air spreading through my body, flowing right into my fingertips and my toes.

As I round the bend, the view opens up so that I can see the Cardew House. I release a breath I didn't realize I had been holding. The tide is well in and so the jewel-like building seems almost to float, suspended between the water and the sky. The sun beats down on the sea, turning it a beautiful turquoise. The cars are still on the drive but, like last night, there are no other signs of activity.

I pick my way down to the beach, which is currently little more than a thin band of golden sand standing between the sea and the lumbering sea wall. At either side, the cove is hemmed in by dark, sea-smoothed rocks, and I clamber across them. The rocks feel warm beneath my bare feet and I jump onto the damp sand. With little concern for my clothes I plunge into the water, wading out until it laps somewhere around my knees. It is bracingly cold, and the shock of it clears some of the stubborn cloudiness in my head. I stand for a moment, feeling myself sinking, the fine sand closing in around my ankles, anchoring me to the seabed.

My skin is itching with the need to know what is going on at the house. It is so close, so tantalizing, that other world of glamour and excitement. I glimpsed it as it sailed through the village last night, and remembering the image of that convoy of cars speeding past me makes my head buzz again, but this time for non-ginger-wine-related reasons. Knowing that they are all over there, knowing that the house is really, truly alive after all this time, fills me with a sense of longing so powerful it is like a kick to the stomach. I dig my toes further into the sand. I have to see it. I have to see them all for myself.

My heartfelt longings are interrupted then by the sound of someone calling my name. I turn quickly, wobbling as I lift my hand to shield my eyes, and realize that the shouting is coming from the top of the cliff. It's Tom, and he looks agitated as he scrambles down toward the beach.

"The dragon's arrived!" he exclaims once he reaches me, coming to a screeching halt that sprays sand in the air. His body quivers like an exclamation mark. This is dark news indeed.

"Already?" I ask with a sinking feeling. The dragon is Midge's other sister, our aunt Irene. She's a gaunt, disapproving woman who looks rather like an overgrown crow. She has been positively swathed in black since the death of our uncle Art over four years ago, and will probably remain so forevermore because Queen Victoria is her role model in all things, despite the fact that she's been dead for almost thirty years. Aunt Irene likes to come and look in on us fairly regularly, just to remind us in a very loud way that we are living like heathens. Presumably, she has arrived to share her thoughts on our behavior at Alice's wedding. I have a feeling they will not be positive.

Tom, it seems, has had a lucky escape. "I heard her coming up the drive," he rattles out, and the shuddering breaths he is taking make it clear that he has legged it all the way here. "She was already moaning *to herself.* She didn't even need anyone else there to have an argument with. I think she was quoting the Bible . . . something about gluttons and drunkards." He rolls his eyes. "And I was there in the kitchen, *innocently* enjoying a piece of my *beloved sister's* wedding cake," he continues, and the outrage in his voice is real, even if his claims that any of us are suddenly beloved seem a bit of a stretch, "and her voice was getting louder and louder, and then she appeared in the doorway and started screeching about how I should be using a plate and cutlery and how I had been raised wild . . ." He finishes with a shake of his head. "I just stood up and made a run for it. I could hear her shouting all the way down the path. Thought I'd better let you know."

"Thanks," I reply. "Did Freya make it out?"

Tom shakes his head. "I don't think so. There wasn't time." He trails off, a haunted look in his eyes, and we both bow our heads for a second, thinking of our fallen comrade.

Freya is almost certainly being berated right at this very moment—for talking too much, and laughing too much, and existing too much. Aunt Irene, it always seems, would like us all to be a lot . . . *less*. Her own house is grim and silent, like a mausoleum. Both her sons (the pinnacle of perfection, of course) are grown up and have left home now, but I remember them as pale, silent ghosts always haunting that horrid place.

Tom's message delivered, he is already on the move again. "I'm going to see Bill," he calls over his shoulder. "Don't go home! She'll be there for hours!"

With a sigh I pull myself from the water and sink to the sand. This is exactly why I need the Cardew House. Looking at it now I feel a pang that I can't go and hide out there, among the books and the shadows. It is blisteringly hot, and the house will be cool and quiet.

Except it won't. Not anymore. As if to confirm this I hear a distant shout. I'm on my feet immediately, watching as three dots appear in the water beside the island. There are people swimming out from the cove. I think they must be racing each other. I can't discern any details; all I can see are flashes of pale limbs and white spray as they thrash enthusiastically through the water. The sound of shouting gets louder, more than one voice egging them on from the sand. The figures turn back toward the shelter of the cove and disappear from view. Cheers explode, reaching across the waves, and the race must be over. I stand frozen as the minutes tick by, watching, waiting, but nothing happens. They're gone.

I kick the sand in frustration. The tiniest glimpses, the glittering promise of that world snatched out of my hands. I want to see it all with an urgency that overwhelms me for a moment. I want the lights and the music and the noise and the excitement, I want the newness and the fantasy. I want to experience things that are bigger than my own life, not just read about them. I want to escape into that dream for a while.

I sit back down, against the rocks this time, seeking some shelter from the sun. I pull my notebook and a short, stumpy pencil from my pocket and chew on it thoughtfully. Then I write about the party last night, and I find myself dwelling on the arrival of the Cardew party, on the girl leaning out of the car. And how her smile seemed like a promise.

CHAPTER FOUR

It's over a week later and my impatience has reached boiling point. Even Midge the Unflappable is fed up with my moping about. "Honestly, Lou," she says, "you're worse than the triplets. Will you get out of the way and do something useful?"

I slam upstairs to my room and write angry, scathing passages in my notebook about how nobody understands me. I try to concentrate on the next chapter of *Lady Amelia's Revenge,* but the words seem to dance about on the page in front of me. I feel unsettled and agitated. It's hard to admit that I'm lonely. Alice and Jack are on their honeymoon in Devon and the realities of an Alice-free house are finally here, pressing in on me.

I do my chores in the morning and I take care of any small jobs that need seeing to on the farm; I pull weeds out of the vegetable garden and I pick ripe strawberries, destined for Midge's kitchen, the juice staining my fingers. I do a truly awful job of darning socks, I mind the triplets, teaching them to sing their ABCs in a noisy, tuneless chorus, and sometimes I help Tom with his schoolwork, but mostly the days just stretch out empty in front of me, while I wait for something, *anything*, to happen. I know that I am simply filling time, rather than doing anything genuinely useful or productive. My life feels too small for me now, like a dress that I have outgrown, cutting into me more and more uncomfortably every day. How long can things carry on like this? Without Alice to talk to and to laugh with, without the distraction of preparing for the wedding—an event that has taken over the last few months—I feel so flat, like all the fizz and energy has gone from my days. I am lost.

Enough.

I squeeze my eyes shut and take a deep breath. It's time to *make* something happen. It's time to take matters into my own hands. And so, with a great sense of relief, I formulate a plan.

As plans go, it isn't a particularly complex one. I slip out of the house later in the evening—the tide is out, which means that the causeway is exposed and so it should be easy to sneak over to the island. I know the place better than anyone, so surely it won't be too difficult to catch a glimpse of what is going on? I'm desperate to see the house transformed. I want to know if the parties are all we read about and if those people, the ones who sped past me at the wedding, can really be as glamorous as they seemed. I want to see that other world, a world that speaks to the restless need in me, chafing against the limits of my own life. And once I've seen it, perhaps my curiosity—the curiosity that's been burning me up all week—will be satisfied.

The night is clear and calm. When I reach the beach, the sea is quite still, its gentle rippling waves filling the air with a muted rushing sound. The Cardew House is lit up like a birthday cake, and if I strain my ears I can just about hear the echo of music and laughter being carried across to the shore. I let the darkness wrap itself around me as I creep along the old cobbled causeway, hugging the shadows at the edges, where rocks jut from the seabed covered in slick green seaweed. I am in the open here, and if I'm unlucky and someone is about, then they could spot me pretty easily. To be honest, the sense of jeopardy only adds to my enjoyment. I feel daring and reckless. I want to laugh as the adrenaline thunders through my body.

As I get closer to the house the noise gets louder and louder. There's just so much of it. There is music playing, the sound of glasses clinking, people shouting and laughing in high, breathless voices. The sound is coming from the back of the house, but at the front where I stand, frozen for a moment and absorbing this wall of sound, there is no sign of anyone. A nearby crunching on the gravel drive jolts me and sends me hurtling—not too daintily—into some shrubbery. A couple in the most gorgeous evening wear sway into view, clearly under the influence of something even stronger than Aunt Cath's ginger wine. I hold my breath. This is what it must be like seeing a lion in the wild. My eyes greedily take in details—the shot of gold silk running through her scarf, the touch of red in his hair, made darker by the oil he seems to have rubbed through it.

"I said, *darling,* isn't a girl allowed a bit of fun every now and then?" the woman shrieks, swaying a little.

The red-haired man wraps an arm around her waist, pulling her close. "And what'd he say?" he slurs, his eyes raking over her in a way that makes my body itch—though whether it's a good or a bad itch I'm not entirely sure.

"He said . . ." The woman gasps, doubled up in mirth. "He said . . . can't you be a little more like Mother?"

"No!" the man howls, dissolving into noisy guffaws and wiping his eyes. "Well, I'm very glad you're not like *my* mother," he purrs finally, pulling her even tighter against his side.

As lines go, I do not find this one either smooth or convincing, but it seems to work on the woman, who is now looking up at him and batting her impossibly long eyelashes. With an impatient growl he pulls her face toward his, and then the two of them are locked in a breathless and—I can't help but feel—rather unnecessarily dramatic kiss. I turn my eyes away.

Leaving them to finish their theatrics in peace, I begin to move, stealth-like, through the newly tidied gardens and around to the side of the house. I'm actually feeling rather proud of my spying skills up to this point, and there is, I know, a good sturdy oak tree a little further on. If I can just pull myself up into its branches, then I will be able to watch what is going on in complete secrecy. I'm beginning to feel like an explorer, navigating new and unfamiliar worlds. I wish I had thought to bring my notebook so I could write some of this down, although I suppose it is too dark to write in it anyway. As I round the side of the house, still patting myself on the back for getting this far, I cannot help but gasp.

Candles in glass jars dot the lawn and hang from the trees, flaming torches have been dug into the ground, and a hazy, romantic glow hovers over the scene in front of me. There are dozens of people gathered on the lawn. Moonlight strikes the rippling water beyond, and the sky is simply bursting with stars, like great handfuls of silver sequins scattered on a swath of black silk. A large platform has been erected at the back of the house and a real jazz band is playing something furious and pulsing that makes my feet itch to dance. Not that I would be up to much compared to the exotic creatures who are already dancing in front of the band—they are spinning, whirling and kicking with such energy that all I can make out are blurs of vibrant colors and clacking strands of beads and pearls. It is everything I've been dreaming it could be, and much, much more.

I realize then that for all my self-congratulatory spy talk I am currently still standing, glued to the spot, with my mouth hanging open for anyone to see. Fortunately for me, the enormous crowd have other things on their minds, and I delve back into the safety of the trees, creeping swiftly toward my chosen perch. Thanks to many years of practice I'm rather good at climbing trees, and you'd be surprised what a useful skill it can be in a pinch. It's only a matter of seconds before I'm shinning easily up the trunk of the old oak and dangling my legs over a good sturdy branch. I can breathe a little easier now—knowing that I can't be seen through the lush canopy of leaves . . . and, anyway, it seems highly unlikely that anyone would be looking up here when there is so much else to be looking at.

I let my own eyes feast on the scene. It's as if I've stepped straight inside a cinema screen. The men look so dashing and expensive in black tie, and the women, with their shingled hair and crimson lips and amazing dresses that swing around their knees, they're beautiful, just like in the pictures. There is champagne everywhere—in the glass saucers that are lifted to those curving crimson lips, in the bottles that are being circulated by waiting staff, and in the loud pops that are greeted by cheers as bottle after bottle is opened. In fact, there is so much champagne, I swear that underneath the music I can hear the bubbles fizzing.

The chatter is loud and excited, and I sit there on my tree branch looking down on all these people, as if they are the sort of exotic birds you might see at the zoo. There's a lot of laughter in the air, and the giggles and guffaws are restless and eager. I sit with my chin in my hand, a happy sigh on my lips, satisfied just to take it all in. Here, finally, is the world that I have only read about. I'm overwhelmed by it—the colors, the lights, the *energy* of it. It's humming and thrumming through me, in time with the music. A man is playing the trumpet, and the shrill, scattered sound it makes is relentless, begging me to move. I feel the tree branch shifting underneath me as my legs swing, just a little.

I don't know how long I've been there when I'm suddenly aware of a tall man moving through the party. Wherever he goes I notice that the shouting grows louder; everyone wants his attention. Women want to touch him on the shoulder or the arm, they want to laugh up into his face. I can't see much of him from my hiding place above the action, although I want to. I watch him for a while, my eyes following his progress. I make out a pair of broad shoulders, a head of thick, dark hair with a slight curl to it. He moves easily, one hand in his pocket. His progress is slow, languorous, as though he alone is immune to the urgent, pulsing music, to the excitement that crackles in the air. At one point he turns his head slightly to one side and I think he is trying to hide a yawn. I am so busy watching him that I don't register at first that he is coming closer and closer to where I am hiding.

I curse under my breath and pull my legs up, flattening myself against the branch as much as I can. Why is he coming this way? My perfect hiding spot is in the shadows, at the edge of the party, and that is exactly why I chose it. I didn't expect anyone to stray this far from all the action.

In the gloom I see the man come to a stop beneath me. There is a scratching noise and the dance of a flame as a match is struck, followed by the glow of a burning cigarette. He turns, lifting his chin, and briefly, his features are illuminated. I glimpse a harsh, angular face with high cheekbones, and a hard mouth set in a straight line. He exhales a long stream of smoke and stands in the shadows, the cigarette dangling loosely from his fingers. I hold my breath and try to hug the tree branch as closely as possible, to melt into it. *Become the tree,* my brain hisses. *I am the tree.*

The man lifts the cigarette to his lips and inhales again. The silence that envelops us seems almost oppressive now, removing us from the party as the world shrinks down to this one dark corner. I am certain that the thundering hammer of my own heartbeat must reach his ears soon, and why have I never noticed before how loud the simple act of breathing can be? I'm almost relieved when the stifling quiet is finally broken by his voice.

"Are you enjoying the view?" he asks, without looking up. My heart stutters, my body freezes. I don't dare to move. "I can't think that a tree branch is the most comfortable way to enjoy a party. Although, given some of the guests, I really do understand the impulse," he adds, and his voice is a lazy drawl, curling through the night air toward me like his cigarette smoke.

With a feeling of intense nausea, I realize that I have been caught.

My options flash through my mind. Should I run away?

How will I manage that with him standing right below me? Should I stay quiet? That won't do much good if he already knows I am here. There is nothing to do now but brazen it out.

"Yes," I say finally, trying hard to match his indifferent tone. I let my legs swing back down so that I am sitting up rather than hugging the tree branch like a demented squirrel. "The view is lovely," I say, and I'm proud of how steady my voice sounds. "And I'm quite comfortable," I add. "Thank you very much for asking." Even Aunt Irene would be proud of my manners, and this thought is enough to make me laugh. So I do.

He turns to look up at me now, and in the moonlight my eyes meet his and the laughter dies in my throat. With a start I recognize those hooded eyes. I have seen them looking out from the pages of many, many society magazines, although before now I had no idea they were a deep mossy-green color. Alice and I have discussed pretty much every detail of his love life and admired every stitch of his clothing. Here is Robert Cardew, in the flesh, and talking to me. Meanwhile I am sitting in a tree, having gate-crashed his party. It's no wonder his face looks so hard and uninviting. I wonder nervously if he will have me thrown out, if he realizes that I'm the one he chased from the house months earlier.

"Are you having a nice time?" I ask desperately, casting around for something to say.

"Not really." He shrugs. He's not looking up at me

anymore, but out toward the water. He doesn't seem terribly interested in my presence.

"Why not?" My question cuts through the air as blunt as a butter knife.

He lifts his cigarette to his lips, and for a second I think he isn't going to answer, that he's just going to pretend I'm not here. Finally, he shrugs again. "I'm bored."

"Only boring people get bored," I say automatically. It's what Pa always says to us when we complain of boredom, usually before he gives us some hideous chore to do. I can feel a blush spreading across my face and down my neck, and I send out a prayer of thanks for the darkness.

"A motto you hear quite frequently, is it?" Robert Cardew asks, and I give a little splutter of indignation.

"I'm not boring!" I exclaim. "And I'm not the one who's bored by all this. You are."

"Perhaps you're right," is all he says. The blandness in his voice gives nothing away. I am certain this is deliberate, and I find it tooth-grindingly frustrating.

I exhale slowly. Perhaps I can use his lack of interest to my advantage; maybe I'll get away with this, after all. I can wait for him to move—just a little bit to the right will do—and then I'll have to jump down and make a run for it. I'm pretty fast so there's a good chance he won't catch me. At least he doesn't seem too concerned by the fact I've gate-crashed his party, and there's absolutely no need for me to tell him I've been breaking into his house for over a year.

"I think you must be my apple thief," he says. "The one with a fondness for Agatha Christie novels."

So much for that plan.

"I don't know what you mean." My voice has a slight squeak to it, and, even though he doesn't move, somehow I know that he hears it and that it's a point to him in this odd game we're playing.

"You left apple cores all over the floor," he says. "Next to a pile of books. It was either you . . . or we have extraordinarily literate mice."

"That could have been anyone," I say lamely. Silence again, as though he's not even going to dignify that one with a response. "Well, you surprised me," I huff then, giving up any attempt at denial and finding myself on the defensive. For whatever reason the profound sense of disinterest with which he seems to view my appearance makes something inside me crackle with anger. "Usually I tidy up after myself," I add.

"Usually?" His voice is silk.

"I might have been once or twice before," I grind out, and even to my own ears I sound like a sulky child.

"Hmm," he murmurs noncommittally, and that crackly feeling grows inside me.

"And, actually, I'm glad I did. I think it's a crime having a library full of books that no one reads," I snap.

He turns to look up at me again, and I refuse to be distracted by his stupid green eyes.

"Yes." He nods thoughtfully. "Although I suppose *some*

people might say that the breaking and entering was the real crime," he continues, looking down again and picking at an invisible thread on his cuff with elegant fingers.

"Technically, the window was already broken," I point out, and I channel Aunt Irene's chilliest, most obnoxiously dignified voice. "So, *if anything,* it was only really entering."

"An excellent point," he agrees, grinding the end of his cigarette beneath his shoe.

"I wish you'd stop agreeing with me in that patronizing manner." I throw my hands up in exasperation. "It's so . . . so . . . *disagreeable.*"

"I know." He looks up at me again, and the ghost of a grin appears on his face, but it is gone so quickly that I could have imagined it. "Do you think we might continue this on the ground?" he asks, his voice once more painfully polite. "It's rather hurting my neck having to look at you up there, and I don't think this getup is the most appropriate choice for tree climbing." He gestures toward his immaculate dinner suit.

"No, it's not," I say, trying to delay the inevitable. I feel anxiety humming in my chest as I realize that I am going to have to give up the relative safety of my tree branch. "I don't suppose you climb a lot of trees," I add.

"Not a lot of them, no. Not anymore, anyway."

"You're missing out," I mutter, and with a sigh I pull myself up onto the branch and clamber down, landing with a slightly dusty thump at his feet. I look up at him with what I hope is a defiant expression, pushing the tangle of my curls out of my eyes and wishing helplessly that I had not snuck out of the house in shorts and Pa's oversized sweater.

(*Oh, yes,* my inner voice pipes up, *if only you had gate-crashed his party in evening wear. Silly Lou, you should have dug out the Chanel.*)

Close to, he is taller and even more impossibly elegant than I first thought. His suit fits him perfectly and he wears it with the ease of a man who spends a great deal of time in a dinner jacket. His face is intimidatingly severe, all sharp angles and firm lines. I try not to flinch beneath his apprais-ing look, and I feel my knees tremble a little—not that I'd give him the satisfaction of knowing it. I glare back at him. Those inscrutable eyes finally hold a glimmer of surprise, and I rub my nose self-consciously before tucking a strand of hair behind my ear.

"You're older than I thought," he says, and for some rea-son I feel myself bristle at this. Did he take me for a silly child? I pull myself up to my full height.

"I'm seventeen," I say stiffly. After all, I am not so much younger than him, although everything about his manner seems much more grown-up.

He seems to consider this for a moment. "Then perhaps you would like some champagne?" he asks.

"Champagne would be delightful," I say airily, as if I drink the stuff all day.

"Wait here," he says, and he bends, just a little, at the waist. "I'll only be a moment." He disappears away in the direction of the crowd.

Every instinct is telling me that now is the time to make a run for it, but somehow I know that's what he expects me to do and so instead I dig my heels in. If he thinks that he intimidates me, then I'll show him how wrong he is. The fact that I shouldn't be here in the first place has become inconsequential. His arrogance is like a challenge that I can't refuse.

By the time he gets back I've almost changed my mind three times, but I'm standing firm, precisely where he left me. He doesn't give me the satisfaction of looking surprised, just holds out a glass full of champagne.

"Sorry that took so long," he says, and his eyes flicker toward the party. "It's a bit of a din in there, and I can't seem to take two steps without someone wanting to talk my ear off."

The glass in my hand is cold to the touch, and I raise it to my lips, feeling the bubbles leap toward me even before the sharp taste floods my senses. My first taste of champagne. It tickles my nose and gives me the tiniest injection of bravery.

"Poor you," I say sweetly. "Although perhaps throwing an enormous party isn't the best idea if you want to be alone." I look up at him over the top of my glass but his face remains stony.

"It's not about being alone," he says. "It's about being with someone worth talking to."

I'm totally thrown, as the sheer arrogance of that statement overwhelms me. This man certainly has a high opinion of himself. I bury my face in my glass, trying to hide my disapproval by throwing back a gulp of my champagne, but I end up spilling most of it down my front instead.

"Anyway, it's not *my* party," Robert continues, and thankfully he seems oblivious to my clumsiness. "It's my sister Caitlin's. I should really introduce you."

"Didn't you want to introduce yourself first?" I ask. It suddenly strikes me as impossibly self-important that he hasn't done so. I mean, yes, OK, I know who he is, but he doesn't *know* that I know. Something about that makes me want to pick a fight.

"How rude of me." He smiles, but it's the smile of a shark before it attacks. "I quite forgot the proper etiquette when one meets someone hanging from the branches of a tree."

"I wasn't *hanging from the branches*," I say acidly. "You make me sound like a monkey. I was perched. Elegantly."

He gives me a long look. I know exactly who he is, but I'll die before I admit it. I glower back at him.

Then he surprises me by reaching for my right hand, bending over it in a little bow and brushing my knuckles lightly with his lips. All the blood in my body seems determined to rush to my cheeks, even though I desperately will myself to look unmoved.

"Robert Anthony Frederick St. John Cardew, your most humble servant," he says, like a character in a Regency novel, and I know, I just *know*, that he expects me to swoon.

"Louise Rose Trevelyan." My voice is little more than a

growl. "And I sincerely hope that you're not expecting me to curtsy."

He looks up and laughs, a short, sharp laugh that seems to have been surprised out of him, and his face is transformed for a second by a sudden lightness that makes him almost handsome. If that's the kind of thing you like, I suppose.

"That's a lot of names you've got," I say, snatching my hand back from his fingers and wiping my slightly clammy palm on my shorts.

"I've got a few more, actually," he says coolly, all that unexpected lightness gone from his face. "But I thought that for the sake of expediency I'd better save them for another time."

"Right," I agree. "Maintain an air of mystery."

"Very important," he says, and then after a pause he adds, "for a good story."

"Ye-es." I eye him nervously. It seems a strange thing to say, and there's something dangerous and self-satisfied in his voice, like a card player about to reveal his winning hand, although his face remains implacable.

"Lady Amelia would approve." His voice is silken, and he's not looking at me.

I almost drop my glass, and I feel the blood leaving my face. "W-what did you say?" My words are little more than a croak. Surely I have misheard what he said?

"Lady Amelia," he repeats conversationally. "I think she'd be firmly in favor of maintaining an air of mystery, don't you? Although she can be a trifle . . . *overdramatic* at times."

I close my eyes for a second, forcing my brain to make sense of his words. With a sinking feeling I remember the notebook that I lost. My eyes snap open, and I can see from the light gleaming in his gaze that he is enjoying this.

The truth dawns on me then, that I must have left the notebook behind the last time I was here, and my stomach lurches as I realize where my notes have ended up. Those fledgling thoughts, those precious scribbles, and it was Robert Cardew who found them. Worse than that . . . he read them. I *never* let anyone read them, no one but Alice, that is, and now this . . . this *man* is making fun of them.

"Overdramatic," I repeat, mechanically.

Robert inclines his head. "I suppose it rather comes with the genre," he muses, and I feel a wave of anger wash over me. I expect my literary tastes are a little low for him, the great big arrogant, patronizing snob.

"I suppose it does," I force myself to say with a lightness I don't feel. A lightness that conceals the simmering, shimmering fury rising within me. "Perhaps you would be so kind as to return my notes to me. Losing them has put me a little behind."

"Well, as much as I enjoyed them, I'm afraid I don't carry them around with me," Robert says glibly, patting his pockets as if to convince me the notebook isn't there.

"Of course not," I grind out, trying to hide how much I'm stung by the joke, by the fact that he's laughing at

something that matters so much to me, treating it so dismissively.

A frown flickers across Robert's face. "I—" he begins,
but I cut him off.

"Well, thanks for the champagne." I keep my voice airy
and drain the rest of my drink before handing the glass back
to him. "I'd better be going."

"I thought I was going to introduce you to my sister?"
I think his voice is a challenge, and this time he must know
that he has won. There's no way I'm staying to talk to him,
no way I'm walking into that party, a scruffy dusty girl who
just fell out of a tree. Not to add insult to serious injury. Part
of me had been quite enjoying sparring with him, I realize, but the joke about my writing has left me feeling small,
slightly ridiculous, and now I want to get as far away from
him as possible.

"Not this evening," I say with all the dignity I can manage. "I'm afraid I have another engagement. Thank you,
Robert." Then, before my courage can fail me, I turn and
sweep off through the trees, leaving him standing alone in the
moonlight.

CHAPTER FIVE

I relive every painful moment of my encounter with Robert Cardew over and over, on an endless loop, for three days. Thanks to the loss of my notebook I feel vulnerable and exposed, as though Robert Cardew has seen some hidden, secret part of me. As the shock of our encounter wears off, the crackling, angry feeling in my chest only increases. Whenever I think about it I get all hot and cross, and I want to kick things. On the other hand, the sight of the party, of the glamour and the excitement, has also lingered in my mind, piercing me with pleasure and longing each time I remember it. I had hoped that my curiosity would be satisfied by my visit, but instead, that little glimpse has left me feeling even more lost and empty.

Then an envelope arrives. The envelope is heavy, and when I run my fingers over it the paper feels more like silk. It has my name and address scrawled untidily across the front in peacock-blue ink. I stand in the kitchen and rip it open with trembling fingers. Inside is a thick, white card edged with gold and engraved with glittering golden words.

ROBERT AND CAITLIN CARDEW INVITE
YOU TO A PARTY IN HONOR OF
LAURIE AND CHARLES MILLER.

JOIN US IN WELCOMING THESE TWO
BACK TO DRY LAND.

CARDEW HOUSE, JUNE 29, 1929.

COCKTAILS AT 9 P.M.

PLEASE WEAR WHITE.

Along with the invitation there is another sheet of thick, creamy paper. It is covered in the same untidy writing that is on the front of the envelope. The words there make me need to sit down rather quickly.

Dear Louise,
 I was <u>too</u> upset to learn from Robert that I missed making your acquaintance at our party the other night. He really is the <u>most</u> odious creature imaginable, I know, but if you could bear to see him

again I would <u>so</u> love it if you could come to our
next get-together as my guest. Come for dinner at
seven, and stay over so that you don't miss breakfast
this time.

I can feel it in my bones that you and I will be the
<u>best</u> of friends. Do say you will come, do! <u>Do</u>!

—CC

I hold the note in my hand, my heart thumping. CC must be Caitlin Cardew, Robert's sister. I lift a hand to my forehead as if to try and rub away the frown that is hovering there. My brain just can't seem to make any sense of this. Robert must have told Caitlin that I gate-crashed their party, that I broke into their house, that I was pretty rude to him after he caught me, that he insulted me (she is quick to point out his odious nature, after all), and her response is to invite me to dinner? I look again at the scrawling handwriting, at the quivering exclamation marks and the words heavily underlined. The spicy and exotic scent of unfamiliar perfume clings to the paper. I rack my brain, but I can't remember seeing pictures of her in the magazines where her brother is such a fixture.

Finally, another thought, as clear and golden as a ray of sunshine, pierces this fog of confusion, and I feel the frown melting from my brow. I am going back! I'm going back to that beautiful, exciting place, and this time I'm going as an invited guest. The only fly in the ointment is that I'll have to see Robert Cardew's infuriating face again, but I suppose at a big party it will be easy enough to avoid him. Perhaps I will even be able to retrieve my notebook before he shares it with anyone else . . . if he hasn't already.

Because of course I'm going to go. Of *course* I am. I run my finger over that final exclamation mark. *Do!* The invitation is another apple in my hand, begging me to take a bite.

I slip it carefully into my pocket now, so that I can take it with me. After almost two weeks I'm going to see Alice. It's the longest we've ever been apart and I can't wait. It feels as if a lifetime has passed, and there is so much to share. Today is to be my first visit to her new house. I wanted to go earlier, as soon as they got back, but Midge told me that the love-birds needed some time to themselves. I felt a little embarrassed then. The books and films always seem to end with the wedding so the delights of the honeymoon occupy an often-visited, if hazy, area of my imagination. It's strange to think that these things are no longer a mystery to my sister.

I make my way over to the house—*Alice's* house, I mentally correct myself—with the invitation burning in my pocket. The house is part of a terraced row of cottages in the middle of the village—squat, ugly buildings of dark stone that were built a long time ago to withstand the storms that roll in from the sea. Alice and Jack's house is sandwiched right in the middle, a narrow slip of a building. There is no garden out front, but Pa made Alice a window box that she has filled with daisies. It stands proudly on the slightly crooked windowsill, and this out-of-place riot of cheerfulness is so much my sister that it makes me smile. I knock on the door, feeling suddenly shy, and it flies open immediately.

"What are you thinking?" Alice demands, sweeping me into a hug. "You don't have to knock like you're some sort of *visitor*."

I laugh into her shoulder, relieved that she looks and sounds the same, as though being married was going to write itself onto her body somehow. "I *am* a visitor, Alice!" I say.

"Oh, but not really." She pulls me through the door.

I stand, looking around me with interest. The room we are in is quite dark, and my eyes take a moment to adjust.

"Gloomy, isn't it?" Alice asks.

"It's—" I start, but she cuts me off.

"Don't say anything, I know it is. It's because the window is so tiny." Alice is brisk. "But it's lovely and cool in the hot weather and it will look much better when I paint everything white."

"What? The walls, you mean?" I rest my hand on the rough stone.

"Everything." Alice's eyes gleam. "The walls, the furniture, the floor."

"Everything?" I echo. "What does Jack think?"

"Jack thinks I should have whatever I want." Alice gives a toss of her head and a wicked smile. "It will be like living in a cloud," she finishes firmly.

"Hmm," I say, unconvinced. "A cloud? Perfect for a pair of lovebirds like you." Alice laughs, and it's a pleased kind of laugh, soft and musical. "So," I say, nudging her in the ribs, "are you going to give me the tour?"

Alice's dimple flashes. "Of course." She flings her arms

wide and speaks in a grand voice. "As you can see, this is the living area and dining hall."

There is a small stone fireplace with two battered arm-chairs pulled up next to it and a pretty blue rug laid out on the flagstone floor. In one corner is a little table with two chairs. "Oh, the cushions look wonderful!" I exclaim. Alice and I saved up and sent off for the material months ago, con-vinced that it was the spitting image of a fancy Liberty print, and Midge has made two blue, floral-patterned cushions to tie onto the dining chairs.

"There's even enough material left over for a tablecloth," Alice says. "And Aunt Irene gave us a pair of silver candle-sticks as a wedding present so we've been dining like royalty all week."

I snort in a very unladylike way. "I doubt royalty have to eat whatever it is you've been cooking." It is well chronicled that Alice has not taken naturally to the domestic arts.

"I'm not that bad," she says now, crossly.

"You once set fire to our kitchen," I remind her. "While making a sandwich."

"It was only a very small fire," Alice mutters mutinously, her arms folded over her chest.

"So, lots of burnt toast, then?" I ask.

This draws a reluctant smile. "Quite a lot," she admits, and she unfolds her arms.

"But Jack eats it without complaint," I simper, clasping my hands together. "For you can do nothing wrong. Love's young dream. You angel, you goddess!" I press the back of my hand to my forehead and pretend to swoon into one of the armchairs.

"Something like that." A smile curls at the corner of Alice's mouth. The secret smile that builds a wall around the two of them.

"So, show me the rest," I say quickly, jumping to my feet. Alice leads me through the back to a very tiny kitchen with a small stove and a wooden cabinet, on top of which her wedding china is proudly displayed.

Beyond this room stands the long, narrow garden, which is currently overgrown in a tangle of weeds and dandelions. "The outhouse is down there." Alice gestures before turning back to the living room and heading up the steep staircase. There are two rooms upstairs—one tiny box room and Alice and Jack's bedroom. Unlike the downstairs it is bright and light thanks to the larger window that looks out over the back garden. Alice has hung lacy net curtains and they ripple slightly in the breeze from the open window. There is also a washstand, a wardrobe, a small chest of drawers decorated with stenciled daisies, courtesy of Freya, and a bed.

My eyes linger here. Alice and I picked out her bedsheets together weeks ago. They are white with little yellow flowers embroidered around the edge. At the time choosing them was just one decision in a long list of other new-house-related decisions, but now they look different. They look like part of a grown-up house, they are sheets for a marital bed—a bed that Alice shares with Jack. I turn my head, catching Alice's eye. She is smirking.

"There's no need to look so horrified," she says. "It's just a bed."

"I know," I reply, leaning casually against the door frame and keeping my voice even. "I've seen them before." There is a crackling feeling in the air. "Oh, Alice!" I burst out. "Was it . . . was it . . . *How* was it?!"

There is a pause as Alice considers my question.

"It was . . . strange," she says slowly. "And then it was . . . lovely."

"Strange how?" I ask, eager for more details. "Lovely how?"

Alice shakes her head. "It was like . . . like we wanted to be as absolutely close to each other as possible. Like no matter what we did we couldn't get close enough until . . . well, it's hard to explain, but you'll see, soon enough," she finishes with a smile. "Unless you plan on being an old maid, of course." She laughs and I do too, though not as easily. I am disappointed—both by Alice's vagueness and by the old maid comment. Something in her words makes me feel uneasy, like there is a clock hanging over me, ticking away, counting down to something I'm not even sure that I want.

"Well, we can't all meet people like Jack . . . there's only one of him in the village," I say with a lightness that I don't quite feel.

"Perhaps you'll meet someone from somewhere else." Alice nudges me with her elbow. "Thanks to the Cardews it looks like Penlyn will be full of eligible bachelors this summer. It's all over the village that they're having enormous parties every night."

"Oh, interesting," I say, keeping my voice as offhand as possible. "I wouldn't know anything about that." My face is a picture of innocence as I reach into my pocket and pull out Caitlin's invitation, fanning myself with it. In the dancing sunlight streaming into Alice's bedroom the gilded paper seems even fancier, even more exotic. Alice snatches it and scans the words, her eyes growing rounder and rounder.

"I missed making your acquaintance at our party the other night," she reads aloud. "What is that about? You've been up to something!" She looks up at me and I blink innocently. "LOUISE!" she squawks, and now I feel like the one with the secret to share, and I hug it to my chest, delighted. "How on earth did *you* get invited to a Cardew party?" Her voice is getting louder and louder. "What have you done?!"

"Make me a cup of tea," I say, stretching my arms and yawning nonchalantly to conceal my smirk. "And I'll fill you in."

In the end it takes almost an hour to catch Alice up, and our tea sits beside us untouched. She wants every detail, particularly when it comes to what everyone was wearing. ("I can't believe you were wearing your tatty old shorts!" she moans, completely horrified, head in her hands.) She asks about the clothes and the music and the drinks, but most of all she asks about Robert Cardew.

"I just can't believe it, Lou!" She shakes her head, sending her blond hair rippling down her back, as she leans forward in her chair. "I can't believe you met him. We've been read-ing about him for so long and now you've actually spoken to him!" She wiggles excitedly in her seat. "Is he as handsome as he is in the pictures?"

"I suppose so," I say grudgingly. "I don't know if I'd call him handsome exactly. And he's quite old."

"He's twenty-three, as you *well know*." Alice wiggles her eyebrows. "That's hardly ancient."

"Well, he seemed older." My voice is petulant. "Probably because he was so arrogant and patronizing and pompous and . . ." I trail off, unable to bring myself to share the hu-miliating manner in which he hurled Lady Amelia in my face. I sniff.

"Well, they're all like that, aren't they, those rich types?" Alice interrupts knowingly. "It's so funny to think of you there, hobnobbing with the Cardews." She picks up the invi-tation again, staring at it and stroking it reverently with her fingertips. "And you're going to go again . . . you're going to be friends with them!" I think that maybe there is a drop of envy in her voice then.

"I could see if you can come too?" I ask brightly, although I already know that I don't want her to. I love Alice, but I want this for myself. I don't want to be Alice's shadow this time; I want my own story, and I feel certain that this is it.

"Absolutely not." She tucks a long golden strand of hair behind her ear. "I'm an old married lady now, and I have quite enough to do. Plus"—she smiles here—"I'd rather spend time with Jack than anyone else . . . even Robert Cardew."

I realize with a pang that she means it. Alice really would rather spend an evening eating burnt toast with Jack than go to a spectacular party thrown by an infamous group of bright young things. This must be what true love does for you.

"But, Alice," I say then, raising a question that has been burning in my brain ever since the arrival of the invitation this morning, "*what* on earth am I going to wear?"

Alice nods seriously, tapping a finger against her cheek. "This is exactly what I've been thinking about too." We sit in glum silence for a moment. "It's a shame you can't wear your bridesmaid's dress," she says. "Do we even *have* anything white you can wear? I can't think." I can see her mentally rifling through both of our wardrobes.

"Nope," I say. "Not a thing. You know Midge doesn't believe in white clothes, not with the state we can get ourselves into. The only white thing I own is that nightdress that Aunt Irene gave me last Christmas, and I can't wear that."

"Oh, yes, you can!" Alice leaps to her feet. I follow suit.

"Alice, you can't be serious!" I exclaim. "I can hardly go to a spectacularly fancy dinner in my nightie!" I close my eyes for a second and shudder at the complete and utter dreadfulness of such an idea.

"You can and you will," Alice says firmly, a Cheshire-cat grin spreading across her face. "Just call me your fairy godmother, because tomorrow, Cinderella, you shall go to the ball."

CHAPTER SIX

The next evening, I stand in front of the mirror as Alice fusses over me.

"Oh, Alice, are you sure about this?" I ask doubtfully, looking at my reflection.

"Absolutely," Alice mumbles through a mouthful of pins. "Now hold still while I have a look."

I am wearing the nightdress.

Just let that sink in for a moment.

I haven't worn it before because, as nightdresses go, it is pretty fancy. As it was given to me by Aunt Irene, it is also the most absolutely proper, modest thing imaginable. Made of fine white cotton, it has long sleeves that taper into tight lace cuffs. The hem falls several inches below my knees and it is high at the neck, trimmed with a little more lace and clasped demurely with a tiny pearl button. Yes, as nightdresses go, it is quite nice. *However,* no matter how fancy the nightdress, there is no denying it is a world away from the slinky, sophisticated dresses I saw at the last Cardew party. It doesn't seem to matter how many times I point this out to Alice. She is ignoring me with a degree of success that I find very irritating, pushing me here and there as she fiddles about with the fabric and consults a magazine that she has laid open on the floor, oblivious to my protests.

Alice is pulling in the waist now, eyeing my reflection speculatively, and then she turns and tugs something from the bag that she has brought with her. My heart sinks even further.

"What . . . what is that?" I whisper.

"It's one of my net curtains," Alice says calmly.

"I can't wear that!" I shriek. She's gone too far this time.

"Thank you very much," Alice snaps. "I spent a lot of time choosing these, I'll have you know."

"Alice." I struggle to keep my voice calm in the face of her obvious departure from reality. "I'm sure it's a lovely curtain. In fact, I admired it greatly when it was hanging in your window, but you can't *seriously* be suggesting that I go to a party . . . a *Cardew* party"—I close my eyes here for a painful moment—"wearing a *nightdress* and a *curtain*?"

"Oh, I'm *sorry.*" Alice is enjoying herself, wringing the sarcasm out of every word. "I had no idea that you had so many white evening gowns just lying around the house." She gestures around the bedroom. "Of *course* you should wear one of those, I'll just ask Midge if she'd mind pressing the Jeanne Lanvin, shall I?"

"I can't go," I say flatly, choosing to ignore her. "That's it. I simply cannot go."

"Nonsense. Just wait a minute and see. It won't look like a curtain when I'm finished." With that she brandishes a pair of scissors. Before I can say a word she has sliced the curtain clean in two.

"Oh, no!" I gasp. "You shouldn't . . . you can't . . . Alice, your lovely curtains!"

"It's for a good cause." Alice is stoical. "There will be other curtains."

I finger the material, knowing how hard Alice scrimped to buy these frothy, feminine scraps of lace for her first home, and I see the determination in her eyes. The damage is done now—the least I can do is see her mad scheme through.

"OK," I sigh. "Show me."

Ten minutes later I have to admit that Alice is not as mad as I thought. She has tucked the nightdress up around my hips and pinned it before winding the larger piece of curtain around like a sash, gathering it up at the side in a large, loose bow, leaving the ends trailing. The end result is quite a modish silhouette, not a million miles away from the picture in the magazine that Alice shows me.

"It's a shame about the long sleeves," I say. "I don't suppose we can cut them off? It looks a bit puritanical compared to what they'll all be wearing."

"It will look worse if we hack them with the scissors," Alice replies. "Anyway, I quite like it. You look different. You just need to pin all your hair up properly and wear my little pearl earrings and it will look very elegant."

I tilt my head to one side, still staring at my reflection. "I don't know," I say, not at all sure that I want to be different. "Do you really think it'll pass?"

"Of course it will!" Alice insists. "You know how much time I spend looking in those magazines. I'm the expert here, trust me. If anything, you'll set the fashion."

"OK," I say reluctantly, because Alice's mania for the society pages really *is* something I can put my faith in.

Alice's dimple appears. "Plus, just think of the thrill of going to a party in a nightdress that was a gift from *Aunt Irene*. I bet that's not what she had in mind when she gave it to you!"

I snort at that. It is quite a pleasing thought, I have to admit. "And what's that for?" I ask, pointing to the smaller strip of lace curtain that Alice is running through her fingers.

"For your hair," Alice replies. "Sit down, please."

I do as she says, sitting in front of her on the floor and trying to relax as Alice's fingers work through my hair, gently untangling my curls. We sit for a long time in silence, and I close my eyes. If I put the Cardew party out of my mind, this feels almost normal. It's a relief to have Alice back in the house.

"OK, done," she says. I open my eyes, stand and look in the mirror.

"Oh, Alice. You *are* clever," I say, raising a hand to my hair. Alice has wrapped the lace strip around the top of my head in a broad band and threaded it through my curls before pinning them up. The effect is really quite pretty, and I think that against the white lace my hair looks a bit darker and less mousy.

"I can't believe you ever doubted me," Alice says as I continue to revolve in front of the mirror, checking my reflection from every angle.

"Now." Alice's voice is brisk and businesslike again. "What are you going to do about shoes?"

I freeze. "Oh, no," I whisper, and the face reflected back at me in the mirror is like a mask from a Greek tragedy. "I don't suppose you've got a pair of glass slippers in that bag?"

Alice shakes her head, exhaling in frustration.

"What am I going to do?" I groan.

"You'll just have to wear your pink ones," Alice says finally. "You can always take them off . . . you usually end up barefoot anyway."

"OK." I nod. "Although I don't think this is really a barefoot kind of event." I can feel the nerves jangling in my stomach.

"You're going to be fine." Alice jumps to her feet, dusting herself off. "And I have to get home. My husband will be wondering about his tea."

"Can't Jack get his own tea?" I ask impatiently. This is a sister emergency, for goodness' sake.

"If you think my cooking is bad, you should see what

77

happens when he's left unsupervised," Alice says as she gathers her things together. I take a deep breath.

"And you're *sure* it's OK?" I ask again.

Alice rolls her eyes. "Yes. Just don't dance too wildly," she adds over her shoulder, already halfway out the door. "You don't want your dress unraveling!"

"Thanks for that," I mutter under my breath, but Alice is gone. I begin shoving clothes into an old carpetbag—after all, I remind myself, I am invited to stay over. I'll need something to wear in the morning. And something to sleep in, of course, another nightdress. The thought makes me giggle, and the sound has more than a hint of hysteria in it.

Midge sticks her head around the door. "Everything all right?" she asks, taking in my appearance. "You look very nice. Where did that frock come from?"

"Alice made it," I reply, biting my lip.

Midge, unflappable as ever, doesn't bat an eyelid at the thought of Alice (who can barely sew on a button) whipping up a whole dress, and I don't really want to go into too many details. Midge is a very relaxed kind of parent, but I realize that even she may have something to say about my going to dinner in a nightdress.

"Well, she did a lovely job," Midge says, and I am so relieved that she seems to think I'm wearing a normal party dress that I want to sit down on the floor and weep. "Do you have everything you need?" she asks.

"I think so," I say uncertainly. "I don't really know what you take to a fancy house party."

"Oh, I'm sure it will be fine. People are just people, Lou. Wherever you go." Midge smiles serenely. She and Pa have treated the invitation with the same casual pleasure that they would an invitation from any of our friends. Sometimes I find their failure to be moved by any of our more outrageous behavior fairly astonishing, but apparently my producing an invitation to dinner from the local landed gentry is nothing to bat an eyelid over.

Just then, Pa appears around the door with a triplet under each arm.

"I found two of 'em, Midge, but I can't uncover the third." He looks me over and gives an appreciative whistle. "Very nice, Lou." Again, I feel buoyed by the fact that he hasn't forbidden me from leaving the house in what is obviously night wear.

"Davy's probably in the pantry again, trying to get into the jam," Midge says, ambling from the room, with the rest of us traipsing behind her.

When Midge opens the pantry door, Davy is indeed sitting on the floor with one small hand plunged into a jar of strawberry jam. From the look of his face and clothing, he has been indulging for some time. He looks up at us, smiling sunnily and waving his jam-covered hands around. "Yum!" he exclaims. "Yum, yum, yum!" He pulls himself unsteadily to his feet, intent on sharing his precious bounty with me.

"Stay back!" I shriek, clutching the carpetbag in front of me like a shield, very aware of the pristine whiteness of my outfit. Pa, ever the hero, darts in front of me despite the fact that he is still holding Joe and Max, who are squawking loudly at their own lack of jam. Davy is now very upset by my rejection of his kind offer and adds his own cries to their chorus.

"You'd better go, Lou," Midge says, scooping Davy up and unceremoniously plonking him in the kitchen sink. "Have a wonderful time."

Pa smiles at me over the heads of the other toddlers, who are both wailing loudly.

I smile back tremulously. Time to go. It's funny that I feel a lot more nervous about going to the Cardew House as a guest than I did about sneaking in uninvited. Still, never let it be said that I shrink from an adventure. Taking a deep, steadying breath, I set out, ready for a closer glimpse of a world I've dreamed about—one that is full of all sorts of possibility.

CHAPTER SEVEN

The early evening is warm enough that I don't need anything over my dress; in fact, the light, soft cotton feels quite nice on my skin as I wind my way down the path to the beach, my fingers skimming the tall grass on either side. All is calm and quiet, but when I finally arrive at the beach it is to find that the tide is in. My heart sinks. I hadn't even thought about it, and I stand dithering on the sand for a moment. What an idiot I am! I can hardly swim over there in my white dress. That would be *quite* the entrance to make, rising from the water with bits of curtain hanging from my wet hair. I will have to drag out the rowboat, and that means that I am going to be horribly late.

Suddenly, breaking the stillness, I hear a distant rumbling

sound. It doesn't take me long to realize that it is coming from the small, sleek motorboat that is bouncing across the water toward the shore. It is a journey of only a few minutes from the island to the mainland where I stand, shielding my eyes from the early evening sunshine and trying to make out who is in the boat.

I feel my heart stutter when I recognize the figure looking out from behind the wheel. It is Robert Cardew. That tingling angry feeling skitters across my skin and I draw my shoulders back. This time, at least, I have the advantage of being where I'm supposed to be, but still something about his presence leaves me feeling off balance.

"Hello," I call from the beach as he comes to a stop in the shallow water, turning the engine off with a sharp click.

"Hello," he calls in response. "Caitlin sent me over for you."

"Good job she thought of it." I am frustrated to find I am babbling. "I certainly didn't and I've lived here forever, well, for my whole life anyway, and you'd think that I would remember to think about the tides but I didn't, so . . ." I trail off hopelessly. He is watching me, and his face registers nothing but cool disinterest. "Anyway," I say, trying to recover some sense of dignity, "thank you very much for coming to get me."

"Not at all," he answers. There is a long pause as I reach for something else to say. "Do you think you might like to get in the boat now that it's here?" he asks.

I glare at him, trying to think of a witty comeback.

"I suppose you could swim?" he muses, turning to look over his shoulder at the house. "It doesn't look too far."

"It's not," I snap, nettled. "I've done it many times."

He raises an eyebrow at this. "Many times, you say. Interesting."

"Well, not *many* times," I correct myself, hastily.

We stand for a second, looking at each other, and finally, he shrugs. "Either way, I think swimming is out today."

"Yes," I agree. "I'd already ruled it out, actually. Just think what a mess it would make of my hair."

"And your very fetching dress," he adds. I look at him suspiciously then to see if he is teasing me, but he's gone back to that blank, polite expression that makes him look quite stern. I slip my shoes off and stuff them into the top of my bag.

I paddle out to the boat and Robert offers me his hand. Slipping my fingers into his, he helps to pull me on board, and I notice that his grip is firm, his skin warm. I take a moment to admire the boat—it's a real beauty, obviously the very latest thing, all dark polished wood and gleaming brass. There seem to be lots of buttons, and I want to press them all to see what they do.

"Do you mind terribly if I have it back?" Robert asks, in that offhand voice of his, and I look up into his face.

With a start I realize that I am still holding his hand. I feel a blush spilling across my cheeks—and not a delicate, rose-tinted blush either, but something that makes my face look more akin to a ripe tomato.

"It's just that I need both of them to start the boat," he points out.

I snatch my hand away. "Of course," I say frostily. "Thank you for your help." With that I sit back on the polished wooden seat with an unladylike bump, to stew over how impossibly loathsome this man is. I take a deep breath and close my eyes, thinking happy thoughts. I feel a smile spread across my face.

"What are you thinking about?" Robert asks, and I realize he still hasn't started the boat.

"I am thinking about kicking you in the shins," I say, opening one eye. "It is very satisfying."

Robert makes a sound that I would be tempted to describe as a snort if I thought that such an elegant man was capable of making such a noise, and without another word he starts the boat and turns us toward the house. It seems he hasn't taken my threat of violence seriously, though I had only been half-joking. It is then that I notice he is wearing loose, dark trousers and a blue shirt, open at the collar and rolled up at the sleeves. Not that I am looking at his arms.

"Oh! You're not wearing white!" I exclaim. After all the difficulties of finding something to wear, have I misunderstood the invitation? I certainly would have felt a lot more comfortable in my pink bridesmaid's dress.

"Pardon?" Robert shouts over the noise from the motor.

"You're not wearing white!" I yell, my voice carrying a hint of panic. "I thought the invitation said . . ."

He interrupts here. "I'll change for dinner once we're

home. Although I'm not a big fan of white tie." He grimaces. "But this evening is another one of Caitlin's mad themes, and it's much easier to just go along with them rather than have her wear you down with endless arguments. Trust me," he says. "I have plenty of experience in the matter."

"Oh, OK," I murmur, wrapping my arms around myself and really feeling the thinness of my dress now that we are speeding across the water with the breeze roaring around us. We're definitely moving a lot faster than I do in the old rowing boat. I desperately hope that Alice has anchored my hair firmly enough as I brush an errant curl away from my face.

"I think I owe you an apology." The words that he speaks next seem to have been pulled reluctantly from Robert's mouth. My head snaps up in surprise. He's not looking at me, but still out across the water toward the house.

"An apology," I repeat suspiciously, not sure that I have heard him right.

With a sharp click Robert cuts the engine, and the air stills around us as the boat idles in the clear water. He turns to face me.

"Yes," he says awkwardly. "About your story."

I feel my body tense. Is he going to make fun of me again? I eye him warily, looking for any sign of teasing.

"What about it?" I ask, trying to sound as though I haven't given the matter another thought.

"I think you misunderstood what I said before," he says, and he reaches up and rubs his chin. For the first time he doesn't seem completely sure of himself.

"Oh?" I raise my eyebrows, sitting very straight on my seat with my hands clenched in my lap.

"Yes, I—" He pauses for a second here. "I didn't mean to offend you," he says stiffly.

"I wasn't offended," I sniff, keeping my voice cold and guarded. "Your opinion of my work is really neither here nor there, but I would be grateful if you would return my notes to me as soon as possible."

Robert presses his lips together. "Of course," he replies, and without another word he starts the engine again.

Minutes later we pull around to the side of the house, drifting into the secluded cove that is one of the island's hidden treasures. There is a small jetty here and Robert ties the boat up before jumping out, grabbing my tatty bag in one hand and offering the other to me. He doesn't say anything, but I know that somewhere on the inside he is laughing at me as he holds his hand out patiently for mine. With a sigh and a great show of reluctance I place my hand in his and jump lightly from the boat. This time I let go of him very quickly.

I begin to make my way toward the crumbling steps that lead up to the house, but then realize that normal guests probably wait to be guided by their hosts, and today, at least, I am determined to be a normal guest. Coming to an abrupt halt, I turn on my heel, only to knock into Robert, who has obviously been following just behind.

"Oh, sorry," I gasp, thrown off by the very nearness of him, and the clean smell of his shirt. "I thought maybe you should be leading the way." The words come out crossly, and they seem to stick in my throat a little.

"Oh, no," he says, taking a step back. "Please, after you." He gestures with a sweep of his arm. His manners are so polished, as absolutely smooth as the glass marbles that Tom carries in his pockets. His unflappability only makes me feel more awkward.

"Fine," I say, scrambling across the sand and plunging up the steps at such a speed that I am left waiting for him when I reach the top. I take a moment to admire the view. The mainland looks so pretty in the heavy gathering light that fills the sky before a sunset. The house positively glows, the honey-colored stones lit as though from the inside. I hear the ripple of the breeze through the trees, and it's like they're speaking to me, welcoming me back. I feel a shiver of anticipation. It's already the sort of evening where it feels like anything could happen.

Robert appears at my shoulder. "It's beautiful, isn't it?" I ask softly.

"I suppose so," he says, running his eyes dismissively over the scene. I suspect that the trees don't speak to him very often. He's probably comparing the scene in front of him to London and Paris and goodness knows where else. He has that air of someone who has seen it all. The thought jabs at me. I'm envious, I realize, that he's seen so much, and annoyed too that he seems to care so little about it all. It's no wonder he gets bored easily. Well, it's his loss if he can't appreciate a gorgeous evening like this one.

"Why did you decide to come back for the summer?" I ask. If he's so underwhelmed by this scene it seems a strange decision.

There's a brief pause. "My sister fancied the change of scenery." His voice is bland. "The sea air makes a pleasant change from London."

"Oh," I say. Hardly a glowing description. The poor house deserves better than "a pleasant change." I feel angry on its behalf.

He looks down. "Thinking about my shins again?" he asks, and I realize we are standing quite close to one another.

I jump to the side like a startled cat and pull myself up very straight. "As a matter of fact I wasn't thinking about you *at all*," I say, very much on my dignity.

We are walking up the drive toward the house when the front door swings open and a girl appears, running toward me to clasp my hands in hers. She looks like a fairy princess, floating in a cloud of white silk and chiffon. White feathers crown her shingled head, although her pale hair looks almost silver in this light. Several strings of pearls are wrapped around her slender neck, and on her feet are the most gorgeous white silk slippers, a bit like you'd expect a prima ballerina to wear. I recognize her at once as the girl who was hanging out of the back of the car that drove through Alice's wedding.

"Darling!" she exclaims, pressing a warm kiss on each of my cheeks. "I'm so glad you're here."

"Louise, this is my sister, Caitlin," Robert says.

"Please, call me Lou," I manage.

"*Lou!*" Caitlin sings, and my poor little name has never sounded so poetic. "I cannot tell you how pleased I am that you decided to accept the invitation."

"I—" I begin, my eyes sliding over to Robert, searching for clues as to how the invitation came about in the first place. I should have asked him when we were on the boat, I realize. "I'm glad to be here," I say finally. "I wasn't sure that I'd exactly be welcome back, after last time . . ."

Caitlin slips her arm through mine, so I don't see Robert's reaction to this. His sister, however, is an open book. "Goodness, don't worry about that," she says, her eyes sparkling as though she's enjoying a great game. "You're not the first gate-crasher we've had, but most of them are terrible, dull things. You, on the other hand . . . you're different, I can tell. A breath of fresh air." She tips her head slightly to one side, assessing me. Whatever she's looking for, she obviously finds it, because she nods approvingly. "Oh, yes, Robert, you were so right," she calls over her shoulder before returning her attention to me. "We are going to be fast friends, I can see it already."

Robert mutters something under his breath, and I think it sounds like, "God, help me." I wonder what on earth he has said to Caitlin.

"Well, I'm glad," I say, and it's true. It's difficult not to fall for Caitlin's charm. She shares that essential quality with Alice, no matter how different the two of them seem on the surface. Strange, I think, that she seems to have more in common with Alice than she does with Robert. Her easy friendliness is a million miles away from his closed-off arrogance.

"You look beautiful," I say to Caitlin now, trying hard to keep the envy out of my voice. I feel shabby and awkward in my makeshift outfit, out of place next to all her splendor.

Caitlin lets go of my arm and skips around in a little circle, a pleased smile on her lips. "It did turn out rather well, didn't it? But you look absolutely delicious. Where *did* you get that darling dress?"

"Um, from my sister," I say cautiously.

"Everyone's going to go mad for you," Caitlin continues with absolute certainty. "You look so fresh, like a little snowdrop. You'll be all the rage!"

I choke down a giggle at this, imagining a rush on net curtains. I feel a pang of queasy nervousness at the thought of meeting all these people. Will they really like me? Or will they take one look at me and see a fraud in a nightdress?

"Robert, take Lou's bag up to the blue room, will you?" Caitlin calls over her shoulder, her voice cutting through my anxious thoughts. "And hurry up and change. It's almost time for dinner."

"Yes, sir," Robert says, but Caitlin is already dragging me into the house. This is it. It's time for everything to really begin.

CHAPTER EIGHT

If the house was beautiful in its abandoned state, now it is positively dazzling. I feel a strange thrill at the sight of this once-familiar space transformed into something so spectacular. We stand for a moment in the entrance hall with its gleaming marble floor and enormous glass chandelier while I look about me. Caitlin is walking ahead, very much at ease in these spectacular surroundings. It is then that I realize Robert has disappeared with the bag that contains my pink shoes. My feet are still bare and—I see with mounting horror— slightly sandy from the walk. I stand frozen for a second. What can I do? I'm going to have to confess to the dazzling fairy princess next to me.

"Um, Caitlin," I say quietly, though it still feels as if my words are bouncing off the polished walls. "I don't know how to tell you this, but I haven't got any shoes."

Caitlin comes to a stop and turns, looking down at my feet. "So you haven't," she says.

Thankfully, she's not reacting like I've committed some horrifying breach of social protocol, and so I take a deep breath. "I—I hadn't got any white shoes," I admit, and my voice is small. "So I wore my pink ones, but I took them off before getting in the boat. They're in the bag that Robert just took upstairs. If you tell me where he's gone, I'll just run up and get them."

"Oh, darling, I wouldn't worry." Caitlin looks completely unconcerned while I feel panic rising inside me. "It's no good wearing them if they're pink. I've been very strict about the dress code, I'm afraid. Robert calls me the drill sergeant, but he doesn't understand." She laughs a little here, her eyes turned down so that I can't see them, but there's something taut about her voice. "The parties have got a little out of control in our circles and, honestly, if everything's not just exactly right, then people simply *pounce* on you." She rolls her eyes here and flashes me a glittering smile. I know perfectly well that what she says is true; after all, I've read about enough of the parties, and every single tiny detail is up for consumption. I've never really thought about this as a source of anxiety before; I suppose I just imagined that the parties sprang up, as wild and spontaneous as the people who attend them. Looking at Caitlin now I realize that isn't really the case. It is interesting, of course, but we seem to be rather moving away from the matter at hand.

"I see," I say, trying to keep my voice even, trying harder to mirror her nonchalant attitude to my footwear.

"I'm sure we can find you some shoes, if you want." Caitlin smiles. "Although I wouldn't bother, if I were you."

"You wouldn't?" I ask, surprised.

"No," Caitlin says decidedly. "You look so sweet with your lovely tanned skin and your bare feet and it suits you very much."

I am torn between pleasure and despair. Is that a compliment? "I can't go into dinner without shoes, Caitlin," I say firmly. What might be seen as an eccentricity in her isn't going to work for me, the interloper from the village.

Caitlin shrugs, and in that movement I see the similarity to her brother. Everything is so smooth and easy. "OK," she says, glancing back down at my feet. "We look about the same size. Wait here." With that she disappears through one of the doors off the hall, reappearing moments later with a shoebox. "There," she says, handing it to me. "But I insist you kick them off for the dancing." She grins. "And I'm your host so you have to do as I say."

"OK, OK," I agree. I open the shoebox, and inside are layers of delicate pink tissue paper, hiding a pair of white silk slippers just like Caitlin's.

"Oh," I gasp. "Caitlin, I can't wear these . . . they're beautiful and you haven't even worn them yet."

"Don't be silly." Caitlin snorts, a most unladylike noise. "I always order more than I need. You need shoes, and there are shoes. Now, stop arguing and put them on so that we can join the party!"

She's right, there's no point in arguing. It's obvious that such generosity is in Caitlin's nature, although a mean little part of me thinks that maybe it's easy to be generous when you have so much. Without further comment I give in and slip the shoes onto my feet. They are a tiny bit too big, but they still feel wonderful. Gazing down at my dainty, expensive feet gives me a little jolt of confidence and I look up at Caitlin, feeling much better. Whatever happens, at least my feet will fit in.

She laughs. "I'm glad you feel better," she says, and it's obvious that my emotions are written all over my face. She takes my hand and squeezes it, surprisingly gentle. "Sometimes I forget how strange we can be," she says. "Sweeping you up like this, dragging you into a party where you don't know anyone. I hope you don't mind?"

"Mind?" I repeat, shaking my head. "Of course I don't mind!" Impulsively, I decide to tell her the truth. "I'm just so excited to be doing something new, to be seeing something different."

Caitlin nods seriously. "Then you should understand exactly why Robert and I want you here," she says, and I am not really sure that I do understand, but her serious face has melted away, replaced by an infectious grin. "Now, let's go!"

She pulls me forward impatiently, casting the shoebox to one side and propelling us into the sitting room.

"I know how much you like *this* room," she whispers so low that only I can hear. This is, of course, the room where she and Robert almost caught me three months ago. It feels like a lifetime ago. I glance at her, but in her face I see nothing but mischievous appreciation for a prank well played. This world feels topsy-turvy, and I don't understand the rules.

Looking around, I can hardly believe that this is the same room I chose as my own—but there is the fireplace into which I have cast many an apple core, and there is the rug that I've spent so much time lolling on. It no longer looks faded or worn but, like the rest of the house, restored to something better and more vibrant. The space feels smaller now, warm and intimate, and the sound doesn't echo. The walls have been papered in the palest blush pink with something that contains tiny flecks of gold, the floorboards have been polished until you can almost see your face in them. There are plush, moss-colored velvet sofas to sink into and a room full of elegant people waiting to talk to Caitlin, and possibly— I think, with a nervous lurch of my stomach—even to me. There are about twenty people milling about, but at this moment, through my eyes, it feels like an awful lot more. The men are dressed in white dinner suits with white bow ties, the women in white dresses almost—though not quite—as spectacular as Caitlin's.

"Everyone, I must introduce you to my friend," Caitlin

sings, and all heads turn eagerly in her direction. "This is Lou." She pushes me forward and I stand awkwardly, not really knowing what to do. Finally, I raise my hand in a sort of feeble wave.

"Hello," I say.

"I have to go and check on the rest of the preparations," Caitlin says to me. "Will you be all right?" She must see the panic in my face. "They're all perfectly harmless, I promise you," she says, "and Robert will be down in just a couple of minutes." She rolls her eyes. "*So* unfair that it takes men so little time to get themselves ready."

"Yes." I manage a weak smile. "Go, go and do what you need to do. I'll be fine."

"I'm sorry about this." She grimaces. "There are just so many things to see to, and there's no one else . . . but later we will get a chance to talk properly. Bernie"—Caitlin turns from me then and calls into the crowd—"come and take care of Lou, won't you, darling?"

A man saunters slowly in our direction. He's wiry and elegant in his white tie, and when his face is still it rests in a slightly sneering look.

"I live to serve," he drawls, and I'm relieved to see the sneer lift a little, replaced by something a bit friendlier. He raises a cigarette to his lips and sweeps into a bow. "By the by, where is that *delightful* brother of yours?" His eyes look eagerly over Caitlin's shoulder.

"Robert's just gone up to change," Caitlin replies.

"And the guests of honor?" Bernie raises an eyebrow.

"Oh, you know Laurie." Caitlin laughs. "She loves to make an entrance. There's not a chance she'll be down before everyone else is assembled."

"Of course," Bernie murmurs, then turns, his eyes running over me with undisguised interest. "Well, come, come, my little chick, let me take you under my wing. We must go and fetch you a drink."

Seeing that I am to be taken care of, Caitlin turns and trips out of the room.

Bernie guides me toward a drinks trolley and gestures expansively. "So, what will it be? They have it all, I think. The Cardews are always very well prepared in the liquor department."

Unfortunately, the memory of the ginger wine is still strong enough to turn my stomach when coupled with my terrible nerves. "I'd just love a glass of soda water, please," I say, hoping that I don't sound too prim. "I'm not a big drinker usually," I add by way of explanation. "I can't keep up."

"Well, that explains why you look so disgustingly *healthy*," Bernie says, pouring the drink and adding ice. "You make the rest of us look positively haggard."

I look at Bernie's face. I guess he is in his early thirties, though I suppose he could be older. He is handsome in a dissipated sort of way, very pale and angular with hollow cheeks and a rather pointed chin. His dark hair is swept back from a high forehead, and he has slim, elegant hands that flutter while he talks. There's something about him that makes me uneasy, a sharpness in his gaze that is at odds with his languorous movements. If anyone is going to out me as an imposter, I have a feeling it will be him. I sip carefully at the drink that he hands me, trying to keep my hands from shaking.

"How do you and the Cardews know one another?" he asks, watching me from beneath heavy eyelids.

"Um, we've known each other for a while," I say clumsily. "How about you?" I ask. "How do you know them?"

"Oh, how does anyone know anyone?" Bernie sighs, waving his cigarette in the air as if to emphasize the ethereal nature of his relationship with the Cardew siblings. "We've known each other for ages. Must have met at one dreary party or another. Sadly, they all blur into one in the end . . . They're endlessly dull, all the parties, you know, but one must make the effort."

"Of course," I mutter into my drink, thinking that it will take an awful lot of parties before I become bored by this sort of evening.

"Always the same parties," Bernie continues, "always the same people. That's why you're so interesting. But then Caitlin does tend to collect the most *fascinating* people," he says, taking another drag of his cigarette.

"Me?" I squeak in surprise. "I'm not interesting." I have to stop myself from snorting with laughter at the very idea.

"But you're *new,* darling." Bernie leans toward me. He smells of violets and cigarette smoke. "And new is *always* interesting." His eyes rake over me, and I shift uncomfortably.

Is this what Caitlin meant? Am I the new, different thing for them?

"Well, all of this is new to me," I say, gesturing around at the party and our glamorous surroundings.

Bernie continues to look at me through half-closed eyes. "You do have a certain . . . *freshness* about you, you know, I can quite see the appeal."

"You make me sound like a pint of milk," I grumble. The feeling that I have been "collected," that I am on display somehow, as if I am a slightly curious object rather than a real person, nettles me, and I draw my shoulders back, lifting my chin. I may be excited to be here, but a girl has her pride.

Bernie laughs softly, reading the emotion in my face. "I apologize." He blows a stream of smoke through his nose. "I just mean that you're something different from the usual. Don't be surprised if you find yourself an object of interest among this lot." He gestures around the room, and I do see that a couple of people are casting furtive glances in our direction. I fiddle nervously with one of my sleeves. I wonder what they see when they look at me. Hopefully not a total fraud.

There is a chorus of greetings from over by the door and I turn to see that Robert has arrived. My spirits lift as my eyes meet his and he begins to make his way over to us. It must truly be desperate times, I find myself thinking, when the sight of Robert Cardew bearing down on me is a relief.

"Ahhh," says Bernie, and I turn to find him looking at

Robert through narrowed eyes as if he wants to unlatch his jaw and swallow him whole. "What a singularly attractive man." He sighs again. Bernie does a lot of sighing, I notice.

"Um, yes," I agree, because it's impossible to deny that *objectively* Robert Cardew is looking quite good, with his cheekbones and his broad shoulders and his dark hair curling over the starkly white collar of his shirt. He makes a very pretty picture. Until he starts talking, of course.

Robert appears at my elbow. "Hello, Bernie," he says. "I hope you're not corrupting Lou already?"

Bernie bats his eyelashes. "I'm sure I don't know what you mean."

"Did Caitlin abandon you so soon?" Robert asks me, not at all perturbed by Bernie's flirtation.

"She didn't abandon me," I say quickly. "She just had to check on some things for the party."

"And she did make sure to leave Lou in my capable hands," Bernie chimes in. "I've been enjoying the opportunity to get to know this friend of yours, Robert. Tell me, how do you know each other? Lou didn't say."

Of course I didn't. What *could* I say, after all? *Actually I've been breaking into his house on a regular basis*? I force myself to meet Robert's eye.

"Lou is . . . an old friend," he says smoothly. "She practically grew up at the house, knows it inside out."

I hide my face by taking a deep swig of my water then, nervous laughter rising to the surface like the bubbles still fizzing in my glass. I'm surprised by this display of humor.

For a moment it feels as though Robert and I are conspirators.

"Oh, really?" Bernie raises an eyebrow.

"Oh, *absolutely*," I sing in my best cut-glass voice, matching his tone. "Old friends. Some of us much older than others." I smile sweetly at Robert, and it's possible that an answering smile tugs at the corner of his mouth, before he gets it back under control.

"Yes," Robert continues. "In fact, Cait must be so pleased to see you again." He turns to Bernie. "Their last visit was so brief, you see, that Lou was practically out the window before they could catch up."

Bernie looks so bemused that I can't stop the laughter rising up and bursting out of me, and this time Robert really does smile. It's a victorious smile, I think, because he's made me break and laugh in front of Bernie, but for some reason I feel like I've won something.

Bernie is looking back and forth between us. "Well, Robert," he says, a slow smile spreading across his own face, "I don't know what you've been thinking about, hiding her away from us all. She's such a breath of fresh air."

"We weren't hiding her from you, Bernie." Robert begins to fix himself a drink. "Lou lives here in Cornwall. She doesn't come up to London terribly often."

Or ever, I mentally correct him.

"And who can blame you, darling, when London is such a dead bore." Bernie is nodding at me sympathetically. "I mean it. When Robert and Caitlin suggested this jaunt to the countryside, I tell you I was positively delirious. What a joy to escape the city, particularly in this *unspeakable* heat."

"I can't imagine being bored in London," I say wonderingly. I've dreamed of going to London for years. It looms large in my imagination, a city of soot and smoke and noise and possibility.

"Lou is of the opinion that only boring people get bored," Robert puts in here, and I glare at him.

"Well, exactly," Bernie drawls, blithely ignoring any insult to himself. "And the people in London are the most dreadful bores of all." He nods at me approvingly as though I have made a very astute observation, and I sneak a glance of triumph at Robert.

Suddenly, the door to the sitting room is thrown open and every conversation comes to a screeching halt. All eyes swing in that direction.

I feel my mouth drop open. Standing in the doorway is the most spectacular-looking woman I have ever laid eyes on. She is tall and voluptuous, far from the ideal figure the magazines splash about, though one look at her is enough to tell you she couldn't care less about that. Her white silk dress ignores the modern lines dictated by fashion and clings to her curves, emphasizing her hourglass figure. Her dark hair is shingled, cut daringly short at the back, and her eyes are enormous, pansy blue with almost comically long lashes. A collar of stunning diamonds glitters at her throat, and despite the warmth of the evening (and the fact that we are currently indoors) she has some sort of white fur stole slung casually around her shoulders. Making sure that all eyes are on her, she shrugs this off, catching it up in one hand and letting the end trail along the floor before turning and dropping it onto a nearby sofa. In doing so she reveals the back of her dress, which is cut into a daringly low V-shape, showing off a good deal of smooth skin. Everything about her and the way she moves is sensual, full of a promise I don't quite understand.

"Well," she says, running her eyes over the stunned crowd. "Don't you all clean up nice." Her voice is warm honey, her accent unmistakable. Here is Laurie Miller, southern heiress and Robert's fiancée.

The thought startles me, and my eyes fly to his face. Of course I know that he is engaged. I know, even, that the party tonight is in his fiancée's honor, but knowing it and seeing it are two different things somehow. It's almost been possible to forget that the Robert in front of me is the same one I've been reading about for so long, but Laurie's presence brings the fact back into sharp focus. There's no way to ignore that a creature as dazzling as this belongs in the pages of a fashion magazine.

If I expect to find any sign of burning passion in Robert's eyes (and naturally I *do*, when confronted by such a goddess) I am to be sorely disappointed. Robert's face shows only the faintest trace of amusement, and he sips nonchalantly from his drink as the others in the room move forward to envelop Laurie in a cloud of noisy air kisses. Robert's eyes slide away, to the clock on the mantelpiece, and—unbelievably—I am sure I see a tic in his jaw, as if he is stifling a yawn. It's a million miles away from the way that Jack looks at Alice.

I am about to speak, to say something to Robert about how stunning Laurie is, when I am stopped in my tracks by the arrival of another person. Walking in behind Laurie is a boy of such golden beauty that I actually feel myself go weak at the knees, a phenomenon that I thought only happened in romance novels. He is, quite honestly, the most good-looking man I have ever seen, and I almost have to pick my jaw up off the floor as he begins shaking hands with people and patting them heartily on the back.

"Who—who is that?" I manage, trying not to sound overly interested.

"Ooh!" Bernie nudges me with his elbow. "Seen something you like?" He grins at me wolfishly.

"N-no," I stammer. "I just wondered. It's not important."

"That is my future brother-in-law," Robert says. "Would you like me to introduce you?"

"Oh, no," I say, my eyes fixed on the floor now. "That's not necessary. I like it over here."

"You like it over here?" Robert repeats.

"Yes," I say, more firmly. "I think that this is a particularly pleasant part of the room and the . . . view . . . of everything is so nice and I wouldn't want to, um, leave off enjoying such a . . ."

"Oh, dear," Bernie sighs, interrupting my rambling. "Another one lost at sea. Not that I can really blame you, of course. He is altogether *too* delicious." He takes a silver case from his pocket and withdraws another cigarette. "Robert," he says. "Put the dear girl out of her misery and call him over. I have a longing to play matchmaker. Two such fresh, young daisies would make a sweet pair."

I stand struggling for words, making small squeaking noises as Robert strikes a match and lights Bernie's cigarette for him.

"Of course," Robert says, and his voice is disinterested. "Charlie!" he calls across the room, and the boy looks up, a grin lighting his face. Instinctively I clutch at Robert's sleeve.

"Robert!" he exclaims, shaking Robert's hand enthusiastically. "What a shindig! Especially welcome after that god-awful journey."

"Glad you approve," Robert responds, extracting my hand, which is apparently still clamped to his jacket, and pushing me forward a little. "I know you've met Bernie, but allow me to introduce Louise Trevelyan. Lou"—he turns to me—"this is Charles Miller."

"Nice to meet you, Louise." He holds out his hand and grasps my own. "But, please, call me Charlie." His accent is glorious. I stare up into the velvety blue eyes, fringed with the kind of long eyelashes that are completely wasted on a man.

"It's nice to meet you too," I say, feeling my temperature rise as his fingers wrap fleetingly around my own. "But, please, call me Lou."

"Lou it is."

Charlie Miller is film-star handsome. His sandy blond hair is cut short and swept back, though an unruly lock falls over his forehead and my fingers itch to push it gently away. He has a strong, square jaw and when he smiles—as it seems he often does—his eyes light up and his white teeth flash. It is all I can do not to ask for his autograph.

"Come on, Robert, leave the children alone to play," Bernie purrs, giving me a very unsubtle wink. "I'm longing to catch up with your fiancée. I must know who dresses her."

"I believe she dresses herself," Robert says, allowing Bernie to lead him away.

Now I am alone with Charlie. My mind races, trying desperately to think of something interesting to say.

"I'm sorry to hear you had a bad journey," I say finally. "Were you coming back from America?"

Charlie nods. "Yes, we were stuck on that ship for five days, and I have to admit that I'm not much of a sailor." He smiles ruefully.

"Oh, I love being on the sea," I say. "Not that I've ever done such a long journey," I add quickly. "My sister and I used to make all these elaborate plans to stow away on one of the ships to America and disguise ourselves as boys so that we could work in the engine room." I grin at the memory. "We never got very far with it in reality, though. Once we'd got through the cheese sandwiches Midge packed us and it got dark, we'd end up turning back and heading home."

"Midge?" Charlie repeats, a frown crinkling his forehead.

"My mother," I explain.

"Your mother used to pack you cheese sandwiches so

that you could run off to sea?" He looks vaguely affronted, and I'm a little surprised by his stuffiness.

I laugh. "Oh, yes," I reply. "She used to wish us happy voyages, and then of course we always came back because by giving us permission to go she took all the excitement out of it."

Charlie looks bemused, but smiles politely. I haven't thought about those games Alice and I played for a long time. What would Midge say now, I wonder, if I told her I wanted to go away? Would she wish me happy voyages? Would I have the nerve to actually go?

"Well, I think you made the right choice to stay on dry land." Charlie's voice is bluff and cheerful. "We finally got in last night but I've been asleep most of the day. All that traveling really takes it out of you, I guess. Still"—his voice brightens—"it means that I'm good and fresh for tonight's party." He smiles again, treating me to another glimpse of those beautiful white teeth. I like the way his eyes crinkle up at the corners. His looks really are quite dazzling, and I blink.

"Yes, it's a breakfast party for you, I suppose, rather than a dinner party," I say.

"Exactly!' he exclaims, laughing loudly, as if I've said something incredibly witty. "Although . . . would it be bad form to drink at breakfast?" He is moving away from me and toward the drinks trolley.

"I don't think so," I say in what I hope is a sophisticated manner. "You are on holiday, after all."

"Can I fix you a drink?" Charlie asks.

"No, thank you." I am still clutching my water.

"Look at all that," he says, eyeing up the bar. "Let me tell you, it's a welcome sight after all the garbage we've been drinking the last few weeks."

"Oh, I suppose so," I agree, sipping my drink and trying not to appear too eager. "I hear that the drinks they're cooking up are positively lethal. I'd love to go to an American speakeasy, though, they sound so exciting."

"Mmm." Charlie inclines his head in agreement. I am disappointed. I had hoped for tales of seedy back room nightclubs, of secret passwords and gangsters, hot water bottles full of whisky and the sound of smoky jazz.

We stand in silence. I can't think of anything else to say, and the quiet stretches out between us. It must be because he's so handsome, I think, that my brain can't seem to find any words. I am focusing all of my attention on the glass in my hand so that I don't stare at him too openly. When I do finally look up, Charlie is glancing about him with an amiable expression on his face, and he seems very relaxed while I'm starting to feel a little awkward. How frustrating that I have no trouble making conversation with the wretched Robert Cardew, but I can't seem to string a few sentences together with this perfectly nice, extremely handsome man. I frown, overcome by a vague feeling that it's all Robert's fault somehow. Then, thankfully, another couple joins us.

Charlie, it seems, is also delighted by their appearance,

as it gives him a chance to start talking about some kind of sporting event that has just taken place. It might be cricket. I'm not entirely sure, but he seems enthusiastic about it. I tune out of the conversation, happy just to be standing there, and to let my eyes wander around the room. I am mentally taking notes, pinning the images down in my memory. I watch as these people talk, and I try to work out how they all know one another. They're very tactile, always touching each other, and their eyes are bright, feverish. It's not just the fine clothes that mark them out as being different from the people I know; it's the way they stand, it's the way they speak. But there's something else too, some restless energy about them all, as if they could vanish at any moment, just throw open the doors and disappear off on their next adventure. They're passing through, tied down to nothing. Free.

As I'm watching them I realize that someone is watching me. I glance to the side and see Bernie standing in the middle of a group. His eyes rest thoughtfully on me, and I smile tentatively. He nods back, a small, knowing smile on his lips that makes me feel as though I have been caught doing something I shouldn't.

At that moment a voice intones, "Ladies and gentlemen, dinner is served in the dining room," and I turn to see an older man in a black suit standing by the door.

"I guess even Caitlin couldn't get the butler into white tie," Charlie mutters in my ear.

"He doesn't look very impressed by us," I whisper. In

fact, the butler in question has the put-upon look of a long-suffering man who likes things done a certain way, and doesn't care too much for all this frivolity.

"Shall we?" Charlie asks, gesturing with one hand toward the door.

"Of course," I reply, and he rests his hand lightly on my back, guiding me forward. The warmth of his fingers through my thin dress is sending little electric jolts up and down my spine, and I feel myself shiver as though I am standing out in a cold breeze.

When we reach the dining room it is to find Caitlin standing behind a chair at the head of an enormous table. The room has been transformed and I think, fleetingly, that Alice might find inspiration here for her cloud-like room.

Everything is white. The floor and the walls have been draped with gauzy white material, the table is covered in a white tablecloth, with centerpieces of white candles and white roses. White chinaware is laid out, and the staff stand to one side in white uniforms. (I guess Charlie is right about the butler; he certainly doesn't seem like the sort of person who would lower himself to wear a costume.)

"Welcome, everyone!" Caitlin cries, over the murmurs of admiration. She is looking very pleased with herself. "Please find your name and take a seat, so that the festivities can begin."

I find the place card with my name on it (silver ink on white, naturally) and take a seat. I am between a woman called Patricia Lester and a scrawny young man who introduces himself as Simon and spends most of the meal staring moonily down the table toward Caitlin. She is sitting next to Charlie, and I have to admit that my own eyes drift that way an awful lot too. We are quite the pair, Simon and I. Unfortunately for my burgeoning crush, Charlie's voice is loud and carrying, and so I hear him talking at great length on a variety of subjects including shooting, fishing, and the correct stance when boxing. He speaks with a puppyish enthusiasm and punctuates his conversation with noisy laughter. He's perfectly nice, but there's something slightly . . . dull about him, something that fails to match up to those film-star looks. Occasionally he catches my gaze and smiles, and I still can't help but swoon a little at the intense blueness of his eyes.

I make more of an effort with Patricia as plate after plate of delicious food is produced (all of it white, of course, from the delicate white soup to the snowy meringues with champagne syllabub), and I am pleased to find a fellow Agatha Christie fan. We get into quite a heated discussion about murder weapons, which ends when Simon finally tears himself away from Caitlin's face just in time to hear my theory that there are nine different ways I could kill the people sitting at this table without getting caught. Simon's face registers his distinct disapproval, and I'll admit that taken out of context it doesn't look good. Still, I decide, Simon is as dull as a stick.

I glance up to the other end of the table then and see that Robert has his eyes on me. "Only nine?" he says, his voice carrying down the table. "I can think of ten."

I look at him in surprise. "I don't believe you."

He shrugs. "It's not your fault," he says, leaning back in his chair. "I have the advantage in knowing that this table contains a hidden compartment."

"Does it really?" I ask, intrigued despite myself.

He nods. "Just the right size for a murder weapon."

"I say," Simon puts in here, looking a bit affronted. "Steady on, Cardew, young ladies present."

"Ah, quite right," Robert says smoothly. "Forgive me, Lou, I didn't mean to upset your *delicate* sensibilities."

I snort at that. His face might be a mask of politeness, but I know perfectly well what he thinks of my sensibilities. I resume my conversation with Patricia, although I can't help running my fingers along the edge of the table in search of the hidden compartment.

To Robert's right, Laurie is in full force, telling an anecdote that has everyone around her shrieking with laughter. I watch for a moment, admiring the way she keeps them all hanging on her every word with seemingly very little effort. Unlike her brother, she doesn't rattle on. She speaks slowly, and the smallest action, the raising of an eyebrow or the quirk of her lips, is devastating. People look at her with an admiration that is almost blinding.

All except her fiancé, that is. For most of the meal he sips his wine and answers questions politely. He has withdrawn, and his face is hard again, his mouth firm, his eyes cold. I see him drum his fingers on the white tablecloth, fiddle with his cutlery when he thinks no one is looking.

Dinner lasts a long time. It seems that no one is in any great hurry, and I am enjoying myself enormously. Outside the long windows it grows dark, and the candles are lit. I feel much more relaxed, almost sophisticated. It is as if the whole evening is happening to someone else, it's so unbelievable that I am here, almost like I am watching it from the outside. Except this time, I remind myself gleefully, I'm not reading about it in a magazine or sitting in a tree, watching the action take place; I am here, I am a part of it. The night seems suddenly to stretch ahead of me, like a dream I can't bear to wake up from, full of possibility.

Finally, our conversation is interrupted by the deep clanging of a bell.

"OK, everyone!" Caitlin exclaims, and she jumps to her feet. "Now it's time for the evening to begin!"

A thrill pulses through me. All of this excitement and apparently the evening hasn't even begun. Caitlin is by my side then, pulling me to my feet and tucking her arm into mine.

"Come on," she says. "The real party is in the orchard."

"I can't believe this *isn't* the real party," I reply, giddy and excited. "I'm having such a wonderful time."

Caitlin looks at my face, which I'm sure is positively glowing. "You really are, aren't you, you darling?" she murmurs. "How nice to see someone enjoying themselves so much."

"But you all enjoy yourselves all the time!" I exclaim. "All the parties, the costumes, the people. How could anyone be unhappy with all of this?"

Caitlin smiles, though it doesn't quite reach her eyes. "Oh, it's my experience that people can be unhappy anywhere," she says, and I hear something in her voice that makes me think for a second that she really means it, but then she gives a little shimmy of her shoulders, almost as if to shake off the gloom, and she's back to the bright, glittering creature of earlier. "Anyway," she continues, "if you've enjoyed the evening so far I absolutely cannot wait to see what you think of the next part. If I do say so myself, it is some of my finest work."

We're outside now and there are lots of cars pulled up on the drive. People must have been arriving for hours and hours. How curious to throw a party that can start without you. I say as much to Caitlin.

"But you wouldn't want to arrive until things have warmed up, would you?" she asks. "There's nothing worse than being early and standing around waiting for people. This way we get to enjoy the full effect." We round the corner of the house and walk through the arched entrance to the orchard, cut into the white stone wall that hems it in.

Then I see exactly what Caitlin means.

CHAPTER NINE

Underneath the inky velvet sky, the orchard glows like a luminous pearl. A white dance floor has been erected in the front, and white ribbons are tied to the trees, which have also been hung with delicate silver apples and pears. Lights twinkle up and down the rows of fruit trees, and it's as if we have stumbled across a fairy grove. In the pale, silvery moonlight throngs of guests drift across the lawn and up and down the tree-lined avenues in their white outfits. Laughter and music fill the air.

"Oh, Caitlin!" I breathe.

"I know!" she says eagerly, tugging me forward. "Let's go!" and we make our way into the crowd. "You see, the orchard is perfect for a bit of privacy," Caitlin explains. "All sorts of secluded corners for wicked behavior." Her eyes twinkle. "Perhaps you and Charlie should go for a little walk."

"I—I don't know what you mean," I splutter.

"Ohhhh, yes, you do." Caitlin wags her finger at me.

"He's *quite* handsome," I admit in a small voice.

"Oh, Charlie's nice enough, if you like that sort of thing, I suppose." Caitlin wrinkles her nose. "Not my type."

"Really?" I ask, surprised. "Why not? What's wrong with him?"

Caitlin looks at me uncertainly for a second, before reaching out her hands to grab a couple of drinks from a passing waiter and handing one to me.

"Oh, nothing, darling, nothing," she says lightly, draining her glass in one long gulp. "He's terribly sweet . . . but a beautiful ninny, that's for sure."

I snort at this. Although it's mean, I have to admit this has been my own conclusion. I sigh. "A *very* beautiful one, though," I say with a little smile.

Caitlin laughs, throwing her head back as she does so. Her laugh is nice, sort of scattered and lilting; it has an untidiness that is at odds with her polished appearance. "Kick off those shoes," she demands now. "You did promise. Let's dance!"

I need no further invitation. The band that was here a few nights ago is back, and they are playing the most wonderful jazz. My feet are already itching to dance, and their music is like a call to arms. Six black musicians are squeezed on the stage, along with an upright piano, a double bass, drums and horns, and they are playing as though their lives depend on it.

The man playing the piano is singing, and his voice is so much better than anything that's ever come out of our record player at home. He's fire and ice, his voice smooth and sensual one moment, then explosive, burning the next. The crowd is going mad. Caitlin is turned toward him, her eyes closed as she sways to the music, a faraway look on her face.

"He's wonderful," I murmur.

Caitlin opens her eyes, as if startled to find me standing there. "He's . . . quite good," she says nonchalantly, and I think she is trying to hide a smile, obviously pleased that she's pulled off such a splendid party.

Not wanting to be rude, I take a long gulp from my glass, not even sure what I am drinking. To my relief, it's sweet and fruity, almost like juice. I do as she says and kick off the white slippers, feeling a pang at leaving them that is slightly eased by the feeling of warm grass under my toes. Caitlin does the same, and I notice that her toes are painted with red nail varnish. We make our way to the dance floor, which is already full of hot, vibrant bodies swaying and spinning to the beat.

The Charleston is an exhilarating dance, a dance full of joy—the joy of being alive, the joy of being right here in this very moment. It is a dance that says that we are modern and unafraid. With a tremendous feeling of relief, I throw my hands in the air and give myself over to the feeling of it. I remember learning the dance with Alice, giggling in the front room as we bashed into each other while Freya critiqued us mercilessly. I feel a pang as I think about that time with Alice. It was before she got engaged, when I had no thought of anything ever changing between us.

Caitlin dances next to me, her hips shaking, her feet flying across the ground. Her red lips curve into an enormous grin as her eyes meet mine. She reaches out and squeezes my hand. I squeeze back, giving myself over to the music and laughing as I turn my face up to the night sky.

A hand appears on my arm. I swing around and find myself laughing up into the handsome face of Charlie Miller.

"I have to dance with the prettiest girl here," he yells above the music, and despite the practiced chivalry in his words I can feel a goofy smile sliding across my face, at this scene unfolding like a dream, like something I would have made up for my book. Charlie is like a cut-out version of Prince Charming, with his straightforward good looks and his easy smile. The music is too loud, too fevered for conversation, and I allow myself to simply enjoy the fantasy. This, I realize, is what I had hoped tonight would be like. A world away from my own life, where I can be someone else, where I can step straight into the pages of my well-thumbed magazines.

The music changes and couples sweep into an energetic fox-trot. Charlie is a good dancer, and I lean against him, more than happy to be led around the dance floor in his arms. What an excellent invention dancing is, I think dreamily. What a wonderful excuse to press up against a handsome man.

When the music ends we switch partners and Charlie

asks Caitlin to dance. I find myself staring up at that terrible drip Simon, but make my excuses.

"I think I need a drink, if you don't mind!" I exclaim, fanning my warm face with my hand.

Simon doesn't even have the good manners to look disappointed; he just shrugs and grabs hold of the next girl along. *Perhaps I'm not completely irresistible after all,* I think ruefully. I catch Caitlin's eye and gesture that I am going to find a drink. She nods, and her lips form the words "Come back soon." I make my way off the dance floor, squeezing through the heaving crowd.

Away from the dance floor the air is a lot cooler, and I take several deep, steadying gulps. The buzz from dancing still rushes through my limbs, leaving me restless, and I go off in search of a glass of water.

Almost immediately, I bump into Robert. Well, more accurately, I trip over his feet. As I'm heading, stumbling, toward an inevitable collision with the floor, one of his arms shoots out, and his hand wraps around the top of my own arm. With a sharp tug he pulls me upright before I can fall.

"Oof." A noise comes out of me and I rock back on the balls of my feet, flustered.

"Hello." He looks down at my flushed face and removes his fingers from my arm, although the warmth of his touch remains.

"Hello," I reply, and I rub at the spot where he caught me, as if I can rub the tingling feeling away. "Thanks for the rescue."

"Not a problem," he says. "Clearly, you're more nimble when it comes to tree climbing than you are on solid ground."

"It was actually your big feet that tripped me up," I point out, because something about the way he says it stirs the combative spirit in me. "And I bet you're awful at climbing trees."

"I used to be quite good, actually," he admits, with one of those rare, eye-crinkling smiles. "It was the only way to get away from Caitlin, when she was following me around all day, wanting to play at tea parties."

I laugh at this, enjoying the image.

"Are you having a good time?" he asks.

"Oh, *yes,*" I sigh, unable to control my enthusiasm, even in front of him. "It's wonderful, exactly how I imagined it. I've just been dancing my legs off and now I'm dying for a drink."

"Let me get one for you," he says, offering me his arm politely. I look at it suspiciously, but we seem to have called some kind of truce for now, so I slip my hand into the crook of his elbow and we make our way through the crowd to the long bar that has been set up against the wall. Behind it the barmen in white jackets are rattling and twirling silver cocktail shakers with a great amount of energy. I watch them for a while.

"You really are enjoying yourself, aren't you?" Robert says then, and I turn to find him looking at me.

"What do you mean?" I frown, wondering if it's a trick question.

"Just that I can see it in your face. You look . . . happy."

"That's what Caitlin said," I admit. "And I told her I didn't understand how anyone could be unhappy when they are surrounded by all of *this*." I gesture around me, Caitlin's words seeming even stranger as I take it in with another frisson of excitement.

"Ah, and what did Caitlin say to that?" Robert asks, and his body seems suddenly very still, his eyes watchful.

"She said that people could be unhappy anywhere," I reply, thinking of the tension in her voice as she said it. His jaw twitches, and his eyes look sad, just for a fleeting moment. I am surprised to feel an immediate, desperate need to cheer him up. There is more going on here than I am being told, that much is obvious.

"Maybe you don't enjoy these things as much as I do because you're just so old and stuffy?" I ask sweetly, widening my eyes and looking up at him.

"What manners." He gives a put-upon sigh. "Twenty-three is hardly old."

"Hmm." I tip my head to one side, considering this. "Then I suppose you don't have to be old to be stuffy after all." I grin. "How interrrresting." I roll the word around my mouth in a good impression of his own drawling indifference.

Robert looks down at me from under raised eyebrows. "Brat," he says, but there's no sting in it.

I stick my tongue out at him as if we are a pair of squabbling children.

121

"What will it be?" the bartender asks us.

Robert looks at me. "Well?"

"Just a water, please," I answer, drumming my fingers on top of the bar.

"A water, and a whisky, please," he tells the bartender, who disappears to fetch the drinks.

"Are you going to dance?" I ask, turning and leaning back against the bar so that I can see all the couples who are currently hitting the dance floor. I wonder idly if he is a good dancer—he carries himself with a kind of grace that makes it seem likely.

"Why? Are you asking?" He looks at me as though he knows exactly what I was thinking. In fact, I think, he looks quite unnecessarily pleased with himself. I expect he's used to girls falling all over themselves wanting to dance with him.

"Oh, no," I say. "I'm sure a man with such a . . . *serious* nature doesn't have much interest in these modern dances."

"Modern dances?" Robert frowns. "You're trying to make me sound old again."

"I'm not *trying* to do anything."

He snorts. "You're not overly concerned with the social niceties, are you?" His gaze sharpens as it rests on my face.

"You don't know anything about me," I say with great dignity.

"I know you're the kind of girl who breaks into people's houses and steals all their apples," he says, taking our drinks from the bartender and handing me my glass.

I suppose I can't argue, but I'd rather not dwell on that

little detail. "I had something to drink when we came in," I say, changing the subject. "It was so sweet it tasted like fruit juice."

"A Mary Pickford." Robert winces. "I warned Caitlin she shouldn't have them circulating because everyone will be falling down drunk before midnight, but she says that's half the fun."

"I like her a lot," I say.

"Who?" Robert asks. "Mary Pickford?"

"No, silly! Caitlin."

Robert smiles, and his face is softer than I've seen it before. "I'm glad. She likes you too. I can tell."

I feel a glow spread through me at his words. "She's done an amazing job on the party," I say, gesturing to the scene that surrounds us.

"Mmm." The noise he makes is noncommittal. He really doesn't seem to be interested in any of it. How strange to be so unmoved by all this splendor.

"Don't you think so?" I ask, exasperated. "Not up to your high standards?" My voice is a challenge. The way he takes all of this for granted infuriates me, especially after Caitlin mentioned—even fleetingly—the pressure that these parties put on her. It's obvious how much hard work has gone into this evening, and yet he is so dismissive of it.

There's a pause; he looks at me and his green eyes are cold. "I couldn't care less about the party," he says shortly. "All this . . ."—he gestures around with his hands—". . . *performance*." His voice is almost angry. "The only

123

thing that recommends it to me at all is that it seems to keep my sister occupied."

"So that you don't have to play at tea parties with her, I suppose?" My voice is acidic. He is so overbearing, I can't stand it. It's as if he can't bring himself to care about anything, as if he's too good for all of it. "I doubt that Caitlin needs to be *kept occupied* like she's a . . . a child."

It is clear that any thawing out that has happened between us is at an end.

"*That,*" he grinds out, "is not what I meant."

We stand in silence for a moment, glaring at one another.

It is then that Laurie appears. "Hello, darling." Her voice wraps around us, low and husky. "I've been wanting you to introduce me to your new friend all night."

I know perfectly well that she is only being kind, but when those sleepy blue eyes look me over approvingly I feel my back straighten and my chin lift.

"Ah, yes." Robert's voice is back to being smooth and polite; the hostility has left his eyes. "Laurie," he says, "this is Lou. Lou, Laurie."

Laurie slinks forward, pressing a kiss to each of my cheeks. She smells like something warm and spicy, almost masculine. It suits her.

"Would you care to take a walk?" Laurie asks me. "Only if you can spare her, sugar?" She turns to Robert, caressing his arm. I am a little stunned to be singled out like this. What could Laurie Miller possibly want with me?

He smiles down at her. "Of course," he says, and I know

he's probably relieved to get me out of his hair. Well, that feeling is certainly mutual.

"I'd *love* that," I say. A look passes between Robert and me that is like a clashing of swords.

Laurie is glancing between us. "Is everything all right?" she asks.

Robert takes her fingers in his hand and presses them fleetingly to his lips. "Of course," he says again, and I feel, just for a second, as if the same wall that surrounds Jack and Alice has appeared here as well. My heart thumps hollowly. Then they both turn their attention back to me, Robert drops Laurie's hand and the feeling is gone.

Laurie and I leave Robert at the bar, where he has already been commandeered by more partygoers, and we plunge into the trees. Almost immediately the noise recedes and we are in a different world. Caitlin has set up sofas, blankets, cushions in between the trees, creating dozens of intimate, secret spaces where it feels as if anything could happen. Some of them even have gauzy white curtains pulled across for greater privacy.

We wander slowly down the avenue, and in one alcove we find Bernie, surrounded by a group of lovely boys who are hanging on his every word. He flutters his fingertips at us in greeting, but makes no other effort at conversation. Further along we find an empty white velvet sofa wedged cozily beneath two pear trees, and Laurie sinks gracefully into its cushions.

"Where did Caitlin get all this furniture from?" I marvel,

perching on the other side of the sofa and enjoying the feeling of being tucked away and hidden from the world, as the branches of the trees curl into one another above our heads.

"No one throws a shindig quite like Caitlin." Laurie smiles, a seductive smile. The practicalities are obviously not of interest to her.

"I've never seen anything like it!" I exclaim, then kick myself for looking too eager. I try to lean back into the sofa in the same way as Laurie, but what looks effortless and comfortable in her leaves me looking stiff and unnatural, like a china doll. In the end I give up my attempts at sophistication and sit like a child, tucking my feet beneath me.

Laurie watches my maneuvers from under her long lashes with some amusement.

"I'm sorry to steal you away from all the action," she says finally, and I flush at her words, hoping that she doesn't think that because Robert and I were alone together there was anything flirtatious going on. That couldn't be further from the truth.

"I wasn't in the action, I was only talking to Robert," I say in a way that I hope is dismissive. Hearing the words out loud, though, I realize they sound a bit too familiar. "I mean, we were . . . he was just . . . talking to me about his sister," I finish weakly.

Laurie doesn't look at all concerned by my rambling, and I relax a little. It makes sense, I think. Even if I *had* been flirting with Robert, I'm hardly a threat to her. I glance over at her again and she looks like one of those expensive white cats, stretched out imperially across the sofa.

"It's so nice to see someone new around here." Laurie's voice is almost a purr as well. "The Cardews do have a habit of introducing one to the most interesting people."

The way she says it makes me frown. It's a bit too close to what Bernie said earlier. I fold my arms protectively across my chest. I am hardly a curiosity to be put on display.

"Caitlin told me all about you," she says then, and I freeze. What version of everything has Caitlin told Laurie? Family friend or trespasser? "About the whole sneaking-into-the-house thing," she clarifies.

My shoulders slump. Oh, *that* version of everything.

"Don't look so downbeat," she says. "I thought it was a riot."

"You did?" I ask hesitantly.

"Sure. You didn't hurt anyone, did you?" She shrugs—an action so languorous it takes fully twice as long as it would take anyone else. "So, what's the problem?"

I tuck a loose lock of hair behind my ear. "I don't know," I say, looking up toward the branches that cocoon us here. Something about Laurie has me opening up to her. There's something hypnotic about her gaze, the lack of judgment there. "No one seems angry about it, but that feels strange, sort of back to front. I shouldn't have done it . . . anyone else would be upset. It *was* wrong." It's the first time I've admitted as much and I realize that it has been worrying me a little.

"Honey." Laurie leans across and pats my arm. "There's enough trouble in this world that you don't need to go looking for more. You can trust me on that one." She reaches into her white stole, where a hidden pocket contains a silver cigarette case.

"I suppose," I say, rubbing my nose as she places a cigarette between her lips and lights it. "You're all very kind," I finish.

Laurie chuckles at that. "Oh, no," she assures me. "We're a lot of things, but kind is certainly not one of them. Believe me, no one would have invited you if they didn't want to. We're all out for ourselves here, don't forget that."

I sit quietly for a moment as Laurie blows smoke rings. I can't tell if she's being serious or not.

"Well, I think you've been kind to me," I say. "And I really don't see what there can possibly be in it for you, but I'm glad that I'm here."

Laurie smiles then. "I think it will be quite the summer," is all she says in response.

"The *whole* summer." I sigh, seeing it stretch out in front of me, daring to dream that I get to be a part of it.

Laurie's eyes narrow a little. "How old are you, Lou?" she asks after a moment.

"I'm almost eighteen," I reply.

"Hmm." She doesn't say anything else for a while, just carries on smoking her cigarette with a calmness that is almost awful. "And what do you plan to do *after* the summer?" she asks.

I freeze.

"I—I don't know," I say, drawing shapes in the grass with my toe. "I'm not exactly . . . that is, I'm a bit . . ." I trail off.

"You're at a loose end at the moment?" Laurie murmurs, and I'm beginning to think that her sleepy gaze is deceiving. She seems to be peeling me back to get at something important, something I'm afraid to admit even to myself.

"Why do you say that?" I ask quickly.

"Something about the way you talk about the summer. Like it's an escape."

I am silent, thinking this over, forced to acknowledge that Laurie is right.

"I guess at some point I'll get married," I say at last.

"Oh?" Laurie arches one elegant eyebrow. "And to whom, may I ask?"

"Oh, no one in particular," I say, rubbing my arms, feeling a sudden chill in the air. It's the first time I've voiced the thought that has been pushing in on me for weeks, maybe months. "My sister—Alice." I exhale. "We always do, or *did*, everything together, and she's just got married."

Laurie dips her head, which I think is her version of an encouraging nod.

"I suppose that's what everyone's waiting for me to do." My voice is small. "That's what girls in Penlyn *do*."

Laurie exhales slowly. "Sometimes it's a good idea to get married." She pauses. "But a woman should have . . . passion. If not for her husband, then for something else."

"Do you have passion for Robert?" I ask, and then I am

mortified by my own question. The idea of Laurie and Robert together is something I can't quite get my head around.

Laurie doesn't seem to mind. "I like Robert a great deal," she replies. "And he and I understand one another. We'll be happy together, I think. But for me passion is for outside of marriage." She says this serenely, as though it's something she's considered carefully. I'm not sure that I know what she means.

"I think Alice has passion in her marriage," I say. "But she's lucky. She married someone she truly loves." I draw my knees up to my chest. "I know that the next thing for me is to get married. I've finished school, I'm the oldest one at home now, and it's *my turn*. But . . ."

"You want something more," Laurie says evenly, as if she is simply stating a fact.

"Yes," I say, surprised. "Yes, I do." I haven't said it aloud before, and it feels almost like a betrayal of Alice to admit it, but Laurie is forcing me to talk about things I have been afraid to look at too closely. "*Is* there something more?" I ask, a note of desperation creeping into my voice.

Laurie breaks into peals of unexpected laughter. "Oh, *honey*."

"It sounds like I found out where the real party is." A deep voice interrupts Laurie's merriment, and I look to see Charlie standing in front of us.

I jump up, and Laurie flings out a graceful hand as though she expects Charlie to prostrate himself at her feet. He settles for squeezing her fingers.

"Hallo, sis," he says. "I came to see if Lou here wants to take another turn around the dance floor?" he asks with a boyish grin. "Caitlin's been looking for you too," he adds.

"Yes, go," Laurie says. "I've monopolized you long enough."

"Won't you come with us?" I ask.

Laurie shakes her head. "I think I'll stay here and see if anyone interesting comes along." She leans back on the sofa and stretches her arms above her head, a wicked look in her eye. "Though, Charlie, be a lamb, will you, and send someone over with some whisky?"

"Sure," Charlie agrees easily, and reaches out to take my hand.

I catch Laurie's eye.

She winks.

We leave then, and Charlie sets off to find the required whisky, agreeing to meet me back at the dance floor. I trail through the avenue, thinking over my conversation with Laurie as my fingertips brush against the line of tree trunks. I'm walking past one of the curtained alcoves when I hear Caitlin's voice.

"Why do you ask me that when you know I can't?" she cries, and her voice is angry.

A low voice answers, though I can't make out what it says, and I understand, suddenly, that I'm being impossibly slow, and that she's in there with a man.

"Why can't things carry on as they are?" I hear Caitlin say with a brightness that sounds almost desperate.

Again, the response is indistinct, a low, insistent hum.

"Darlllling," she says, stretching out the word, and her voice lingers in the air, soft and persuasive.

I leap back at the intimacy of her tone. Whatever this is, it is definitely private, and I feel like an intruder. I start to walk away, and Caitlin's untidy laugh drifts behind, chasing after me through the tree-lined avenue.

I am caught by a couple of people who are keen to know who I am and how I know the Cardews, and I can feel their greedy curiosity like fingers running across my skin. I answer vaguely, politely, but this only seems to increase their interest. By the time I reach the dance floor Charlie is already waiting for me, but the music has stopped.

"The band are taking a break," he explains. "They'll be back in a minute. Can I get you a drink?"

I shake my head. "No, I'm fine, thank you," I say.

Caitlin reappears then, all glittering eyes and flushed cheeks. She's a girl with a secret, and I wonder if one day she'll tell me what it is. For now, she grins at us. If I didn't know better I would think nothing of it, but her grin has that same bright, brittle quality that I heard in her voice earlier, and I'm certain that there's something anxious behind it. "What are we all standing around for?" she demands. "Where's the music? Let's dance!"

And then, as if she's made it happen with sheer force of will, the band starts playing again and I'm able to lose myself in the music.

I dance all night. In fact, I dance well into the morning.

The music is pulsing and insistent, making it impossible for me to walk away. It seems to fill my body with a kind of fierce energy that I can't ignore, tethering me to the dance floor.

For the rest of the night Caitlin and I are rarely more than a few feet from each other. Like magnets irresistibly drawn together, we spend the evening shouting and laughing over the music. I have never had a close female friend besides Alice. I suppose that with her around I never felt the need to find one—I definitely never experienced any sense that I have been missing out on something important. But now with Caitlin I feel something strange . . . it's almost like a crush. I want to be near her, I want to make her laugh, I want to hear her thoughts on . . . well . . . *everything*. I hadn't realized before tonight that this can happen, that you can fall in love with your friends.

Finally, finally, the party begins winding down. People disappear to find a bed to fall into (alone or together) and the roaring sound of departing motorcars cuts across the music. I am almost asleep on my feet when Caitlin takes pity on me. The band has stopped playing, but music is drifting out of a gramophone, and Caitlin is still whirling around like a spinning top, showing no sign of quieting down at all. Her eyes are unnaturally bright.

"Charlie! Will you show Lou up to her room?" Caitlin catches him by the arm and looks up at him beseechingly.

"I'm fine!" I insist. "I can go on for hours yet." This statement is unfortunately undercut by a yawn so big that it sets me swaying. Caitlin laughs and twirls off, diving into the small group that seems to have no intention of sleeping ever again.

Someone else is calling Charlie's name and I see him glancing over in their direction.

"It's honestly fine," I say, patting his arm. "I can find my own way back."

"Are you sure?" he asks, looking down at me.

"Oh, yes." I laugh. "I know my way around this place pretty well."

"Well, OK, then." Charlie smiles. "I'll see you in the morning."

"Goodnight," I call over my shoulder, already making my way out of the orchard and toward the house.

I'm surprised to come across a man on the front steps, hunched forward and smoking a cigarette. A pool of light from the open front door falls over him.

"Hello," I call as I walk toward him.

The man lifts his head and smiles at me; his smile is a friendly flash of white teeth that reveals a perfect dimple in his right cheek, his eyes are large and dark, his skin is burnt umber. It's the singer from the band. I hesitate a little. Penlyn isn't exactly a melting pot, and outside of my beloved jazz records we don't see a lot of black faces here.

"Hello," he replies, jumping briskly to his feet as I get nearer. "Sorry for sitting here in the dark, I'll get out of your way." His careful politeness leaves me thinking that he saw the hesitation in my face, and a wave of shame washes over me.

134

"Don't be silly," I say, returning his smile. "How can you possibly be in my way? These stairs are wide enough to support a full marching band." I eye the stairs speculatively. "Although, now that I think about it, some of the guests are weaving about enough to need the full range of the space." I peep back at him. "Not me, though. I only had one Mary Pickford."

"Mary Pickford?" the man repeats, and his nose scrunches up in confusion.

"Those pink drinks," I clarify. "The ones that people have been knocking back with a little too much abandon."

The singer laughs, and even his laughter is musical. "Oh, yes." He nods. "I've . . . er . . . noticed a few people enjoying the benefits."

Just then, as if perfectly timed, a loud retching sound emanates from some nearby shrubbery.

Our startled eyes meet and we both dissolve into a fit of giggles that we try—unsuccessfully—to keep quiet.

"We shouldn't laugh," I whisper, remembering with a lurch the morning after the ginger wine. "They're going to feel dreadful in the morning."

"I don't think we've met before," the singer says then, holding out his hand to me. "I'm Lucky."

"Lou," I say, placing my hand in his.

"Lou, huh?" Lucky's nose crinkles again, and his voice is quiet but friendly. "Is that short for something?"

"It's short for Louise," I reply.

"Oh." His eyes light up. "Like the song?"

"Yes." I nod. "Like the song."

"We didn't play that one tonight." He tips his head to the side a little. "I wish I'd known. I'll have to owe you one."

"You're really wonderful, by the way. I love the way you play," I say breathlessly, cringing a little at how unsophisticated that sounds.

"Oh, yeah?" He looks pleased.

"Yes," I say foolishly, because I don't really have any words for what the music has meant for me tonight, for the way it seemed to respond to the restless need in me, for the sense of freedom it gave me to dance. I think he understands, though.

"That's always nice to hear." Lucky's voice is warm, and I feel a bit less silly.

"We don't get to hear a lot of jazz in Penlyn," I say. "Only on the record player."

Lucky looks surprised. "You're from here?" he says. "You're not . . ." He trails off and his eyes dart back toward the last remnants of the party. There are still enough people dancing and talking to make quite a bit of noise.

"One of them?" I say, and I force my voice to sound relaxed. "No." It hurts a little, but it's the truth. My evening of pretend is almost over, and the thought cuts through me.

Lucky doesn't reply to that, just nods thoughtfully and lifts his cigarette to his lips. It's gone out so he lights it again.

"I'm afraid we're stuck here at the moment," he says then, and points out to the causeway, which is underwater. "We have to wait to get the van over with all our equipment."

"I suppose that's a strange problem to have," I say.

His smile is rueful. "Not one we've run into before, that's for sure. This place is pretty wild." He looks around him as though taking it all in for the first time, and then he shakes his head and lets out a long breath. Some fleeting emotion flashes across his face, but I can't make it out in the moonlight.

"The Cardew House," I say, coming to stand beside him. "It's a magical place. It gets under your skin." I look around now as well, and the beauty of the house works like a cocktail, warming the blood in my veins.

"The Cardew House," he echoes, but his voice is hollow, as though he doesn't see what I do. There's a pause as he finishes his cigarette. "It's certainly not the sort of place you want to walk away from." He sighs.

"Not if you can help it," I agree. "But I guess we can't stay forever." I feel my heart lurch at that.

"I guess not." Lucky sounds sad about it too.

"Anyway"—he takes a step away—"I'd better get back . . ." Lucky gestures to the van, where I can see the rest of the band are packing their instruments away.

"Oh, yes," I say. "It was nice to meet you. I really did love your music."

He puts his hands in his pockets and saunters past, a pleased smile clinging to his lips. "It was nice to meet you too, Louise," he says, and as he turns and walks away, I hear him singing softly, in his beautiful voice, that song with my name.

I stand under the blanket of stars, listening for a moment. It's the perfect end to a perfect evening, and I wander inside with a huge smile on my face.

Until I realize that I have no idea where I'm going.

How can I have forgotten that I haven't been shown which room I'm staying in? What was it that Caitlin said earlier? *The blue room.* But they've redecorated everything. I don't know which room that is. My heart sinks.

It sinks even further when I hear someone clearing their throat behind me.

Turning, I see Robert leaning against the door frame, his arms folded, his white bow tie undone and an inscrutable look on his face.

I groan under my breath.

"Are you lost?" he asks.

"I don't know which room I'm staying in," I grind out.

"And here I was thinking you knew the place better than we did," he says, walking toward me.

I stay quiet. Mostly because I'm worried about what words might come out of my mouth if I don't. Why does he make me feel so cross all the time? His dismissive words about the party and his sister still ring in my ears.

"Follow me," he says, and he walks past me and up the stairs, his jacket thrown over one shoulder. His strides are long, and he takes two steps at a time, leaving me scrambling to keep up with him. We walk down a long corridor and he stops outside one of the doors. "Here we are," he says unnecessarily. "The blue room."

"Thanks," I say, reaching for the handle. And then, because my parents raised me well, I turn, my back against the door, and force myself to look up at him. "And thank you for inviting me tonight. I had a wonderful time."

He leans one shoulder against the wall and looks at me for a long moment. Those green eyes are enigmatic. He's standing so close to me that I'm sure I can see little flecks of gold in them.

"You're welcome," he says. And then he straightens up and walks away.

I stand for a moment, leaning against the door, trying to catch my breath. It must be warm in here, I think, after being outside. I turn the handle and stumble into the blue room.

It is slowly dawning on me that the room I am standing in is the grandest I have seen yet. It is at least four times the size of my room at home. The walls are papered in broad blue and gold stripes, a small chandelier drips with crystals from the ceiling and an enormous four-poster bed hung with blue drapes dominates the space. My ratty old bag sits on top of the luxurious crisp, white covers looking completely out of place. I move around, touching the gleaming, polished furniture, breathing in the smell of beeswax. I hover over the pretty dressing table, examining the many glass jars and bottles that have been arranged there, and spray myself with a bottle of expensive floral scent.

There is another door to my right and I push it open, totally floored by the discovery that I have my own bathroom, complete with an enormous sunken bath and gleaming gold taps. I let out a little squeak then, running my fingers over the marble surfaces. There is a large mirror along one wall, and I catch a glimpse of my reflection: wild-eyed, pink-cheeked and bedraggled. My hair has worked itself loose (even Alice's skill as a hairdresser can't hold up against hours of frantic dancing) and, I note sadly, it has not done so in a carelessly attractive way, instead unraveling into a frizzy tangle. I have no idea where the lace band has disappeared to, but it is definitely long gone. With a sigh I close the door on the bathroom and walk over to the window, pulling back the heavy blue curtains.

The sky is just beginning to lighten outside, and my room looks out over a restless turquoise sea. I sink into the plush window seat, bringing my knees up to my chest and resting my head back against a cushion. I watch as the first struggling rays of the day pierce the sky, casting a warm glow across the water. I watch for as long as I can, fighting against the heaviness in my eyelids, not wanting this single, magical night to end. Then, finally, when I can't watch anymore, I fall asleep underneath a sky painted gold.

CHAPTER TEN

When I wake several hours later I am groggy and disorientated. My neck is hurting and I realize that I am still squished up in the window seat. I unfold myself and stand, stretching my cramped limbs. I eye the beautiful, cloud-like dream of a bed with regret. Trust me to miss my opportunity to sleep in that. I could try to go back to sleep now, I suppose, but as I trail my fingers over the white sheets I realize I am not a bit tired.

I pad silently over to the door. I am still wearing my dress from the evening before, and I think now that the nightgown has finally fulfilled its destiny. Perhaps I could start a line of party dresses that also double up as pajamas. It certainly makes falling into bed (or window seat) at the end of the evening very straightforward.

Opening the bedroom door a tiny crack, I listen carefully for any sign of life, but there is none. Everything is completely silent. Obviously this is not a household of early risers . . . in fact, for all I know they could all have only just gone to bed.

It seems the perfect opportunity to luxuriate in the amazing bathtub. It would be rude not to, I reason, and who knows when such a chance will present itself again? I turn the taps on and gleefully pour in great big splashes from every single pretty bottle that lines the side, finally sinking into the warm, fragrant water with a happy sigh.

Lying back in the bath, I go over the events of the previous evening in my mind. The lights and the noise and the colors arrange themselves into a dazzling collage as images press in, one on top of the other. I feel my limbs relaxing beneath the warm water, and I play out various scenes in delicious detail. I remember stepping into the orchard and entering a fairy tale. I am almost afraid that the memory of it must have been a dream, but looking around me now I know that it was all wonderfully real. I turn the night over in my mind, and realize with a twinge of sadness that it is already a memory, something fragile to be pulled out and admired, but no longer something to look forward to, to live in. I wonder if I will come back here, and if this is the beginning or already the end of my adventure. My fingers curl at that, and I shut my eyes tightly, sending out a silent wish that it doesn't all end here.

I frown now, thinking back over my conversation with Laurie. It is one thing to acknowledge that I want something bigger than the life I know in Penlyn, but it is another thing entirely to work out exactly what that is. I think about Alice and how happy and certain she seems, but no matter how hard I try I can't imagine myself in her position. Something about that makes me feel sad, as if the gap that has opened between my sister and me suddenly yawns even wider. I've always followed in Alice's footsteps. I don't really know how to blaze my own trail. And even if I did, by choosing something different, will I somehow be saying that I think she chose wrong? Will she be hurt? Will Midge and Pa? If I leave Penlyn behind, will that mean turning my back on my family?

Shaking my head, as if to dislodge all these difficult questions, I pull myself from the water and wrap my body in the thick, fluffy towels that have been laid out. After running a comb through my hair, I pull on a pale blue dress that is one of my best and usually reserved for Sundays (though it looks decidedly underwhelming in the context of my surroundings). I dab on some more of the heavy, exotic scent, but for some reason I think it smells all wrong on me. Then, finally, I sit on the bed, unsure what to do next. The answer comes courtesy of my stomach, which gives a deep and emphatic rumble. I need to go on the hunt for breakfast.

Tiptoeing down the staircase, I still can't detect any sound to indicate that the rest of the household have yet risen from the dead. I hesitate on the bottom step, undecided about whether I should head back to my room or press on. In the end hunger wins out over shyness and I make my way through to the dining room. Sunshine streams through the huge windows, and there is no sign at all of last night's party, as if the whole thing really has been some sort of dream. Robert is already in here, the newspaper in his hands, a cup of coffee and a plate of toast on the long table in front of him. I pause, but then he looks up and I'm caught staring at him.

"Good morning," I say, hovering on the threshold.

"Good morning," he replies, getting to his feet, because even early in the morning, even just with me, his manners are impeccable. "I wasn't expecting to see another soul for hours yet. Come and sit down. Would you like something to eat?"

My traitorous stomach rumbles loudly. I try to look unconcerned.

"I'll take that as a yes," he says. "What will it be?"

"Whatever you have is fine," I reply cautiously, slipping into the seat next to him at the table. I glance suspiciously at his face, but it is a mask of politeness.

"We have everything," says Robert. "So you choose. Eggs? Bacon? Toast? Fruit? There are some little pastry things that Caitlin can't get enough of."

"Little pastry things sound lovely." I am using my most extra-polite, best-behavior voice. "And a cup of tea, please."

The disapproving butler materializes then, looking as starchy as he did the night before.

"Ah, Perkins," Robert says smoothly. "Miss Trevelyan would like a cup of tea and some of those pastries that my sister has a mania for."

"Very good, sir," Perkins intones, and I smile hesitantly as his eyes slide in my direction. They keep sliding, as though I am not there at all, as though I have become one with the wallpaper. His face remains impassive and he disappears soundlessly toward the kitchen.

"That man makes me nervous," I mutter under my breath.

Of course Robert hears me, but instead of making fun of me as I think he will, he leans forward conspiratorially. "I know what you mean," he says in a low voice. "Perkins has that effect on everyone."

"You don't seem to be nervous around him," I say, surprised.

"Don't I?" The corner of his mouth tugs up a little. "Well, that's good to hear. I've been practicing. Perkins has worked for my family since before I was born, and I think he still sees me as the naughty boy who tried to decorate our antique dining table with my paint set."

"Did you really?" I tip my head to the side and look him over consideringly. I can't imagine the elegant man in front of me as a naughty child.

"I did." Robert nods. "I was three at the time, I believe, and I thought it would be a nice surprise for my mother."

"And what did she think of that plan?" I ask.

"She thought it was hilarious, as I remember, but Perkins took a different view of the subject."

"She sounds nice," I say.

There is a pause, and Robert fidgets a little in his seat.

145

"She was," he says finally. "She died a year later, when Caitlin was born."

My hand shoots to my mouth as if I can shove the words back in. I cannot believe I used the present tense when I know perfectly well that Robert's parents have both passed away. Sometimes I forget that I know so much about him—that the gossip columnists' darling sits in front of me. "I'm so sorry," I say, and the words feel inadequate.

"Well, it was a long time ago." Robert clears his throat. "And how is it that you are up and bright-eyed so early?"

"What time is it?" I ask, stretching my arms above my head and leaning back in my chair. "I have absolutely no idea. Time seems to lose all meaning once you're here. It's like Wonderland."

"I believe it's just gone eleven," he replies.

"Eleven!" I exclaim. "That's not early! I can't believe I slept so late."

"Anything before midday is practically the middle of the night around here," Robert says. "And I shouldn't think you got to bed much before four."

"Eleven," I repeat, shaking my head, but Robert has already returned his attention to his newspaper. No wonder I'm starving.

And then, as if by magic, Perkins appears again, carrying a tray full of dainty pastries and a steaming silver teapot.

"Thank you very much," I say, smiling up at him in what I hope is a winning manner.

"Will that be all, madam?" His voice is icy.

Unfortunately, I have already stuffed one of the pastries right into my mouth. "Oh," I mumble through a mouthful of food, realizing with a sinking heart that he is addressing me. "Yes. Thank you." I swallow nervously.

Perkins disappears and I pour myself a soothing cup of tea, glancing up at Robert as I do so. Here, in the soft light of the morning, he seems much more relaxed, almost—dare I say it—friendly. I eye him suspiciously for a moment, but he just sips calmly at his coffee, his long legs sprawled in front of him.

"Why are you being so nice to me?" I ask, deciding to take the proverbial bull by the horns.

Robert sighs, carefully placing his coffee cup back in its saucer. "You make me sound like an ogre. I'm always nice to you."

I snort.

"I am!" Robert retorts, nettled. "I've been perfectly polite. You're the one without any manners."

"And that's you being polite, is it?" I ask. He looks put out, and I pick up another pastry and nibble at it. It tastes of honey and almonds. "You have teased me," I start, counting off on my now sticky fingers, "you have been condescending and high-handed, and, worst of all, you made fun of something . . . something that is important to me." I flounder a bit there.

"I'm sorry if I've offended you," Robert says stiffly after

a pause, and I can see that he's really bothered that I insulted his manners. "I did try to apologize yesterday, but I can see that I didn't do a very good job."

"Oh, don't," I groan. "When you do that icy polite thing I think it's the most obnoxious behavior of all." I feel my temper rising as I sit back in my chair and fold my arms.

"Well, then, I don't know what you want from me," he says, exasperated. It's probably the most animated I've seen him, and despite my irritation I realize I am quite enjoying this.

"Noooo," I say thoughtfully, deliberately stretching the word out between us. "It's quite complicated, isn't it? It seems like either way you make me cross. But then, I seem to make you cross too, so I suppose we're even."

"You don't make me cross," Robert says crossly.

"Mmm." I make a soothing sound of agreement.

There is a pause as Robert glowers at me, and then he seems to catch himself, and he laughs—just a little, and very reluctantly.

We sit quietly for a while, and I look about me with interest. Now that all the gauzy white material has been removed I can see that the dining room has been left largely the same as it was. The pale, buttery paneling on the walls has been repainted, and there are new, spring-green curtains hanging at the side of the French windows, but it is still recognizable as one of the rooms I have haunted. It is a bright, cheerful space, perfect for long, lazy breakfasts, and as the sunlight spills across the table I wiggle contentedly in my seat.

"You always do that, you know." Robert's voice cuts through my observations.

"Do what?" I ask, turning to face him.

"Look about with those big eyes of yours like you're taking in every single tiny detail." He widens his eyes, presumably to demonstrate the way he thinks I goggle at the world.

I flush, and not just because he said I have big eyes. (Not exactly a first-class compliment, I know, but you have to take what you can get in this life.) "I'm just observant," I mutter, unsettled.

"Oh, I had noticed." Robert's voice is dry. "I suppose it's the writer in you."

My mouth falls open. "I—" I begin, but the word is a wheeze. "I don't think *you* should be talking to me about my writing."

"That reminds me," Robert says, and he stands and goes to the sideboard, where he opens a drawer. He pulls something from inside and comes around the table to place it carefully next to my elbow before returning to his seat.

I stare at the object by my side. My eyes flicker to his face and his expression is hard to read. Sitting next to my elbow is a thin blue notebook. I don't need to open it to know that it's the one I lost, the one that contains several chapters of *Lady Amelia's Revenge*. I don't know what to say.

"Thank you," I manage. "For returning it, I mean, not for reading it." My voice is as icy as I can make it.

Robert, at least, has the good grace to look a little guilty. "I really am sorry about that," he says, and then he frowns.

"Not that I read it, but if I gave the impression I was making fun of you."

It's a strange sort of apology. "You're not sorry you read it?"

He shrugs. "You left it behind and I found it," he says. "I didn't know what it was," he continues, "so I . . . read it."

"So you read it?" I repeat again. My conversation is not exactly sparkling, but I'm finding it hard to think straight. I realize now that my crossness has been replaced by something else. I so desperately want him to say he liked it.

He nods, and holds his thumb and finger apart. "I only read a little. Not all of it."

"Right," I say, trying to ignore the pang of disappointment that I feel. "Right."

"And I stopped reading as soon as I realized what it was," Robert continues. "I'm not one to pry in other people's private affairs."

"Oh," I say, and my voice sounds a little hollow. "Well, good." I run my fingers over the blue notebook.

"Mmm." He sips at his coffee indifferently. "Although if I'm being completely honest, I should say that I stopped reading *almost* as soon as I realized what it was."

"Almost?" My voice is dangerous. "What does *that* mean?"

"It means I thought it was interesting," he says, lifting his newspaper and disappearing behind it. "So I might have kept reading for a page or two." He knows that I want to talk to him about it, the beast. He's going to make me ask him what he thought of it, but I won't, I won't. I screw my hands up into two trembling fists.

"Do you know?" I say after a moment, and I'm surprised to find that my breathing is uneven. "I would very much like to screw your stupid newspaper into a ball right now."

"I'm sure you would," he says politely.

I sit blinking at the plate of food in front of me. I lift my cup of tea to my lips and realize that it is empty, so I place it carefully back onto the saucer. I take a deep breath. I can't help myself. "You thought it was interesting?" I ask finally, and my voice sounds thin and reedy.

He lowers the newspaper. "Actually, I could hardly stand to put it down," he says. "But I did." He picks up the paper again, and his voice drifts pointedly from behind it. "Because it was the *polite* thing to do."

I sit stunned for a moment. He couldn't put it down. Those simple words are a gift. Something in his matter-of-factness is more convincing than any string of superlatives would be. Aside from Alice, no one has read any of *Lady Amelia's Revenge*, or any of my writing really. Sharing it feels like sharing a part of myself—an impossibly tender, fragile part of myself that might not recover if it was broken. And I can't quite believe that the person I am sharing it with is Robert Cardew.

I'm glad the newspaper is between us so that I can't see his face. I know my own expression probably gives away my every emotion. Tentatively, I place my hand on the blue notebook and push it toward him.

"Perhaps you should keep reading, then," I say, trying to keep my voice offhand even as the blood is pounding in my ears. "If you really want to."

The notebook sits for a second on the table between us. It feels as though I have offered up my throat to a man with a knife. Robert slowly reaches across and his fingers close around the book. He tucks it carefully into his jacket. "Thank you," he says. "I'd like that. Is there any more?"

"There will be," I say. "Perhaps."

I release the breath that I was holding and help myself to another pastry. They are buttery and flaky and delicate . . . almost as good as something that Midge would make. It must be because I am distracted, my mind still trying to absorb the idea that he liked my writing, that I inform Robert of the fact.

"And who is Midge?" he asks.

I swallow another mouthful. "Midge is my mother," I say, and then, to fill the quiet that follows this pronouncement, I find myself telling him a story about the time Gerald the car broke down and had to be towed back to the farm by Mr. Cobbett's big shire horse while Freya sat in the back wearing a hastily assembled newspaper crown and waving at people like the queen. When we finally got home we had accidentally amassed a bit of a parade behind us. Midge shrugged, flung open the kitchen doors and threw one of the best parties Penlyn had ever seen.

The story makes me laugh, and I look up to see that Robert is smiling. A real, proper smile. My teacup clatters in its saucer. It's extraordinary what a difference that smile makes to his face. He looks so young and lit up. I find that some of my earlier crossness has melted away and, in fact, I'm feeling quite in charity with him.

"What's the matter?" Robert asks.

"Oh . . . nothing," I say nonchalantly. "I'm just not sure I've seen you smile properly before. You should do it more often, it suits you."

"Oh, rrreally?" Robert drawls, clearly very pleased with himself.

I roll my eyes. "Don't get too carried away." I throw a chilly look at him across the table. "I only meant that it was an improvement on the scowl you usually wear."

"I do not *scowl*," Robert says.

I snort into my tea. Then, because it is sitting untouched in front of him and I am still hungry, I reach out and pinch a piece of Robert's toast.

It is at this point that Caitlin drifts in, and I am happy to see her.

"Good grief." Robert's voice is dry. "Do my eyes deceive me or can that be my sister gracing the breakfast table before noon?"

Right on cue the clock begins to strike twelve.

Caitlin sprawls into one of the dining chairs and slumps down, resting her elbow on the table and her chin in her hand. "Ha ha," she mutters, her eyes half-closed. "Very funny, I'm sure. Doesn't it bother you that your sister is actually, definitely dying?" She groans. "Oh! Perkins," she exclaims as the man himself appears like a silent and dour-faced genie. "Be a darling and fetch me a Bloody Mary, will you? Very bloody, if you get my meaning . . . the sort of thing Dracula would take a liking to. And . . . thinking about it, make a pitcher, will you?"

"Of course, madam," Perkins intones gloomily.

Caitlin lets out a whimpering noise and rests her head against the tabletop.

"Are you OK?" I ask, looking at her limp figure.

She lifts a hand weakly in response, then lets it fall to her side.

I look at Robert. "What does that mean?" I ask.

"It means I was right about the Mary Pickford cocktails," he says, and I can detect just a hint of big brotherly self-satisfaction in his words.

Judging by the hand gestures Caitlin is making, so can she.

"Why are you both looking so disgustingly cheerful?" Caitlin asks finally, after downing half of the bright red drink that Perkins brings out for her.

"We didn't drink as much as you," Robert says matter-of-factly. "I'm not sure anyone did."

"Hmm." Caitlin sniffs at this, but the color is coming back into her cheeks now, and she looks a lot more alive. I inform her of this fact and she shakes her almost-empty drink at me. "Dear old Perkins could wake the dead with a couple of these," she says.

"And he's had to do so on more than a couple of occasions," Robert puts in.

Caitlin ignores this. "So, Lou," she says, suddenly awake, her eyes boring into mine, "I trust you found your room all right last night?" She is smirking, and I realize then that she thinks Charlie saw me back to my room. For some reason I don't want to mention that in Robert's presence. Thankfully, he has returned his attention to his newspaper.

"Yes, thank you," I answer.

"And that your escort didn't behave in an . . . untoward fashion?" She giggles.

"Of course not," I hiss, mortification running through my veins.

"Shame." Caitlin pouts.

Robert rustles his paper. "What are you talking about, Cait?"

"Nothing, just that Charlie seemed *very* keen to see Lou to her room last night."

"Hmmph." Robert makes a sort of grunting noise and doesn't say any more.

I glare daggers at his sister, trying to communicate that I would rather talk to her about last night when we are alone. She rolls her eyes at me, but seems to get the message.

"Fine, fine," she says. "I believe you . . . millions wouldn't, but I do." She pours herself another glass of the vibrant red drink. "Has my brother been keeping you entertained?" she asks.

"I've been delightful company," Robert answers before I can say anything.

"I think that's overstating it," I mutter.

"I thought we had a very nice chat," Robert says. "You only threatened to destroy my newspaper once, and I didn't even offer up a word of protest when you ate all my toast."

"Oh, that was very big of you," I reply.

"Oof, my head is still hurting too much to listen to all this back-and-forth," Caitlin interrupts, and Robert goes back to his reading with a smirk. "So, what shall we do with this glorious morning?" she asks.

"Morning," Robert's voice drifts out helpfully from behind the paper, "has finished."

"You know what I mean." Caitlin waves a hand dismissively. "I think we should go down to the beach and sunbathe." She turns to me. "Having a tan is getting to be so fashionable." She sighs. "But I just seem to turn pink and then white again. Not like you and Laurie."

It feels good to be paired with Laurie, even if it is only because I spend so much time scampering about outside. Also, despite my best efforts to stay informed, I had no idea that tanned skin was coming into fashion. I make a note to inform Alice later.

"I haven't brought my swimsuit," I say.

"I have a hundred suits, so of course you can borrow one of mine."

"Thank you," I manage. "What about the others?"

"Well, they have their own suits." Caitlin's head tilts to one side.

"You know what I mean!" I exclaim.

"They'll all join us eventually." She smiles sweetly. "Is there anyone in particular you are wondering about?"

I push my chair back and get to my feet, deliberately ignoring this. "Shall we go?" I say.

Caitlin stands as well. "Yes, let's." She moves toward the door. "I think you and I have a *lot* more to discuss, anyway."

An hour later I am sitting on the golden sand, feeling self-conscious and adjusting the strap on my borrowed bathing suit. It is red, a lot more daring than my own, and I'm not used to wearing something that leaves so little to the imagination. Not that anyone else seems to be paying much attention. I look down at my flat chest. There isn't *that* much to pay attention to, I suppose.

I lie back, propping myself on my elbows so that I can look out over the sea. It is a perfect late-June afternoon, and the water shimmers invitingly. The cove is quiet and secluded, and the sun feels good on my skin. I am happy to be here, to put off my return home for as long as possible.

I sink back next to Caitlin, holding up my hand to shade my eyes and watching the light dance through my splayed fingers. We have enjoyed a lengthy gossip about the night before, and I find myself surprisingly relaxed in her company. Now, Caitlin is flicking through a magazine and I wonder sleepily if I should go and find something to read in the library. Suddenly something drops into the sand next to me, making me jump. It is a book. I pick it up and squeal with delight. It's *The Seven Dials Mystery,* the latest Agatha Christie novel.

A shadow falls across my face, and I see that Robert is standing over me. "I thought it was time the library was updated," he says.

"I've been wanting to read this for ages," I say, sitting up. My eyes linger for a moment on his broad shoulders before I turn quickly back to the book in my hands.

The quiet is broken by a whooping sound and the appearance of a group from the house party. Here is Patricia, and her portly husband, Jerry, and trailing behind them is Laurie, whose bathing suit is so scanty that it makes mine look practically Victorian. She is wearing a gorgeous silk robe over the top, but it hangs open, rippling at her sides and doing little to cover anything up. She positively undulates across the sand, a beautiful paper parasol decorated with pink cherry-blossom resting against one shoulder.

"Hullo!" exclaims an excited Jerry, who is casting not-so-subtle admiring glances in Laurie's direction. "Isn't it a smasher of a day?"

"It's lovely," I murmur.

Robert is talking to Laurie. She gestures back up the steps, and I see that Charlie is slowly making his way down to the beach, struggling to carry something bulky. Robert goes over to help with what I eventually realize is a lounger for Laurie to recline upon so that she doesn't have to lie in the sand.

"Oh, what a good idea!" Caitlin exclaims. "I don't know why I didn't think about it."

"You can have this one," Charlie pants eagerly, depositing it at her feet.

"Oh?" Laurie arches one perfect eyebrow. "And what am I supposed to do?"

Charlie grins. "Your darling fiancé can go and fetch one for you, of course." He runs a hand through his blond hair and puffs out his cheeks in mock exhaustion. "I'm certainly not doing that again."

Laurie looks expectantly at Robert, who rolls his eyes. "Fine," he says, kissing her lightly on the cheek. "I'll be right back." It's strange, but the crackling feeling that you can't miss between Alice and Jack isn't there. Laurie and Robert are warm with each other, affectionate, but their romance isn't how I imagined it would be. I remember what Laurie said last night, about passion being for outside of marriage, and I wonder again precisely what she meant by it. She and Robert are not at all the characters in the great romance that Alice and I made them out to be when we read about them. It's almost a disappointment.

Charlie stands in front of us too, and I can't stop myself from staring at him. He looks like he's been chiseled out of marble. No, I correct myself, marble is too delicate, too refined. Charlie's skin is golden-brown and he sort of glows. I don't know how to describe it. He looks like an advert for good health.

For a second our eyes meet and I feel tingles spreading through my body. He really is *impossibly* good-looking, and that fantasy is hard to give up. I wonder briefly if the tingling feeling is the thing that crackles between Alice and Jack, but I don't think it is . . . not precisely.

I sit back on the sand and lift the book Robert has given me, determined to appear absorbed and interested in that, rather than tingling feelings. I read the same sentence over and over again, letting the waves of conversation wash over me. Charlie and Jerry seem to be chatting about shooting again, and although I try to follow the conversation for a while, I have to give up because it really is unspeakably dull. Laurie, Patricia and Caitlin are perched on Caitlin's sun lounger like a row of dazzling birds of paradise, gossiping about the people in Caitlin's magazine. The conversation goes something like this:

CAITLIN: Well, I'm not surprised to see *her* in here.
PATRICIA: No, did you hear . . . ?
LAURIE: Honey, *everyone* heard.
PATRICIA: So indiscreet.
CAITLIN: And that *poor* man.
LAURIE: Oh, I don't think he's too downhearted.
PATRICIA: No! You don't mean . . .
LAURIE: Sure. It's been going on for weeks.
CAITLIN: Well, that doesn't surprise me, with what happened at the opera.

And on and on they speak in gleeful, urgent half sentences, never actually saying anything that I can follow.

I'm surprised to find that they read the same magazines that Alice and I do. I wonder again why Caitlin isn't a fixture in them herself—she seems the perfect poster child for their glamorous world.

I am still trying to concentrate long enough to get started on my book when Robert reappears with Laurie's sun lounger.

"Wonderful, thank you, sugar." Laurie promptly moves to her new seat, tipping her head back and closing her eyes. Within moments she is asleep.

"Would you like me to fetch one for you, Lou?" Robert asks politely, and all eyes turn to me as though everyone is just remembering that I am here. I jump to my feet and brush the sand from my legs.

"No, thanks," I say awkwardly, trying to cover my exposed body with my arms. "It's so warm, and I just can't seem to sit still. I think I'll have a swim."

"Hey, that's a swell idea," Charlie exclaims. "What about you, Caitlin? You want to swim with us?"

"Oh, no." Caitlin waves a hand, not lifting her eyes from her magazine. "I'm perfectly happy as I am, thank you. Well, almost. Robert, do you think you could send someone down with some drinks? This heat is making me thirsty."

There is a murmur of approval for this plan.

"Just me and you, then, I guess." Charlie looks at me.

"Yes. I guess," I echo. I think he sounds a little disappointed, and I try not to take it personally.

As I wade in, the initial bite of the cold water almost knocks the air out of me. At my side I hear Charlie mutter something rude below his breath.

"Are you OK?" I ask.

"It's pretty cold," he says, through gritted teeth.

"It's worse if you take too long about it," I explain. "The only way is to rush in all at once."

Charlie inches forward. "I don't know . . . ," he says.

"Just do it!" I plunge in, throwing myself into the sea and feeling the shock of the cool water wrapping itself around me. "It's not that bad!" I call back toward Charlie, who is still standing with the water around his knees. "It's just because we've been sitting in the hot sun. It's warmer out here." I swim a few brisk strokes, the feeling returning to my legs. It really isn't bad at all. Swimming in the winter, now *that* is the kind of cold that strips you of thought and words; this just makes me feel fresh and awake, all fizzy and alive inside.

Charlie doesn't look convinced, but, taking a deep breath, he flings himself further into the water and swims toward me. "You English are crazy," he says through chattering teeth. "This isn't the kind of ocean that human beings should be swimming in. Leave it to the polar bears, I say."

"Don't be a baby!" I laugh, splashing him.

A grin lights up his face and he plunges toward me, returning the favor.

I squeal and dart away. I am a strong swimmer—living here I've been swimming since almost before I could walk, but in this moment I decide I don't want to swim *too* strongly.

After all, playing in the water with a gorgeous man is the stuff dreams are made of, and it would be rude of me not to make the most of such an opportunity.

I let Charlie catch me, and he wraps a strong arm around my waist, holding me firmly while he splashes me with more water. I squirm and kick my legs, sending a spray of salt water over us both.

Charlie is laughing and his eyelashes are wet and clinging together. I rest my palms lightly on his shoulders, and even in the cool water he feels warm.

"How about a race?" he asks, his arm still holding me close to him.

"Sure," I say, desperately hoping he can't feel how hard my heart is beating. "Where to?"

"That rock over there?" Charlie pulls his arm away and points to an outcrop of rocks rising from the sea about fifty yards away.

"OK," I say. "See you there!" and without another word I swim off. I hear an exclamation behind me.

I win the race easily, my fingers skimming against the craggy rocks with whole seconds to spare.

"I win! I win!" I crow as I splash about in the water, ever the demure and graceful lady. I turn to look out toward the village. There is the beach where I stood watching a race just like this one and desperately wishing I could be part of it, and now here I am, really here.

"You're fast." Charlie shakes his head. "I'll admit that, but I demand a rematch. Race you back to land." And this time he leaves me behind, turning and plunging back toward the shore.

Even with the head start he doesn't stand a chance. Taking a deep breath, I dive down under the water, kicking forward and feeling for all the world like a mermaid with my hair streaming out behind me, moving swiftly over the bed of golden sand. I swim far enough that I overtake Charlie before surfacing in front of him. "Hey!" I hear him shout, but his protests are snatched away by a dancing breeze and I carry on moving forward, slipping through the water. I can hear the others on the shore shouting and cheering, and as I stagger out onto the sand I see that Caitlin has jumped to her feet.

"You did it!" she squeals, throwing herself at me. "You were amazing!"

I laugh, trying to push the tangle of wet hair out of my eyes. Someone hands me a towel and I look up to see it is Robert.

Charlie has reached the sand now and he is shaking his head in disbelief. "I can't believe you're so fast," he pants, and I feel myself glowing at the admiration in his eyes. "It's like racing a fish."

Hmm. My face falls. I'm not sure I like that comparison, actually.

"Don't compare Lou to a fish!" Caitlin exclaims hotly, like a true friend.

"I was just saying she swam like one." Charlie holds up his hands in mock surrender. "Gosh, it was *supposed* to be a compliment."

I shrug. "My sister and I always raced a lot," I say. I can't resist smirking at Charlie. "She's a lot harder to beat."

Everyone laughs at this.

"Now I have no trouble believing you swim out here to the island on a regular basis," Robert says. "You looked like a sea sprite out there."

"It's just the way it is if you grow up here," I reply with another shrug, a little thrown by what I *think* is almost a compliment. "You're always in the water, or on the water. I love the sea."

The rest of the afternoon seems to melt away in a lazy, golden haze of reading and drinking and aimless chatter. I feel the night before catching up with me, and I lie back in the sand with my eyes closed against the sun.

"It sounds terribly dull down here." A voice rings out moments later, and I lift myself on my elbow to see that Bernie has arrived, carrying two big bottles of champagne. Trailing behind him and carrying a big wicker picnic basket is one of the handsome young men I saw him with last night. "I'm glad we didn't bother to drag ourselves out of bed any earlier, if this is the state of things."

"If you're not careful, Bernie, you're going to turn into a vampire," Patricia says. "It's practically evening again."

Bernie bares his teeth as though showing off a pair of fangs. "I always have been something of a creature of the night," he says. "It's when all the best things happen. Who needs all this sunlight and fresh air?" He shudders. "Give me a dark, smoky corner any day of the week." These last words are practically a purr, directed at the man beside him, whose cheeks flush pink. "Anyway, darlings," Bernie continues, "there's no need to nag me when I've rustled up such a lovely feast!" Bernie throws his arms open as though he has carefully prepared each dish himself and expects a round of applause.

Caitlin rolls her eyes. "I think Eustace is the one who's done the heavy lifting there," she says, smiling at the boy who is staring worshipfully at Bernie.

"Not to mention Mrs. Vickers in the kitchen," Robert drawls.

Bernie falls gracefully onto the end of Laurie's lounger, one leg swinging easily over the other. "Semantics, my dears," he says, already pulling the cork from one of the champagne bottles. "Semantics. After all, I was in charge of the most important bit." His sentence is punctuated by the popping of the cork, and Caitlin rushes forward with a glass.

The champagne is poured and we all stand (except for Laurie, who is still lounging). I feel the sand between my toes, and the late afternoon sun overhead. My body is loose and relaxed—tired and awake all at once.

"Well," Bernie says, raising his glass. His eyes meet mine, fleetingly. "Here's to a long and beautiful summer. May God bless her and all who sail in her."

CHAPTER ELEVEN

When I arrive home in the early evening I feel as though I am a different person than the girl who left the house only twenty-four hours ago. Everything about the walk back to the farm and even the house itself seems somehow the same but different, and I know that from now on my life will be split into two distinct periods: *Before the Cardews* and *After the Cardews*. I drift through the kitchen door in my blue dress, deliciously aware that I am wearing Caitlin's red bathing suit underneath it and hugging the secret to me like a talisman. I am ready to answer thousands of questions, to relive every single tiny moment in terrific detail, I am ready to tell my tale of glamour and adventure to a spellbound audience. I have mentally compiled a list of a hundred shimmering, magical details with which I will enrapture my listeners. I will, of course, be gracious about the experience, I decide, sharing it with all of them, but not in a boastful way.

Freya is sitting at the kitchen table, wearing a patchwork cloak and dozens of ribbons in her hair, her nose in a book. "Oh, you're back," she says, with a yawn. She turns a page.

"I am," I reply.

There is a long, empty silence. I clear my throat, noisily, but Freya's eyes don't leave her book. Her lack of enthusiasm is like a big bucket of cold water. I sigh. Where was Alice when you needed her?

"Oh!" Freya exclaims, turning to me. Finally, my moment has come. "I almost forgot to say, Midge is waiting for you in the other room." Freya turns the page. "And also, if you see Tom, can you give him a swift kick for me? He spilled ink on the new costume I was making for Cleopatra and he's been skulking in the shadows ever since." Her eyes remain glued to the book in front of her, but her tone is icily murderous.

I can't blame my brother for hiding away. Freya is notoriously protective of her costumes, and I know from experience that the threat of violence is not a hollow one.

Pa appears in the doorway then, wearing the oil-stained overalls that signal car troubles.

"Oh, dear," I say. "How is Gerald?"

"Gerald is just fine," Pa replies. "Though he *is* being a touch temperamental and I promised I would give Mrs. Penrith a lift over to see her son in Penzance." Because Pa is one of the only people in the village to own a car, this kind of thing happens quite a lot, and so Gerald's temperament is of great importance to many people who rely on Pa's ability to keep him running. In Penlyn, people ask after Gerald more than any other member of the family.

"Gerald's *always* a touch temperamental," I say, feeling a twinge of frustration at this familiar tale. It just feels so . . . *normal* after last night. It seems as if everything should be different, but I'm home and it's as if nothing happened at all.

"Did you fix him?" Freya asks. "Mrs. Penrith will go spare if her precious Bobby has to go without his weekly fruitcake."

"We had words"—Pa smiles, a soft, crinkly smile—"and I'm pleased to say that Gerald has decided to live to see another day." He finds a dishrag and begins wiping his hands on it, leaving streaks of oil behind. "Your mother is looking for you, Lou," he adds.

"I *did* tell her," Freya pipes up.

"I just walked through the door!" I exclaim. "I will go through now."

"And I will go and fetch Mrs. Penrith," Pa replies.

"And I will go and purse the ducats straight," cries Freya. Then, shaking her head at our blank faces, "*The Merchant of Venice,* act one, scene three?" Pa and I still say nothing and she shakes her head once more. "Philistines," she mutters. Freya takes Shakespeare very seriously. She memorized Lady Macbeth's sleepwalking scene when she was eleven and her performance is, to this day, the most chilling thing I've ever seen. Tom had nightmares for a week afterward.

I exchange a look with Pa and then make my way through

to the sitting room, where Midge is sitting in an armchair looking the very picture of domesticity. The baby is asleep in a bassinet beside her and she is knitting something. Or, at least, she is trying her best to do so. For some unknown reason Midge finds knitting a terrible challenge, but she can't seem to accept the fact that while there are a million other things that she is good at, she cannot knit to save her life. Instead, she insists on knitting us lumpy and misshapen items of clothing on a regular basis. I groan under my breath, eyeing the bobbly lilac creation in her lap and hoping that it isn't destined for me.

It is then that I notice, with a sinking heart, that Aunt Irene is sitting across from Midge like a malevolent bat, her mouth set in a thin and disapproving line. I curse Freya and Pa in my head for offering up no warning about this. It is, at best, unsportsmanlike. This appearance also probably explains Midge's desire for me to join her *as soon as possible.* Aunt Irene's presence is certainly not the ideal welcome home, although I am determined that it will not dampen my spirits.

"Hello!" I exclaim, breezing in and kissing Midge on one warm cheek. "Aunt Irene! What a nice surprise."

"Oh, it is, is it?" Aunt Irene says acidly.

I turn to Midge questioningly and she gives me the tiniest roll of her eyes. Obviously her older sister has come over to disapprove of something—it is one of her favorite pastimes.

"You're back, are you?" Aunt Irene sniffs, and it becomes painfully clear that today the full force of her disapproval is reserved for me. These kinds of rhetorical questions are always part of the warm-up to a good scolding.

"Yes," I say unnecessarily. "I am." So far the fact that I am back seems to be the only thing my family is interested in, so I'm relieved when Midge asks if I have had a nice time.

"It was wonderful," I say, unable to keep the emotion out of my voice, even though I know that Aunt Irene won't like it. I sit down next to Midge's chair and rest my head against her knee, as I have done since I was little when I wanted to talk to her about something.

"That's good, then," she says placidly, smoothing the hair back from my face. "I was just telling Irene how nice it is that you're making new friends."

A hissing noise comes through Aunt Irene's teeth, one that makes her sound like an angry cat.

"Everything was so beautiful, Midge," I carry on, choosing to ignore the black cloud of displeasure lurking in the corner. "It's like something from a fairy tale seeing the house all woken up like that."

"And did they feed you well?" asks the ever-practical Midge, for whom good food is always the top priority at any social event.

"They did." I nod. "And, oh, it was so funny last night. For the party everyone came dressed in white and everything was decorated so beautifully in white and silver, and then at dinner all the food was white, every single course."

"Ridiculous!" Aunt Irene spits as if it is the filthiest word she knows.

"And the party was in the orchard and the place was hung with lights and silver fruit, and there was dancing," I continue stubbornly.

"Dancing!" Aunt Irene puts in here, and it seems she has found a dirtier word than "ridiculous," after all.

"Yes." I nod innocently. "Dancing. To jazz music."

But this is a bridge too far for Aunt Irene, who visibly swells. "Did you hear that, Midge? *Jazz music!* Did you hear what she said?" If I was writing Aunt Irene as a character, I'd probably give her a cane that she would slam into the floor at this point for emphasis. As it is, Aunt Irene makes do with flinging her hands in the air.

"Yes, I heard perfectly well, thank you," Midge says. "I don't care for it myself, but according to the children it's all the rage."

"You said you quite liked Jelly Roll Morton when Tom played you the record," I point out helpfully.

"Yes, that's right." Midge nods. "I remember. It was very jolly."

"*Midge!*" Aunt Irene's indignation lifts her from her seat and she stands, outraged, in the middle of the room. "How *could* you? *Jelly roll,* indeed!"

I have to stifle a giggle here at the way Aunt Irene says the words "jelly roll," and her eyes snap in my direction.

"I don't see that there's anything funny about it, Louise," she barks. "It's uncivilized is what it is. It's not proper for a girl like you to be dancing around to that . . . that *sort* of music. And I certainly can't believe that you allow it in the house, Midge."

"Oh, calm down, Reeny," Midge says, clacking away with her knitting needles. "We were all young once . . . even you, as I recall."

"You're still young, Midge," I say affectionately because it is the truth, however hard she tries to make out that she is an old matron. The same cannot be said of Irene, who is ten years older than her sister, and looks and acts another ten years older than that.

"So, you've been off dancing and drinking and doing goodness knows what with those troublemakers," Aunt Irene snaps, turning her attention to me.

"They're not troublemakers," I say, biting back laughter again and thinking that Caitlin would probably quite enjoy the description. "It was just a party," I add, deciding to leave the more salacious details out until Aunt Irene is gone.

"*Just* a party." Aunt Irene falls back into her seat with a thud. "Their parents must be turning in their graves, the way those children behave."

"Did you know them?" I perk up then, interested to hear about Robert and Caitlin's parents.

"Not personally." Irene sniffs. "Though their reputations were absolutely spotless, of course. A credit to the village, they were."

"Lady Cardew died when Caitlin was born," I prompt.

"That's right," Aunt Irene says. "And poor Lord Cardew,

left with those two little children on his hands. He never re-married, you know, and it wasn't because there wasn't inter-est, believe me." Her eyes are gleaming now. Aunt Irene can play the Victorian widow all she likes, but there is little she enjoys more than a good gossip. And Lord Cardew's decision not to remarry obviously meets with her approval, lifting him up somewhere near sainthood. "He served with distinction during the war, of course, as you'd expect," she carries on.

"And when did he die?" I ask.

"Only a couple of years ago," Aunt Irene says thought-fully. "Not long after your dear departed uncle." Here she lifts a handkerchief to her dry eye, as is her habit when she mentions Uncle Art. Midge and I remain quiet, because to speak too quickly after Uncle Art's name has come up is to be branded ungrateful, unfeeling, and to receive a sharp lec-ture on the respectful treatment of one's elders.

"How did he die?" I push further, breaking the silence after what I judge is an appropriate amount of time.

Aunt Irene's eyes glint dangerously, but fortunately, her love of gossip wins out over her sense of propriety. "I'm not sure," she says. "Some sort of accident, I believe. Riding, I heard . . . so surprising, because he *was* a great horseman. Poor man. We didn't see much of him around the village after Lady Cardew died," she adds. "Just the occasional summer holiday with the children. They seemed to lose their enthusiasm for the place after her passing—she was so fond of Penlyn. A real lady, she was, not like those young good-for-nothings."

Unfortunately, this reminder of the children brings her

back around to her original grievance. "And it isn't proper for you to be up there at the big house, all high and mighty," she snaps. "You don't belong with them."

"Those things don't matter anymore," I say lightly, waving my hand. I try not to let Aunt Irene's words faze me, but I can't help thinking about standing on the front steps with Lucky last night. Caitlin and Robert and their friends were so welcoming, but when it came down to it I *wasn't* quite one of them. I even know that it's *because* of that fact that I was invited . . . someone new, someone different.

"Oh, yes, those things do matter, my girl, and the sooner you realize that the better. It's not right," Irene says. "If you keep on with that lot, people will think you're no better than you ought to be."

"Irene!" Midge exclaims. "Really, that's enough." Even I am surprised by that remark and the accompanying sour-lemon face. It burns me up that crotchety old ladies like my aunt think that just because young people like to dress up and go to parties that they're somehow loose or morally questionable.

"I'm only saying what others will think." Irene scowls.

"I don't care what anyone else thinks," I say mutinously.

"Oho!" Aunt Irene waves a finger in my direction. "That's all well and good now, but what about in a few weeks' time when they all go back to London and leave you behind with your reputation in tatters? What will you do then? You ought to be finding a nice boy to settle down with, not running around with those . . . those . . . *reprobates*."

I feel something hard lodging itself in my chest.

"Leave her alone, Irene," Midge says wearily. "If Lou likes these people, they can't be as bad as you think, and they've certainly been very welcoming to her. You're getting yourself all worked up over nothing."

"This is all your fault, Midge," Irene continues, turning on her, getting into her stride now. "You let all those children run wild, getting into mischief and doing whatever they like. It's a miracle your Alice managed to catch an upstanding boy like Jack."

"Alice could have had her pick of anyone, and Jack's been in love with her since we were children," I exclaim hotly.

"Well, more fool him, then," Irene bites off. "You're certainly going to have to buck up your ideas if you don't want to end up an old maid. *You* haven't got your sister's looks to fall back on."

Oof. That one hurt.

"I'm not going to end up an old maid!" I hiss, jumping to my feet. "I'm only seventeen, for heaven's sake. Just because you don't remember what being young feels like, there's no need to try and turn my life into a tragedy." I am sick of this. Why does the sum total of my ambition have to be getting married, anyway? Doesn't anyone else think there is more to life? That I have something else to offer?

"Lou's right," Midge says firmly, placing a soothing hand on my arm, and I feel my heart fill with love for her. "And there's no harm in her having a bit of fun before she settles down."

I frown, the hard feeling returning in my chest. I wonder

what "settling down" means exactly, and when it is supposed to start.

Aunt Irene sniffs again. "You'll see I'm right in the end," she mutters darkly. "Then you'll all be sorry."

Just then we are interrupted by the door flying open, and Alice barrels in.

"Where is she?" she screeches, and then her eyes fall on me. "Oh, Lou, I heard you were back . . . you have to tell me everything! You have to tell me everything right now! I've been dying, I tell you, just dying!"

Aunt Irene lifts her eyebrows. "You see," she says smugly. "Wild, the lot of them."

"Oh, hello, Aunt Irene," Alice sings sunnily. "Didn't see you there. You won't mind if I borrow Lou for a bit, will you?" and with that she is tugging my arm and pulling me from the room back toward the kitchen.

Freya must have gone on the hunt for Tom, because both she and her book are gone. Alice closes the door firmly behind us so that we can no longer hear the tirade against our abysmal manners that Aunt Irene is pouring into Midge's ear. I feel a pang of guilt. It's not fair that Midge has to put up with her sister when she gets on her high horse. Midge might have the patience of a saint but sooner or later even she loses her temper with Irene. Still, selfishly, I am relieved that at least I don't have to listen to her anymore.

"Thank God for that," I say, rubbing my shoulder where Alice has nearly pulled my arm from its socket. "I couldn't stand being stuck with her for another minute."

"Is she playing the dragon with you about the Cardews?" Alice asks, perching on the edge of the big kitchen table. "She's been rattling on about it ever since she found out."

I groan. "Is it really all over the village?" I ask, moving over to the stove to boil water and make some tea. I need it.

"Of course." Alice grins. "It's the most exciting thing to happen for ages. Everyone wants to know what they're up to over there . . . including me! Now, come on, don't leave out a single, tiny detail. Dish."

"Oh, Alice." I swoon against the kitchen counter. "It. Was. Amazing."

"I knew it!" She claps her hands together. "I knew it would be. Tell me everything."

And so I bring over a pot of tea and a plate of biscuits, and I do. Or, at least, I tell her nearly everything. What I don't tell her is about the tempest of longing that the visit has unleashed inside me. I've peeped into that world now and it hasn't satisfied my curiosity, it has only stirred it to greater heights. I want more; more life, more light, more of everything.

Alice hangs on every word, and I revel in the feeling of having an appreciative audience. "Will you go back?" she asks finally, cutting right to the heart of the thing.

I try to look offhand about it. "I think so," I say carefully. "Caitlin says I have an open invitation to drop in whenever I like."

Alice's eyes are round. "Really?" she asks.

I nod, taking a sip of my tea. What Caitlin had actually

said was that she expected me to be over all the time and that they wanted me for as much of the summer as possible. This was eagerly echoed by the rest of the party, although I couldn't quite understand why. I mean, I know why the whole thing is exciting for me, but not what I have done to elicit such enthusiasm from them.

"I don't know quite what to do, though," I say. "It wasn't an actual invitation with a date or time or anything. Do you think I can really just turn up?" I try not to sound too hopeful, but the idea of spending the entire summer in that vibrant, exciting world makes me fizz inside.

"Hmm." Alice wrinkles her nose. "I'm not sure. It sounds like they want you around, so maybe?"

"I think I'm a bit of a novelty," I mutter then, forcing myself to say the words, thinking back to what Bernie had said about new being interesting, about that feeling of being on display. I don't really want to dwell on it too much.

"I suppose that makes sense," Alice agrees. "I doubt they spend a lot of time with farmers' daughters."

I definitely don't like that. It sounds too close to what Aunt Irene said.

"Things like that don't matter anymore," I say again, though without as much conviction.

"Well, not as much as they used to, no," Alice says, and we drink our tea in silence for several moments.

"Alice . . . ," I begin tentatively. "Do you ever think about, I don't know, leaving Penlyn?"

Alice frowns. "What do you mean?" she asks.

"Well," I say slowly. "You love clothes so much, you could go and see things, you could work in a shop or for a designer."

Alice laughs. "Oh, yes?" She wiggles her eyebrows. "And what about the small matter of my husband?"

"He could go with you," I suggest.

Alice is shaking her head. "Are you being serious?" She looks puzzled. "Jack's a fisherman, Lou. He's going to inherit his father's business. Why would we go somewhere else?"

"For you!" I exclaim. "So that you could do something exciting!"

"I *am* doing something exciting," Alice says simply. "I don't want to leave Penlyn. I like it here. What's got into you, Lou?" Her brow is creased in concern.

"You're right," I say hollowly. "Nothing's got into me. I'm fine, honestly." I play with my teacup. "So, you're happy?" I ask in a small voice.

"Of course I am!" Alice exclaims, her hands thrown up in the air. "Can't you tell?" And she's right, she *is* happy, and I *can* tell. She is absolutely glowing with it. She looks just like a newlywed should look.

"Yes," I say. "And I'm glad. Sorry, I'm just being silly."

"That's all right," Alice replies, getting to her feet. "I have to get home, but come over for dinner this week. I'll get out the candlesticks for you . . . if you're not too busy spending time with your new fancy friends to see us little people," she adds, and there's something in the way she says it that hangs awkwardly between us.

"Of course." I hug her tightly, trying to ignore the strange atmosphere, and then she disappears through the door and out into the night. I slump back into my seat and stare glumly into the bottom of my empty teacup as though I am hoping to find some answers there.

"Oh, you're back," a voice says, and I look up to see Tom standing in the doorway.

"That does seem to be the consensus," I sigh.

"Haven't seen Freya about anywhere, have you?" His eyes dart nervously from side to side.

"She was in here a while ago, but I don't know where she went," I say. "I heard about the costume, though."

He groans. "Oh, well, that's it, then, if she *knows* then I'm as good as dead."

"I can't believe you're afraid of our little Freya," I tease.

Tom snorts. "Oh, yes, you can, or would you like me to tell her it was *you* who ruined her costume?"

"You wouldn't dare," I hiss.

"Not so funny when the shoe's on the other foot, is it?" Tom says smugly, before his face falls. "Well, better tell Midge I'm off staying at Harry's house until the storm passes. A couple of days should do." Tom strides across the kitchen and vanishes into the pantry.

"Aunt Irene will love that," I call. "You disappearing without asking permission or anything. She's already going on and on about how wild we are."

"Is that old crow here again as well?" Tom asks, his horrified face sticking around the pantry door. "All the more

181

reason to beat a hasty retreat. Send up a white flag when it's safe to come home, won't you?"

"How about I hang a pillowcase out of my window instead?" I ask.

"Perfect." He emerges from the pantry clutching a currant bun from which he takes an enormous bite. "Right, I'm off," he mumbles, turning for the door. "Oh," he says through a mouthful of crumbs. "I forgot to say. There's someone here to see you. He's waiting outside."

"What! Who?" I ask, jumping to my feet.

"Dunno. Some posh bloke." Tom shrugs. "I can't pay attention to every little detail, I'm not your butler," he huffs. "Anyway, see you later."

"Oh, hello, Freya!" I say loudly, looking past his shoulder.

The blood drains from his face and he swings around to find that no one is standing behind him. "That's just cruel," he says. "You shouldn't treat your own brother so badly. I am your flesh and blood, you know."

"More bad luck on my part," I grumble, but Tom is already gone.

I step outside, and I don't know why my heart is beating faster or who I expect to see standing there, but it's certainly not the figure before me.

"Bernie?" I call out, and he turns around, his light, pale suit easily visible against the navy-blue sky. He sweeps a rather jaunty hat from his head and grins wolfishly.

"Hello, Lou," he says.

"What are you doing here?" I ask, and the question

182

sounds rude, abrupt. "Sorry," I say quickly. "I just meant it's a surprise to see you. Is everything OK?"

His smile grows wider. "Everything is fine," he says. "I've simply dropped around as a messenger. Perhaps you and I can take a little walk?" He holds his elbow out to me, and I hesitate before slipping my hand into the crook of his arm. There's something so knowing about Bernie that I find it a little unnerving.

"Caitlin asked me to drop over and invite you to dinner tomorrow," he says softly as we walk along the coastal path.

"Oh!" The noise that comes out of me is one of undisguised pleasure.

Bernie ducks his chin. "Yes, Robert pointed out that you aren't used to our ramshackle behavior, and so the hopelessly vague invitation that Caitlin offered up might put you in an awkward spot."

How surprisingly thoughtful of Robert, I think, and again I have the sense that Bernie can read my mind. He chuckles. "Oh, you'll find that Robert can be most charming when he puts his mind to it," he says.

"Not on the evidence I've seen," I grumble.

Bernie makes no response to that. We round the bend in the path and now the Cardew House is in front of us lit up, the reflection of the lights dancing in the water.

"I'm a terribly selfish person," Bernie says then, rather unexpectedly. His eyes are trained on the house.

"What?" I stumble. What am I supposed to say to that?

Bernie looks down and smiles at me. "Oh, I am, darling.

I like to please myself, and I'm afraid I'm not awfully careful with people's feelings. But the Cardews . . ." He trails off here, and reaches into his pocket for a cigarette case. He offers one to me and I shake my head. In a graceful movement Bernie lifts a cigarette to his lips and lights it with a silver lighter. He inhales. "The Cardews are my *friends*." He places an emphasis on the word that makes it clear Bernie doesn't consider many people in this capacity. The Cardews are special. "And those two have been through a lot." Bernie is still looking out at the house and I have gone very still beside him. His words are hypnotic. "I do not care for many people, Lou, but I care for them." He finishes, turning to me.

This serious, careful Bernie is completely at odds with the man I met last night. With a start I begin to think I understand. Bernie is being protective of his friends. But why?

"They've been kind to me," I say carefully. And it's true. Even though I hardly know them.

Bernie looks at me through narrow eyes, and finally he nods. "One can't be too careful," he says, and his voice is tinged with weariness. "The vultures are always circling, and the press . . ." He trails off and clears his throat. "When someone new arrives, someone entirely unknown, you understand, it puts one at a disadvantage." He smiles, showing his teeth. "I am not used to being in the dark about people, but I confess that you are a mystery to me."

"I promise you, I'm not the least bit mysterious," I reply quickly.

"And you're not in contact with the press in any way?" Bernie asks. His voice is soft and silky, but I know there's steel behind it.

I'm surprised by the question. "Of course not!" I exclaim. "Why on earth would I be?" I gesture back toward the farm. "I don't know if you've noticed, but I'm not exactly in the middle of things here. I'm hardly at the hub of some bustling metropolis crackling with news." I fold my arms. "Besides which, I'd never sneak to the papers about anything even if I were."

Bernie smiles a little at this.

"Why . . . why *isn't* Caitlin ever in the papers?" I ask hesitantly.

Bernie exhales a stream of smoke. "Because of Robert," he says finally. "Robert is the sacrificial lamb when it comes to the press. He lets them run what they like on him. But they can't go near Caitlin."

"Why not?" I ask, and my voice is little more than a whisper. There is something underneath Bernie's words, something slippery and secret.

"Caitlin is . . . a trifle *delicate*." Bernie shifts beside me. "Which is why I wanted to talk to you, to make sure . . ." He leaves his sentence trailing in the air, but this time the meaning is clear. He wants to make sure I won't hurt her.

"I—" I begin, and I take a deep breath. "I'm not completely sure what you mean," I say, although I do think there's more going on with her than meets the eye, but I want to reassure Bernie somehow. "But, if it helps . . . I just want to be her friend." The words sound small, but they are true, and they mean something to me.

I think Bernie understands that. I think neither of us has a large group of friends—not real, true friends anyway. I have always had Alice, I suppose, so I've never really thought about it, but Bernie's reasons must be different.

"Good." He throws the cigarette to the ground, grinding it under his shoe. The smile he gives me now reaches his eyes. "Then I look forward to seeing you tomorrow. We all do." With that he takes my hand and lifts it to his lips with exaggerated chivalry.

I feel like I have passed some kind of test. Bernie tips his hat to me once more and saunters off down the path, back toward the causeway. He looks so untroubled that it is as if the conversation never took place. I stand for a moment, looking out at the island before turning for home.

Over the top of all the emotions stirred by my conversation with Bernie, one thought clamors to the front. I am going back. *Tomorrow.* I hug the news tightly to my chest. They do want me. Aunt Irene is wrong about them, just as she is wrong about me. I feel something heavy lifting off me as a fierce desire fills my body.

Change is coming, I can feel it crackling in the air around me, and I know that I am dancing on the edge of something new and deliciously unknown. The rest of the summer reaches out before me and I decide that I will take everything it has to offer with greedy, outstretched hands.

PART TWO

"There was music from my
neighbor's house through the
summer nights. In his blue gardens
men and girls came and went like
moths among the whisperings and
the champagne and the stars."

—F. Scott Fitzgerald, *The Great Gatsby*

CHAPTER TWELVE

It has been five weeks since that first party and I have barely been home. At first I stay over at the Cardew House for the odd night, but soon I begin to disappear from the farm for three or four days at a time. Caitlin has renamed the blue room "Lou's room" and each time I arrive there seems to be some new little luxury waiting for me—a silk scarf, some chocolates, or a new bottle of scent. Waking up in that big cloud-like bed—just as comfortable as I hoped it would be—I marvel at how lucky I am and, although I know it can't last forever, like Cinderella I am happy simply to enjoy the time I have at the party—every last bit of it.

The Cardews plan to leave Cornwall and return to London at the end of the month, which leaves me three more weeks of freedom. It's strange that I think of it that way, I suppose, but I do—here, I'm gloriously free from reality, free from decision-making, free from all thoughts of the future. If there is one thing that the Cardews and their friends really excel at, it's living in the moment. Why think about tomorrow when there is so much pleasure to be squeezed out of today?

Plans are rarely made, but whims are often followed. We burn the candle at both ends, and even at our most languorous and lazy—even when it seems we are doing little more than lolling about—I feel an electric pulse running through us all. Perhaps it is the weather, so hot as to make me feel feverish, but there is an undeniable energy about the place that crackles more and more intensely as the weeks pass. We are a powder keg waiting to explode.

And if we are all burning, then Caitlin is burning the brightest. She is always moving, always talking, always dancing. She is also thinner than she was when she arrived, and I rarely see her eat anything—although a drink is never far from her reach. I notice that Robert sometimes prepares food for her, quietly peeling fruit and placing it next to her so that she eats it, absently, without pausing in her excited conversation. It's one of many small actions that remind me of Bernie's word, *delicate.*

People come and go from the house, and Robert is away often, for days at a time, seeing to the murky and mysterious world of "business" in London. He comes back from these trips more tightly wound, more serious. As a result, I haven't seen as much of him, but we are getting on a little better, our bickering only occasionally erupting into something more serious. Between his surprising tenderness toward his sister and his love of Gothic fiction I am beginning to think it's possible that I *might* have judged him a little harshly. At least, I start to until he says something to deliberately antagonize me.

Caitlin has yet to leave the island at all. She has firmly planted herself here, and she surrounds herself with people. They buzz around her all day like little bees around their queen.

There has been plenty to enjoy. More parties, of course, and dinners, and—when Robert is home—trips to Penzance in the shiny blue car with the roof down. There has been swimming, and games on the beach, and music in the evenings, and cocktails on the lawn. There has been dancing around the sitting room to the latest records, playing cards and trading jibes, and curling up in corners reading all the new additions Robert has bought for the library. My life has, in short, turned into one long, pleasure-seeking holiday, and why on earth would I be anything other than ecstatic about it?

The island keeps us safe in our fantasy—cocooned, and far removed from the brisk realities of the outside world. When the tide comes in and the water kisses the sand down in the cove I breathe a sigh of relief that I have been marooned again. I feel the hours slipping dreamily through my fingers, and the pleasure and pain of it is almost too much to bear.

The evenings that I enjoy best of all are the ones where all the guests disappear and Caitlin, Robert, Laurie, Charlie and I eat dinner outside, at a long table pulled out underneath a cloud of honeysuckle. Moths reel overhead, drunk on moonlight, as we talk until the candles on the table gutter and burn down. The evenings are warm and intoxicating, and we laugh and use our fingers to tear into the perfectly ripe figs that the orchard offers up like a gift.

One afternoon at the beginning of August, though who knows precisely which, as the days melt effortlessly into one another, I am on one of my visits home when Alice drops by. Every so often I duck back to the farm to show my face and take care of some of the chores that I have been willfully neglecting, while placating Freya, who has taken over quite a lot of them on the promise of payment in books and new fabric for her Medusa costume. I should feel guilty about it, I know, but I don't really. Perhaps it's because without my presence, the farm and everything on it seems to continue to run just fine; in fact, it has been rather bruising to my ego how dispensable I seem to be.

Pa seems largely oblivious to my whereabouts anyway, and Midge accepts my disappearances without question. At first I feel I need to ask her permission, but after a while she tells me that she has enough to worry about, what with Freya and Tom trying to kill each other, the triplets wriggling their way into mischief at all hours of the day and night, and the baby teething. I am a sensible girl, she says, I can do what I like. I am glad that Midge thinks this, but I certainly don't feel sensible. What I feel is giddy and reckless. I feel like turning cartwheels in the sand.

At this particular instant I am having a rare moment of quiet, sitting in the meadow in front of the house alone and writing in my journal. A shout splits the air and I look up to see Alice cutting along the path through the field toward me. Her hair spills over her shoulders and her pale blue dress is hiked up as she walks barefoot along the dusty path. She looks for a moment like she has dropped out of another century, she is such an ideal picture of a rural beauty—almost as if she should be holding a crook and followed by a line of gamboling little lambs. I haven't seen much of Alice in the last few weeks, and that feels odd, agitating—like an itch I can't scratch. It is difficult to put my finger on what has shifted in our relationship, but it is clear that something has, something important.

"Hello!" I call, lifting a hand to my eyes and I am surprised by the flutter of nerves in my stomach. Why would I feel nervous about seeing Alice? I shake my head, as if to shake the feeling loose.

Alice comes to a stop just in front of me and for a moment I think that she feels the same awkwardness, but then she smiles her Alice smile and flops down in the long grass beside me. "What are you writing?" she asks.

"Nothing really," I say, casually closing the journal. "Just some notes. Story ideas."

"That's great." Alice tugs at a long blade of grass. "It's been ages since you've written anything. I'm still waiting for the further adventures of Lady Amelia."

"Oh." I cough awkwardly. "Yes. I have actually written a bit more of that."

"Have you?" Alice's voice is surprised but pleased. "That's good," she says lightly. "I thought you'd forgotten all about her."

"Actually, I thought *you* probably had," I say honestly. "I thought you'd be, you know, too busy for that now."

"Too busy for Lady Amelia?" She turns to me, indignant. "Of course not. So, can I read it?"

"I—I don't have it here." I stumble because the conversation feels like it's moving into dangerous territory somehow. "It's at the Cardew House." There is a long pause and I shift my feet. I feel Alice's eyes move to my toes, and to the ruby-red paint gleaming on the nails.

"I see," she says.

"But next time I come back I'll bring it for you . . . ," I begin eagerly, too eagerly. "I'm actually just about to head over so I could—"

Alice interrupts with a wave of her hand. "Oh, no, don't worry," she says, and again her voice is as light as the snowy meringues that Midge whips up. "I'll read it at some point, I'm sure. I'm actually quite busy at the moment with sorting the house out. I've finally started digging out the garden and Pa promised me some seeds." She pushes herself to her feet. "I should go and find him." She stands above me, and her smile is gone now. A small crease of worry mars her lovely face.

I nod. "Of course," I agree, and my voice sounds a little hollow. I hold out my hand and Alice takes it, helping me to my feet. I keep hold of her fingers for a moment, giving them a gentle squeeze. "I can't wait to see what it looks like when you're finished," I say.

Her face softens. "Yes, I'd like that," she says, and then she lets go of my hand.

"I suppose I'd better go as well," I murmur.

"Yes." Alice dusts off the front of her dress with brisk hands. "Well, have a nice time, then," she says, not quite looking at me.

"Thank you," I say, wondering why our voices have gone all stiff and polite again. "Good luck with the seeds," I call after her as she walks toward the house. "Although," I add, my voice getting louder, "if you actually manage to grow anything after the way you slaughtered those sunflowers I'll be amazed."

Alice burbles with laughter and I immediately feel lighter. "How on earth was I supposed to know you could *overwater* the things?" she shouts back over her shoulder, and she lifts her hand in a jaunty wave.

I return the gesture and set off once more, bound for the Cardew House. As I walk I think about Alice. It feels as if our once-familiar rhythm has been thrown off, always a beat ahead or behind one another.

But there is no room for unpleasant things in my life at the moment. I am keeping all uncomfortable thoughts firmly at bay, defending myself against them with endless wish fulfillment. These thoughts may mostly be about my own future, but they include my relationship with Alice as well. In an increasingly hard-to-ignore corner of my brain I know that things will be different after the summer is over, so for now I am living like a mayfly, enjoying my brief time in the sun and turning away all ideas of tomorrow.

I hustle along, over the causeway, feeling my worries slipping away with each step I take toward the house. When I reach the front door I turn the handle, letting myself in without ceremony. I go to the sitting room first, although I don't expect anyone to be there. On such a nice day they're probably down at the beach, so I will collect my book and join them. I am humming, my footsteps ringing through the hallway as I walk.

I open the door and stop abruptly on the threshold. I'm surprised to find Robert inside, sprawled in one of the armchairs with a book in his hands. He's been gone for most of the week, and the sight of him gives me a strange jolt of pleasure that leaves me feeling flustered. I have found that as the weeks pass I look forward to his homecoming more and more. I don't know why. Probably because Caitlin is obviously so much happier when he's around.

"I was reading that," I say, pushing the feeling away as I make my way into the room.

He gets to his feet, the book hanging from his fingers. Despite the warmth of the day he is smartly dressed, and he looks as sharp and polished as a piece of silverware. We must make an odd picture as I stand in front of him in a worn green dress that's slightly too small for me, my hair a tangle of sea breeze. He reaches inside his jacket pocket and pulls out a blue notebook, and I feel a pang of guilt about the conversation I have just had with Alice, mixed with an undeniable sense of pleasure, though I try to keep all sign of that out of my eyes.

It is not the same blue notebook that he had before. In fact, I have written several more chapters of *Lady Amelia's Revenge* and passed them on to Robert. I don't like to admit to myself how much his quiet enjoyment of them means to me. Some evenings we have even sat together, me writing and him scribbling away in his own notebook—probably dull-as-dishwater matters of business, but still, there has been something companionable about it. I take the book from him. "Well?" I ask, studiously disinterested.

"You certainly caught me out with the red herring of the missing key," he admits, sitting back in the chair, while I flop into the sofa across from him. "But I don't think much of this new character." He looks at me from under his eyebrows.

"Oh?" I manage faintly.

"Yes," he says. "This wicked Lord Marvell is a bit much, if you ask me."

"Oh, really?" I keep my voice polite, but I still can't meet his eye.

"Really." Robert's voice is dry. "So obnoxious and arrogant. I can't imagine where you found the inspiration for such a villain."

"Mmm," I choke.

"I actually rather liked him," Robert continues silkily. "Poor fellow's probably misunderstood. Just after a bit of peace and quiet . . ."

I can't fight the laughter anymore, and it erupts from me as I finally look up. His green eyes are laughing too, I think, though he is much better than me at keeping it held in.

"*Not* a very flattering portrait, thank you, Louise." He tries to sound disapproving.

"I don't know what you mean," I say innocently. "Did you see something of yourself in Lord Marvell?"

He says nothing, only treating me to another stern look.

"How was London?" I ask.

Something sad passes over his face now, and he raises a hand, rubbing his forehead in a gesture of weariness. "London was . . ."—he breathes out—". . . exhausting." He says it quietly, like a confession. It is unlike him to sound so . . . vulnerable. I still find him very hard to read, and like his sister he has yet to confide in me. At times I feel like I know him a bit better now, that he has unbent just a little toward me over the weeks, but at others it's as if he's still a stranger— shut off and remote.

I lean forward. "Is something wrong?" I ask. I want to reach out and touch his hand, but I don't.

He looks at me, and for a second I think he is going to open up, to tell me the secret sorrow that he is carrying, but then he smiles. It is not a real smile, just a curling of the lips. "Oh, no," he says lightly. "Just too many late nights, a lot of boring parties."

I nod, pretending to believe him. It is clear to me—it has been for some time—that the Cardews are hiding something. There is something dark that sometimes flickers around the edges of this golden daydream that we're living in. Something that makes Caitlin hum like a bulb about to shatter, something taut in Robert's eyes when he looks at her. Part of me wants them to trust me enough with whatever it is, but another cowardly part of me chooses to ignore it, to add it to the list of troubles that I am casting aside. It is, I realize, what they are doing too, carefully removing anything that doesn't fit into the world we are making, one lit by pleasure and indulgence.

At that moment Caitlin and Laurie step in through the open French windows, arm in arm and deep in conversation about a mutual acquaintance who has evidently been up to something scandalous.

"Robert!" Caitlin comes to a halt, a smile splitting her face before she rushes to embrace her brother. He wraps his arms around her, and over her head he glances at Laurie. Laurie nods her head just a little. Then she notices me intercepting the look, and her smile widens to include me.

"And Lou's back as well," she says. "The whole family together again."

"And now that you're *finally* all here, shall we go and have drinks on the lawn?" Caitlin asks, tucking her hand into mine and pulling me along in her wake. I follow her into the sunshine.

CHAPTER THIRTEEN

Two days later, I am still here on the island. The day is one of the hottest so far and I am sitting out on the beach. Robert disappeared again this morning, and Caitlin is off making long, gossipy phone calls in the cool of the house. The others have been coming and going, but I am feeling lazy, weighed down by the heat. It is the kind of heat that wraps itself around you, and that shimmers in the distance, sending ripples through the air. There isn't even a whisper of a breeze coming in from the sea, and I pull my hair away from my sticky neck. Even in my thin summer dress my body feels hot and sleepy. I am toying with the idea of throwing myself into the water, or of getting up in search of a cold drink that, on the one hand, will stop me from dying of dehydration, and on the other involves me actually moving, when I hear a voice call my name.

I turn to see that Caitlin is skipping down the steps toward me. She stops in front of me, and the close-fitting straw hat on top of her blond head is one that I haven't seen before. Pale blue silk flowers adorn the brim, matching her cobweb-light dress.

"New hat?" I ask, looking up at her. She stands in front of the sun, and the relief of the temporary shade that is cast over me is immediate. The light flares gold around her silhouette, and she scrunches up her nose in appreciation of my comment.

"I had Robert bring it back from London," she says. "You always notice when I'm wearing something new. It's so nice."

"It's easy." I wince as she moves to the side and the harsh light nearly blinds me again. "You're always wearing something new."

"You sound just like my brother." Caitlin rolls her eyes and slips down beside me. "Next thing, you'll be telling me off for my *extravagant spending.*"

"No!" I exclaim, surprised. "Does he really?" I've never heard Robert mention money before. In fact, I don't think I've ever heard any of them mention money. And he's always happy to indulge his sister—to indulge all of us, I suppose; after all, Agatha Christie novels don't grow on trees, and he rarely fails to bring back a book he thinks that I will like when he returns from the city. It's the sort of gesture that threw me at first, but over the last few weeks I've noticed that, just as Bernie told me, Robert *can* be surprisingly thoughtful: remembering throwaway comments, asking after Freya's theatrics or Tom's cricket match, anticipating what his sister or her guests might need in his absence so that Caitlin doesn't have to worry.

Caitlin bares her teeth in a grimace. "Such a bore," she says, her toes burying themselves in the sand.

We sit in companionable silence for a minute. Caitlin leans back, tipping her face toward the sunshine, and I pick up my notebook, reading through what I've written.

"Are you really not going to let me read it?" Caitlin asks, and her mouth is a rosy pout.

I shake my head. "Not a chance."

Caitlin huffs. "You let Robert read them! I can't believe you let Robert read them but not me."

Nor can I. I shrug to cover my own confusion at this mysterious situation. "He didn't give me much choice," I say mildly. And that's true enough . . . at least about the first chapter. After that I don't really know how it's happened. All I do know is that the writing is like a fine, silvery thread that connects Robert and me. It's special and it's private, and it feels like it could be easily broken.

"I see," Caitlin says. "So I have to steal it if I want to read it."

"But you wouldn't do such a thing." I elbow her lightly in the ribs, noticing again how slight she feels. "Because unlike your horrid brother you have a scrap of decency left in you."

"I love the way you and Robert bicker," Caitlin responds,

looking at me through half-closed eyes. "Especially when it's obvious that the two of you are thick as thieves."

"We are not," I protest, mortified that I can feel the heat rising in my cheeks. Hopefully the warm weather will cover it up. "He's hardly ever here, for one thing, and when he is we're always finding something to argue about."

Caitlin nods. "I know, and I think it's wonderful."

"Do you?" I ask, confused by her response. "Why?"

"Robert needs someone to argue with." Caitlin grins. "Someone who doesn't let him be so stuffy. He never used to be like that, you know . . . *before* . . ."

The word *before* hangs in the air over us, and Caitlin draws circles in the sand with her finger.

Before means before their father died, I know. The ellipsis that comes after that word is never expanded upon. The subject of their father seems to be off-limits for both siblings, and whenever he is mentioned—which is not very often—something big and heavy fills the air. I know very little about his death. Aunt Irene—when she can stoop low enough to stop disapproving of me for five minutes—loves nothing better than to gossip about my new friends, but even she knows little outside of the fact that he died a little less than two years ago at their country house in Derbyshire. What I do know is that their decision to come to Cornwall now is somehow connected to it all, as well as to Caitlin's health.

"Do you have to go back to the farm today?" Caitlin wheedles, changing the subject. She always calls my house "the farm," never refers to it as my home. She speaks as though my trips there are visits, leaving something behind rather than returning to it.

"Yes, I do," I say firmly, putting my notebook aside. "I haven't been home in almost three days. I need to make sure that Freya hasn't burned the house down trying to hold a séance."

Caitlin giggles. "Did she really do that?"

"Almost." I smirk. "Fortunately Pa was on hand and he put the flames out before they reached the curtains."

Caitlin rolls her shoulders. "I'm completely in love with your family," she murmurs, her eyes closed.

"You haven't met them," I mutter, but there's a pang of something in my chest. Guilt, perhaps? Or homesickness? Surely not. Whenever I do go home I find everything exactly as I left it, which is somehow comforting and frustrating in equal measure.

"But I feel like I know them so well." Caitlin tips her head thoughtfully to one side. "I love hearing you talk about them. They're like characters in a story; I can hardly believe they're real."

I get to my feet, brushing the sand from my legs and holding out my hand to haul Caitlin up. What she says rings in my ears. It was not so long ago that I felt that way about Robert. I frown. Now, none of them fit neatly into the character molds I had built for them in my mind. I was a fool to think that they could be pinned down like paper dolls. It's as silly as thinking the same of Freya or Tom or Alice.

"Tide's out," I say, smothering a yawn with the back of

my hand. All of this late afternoon sunlight is having a soporific effect. "It's now or never, but I'll be back soon."

"Tomorrow?" Caitlin asks, and her eyes are enormous, pleading.

I laugh. "Yes," I say, the word singing from between my lips. "Tomorrow."

I wind my way back to the farm. My limbs are weary—sun-soaked and heavy. I am looking forward to the cool embrace of the farmhouse. When I finally make my way up there, the scene playing out in the front garden stops me in my tracks.

Freya, Tom and the triplets are having a rather slapdash game of cricket. Or, at least, they are attempting to. What really knocks the air out of my lungs is that there is someone else playing too, someone tall and dark and ordinarily much too sensible to play cricket with a group of rowdy schoolchildren.

"Thank goodness you're back, Lou," Tom calls, spotting me. "The triplets are *supposed* to be fielding but they just keep sitting down. I think they've been picking daisies." The disgust is evident in his voice. "What's the use in having brothers if they refuse to grow up?" he grumbles.

"What are you doing here?" I blurt out, eyeing Robert in alarm and ignoring my brother. I've been doing such a good job of keeping my two worlds completely separate that the sight of Robert here with my family is almost incomprehensible—as if the two can't exist in the same space and time.

"Well, that's a nice welcome," Robert replies, but I think he looks a little sheepish.

"Sorry," I say, and I'm still floundering, completely thrown. "I was just surprised to see you. I thought you'd gone back to London. Is everything OK?"

"Everything's fine." He squints at me. "You're very red," he says. "Are *you* all right?"

"I'm hot," I snap, and suddenly I'm not quite sure what to do with my hands, so I fold my arms across my chest. "It is about a million degrees today. Hadn't you noticed?" Although looking at him now, I realize the answer is probably not. He is wearing light trousers and a white shirt. He looks smooth and clean. I, on the other hand, am red, frizzy and covered in ink stains.

"I had to go to the mainland to sign some papers and when I bumped into your father in the village I thought I should introduce myself," Robert is saying. "We got talking and he invited me to tea."

I stand for a moment, processing this. Then I hear the familiar rumble of Gerald approaching. Looking over my shoulder, I see Pa come to a stop behind me.

"Well, Robert," Pa calls, jumping lightly from the car, "I told you they'd take care of you. It seems you've settled in."

"Robert is an excellent fielder." Tom nods, pushing back the too-big rim of a panama hat that I now recognize as one of Robert's.

"And he says we can go and visit his library, Pa!" Freya, resplendent in a headdress full of carefully stitched snakes, hangs on Pa's arm and looks up at him with starry eyes.

"That's very kind of him." Pa smiles down into Freya's pink face and then over at Robert.

"It's my pleasure." Robert grins, and I realize with a start that with his dark curls disheveled, his cheeks slightly pink from running around, and his eyes bright, he looks much younger than usual. He is standing differently too; he seems less coiled up, more loose-limbed and relaxed. I am finding it difficult to meet his eye, and I can feel my already overheated face heating up even further. It's just too strange seeing him here. I never thought of him as fitting into my real life; he was too remote, too neat and tidy, yet now he looks . . . happy. I thought it would feel like an intrusion, having him here, but it doesn't. And, I suppose, on the other side of that, I wanted to keep the Cardews to myself. With them I get to be someone new, someone who doesn't exist only in the context of my family, of where I'm from.

"Will you stay for dinner, Robert?" Midge calls out through the window. And now I *do* look at him, my eyebrows shooting up. He smiles, and I think his expression is rueful, as though he knows that I'm surprised he's made himself so at home. He *has* been busy, I think; in fact, he seems to be on very friendly terms with the whole family.

"Yes, do!" Tom exclaims, rather proving my point. "I can show you that model car I was telling you about." The whole thing is making my head swirl. Seeing Robert Cardew here, it's like . . . I don't know . . . like seeing a tiger on the farm.

"I wish I could," Robert says, and to my surprise his voice seems full of genuine regret, "but we have guests for dinner this evening and my sister will be wondering where I am." He looks out at the sea. "The tide's out, so I should head home."

"Perhaps you could come over for Lou's birthday next week?" Freya says hopefully, and I shoot her a look that I hope communicates that she should shut up. "What?" she hisses. "He is your friend, isn't he?"

Robert's eyes meet mine, and I shift uncomfortably. Is Robert Cardew my friend? The word doesn't fit right; it's too polite, too bland. It's too much and too little all at once. In some ways I feel as though I know almost nothing about him. We bicker and we tease each other, but underneath that there is an understanding, something small and precious that I can't quite define.

"That would be very nice," Robert says finally. "But now I had better be going. Thank you so much for a lovely afternoon, and such wonderful food, Mrs. Trevelyan." He lifts his hat from Tom's head and places it back on his own.

Midge has appeared in the doorway now. "Don't forget this!" she exclaims, holding out a jar of ginger jam for him to take home. My eyes widen at this, the ultimate gesture of acceptance from Midge.

Robert takes the jar from her and thanks her warmly. "Everyone will be fighting over it at breakfast tomorrow."

"Come back again soon," Midge says, squeezing his hand.

I can't take it all in. Robert, here with my family. I am sure my mouth is hanging open, but I just don't seem to be able to get my head around this collision of my two very separate worlds. "I'll walk you down to the causeway." I hear my own voice before I know what I'm saying. "If you like?" I finish awkwardly, scratching my elbow.

"Yes," Robert replies. "I would like that."

He says another goodbye to everyone, and we wander back the way I have just come, along the path toward the village.

"I hope you don't mind that I'm here?" he asks.

"No, of course not," I say quickly. "It's just a bit strange. Seeing you, in my world, I mean."

"Is it so different, this world?" Robert asks, and his face is difficult to read.

"In some ways, no, but in others, yes." I shrug. There's another pause. "We have many customs that may seem foreign to outsiders," I add, attempting to lighten the mood.

"Oh, really?" He raises an eyebrow. "Like what?"

"Well, for example, here in my world," I say, gesturing around us, "it is traditional for you to address the women of the house as 'Your Magnificence.'"

"I see," he says seriously, but a smile tugs at the corner of his mouth. "Anything else? I wouldn't want to embarrass myself in front of your mother."

"Queen High Magnifico," I correct him.

"Indeed," he says, bowing slightly at the waist. "Our most illustrious ruler."

209

We are walking side by side, and our arms are so close together that occasionally I feel the light brush of his shirt-sleeve against my skin.

"Of course it's expected that you bring gifts for the second daughter of the house," I say, looking up at him from underneath my eyelashes. "Nothing *too* extravagant, you understand . . . diamonds, rubies, motorcars and suchlike. Trifles, really."

Robert puts a hand on his chest. "Unfortunately I left my diamond-encrusted motorcar at home this time. Will I be welcome back?"

"Oh, I should think so," I say. "Although there's every chance you'll be fed to hungry triplets," I add.

"Sounds terrifying," Robert murmurs. And then we both laugh.

I have to admit that Robert's laugh is wonderful. It's warm and rich, and all the more rewarding for being so hard-won. I have noticed that I seem to be able to make him laugh more than anyone else, and that is a prize that gives me a sense of deep and lasting satisfaction.

"So." Robert speaks, after a moment of silence. "Your birthday? You kept that quiet."

I groan. "Only because I don't want anyone to make a fuss."

"But you only get one eighteenth birthday," Robert says. "You *should* make a fuss. And, anyway, you won't have any choice in the matter once Caitlin finds out."

"And how is Caitlin going to find out?" I ask sharply.

"A little bird might tell her," Robert replies innocently.

I scowl. "You look like a pretty big bird to me."

"I certainly won't tell her if you don't want me to," Robert says slowly.

"Good," I say.

"Of course . . ." He trails off.

"What?" I ask suspiciously.

"If Caitlin found out *after* the fact, that you hadn't told her about your birthday, she'd be upset." He stops and looks me right in the eye. "*Very* upset. And"—he lifts a finger—"if she found out that I knew about your birthday and didn't tell her, she would make my life . . . uncomfortable." He sighs heavily. "But if you still don't want me to say anything, I suppose I can keep it to myself."

"Fine," I huff. "You can tell her, but please don't let her do anything too over the top."

Robert laughs. "I'm sorry, have you *met* my sister?! I can tell her, but I think you'd better brace yourself. Once she's got an idea in her head there's no getting rid of it."

I grumble a little at this, but even I know that I am being ungrateful. I'm just not sure that a party for me is such a good idea. I love the Cardews' parties, but the thought of being at the center of one of them is a little overwhelming. That's precisely why I kept my birthday a secret in the first place. I know where I am happiest, and it is somewhere between watching from a tree branch and being the star. When I first appeared at the Cardew House I was something of a novelty and that made me uncomfortable, disposable, but—thanks to my innate dullness—the shine seemed to wear off pretty quickly and most people lost interest in me as I became part of the furniture. Not the Cardews, though, nor their immediate circle. I could have been discarded after a week or two—I was under no illusions about that, as I saw it happen to others who came and went—but for some reason I have been admitted to their group. I still can't really believe it, but I am their friend. It is an exhilarating, addictive thing, especially when I am more used to being grudgingly included in things as "Alice's sister."

"Seems like you've won over the whole Trevelyan clan," I say then, changing the subject.

"I had a lot of fun," Robert says, walking on again, his hands clasped behind his back. "Your family is very nice."

"Oh, yes," I agree, rolling my eyes. "When they're not driving me mad they're an absolute delight."

He smiles a little at this, but the smile doesn't quite reach his eyes. "Well, I think you're lucky," he says, and if I didn't know better, I would think his voice is almost wistful. "It must be nice having a big family."

"It is," I say carefully. "But you have Caitlin."

"Yes," and the word is an exhalation. "I have Caitlin."

We have reached the beach now, and the causeway stretches out across the sand, back to the house. Even now that I am spending so much time there, my heart aches a little at the sight of it.

"So, remind me, who's coming for dinner tonight?" I ask.

Robert sighs. "Oh, just some people from town. It's going to be terribly dull. Why don't you join us?"

I laugh. "Thank you very much; who could resist an invitation like that?"

"It will be a lot less dull if you're there," Robert says, and even though it is perfectly innocent, the words hang between us, just for a second, as if they mean something more. And then, just as quickly as it appeared, the moment is gone.

"I've only just left," I say lightly. "But don't worry, I'm coming back tomorrow to beat you at cards."

"Because you cheat at cards," Robert replies automatically.

"No one needs to resort to cheating to beat you, Robert Cardew."

"Bye, Lou." His voice is firm, blithely ignoring my dig, and he turns and walks down the causeway. "See you tomorrow," he calls over his shoulder.

"Goodbye, Robert," I shout after him, and I stand for a moment on the beach, watching him disappear toward the big house, before I turn to make my own way home.

CHAPTER FOURTEEN

When I arrive the next day it is pretty much as expected.

Caitlin is already waiting for me by the front door when I turn up. The light in her eyes is militant. "Lou, you absolute wretch!" she exclaims, grabbing my arm and shaking me a little. "I cannot believe that you didn't tell me . . . ME, your dearest, most devoted friend, about your birthday."

"It's not a big deal," I say, rubbing my arm. "I didn't want to make a fuss."

"Is it or is it not your eighteenth birthday?" Caitlin asks crisply, turning on her heel.

"It is," I sigh, following her into the house.

"Aha! So you admit it!" Caitlin whirls around to face me,

her long cigarette holder pointed at me accusingly as if she is Hercule Poirot himself.

"I never denied it is my birthday next week," I say patiently. "You didn't ask. I just didn't . . . make you aware of it."

Caitlin looks at me through narrowed eyes. "And why not?"

"I don't know," I say. "I didn't want you to think I expected anything . . ." I trail off.

Caitlin snorts. "Louise," she drawls in a low, slow voice as though explaining things to a simpleton, "you are our dear friend. It is your birthday . . . and your eighteenth birthday, at that. Of *course* we're going to make a fuss."

We enter the drawing room where Robert is sitting, smoking a cigarette and reading a book.

"I told you so," he says, getting to his feet, as he does whenever I enter the room.

Caitlin inhales on her cigarette and makes her way over to the bar, where she tops up her glass with a generous splash of something clear. I very much doubt it is water, and she knocks it back in one quick mouthful.

"Of course, you haven't given me a lot of time . . . ," she says, staring into the middle distance. "However." Her eyes snap on to me and a smile begins to spread across her face, one that makes me feel decidedly nervous. "I think I may have an idea for something *truly* spectacular."

"As opposed to all the other parties you've been having?" I ask, tucking my feet underneath me.

"Oh." Caitlin waves one hand in the air. "Those things? No, those are more like gatherings, really. This, this will absolutely be the event of the summer."

"Caitlin," I say warily.

"Yes, Caitlin," Robert echoes, and his voice is a warning. "Please don't go wild."

"Oh, hush." Caitlin pouts. "You know perfectly well that we always host the biggest party at the end of the summer in London. It's tradition, and *everyone* looks forward to it. Everything about it has to be completely, utterly perfect." I don't like the reminder that we are approaching the end of the summer, that this will all be gone too soon. My birthday is starting to feel like the beginning of the end rather than something to be celebrated.

Robert sighs, but looking at Caitlin's animated face, his expression visibly softens.

"But—" I begin, determined I'm going to have my say.

"Yes, yes, darling," Caitlin says sweetly, dismissing me with a wave of her hand. "Robert already told me. You don't want all eyes on you, and I've found a way around that." She shivers then, as though possessed by some intoxicating secret, and her eyes have taken on a lustrous shine. "And a truly delicious one at that."

"Well, are you going to keep us in suspense, or are you going to tell us?" Robert asks, stubbing out his cigarette in the heavy glass ashtray beside him.

"I don't know," Caitlin says petulantly. "I don't think

either of you are being very enthusiastic about my brilliant idea."

"Yes, we are," I say, and my eyes meet Robert's.

"So enthusiastic," he says obediently, with all the enthusiasm of a rock.

Caitlin looks at us both for a moment and pauses dramatically, her hands stretched out in front of her. "A masquerade!" she exclaims finally, clapping her hands together like a child at the theater.

"A masquerade?" I repeat.

"Yes!" She sits down on the sofa beside me and takes one of my hands. Her eyes really are very bright and I can smell the alcohol that she has just drunk on her breath, sweet and sharp at the same time. "It's perfect," she continues. "We'll have a costume party, and everyone will wear masks. You won't be the center of attention because you'll be incognito." She sits back with a look of great satisfaction on her face. "Plus, people always behave *absolutely terribly* when they wear masks." Her voice is gleeful. "It's so much fun." She looks about expectantly as if waiting for a round of applause.

"It does sound quite exciting," I say cautiously, turning the idea over in my mind.

"Oh, *now* Lou thinks it sounds exciting . . . now that she knows people are going to behave badly," Caitlin teases. "Is there anyone in particular that you would like to be badly behaved with?"

As if on cue, the door opens and Charlie appears. Caitlin

217

dissolves into giggles as he stands in the doorway looking bemused.

"What did I miss?" he asks.

Despite my protests to the contrary, Caitlin remains convinced that I have a thumping great crush on Charlie. Sometimes I wish she was right. Although his good looks alone are almost enough to turn my knees to water, my initial impression of Charlie proved to be correct. He is sweet, good-natured and gorgeous, but he is also absolutely dull. Trust me, there's nothing that will kill a burgeoning infatuation dead quicker than having to spend thirty minutes listening to the endless list of attributes necessary in the perfect trout bait.

"You didn't miss anything," I say to Charlie now. "Caitlin is just happy because she's planning a party."

Charlie comes into the room and sits in one of the chairs, his legs crossed. "When is Caitlin ever not planning a party?" he asks, reaching into his pocket for his cigarette case.

"This is a special party," Caitlin says gleefully, nudging me with her elbow. "This is for Lou's birthday!"

"Is that so?" Charlie's voice is mild as he lights his cigarette and lifts it to his lips. "Well, many happy returns," he says.

"It's not until next week," I reply.

"What's not until next week?" Laurie has arrived. Both men get to their feet, and so do I, so that I can accept a warm kiss on each cheek. Laurie always greets me as though we haven't seen each other for months.

"What's not until next week?" Laurie repeats once we are all sitting down again and she has made sure that Robert is fixing drinks.

"Lou's birthday," Charlie says.

"And we're having a party!" Caitlin exclaims.

"It's not a big thing," I mutter, but Laurie ignores me.

"What kind of a party?" she asks, as Robert places a whisky and soda in her hand. She wraps her fingers around his wrist and gives it a little squeeze in thanks.

"I was thinking a costume party," Caitlin says, then she lowers her voice so that it is almost a whisper. "With masks."

Laurie nods, taking a sip of her drink. "That could work," she says, and a slow, Cheshire-cat grin spreads across her face. "All bets are off when people wear masks. They go crazy."

"Just what I said," Caitlin agrees with some satisfaction.

"But can you pull it together in under a week?" Laurie frowns. "There's so much to do."

"Oh, I don't want you to go to too much trouble . . . ," I start, but Robert leans over the back of the sofa, interrupting.

"I wouldn't bother," he says to me. "Those two are in planning mode now. You're not going to get any sense out of either of them." He hands me a glass, a soda water bubbling furiously over ice cubes. The glass is heavy, beautifully engraved. Suddenly, I have the overwhelming urge to wrap my fingers around his hand, as Laurie did. I can almost feel his warm skin tingling beneath my touch. Instead I bury my flushed face in my glass.

219

"Thank you," I murmur, my heart thumping irregularly. What is wrong with me?

"Of course I can pull it together," Caitlin is saying. "It will be perfect. Every single detail will be absolutely *perfect*."

"Caitlin," her brother says again, and his voice is a gentle warning. "Don't take on too much—"

"Psssh." Caitlin dismisses him with a wave of her hand. "It will be a true Cardew event, just like Mother and Father used to have here. Perfect." Her eyes are glittering, enormous in her thin face.

I see a frown flicker across Robert's brow. It's the first time I've heard Caitlin talk about her mother at all, but the moment passes quickly and then Caitlin and Laurie are talking about color schemes.

"Will Lucky's band be available to play, do you think?" Laurie asks.

"Oh, yes," I say, turning my face away from Robert. Lucky's band haven't played here since that first party, but I still remember how wonderful they sounded. I think I could get on board with the party if I knew that they were playing.

Caitlin's smile remains, but it seems to dim, just a fraction, as it has occasionally in the past when she thought no one was watching. Perhaps it's my imagination. No one else seems to notice, but I feel my pulse quicken.

"I don't know," she says, and she fidgets with the bangles on her wrist. "They're pretty booked up these days."

"It's your own fault for bringing them into fashion," Laurie drawls.

"You really shot yourself in the foot there," Charlie puts in cheerily.

"Hmm." Caitlin is noncommittal, still focused on her bracelets. She won't meet my eye, and I wonder what I would find there if she did.

"Well, perhaps Elodie could be persuaded . . . ," Charlie begins, but he is interrupted by a light knock at the door, and Laurie surges to her feet. The movement is graceful, but the speed is out of character. Her face lights up, eager.

"Speak of the devil!" Charlie exclaims.

I turn questioningly to Caitlin, who opens her mouth to explain, but before she can do so Laurie pulls the door open.

Standing on the other side is a remarkable-looking woman. The vibrant red of her dress highlights the deep bronze of her skin, and her soft, dark hair is coiled on top of her head. She is not exactly beautiful, but extremely striking. She's slight, small, even, but she radiates a self-assurance that seems to occupy a lot of space. A smile curls upon her lips as she looks around the room.

Laurie appears at her side and takes her hand. "The only person you haven't met is Lou," Laurie says, and she gives Elodie a little push forward. "Lou, this is one of my dearest friends, Elodie Marchant. She arrived this afternoon, but she's been resting." Laurie's eyes glow. "Elodie is visiting for a little while, from Paris."

Elodie leans toward me and places her hands at the top of my arms before delivering the two kisses on each cheek like a blessing. She smells like heavy, dark red roses.

"Lou," she says, and her voice is deeper than I expected. "It is so good to meet you, finally. Laurie has talked about you in her letters."

"I can't imagine Laurie taking the time to write letters to anyone," I say without thinking, and Elodie hoots with laughter. It's true, though, Laurie is kind and generous, but she's also catlike—elegant and languid, more likely to throw a comment into someone else's letter than to make the effort to write one herself.

"*Bien sûr*," she says. "Laurie said you were a sharp one."

Lively chatter fills the air, as Caitlin and Charlie catch up on Elodie's news. In the shuffling of seats Robert has ended up sitting next to me.

"Caitlin and I have met Elodie a few times," he says in a low voice. "I think you'll like her. She's a terrific musician."

"What are you two whispering about?" Caitlin asks, and I jump as though I have been caught doing something I shouldn't.

"Robert was just telling me that Elodie is a musician," I blurt.

Elodie nods. "Yes, indeed." Her hands flutter by her side, and she straightens the hem of her dress. "I am a singer."

"She's wonderful." Charlie's voice is full of admiration.

"They call her *Alouette*," Laurie puts in. "It means 'lark.' She's a perfect little songbird."

"You must sing at Lou's party!" Caitlin sits forward and claps her hands. "I see now that is what Charlie was going to suggest before you arrived, Elodie!"

"But of course," Elodie agrees graciously, with a dip of her head. "I would love to."

"It's Lou's birthday next week," Laurie explains. "Caitlin is going to host a masquerade."

Elodie's eyes light up. "Perfect," she breathes. "A masquerade is always so exciting, no?"

"So I keep hearing," I reply warily, as the others dissolve into laughter.

The subject changes and Elodie and Caitlin begin discussing the newest French fashions.

"That reminds me," Laurie interrupts here, "what are we going to do about clothes for the party?" She pauses thoughtfully. "You know, I have something amazing on order in London that would be just perfect. Perhaps I can send the driver for it?"

"Well, I have nothing," Caitlin says decisively. "Absolutely nothing. I've been practically living in rags as it is."

Having spent a lot of time in Caitlin's room, rifling around in her enormous walk-in wardrobe full of extremely beautiful clothes, I think this is something of an overstatement. Laurie, however, is nodding sympathetically.

"This is what happens when you spend an extended period out here in the sticks." She looks at me and raises her glass. "Not that it doesn't have its benefits, of course, sugar."

Caitlin is tapping her cheek thoughtfully. "Of course you're right," she says finally. "And it's not just the clothes. There will be so much to organize. And we'll have to get the word out to make sure we draw a big crowd. It's quite late in the day to throw something spectacular together."

"It sounds impossible," I say. "It's a nice thought, Caitlin, but really, I don't mind. Why don't we have a small party here, just us?"

"Impossible?" Caitlin repeats, arching one delicate eyebrow. "That word is not in my vocabulary. No, it's certainly not impossible." She is leaning forward now, and she has that look in her eye, the one that I know spells trouble. "It simply means that I will need to go to London for a couple of days," she says.

"London?" Robert shifts forward in his seat. "Is that really necessary?" The movement seems a little anxious, his green eyes searching her face. "I'm not sure that you need to—"

"Of course it is!" Caitlin sings. "We can pick up your dress while we're there, Laurie."

"We?" I say, glancing toward her brother. "Is Robert going with you as well?"

"No, silly." Caitlin's eyes meet mine. "You are."

CHAPTER FIFTEEN

Two days later I am on my way to London. I am not quite
sure how it has all happened, and yet here I am in the back of
a chauffeur-driven car with Caitlin, off for my first ever trip
to the big, shining city that has loomed large in my imagination for years.

Unbeknownst to me, Caitlin sent a note to Midge on the
evening she came up with the idea, explaining that she and
"a few friends" would love to throw me a birthday party. If
Midge and Pa had no objections, the note continued, she
would like to take me to London to oversee the preparations
and to make sure that everything was to my liking. When
confronted with that gold-plated, ivory paper and Caitlin's
scrawling enthusiasm, punctuated with so many exclamation

marks, Midge was helpless to refuse. (Not that I think she would have protested much anyway, but such a kind letter left even Aunt Irene [almost] silent on the matter.) And so, by the time I arrived back at the farm, everyone knew I was leaving the next day for London.

Which brings me here, sitting back in my plush seat as I watch the world slip by through the window. Caitlin is next to me, chattering brightly about the people she most wants to avoid while we're here, on the understanding that they are *the most dreadful bores, darling.* There is something jittery about her high spirits, which seems to be growing with every mile we cover. I am beginning to worry that this trip might not be the distraction that Caitlin needs, but rather that we are throwing ourselves into the path of some danger that I don't understand.

We are headed to Mayfair, I know that much, although I don't really know where Mayfair is or what it entails. What I do know is that we are going *shopping,* and that Caitlin keeps saying the word *shopping* as if it is in italics, and that this way of saying it sends a delighted shiver down my spine. We are going to go and see about the clothes, and we are also going to go and "show our faces" around town. This is another thing that I don't quite understand, but I am excited about it all the same. The whole trip seems impossible somehow. While I have just about started to get used to the idea of being at the Cardew House, I wasn't prepared for the speed at which things have happened. A trip that would have taken me an awful lot of preparation is thrown hastily together by Caitlin in the course of a couple of phone calls, and so, while only a few short days ago I had no thoughts of going to London at all outside my persistent far-fetched fantasies, gathered up over many years, now I find myself pulling up outside an elegant mews house on a quiet, leafy street.

"Thank you, Franks," Caitlin sings to the driver as she sails out of the car, fitting a gleaming silver key into the lock on the front door. "Please bring the bags in and take them upstairs."

I step cautiously into the house behind her. The floor is laid with black and white tiles, and a curved white staircase runs up one wall. The space is light and airy, with high ceilings, and there is a table in the center, on which a vase full of white lilies fill the air with their heavy scent.

Caitlin is a whirlwind, disappearing into the rooms beyond, and I follow, my eyes wide, as I take in every detail. "Well, everything looks in good order." Caitlin shrugs off her light jacket and throws it onto the back of a pale green covered sofa. "I know it's small, but there is no point in opening up the big house for only a couple of days." Her voice is bright, although her smile falters a little. "I prefer it here anyway, the big house is . . ." She trails off here, and I think she looks a little pale. "Too big," she says finally.

"I don't think I'd call this small, Caitlin," I reply, gazing around at the perfectly proportioned rooms, the pretty, modern furniture and the walls covered in elegant framed sketches. There are more flowers in here too—fat, pink roses

227

that remind me of Alice's wedding day. Thinking of Alice makes me feel uneasy. I haven't seen her since that day at the farm. Does she even know that I am in London, that I'm about to enter the hallowed halls of fashion? Probably, but not from me, and that feels wrong.

I turn my attention back to the room that we are standing in, struck once again by the easy elegance of it all. I allow myself to shrug off any difficult thoughts, to simply enjoy the moment. "I think it's heavenly," I breathe.

"Oh, I'm so glad you like it!" Caitlin claps her hands together. "It's going to be such fun. There's no staff here at the moment, so we'll fend for ourselves, but as we'll hardly be at home that won't matter."

"If there's no staff, then who put out all the flowers?" I ask, moving over to take a closer look at one of the sketches that line the walls.

"Oh, I have a woman come and tidy, of course," Caitlin says airily. "I hadn't even noticed the flowers." Her eyes flicker in their direction. "How nice." Caitlin takes the smoothness of the way her life runs for granted, I know, but it is still a little jarring.

I look more closely at the picture on the wall. It is a charcoal sketch, deftly drawn and simply full of life. The lines almost tremble with energy. It speaks to the restlessness inside me, and I am overwhelmed by how intimate the feeling is, as though I am seeing a part of myself set up in a frame for everyone to see.

"Why, this is the house in Cornwall!" I exclaim.

"Do you like it?" Caitlin asks, coming to stand beside me.

"Of course I do," I reply truthfully. "It's beautiful."

"It's one of Robert's," Caitlin says, and she is smirking, waiting for a reaction.

She gets one. "Robert's?" I echo, my mouth falling open. I am silent for a second, staring at the picture. "I had no idea that Robert could even draw," I say.

Caitlin nods. "Oh, yes. He doesn't do it so much anymore, but there was a time when he was always sketching and painting." Her smile falters a little here. "Before our father died," she adds.

I reach out and squeeze her hand. She squeezes back.

"It's a shame that Robert stopped," I say tentatively. "He's obviously very talented."

"Mmm." Caitlin's eyes are fixed on the drawing. "I suppose he felt that he had to be a more *serious* kind of person after . . ." She trails off here, and I think perhaps she is going to cry, but instead her face is tight and pale, curiously empty. "Anyway, Robert was suddenly in charge of everything. He was different then." She pauses, and her voice is hollow as she adds, "I suppose we both were." The way she says it makes my heart ache for the two of them.

"So." Caitlin rallies. "Now I have something over you, and that means you have to do exactly as I say."

"Everyone does that anyway," I say, rolling my eyes. "And what exactly do you have over me?"

"Fail to heed my commands and I shall tell Robert exactly how talented you think he is."

I groan. "His ego doesn't need that kind of inflation," I protest, relieved to see her smile again.

"True." Caitlin bats her eyelashes. "But you're a wild card. And I have a particularly decadent trip planned for us, so I need the insurance, just in case you chicken out of anything."

"When have I ever chickened out of anything?" I protest.

"Very true," Caitlin agrees. "This is one of the reasons I love you. Now," she says, "my first commandment is that you go and freshen up. We'll go and have some lunch, but first we have a *lot* of shopping to do."

"Aye aye, captain," I say, giving her a little salute.

"I'll show you to your room," she says, tripping ahead of me and up the stairs. There are three bedrooms on the second floor. Mine is pretty and painted primrose yellow with a large window that looks out onto the street. It also has its own bathroom, though nothing as extravagant as the one at the house in Cornwall. It's almost ordinary enough for me to pretend that it's mine, that this is my own real life, living here in London in my little primrose room. The thought is like pulling my most precious, deeply cherished daydream out into the light. I sigh. That daydream may be beyond my reach, but the city isn't, and I can't wait to get out there and explore. All of London waiting for me, just outside the front door. Excitement wriggles up and down my spine, and I feel like dancing.

When I arrive back downstairs, Caitlin is sitting on the sofa, waiting, her fingers drumming impatiently on a cushion. "Thank goodness," she exclaims. "I'm absolutely itching to get going. Shall we?"

"Let's," I say, feeling a wave of excitement crash over me. "Where to?" I ask.

Caitlin slips into her jacket and waves a reproving finger at me. "All will be revealed," she says. "Please follow me."

With this she makes her way to the front door while I trail dutifully behind. The ever-patient Franks is waiting in the car, and he leaps out to open the door for us. "Carradice's, please, Franks," Caitlin calls as she slides gracefully into the back seat. I clamber in behind her.

It is a very short drive to our next destination, and I just about refrain from sticking my head out of the window. Once we turn off the quiet road where Caitlin's house is, we seem suddenly to be in the middle of so much noise and movement that it leaves my head spinning.

There are cars everywhere, honking at each other, and great red buses that have no roof on top of them and are simply bursting with people. The roads are wide, and the buildings that line the sides are so tall that they seem to reach into the few clouds that float in the otherwise blue sky. It is hot, and loud, and crowded, and for a moment I am overwhelmed by it all, and then I am desperately greedy for more.

The car pulls up only a few minutes later outside a tall, elegant white shop front in the middle of a long row of shops. Above the window on the ground floor a gray marble sign declares in large art deco lettering that the store is, in fact, the Carradice's that we are destined for. When we step out of the car I fly to the glass window in front of me as though pulled there by an unseen force that I am helpless to resist. Displayed behind the glass is a mannequin wearing a truly beautiful gown of red silk trimmed with gold and silver beads in a trailing ivy design.

"Oh," I sigh. "Caitlin, look at this," and I press my fingers against the glass, longing to reach out and stroke the material, imagining the inky feeling of the silk slipping between my fingers. I lift my hand from the glass and realize that I have left smudgy fingerprints there. Horrified, I try to rub them away.

Caitlin turns toward me. "What are you doing, Lou?" she asks, as though I am a naughty child that she has been charged with. She doesn't wait for a response. "Come on!"

Once we are through the door things seem even more wonderful. The floors are white marble and so are the walls, inlaid with a beautiful gold pattern and draped with whisper-thin white silk. There are glass cabinets edged with gold, holding gloves and jewels and all sorts of other beautiful things. Two sides of the walls are clad in mirrors, reflecting back all this shimmering luxury, and a thousand Lous stand wide-eyed in the middle of it all. I take a proper look at myself then, my face a small pale moon, my clothes scruffy and out of place.

"Ahhh, Lady Cardew." A young woman drifts forward from behind one of the counters, her heels clipping across the floor. "How nice to see you again. I believe Madame Carradice is expecting you?"

"That's right, Celia," Caitlin says, shrugging off her jacket and handing it to the woman. "And this is my dear friend Lou."

Both women turn to me, and Celia, the consummate professional, does not betray by the merest flicker of an eyelid that I am not the usual type to frequent such an establishment.

"May I take your coat?" she asks, and I slip my arms out of my thin cotton jacket, rubbing my hands down my sides to try and smooth the crumpled dress underneath.

Celia smiles, and her smile is smooth and flat, a glossy red act of politeness. "Madame is waiting for you upstairs."

"Perfect." Caitlin grabs me by the arm. "I'll lead the way." And she pulls me through a door at the back of the room that opens onto a white spiraled staircase, lined with more mirrors.

"I'm really enjoying looking at myself this much," I mutter. The difference between me and Caitlin has never been more apparent, and I don't need to see my reflection beamed back to me from every surface to know that I don't measure up, that I don't belong. Surrounded by all these mirrors, I have never felt more plain, more of an imposter.

Caitlin stops and fluffs her hair, blowing her own reflection a kiss. "I know just what you mean," she says.

"I don't think you do," I murmur under my breath.

"Oh, hush," she chides, and again I feel like her unruly charge. "Now let's go and see what Madame Carradice has to offer today." With this she hurries up the stairs.

At the top we reach another black door, and Caitlin pushes her way through as if she owns the place. Standing waiting for us in the long room is an older woman of breathtaking elegance. I am not quite sure what it is about her that looks so expensive and so absolutely right. She is wearing a simple black dress, with sheer stockings and only a single string of pearls. Her hair is dark, streaked with gray and pulled back into a chignon, and she wears little makeup. But there is something about the way she stands, about the way her dress falls and the way she wears it that makes you stop and look at her.

"Madame Carradice." Caitlin moves forward, grasping her hands as they exchange a kiss on each cheek. "And as you see I have brought my dearest friend, Lou, with me today." Caitlin turns and gestures for me to step forward. I do so reluctantly, feeling myself shrink beneath Madame Carradice's steady gaze.

Her eyes rake over me, and I feel her notice every single stitch on the hand-me-down dress that I inherited from Alice.

"I see," she says slowly. But what, precisely, she sees I have no idea. I give her a tentative smile, which she does not return.

At that moment there is a tap at the door and Celia arrives with a tray of champagne glasses and an open bottle. I accept a glass, grateful for something to do with my hands, and take a nervous swig before sinking into a plump pink chair. Celia disappears back the way she came, leaving us once more alone with Madame Carradice.

"Well, first of all," Caitlin begins, sipping her drink, "we have something of an emergency. It is Lou's eighteenth birthday in just a few days' time, on Friday, in fact, and I plan to throw an *extremely* lavish masquerade party at our house in Cornwall to celebrate."

Madame Carradice nods, unperturbed as she perches on the edge of her own seat.

"So I will, *of course,* need something ravishing to wear for that," Caitlin says.

"Of course." Madame Carradice nods again, and a gleam of interest has appeared in her eyes.

Caitlin inclines her head. "And the other thing is Lou here."

I am taking a sip of my champagne when she says this, and I find myself choking over it in a not very ladylike fashion at this unexpected mention of my name. "Me?" I splutter.

"Yes, you." Caitlin is brisk. She turns to Madame Carradice, her eyes wide and appealing. "We will need a few things—a couple of day dresses, and something to wear this evening. It's very important that we both look our absolute best this evening. *Very* important."

"Caitlin!" I exclaim. "What are you talking about? I— I'm afraid this isn't . . ." I trail off, mortified, trying to avoid Madame Carradice's eye.

"Don't be silly, Lou," Caitlin says impatiently. "It's my gift to you, for your birthday."

My head snaps up then. "Oh, no!" I wheeze, wishing I could sink into the ground. "That's so kind, but I couldn't."

Madame Carradice is completely still, silent, her face a polite blank.

"Nonsense," Caitlin says. "You said that you were going to let me have my own way and this is what I want. It will make me very happy. It *is* your birthday, after all," she wheedles.

"Well, I . . . ," I flounder.

"And I *suppose* if you say no, then there's a good chance I may remember to tell Robert that you think he's an artistic genius," she says, dropping her eyes innocently and toying with her champagne glass.

I laugh at this, I can't help it. "The word 'genius' never crossed my lips," I say.

Caitlin eyes me expectantly.

"OK," I say finally. "If you're sure. One dress. It's really so generous of you . . ."

"That's enough of that." Caitlin waves my thanks away impatiently and returns her attention to Madame Carradice. "So, Madame," she says earnestly, "we place ourselves *entirely* in your hands."

"Very well." Madame Carradice nods, refilling our champagne glasses. "We'll begin by taking the young lady's measurements, and then I will show you some samples. I think . . . yes, I think I have just the thing." She is tapping her finger against her cheek, and then her face breaks into a sudden smile that takes me by surprise. Her smile is crooked and something about its imperfection is reassuring.

"If you would come this way." She turns to me and gestures toward the back of the room with her hand.

Standing, I follow her as she slips behind a pink curtain. I find myself in a luxuriously decorated changing room. "If you could just slip your dress off," Madame Carradice says, picking up a tape measure from a small table, "then I can get your measurements."

"Of course," I say hastily, fumbling with the buttons on my dress and battling the intense waves of mortification that I am feeling over the tattered state of my undergarments.

Madame Carradice makes no comment, but begins taking the measurements with cool, practiced movements.

"Oh, yes," she says, "I have quite a lot to choose from that will need very little alteration." She looks pleased. "You may put your dress back on now," she adds.

I realize I am still standing in my underwear. "Yes, of course," I mutter, pulling the dress over my head in one jerky movement.

Madame Carradice sweeps the curtain aside and we emerge back into the room where Caitlin is waiting. A lot has been happening during the brief time we have been away, and we find her surrounded by bolts of beautiful fabric, their colors glowing in the lamplight, as though she is sitting in the middle of a rainbow.

I sit down next to her, my hand reaching out as if it has a mind of its own, to run the silky cloth through my fingers. "Beautiful," I breathe.

"Which one do you like?" Caitlin asks.

"Oh, all of them," I say. My eyes fall on a pale green silk organza. It is so delicate, so light, and it reminds me of the sea around the island. "I love this," I say.

"Seafoam." Madame Carradice nods approvingly.

"I'm sorry?" I say.

"Seafoam," she repeats. "It's the name of that particular color. One of my favorites."

"Oh." My fingers linger here as I turn the word over in my mind. *Seafoam.*

"Now, I have some samples to show you, and some things for you both to try," Madame Carradice says, and she claps her hands. A girl steps out from behind the pink curtain wearing a beautiful dress. It has a layered skirt of black silk and tulle, and a body of black-and-gold brocade with little gauzy cap sleeves. The dress is quite long, falling several inches above her ankles.

"I thought perhaps this might meet with your approval for this evening," Madame Carradice is saying. My eyes are glued to the model as she walks toward us and twirls around. The skirt floats out around her, and the gold in the brocade shimmers. I sigh. It is lovely.

"Lou?" Caitlin asks.

"Oh, yes," I say. "You'll look wonderful in it."

"Not for me." Caitlin laughs. "For you."

I turn to see that both she and Madame Carradice are looking at me.

"It will need hardly any alteration to fit," Madame Carradice says. "You have almost identical measurements to Lacey." She gestures toward the model, who has come to a stop in front of us.

I find this hard to believe. Lacey looks elegant and mature in the dress, as though she belongs in it, as though she belongs here in this shop. Is it possible that I could look like that?

"For me?" I say at last.

"Oh, for heaven's sake." Caitlin rolls her eyes. "We can't keep doing this. Do you like it?"

"I love it," I reply, and the answer is a truthful one. "And . . ." My eyes gleam. "I could wear it for my birthday party as well!"

"Fine," Caitlin says. "That's decided, then," and with that Lacey trips back to the changing room while another beautiful girl appears wearing another beautiful dress.

The rest of the afternoon passes in a blur, and by the time we leave we are followed out to the car by people carrying great piles of packages. I can't tell you what we have bought, and how much of it is meant to be for me. (Although by the time we leave, my old dress has been consigned to the bin and I am wearing a new pale pink summer dress that makes me feel incredibly sophisticated.) Over the last few weeks I have resisted Caitlin's offers to borrow her clothes, clinging stubbornly to my own scruffy dresses and shorts rather than risk feeling like a doll that she is dressing up. One afternoon in Carradice's seems to have blasted these intentions to smithereens. I am a little uneasy about it, but at the same time I know that I can hardly run around London with Cait-lin Cardew, and go out on the town this evening, in my own clothes. It's easier to feel all right about it here, surrounded by so much, to feel that taking a tiny bit of it for myself isn't so bad.

"Well, I don't know about you, but I'm exhausted," Caitlin says, though the way she talks is anything but—it's breathless and on edge. "We'd better go and have a quick bite to eat, then take a nap before this evening."

"Where *are* we going this evening?" I ask.

"Oh, the usual," Caitlin says, and her expression is one of, if not boredom, then resignation at least. "Cocktails first, then a club or two." She drums her fingers on the seat beside her, an anxious tap, tap, tap.

"It sounds wonderful," I say, and I wonder if her restless-ness is part of being in London, if she's as affected by the spirit of the place as I am.

"And Bernie and some of the others will be around, no doubt," Caitlin adds brightly. "They'll be *thrilled* to see you."

"Oh, good." I'm a bit relieved to hear this; here among this desperate press of anonymous people I'm beginning to feel just a little overwhelmed. It will be nice to see some friendly faces.

"Let's have a quick lunch on the roof at Selfridge's," Caitlin says decisively. "It will be heaving, of course, but on such a beautiful day it's a nice way to see the city. I think you'll like it. That way we can order some party supplies on our way out. They know what I like."

After we make our way through the store (where I manage to stop Caitlin only six or seven times to look at something extraordinary) and up in one of the mahogany-paneled lifts, the roof garden is a complete and utter vision. There are flower beds, and benches, and still pools of water, and stone urns full of a riot of tumbling pink and yellow flowers. Along one side of the roof is a long pergola covered in ivy, under which tables with white linen tablecloths are set up for lunch.

The view is extraordinary, literally stopping me in my tracks. You can see all of London laid out before you like an impossibly detailed map, and it seems to reach on and on forever. I cannot believe the size of it, or the number of people it must hold. More people than you could imagine, all living their lives in this vibrant, bustling metropolis. I feel then, so sharply that it is a knife in my belly, that I want to be one of them. The life and the noise of the place is already getting under my skin, and it speaks once more to that restless feeling inside me. *Here,* a voice inside me says, *this place.* In London I might find what I have been looking for. Here, I see open doors and opportunities that I could never have at home. The world is, after all, a lot bigger than Penlyn, and I am getting just the tiniest taste of it. And then it will be back to reality. Only a couple of weeks of summer remaining . . . how will I ever be able to go back?

"Thank you so much for bringing me here," I say.

Caitlin reaches across the table and squeezes my fingers. As she pulls her hand back she knocks her glass, sending it crashing to the floor, where it shatters loudly. Several waiters leap forward at once. "Oh dear." Caitlin smiles vaguely. "I'm sorry. I seem to be a little clumsy today."

"Please, don't worry, madam, I'll fetch you another," one of the men says, whisking the mess away so efficiently that mere seconds later it is as though the breakage never happened.

"Is everything OK?" I ask quietly. "You seem a little . . . on edge."

"Do I, darling?" Caitlin lights a cigarette, but I notice that her hand is shaking, just a little. "I think I'm a bit tired," she says. "And hungry. I'll feel better once I have something to eat."

Right on cue our food arrives, and although it is delicious Caitlin only picks at her plate. I rattle on and on, making conversation, but she is quiet, withdrawn, and certainly not herself.

When we arrive back at the house she goes to lie down for a while, and I decide to do the same. I don't think there's any chance that I will sleep, so I am surprised to find myself being woken up by Caitlin a couple of hours later.

"Come on, darling!" she sings. "We have to get ready for a big night on the town."

"What time is it?" I ask groggily.

"Just gone seven," she answers, "so we must get a move on." Her movements are rapid as she flutters around the room, like a butterfly refusing to land in one spot for any amount of time. The nap seems to have helped, at least.

Caitlin helps me to get ready, and I slip into the beautiful black-and-gold dress, the whisper-thin silk stockings and the new black shoes as if I am in a daze. The dress fits perfectly. Caitlin pins my curls up, leaving a couple loose, curling over my shoulders, and she lets me borrow her red lipstick. I look into the mirror and see a girl I hardly recognize.

Madame Carradice had been right, the dress does fit me as it had fit Lacey, and when I move I know that I am walking differently—like someone who knows more, whose body belongs in a dress like this. I stroke the delicate tulle skirt, twirling around and feeling the material twirl with me, and I feel expensive and glamorous. I feel like someone else in this dress, and the sensation is at once liberating and unnerving.

Caitlin wears a gold, fringed dress that moves when she does, hugging her too-thin body and dazzling the eye when it catches the light. Around her head is a gold band, and gold bangles jangle on both of her wrists. Her eyes are lined with black kohl, and they dance wildly.

She is certainly full of energy, whirring around, playing records, mixing drinks and talking a mile a minute, but somehow she is just *too* sparkling. Her whole body sizzles with nervous excitement, as though she is readying herself for something—only I can't work out what it is. I don't know if I should worry, or if it's just excitement at being in the city. I'm so turned around by it myself that *I* can hardly keep still.

My own excitement about the evening seems to feed hers, and we are both wound so tightly by the time we leave that I find I can't sit still in the back seat of the car. As we pull away from the house my breath catches in my throat. It is getting dark and the streetlamps are lit, giving everything—to my eyes, at least—the feeling of being in a story. "I wish it was foggy," I breathe.

"What?" Caitlin asks.

"Like in a novel, you know," I explain. "Foggy old London town, with the streetlamps lit and adventure in the air."

Caitlin dissolves into giggles over this, although I hadn't really been joking. "Oh, there's adventure in the air, all right," she says at last. "Just you wait."

CHAPTER SIXTEEN

"Caitlin looks on good form tonight," Patricia says later, as we are shown to our table in the Candlelight Club, and we all look over to where Caitlin stands surrounded by men in glossy black dinner suits. She seems to be flirting with all of them at once, and they look at her with naked greed on their faces, as though they want to gobble her up. It makes me feel uneasy, protective. I don't think that Robert would like it if he were here.

"Yes," I say. "She seems very . . . energetic."

"But who is it for, darling?" Bernie asks me in a low voice, waving a finger in her direction. "Who is this whole show for?"

"For?" I frown. "I don't think it's for anyone, is it?"

Bernie's face is hard to read as he reaches for a cigarette.

At that moment Caitlin breaks free of her group of admirers and makes her way over. She shimmies through the crowd, the light bouncing off her golden dress. Heads turn as she passes and I note—not for the first time—that whatever "star quality" is, Caitlin Cardew has it by the bucket load. Eyes are drawn to her like moths to a flame, and she is a flame burning very brightly indeed. The room is smoky, and busy, and obviously full of money. The crowd around us are dripping with jewels and everyone seems to know each other. As she makes her way through the hordes, people keep catching Caitlin by the arm and squealing at the sight of her. Caitlin, for her part, delivers hundreds of crimson kisses onto waiting cheeks and makes fleeting small talk as she drifts by.

"Insufferable bores," she whispers as she appears beside me. "The whole lot of them. Now I remember why we left London behind in the first place." She slides into the red velvet seat that is pulled out for her and draws me down beside her.

"Well, Lou, have you invited them yet?" she demands.

"Invited us?" Bernie looks at me. "Invited us to what, might I ask?"

"I didn't know I was supposed to invite them." I laugh. "It's your party, Caitlin."

"A *party*?" Bernie breathes, exhaling a cloud of smoke.

His sleepy face perks up at this. After all, a Cardew party is not to be missed. Even I know that much.

"Yes," Caitlin says, "and it's *not* my party, it's Lou's party. Her birthday party. We're throwing it at the Cornwall house on Friday."

"Sounds delightful," Patricia drawls, "and it's always nice to get out of the city."

"It's going to be spectacular," Caitlin says firmly. "My best work yet. A masquerade."

"Ooooh, masks." Bernie shivers with exaggerated delight. "Wonderful inventions," he murmurs, turning to me. "They're carte blanche for bad behavior, you know."

"So I keep hearing," I groan. "It seems to be something that everyone finds exciting, although if you've all been on your good behavior so far I dread to think what this party will be like!"

"Oh, it will be outrageous," Bernie promises. "Quite the eye opener for you, my little daisy."

"I think my eyes are pretty well open, thank you." I bat my eyelashes at him, determined not to let my irritation show. These kinds of comments make me feel like I've been cast in the role of the unsophisticated innocent, and I hate thinking that this is my appeal. It cuts a little bit too close to Aunt Irene's warnings.

"We'll see," he says, looking at me with his eyes half-closed and a dangerous smile on his lips.

"Anyway," Caitlin says, drawing the attention back to

herself, "I'm telling *you*, Bernie, because it saves me having to do the rounds. All the right people will know within the hour, I'm sure."

"Well, that's charming," Bernie pouts.

On a stage above the crowd of dancers a band is playing some of the foot-tapping jazz I find so irresistible. "You really do look gorgeous tonight," Caitlin says, looking me over with a critical eye. "Doesn't Lou look absolutely gorgeous tonight?" Caitlin demands loudly, looking around at the rest of the group, who are filling up the table.

All eyes turn in my direction, and I shrink beneath the attention. They voice their enthusiastic agreement.

"So *why*," Caitlin cries elaborately, as though she is acting in a pantomime and riling up the crowd, "hasn't anyone asked her to dance yet?"

"Probably because we just walked through the door," I grind out from behind a fixed grin. I am not enjoying Caitlin's campaign very much. But it is too late for that; three of the men who have been fawning over Caitlin leap to their feet, arguing over who will get to dance with me first. I try not to roll my eyes.

"Bernie?" I say, holding out my hand.

"I do love a woman who does the asking," he murmurs, wrapping his elegant fingers around my wrist and guiding me to the dance floor.

"I don't know why she's making a fuss," I grumble as he places his arm lightly around my waist.

Bernie is a graceful dancer, but then I can't imagine him

volunteering to do anything that he isn't good at in front of an audience. His hand rests delicately on my back, barely touching me, and his steps are light and precise as he guides me around the dance floor without seeming to guide me at all.

"Is something . . . wrong?" he asks softly, his eyes straying toward Caitlin, the crease reappearing between his eyes. I am struck by how strange it is to see such worry in Bernie's sleepy eyes, and I feel my heart quicken beneath my beautiful new dress.

"I don't know." My own eyes follow his. "I think so, but I don't know what. She's like a violin string pulled too tight," I say finally.

Bernie briefly closes his eyes, and I see him swallow. I am startled. Is it really so serious as this?

"She shouldn't have come to London," he mutters, almost to himself. "Not after what happened."

"What do you mean, *after what happened*?" I ask quickly.

The look Bernie gives me is enigmatic. "I don't think that's for me to say."

I am quiet for a moment. I know that Caitlin has her secrets, but I'm sad that she doesn't feel able to trust me with them. I feel as if Caitlin knows everything there is to know about me.

"Don't frown, darling," Bernie scolds then. "You'll give yourself wrinkles." He makes a visible effort to paper over the cracks in his smile. "I'm sure it will be fine. And you're off home tomorrow . . . Robert will see her right, don't worry."

I feel myself relax a little at this. Like Bernie, I realize that my faith in Robert is absolute. Well, when it comes to Caitlin, anyway.

We dance for another couple of minutes, although I feel like I am hardly aware of the music or the steps. Poor Bernie winces more than once as I stand on his toes. When we return to the table Caitlin is still seated, and she is telling a story that has the rest of the group in stitches. I feel a further loosening in my chest. Perhaps Bernie is wrong; looking at Caitlin now she looks like a beautiful young woman enjoying a night on the town. She catches my eye and grins.

"Why are you wasting yourself on Bernie when you look so lovely?" she asks gaily, spilling some of the drink in her glass as she waves her hand at me.

I slip into the seat next to her. "I'm not wasting myself," I say. "Bernie is a lovely dancer."

Bernie bows. "The lady is not wrong there," he says, gesturing for the waiter and ordering a bottle of champagne.

"And I danced with him because he's the only man here that I know," I can't resist adding.

"Ouch," Bernie exclaims, clapping a hand to his chest and swooning a little against his chair. "My poor wounded pride!"

"You know what I mean," I snort.

But Caitlin has already moved on. "Now," she says more loudly, turning back to the rest of the group, "what does a girl have to do to get a drink around here?"

A cheer goes up around the table. At that moment a

friendly looking man with sandy hair stops next to me and asks me to dance. I glance toward Caitlin.

"Go, go!" she exclaims. "In fact, I think I'll join you, just as soon as I've had another drink."

I sneak a look at Bernie and he nods encouragingly.

"Go on, little daisy," he calls. "Show London what you're made of. Enjoy yourself."

"Yes, Lou." Caitlin grabs my arm and looks up at me. "Dance! Enjoy yourself; that's why we're here, after all!"

My body hums with indecision. I look at Caitlin, who has already turned to make animated conversation with Patricia. I know that really there's nothing more I can do. If Caitlin wants to open up to me, it will be in her own time—I can't force her, but it's hard to just walk away. A small, selfish voice in my head reminds me that this could be my only chance to experience dancing in a real London nightclub. What happened to grabbing everything the summer has to offer? The man by my side offers me his arm, and after another moment of hesitation I put my hand on his sleeve. I make my way over to the dance floor with my partner just as the band start playing a red-hot Charleston.

"I'm afraid I'm not the greatest dancer," the sandy-haired man says, with a rueful grin. "I'm Joe, by the way."

"Lou," I say, shaking his outstretched hand. He is quite good-looking, I think, and he has a nice smile.

He isn't kidding about the dancing, though. In the end we have a lot of fun, as I try to teach him some of the steps and correct his many, many toe-crushing mistakes.

The next song brings Caitlin screeching onto the dance floor. With her by my side I feel my euphoria grow. As Caitlin dances next to me, shouting along with the singer while the fringe on her gold dress shakes and trembles, I forget about worrying over her. In this moment she is simply a carefree, sparkling girl. Joe tries to keep up with us, as does the next man and the next after that, but no one can match our pace, no one is enjoying the music more than we are.

Finally, exhausted, we go back to our seats for a break. My brain feels slightly fuzzy around the edges, and everything has taken on the sort of soft candlelit glow that comes with an evening you know you'll remember for the rest of your life.

When the barman delivers our drinks he also brings a silver platter of cold roast beef sandwiches. I reach for one, taking a big hungry bite.

"How did he know to bring these?" I ask, my mouth full. "I'm starving."

Caitlin bursts out laughing. "It's so they can serve the drinks," she explains in a very patient voice. "The law is that they can serve alcohol until twelve-thirty, but only if they are selling food too." She shrugs. "They usually just get left."

I stop eating, feeling my face fall. "Oh." I swallow. "So I shouldn't be eating them?"

"Of course you should if you're hungry," she says. "In fact, I'll join you." And we sit, companionably chewing on our sandwiches. "You know," she says, "these aren't actually too bad. Who'd have thought you could actually eat the food. You see?" She wags her finger at me. "I learn something new from you every day."

"Like you should eat the sandwiches that you're paying for?" I ask.

Caitlin slips her arm around my shoulder and pulls me toward her, the top of her head resting against mine. "You're my best friend, you know," she says. "You're the best one. Better than all these lot." She gestures around the room at the animated crowd, her movements just a little unsteady.

"I've never had a best friend before," I say. "Apart from Alice, I mean." The thought that Caitlin Cardew would call me her best friend is dazzling. I wonder what that means to her; I wonder if things will still be the same between us after the summer is over. And I wonder why, if she really means it, she won't trust me with whatever weight she is carrying.

Caitlin pouts. "I still haven't met this Alice. I want to meet her!"

"You can't meet Alice," I reply quickly.

"Why not?" Caitlin demands.

I don't know the answer to that. Or maybe I do, but I don't want to say it. "Because you'll like her better than me," I say finally, and I am more than half-serious. I pick up another sandwich.

At that moment Patricia comes swaying up to the table, one arm around the waist of a handsome boy not much older than me. He is looking very pleased with himself, as is Patricia. I wonder what her husband would think about it, but no one else seems worried.

"She's eating the food!" Patricia exclaims, catching sight of me and falling into peals of laughter.

I roll my eyes. "Is it really so strange?" I ask. "You should have one. They're good."

Patricia laughs even harder at this, swiping at her eyes with her fingers and smudging her heavy makeup in the process. "Are we moving on soon, darling?" she says to Caitlin.

"Moving on?" I ask.

"Yes," Caitlin sighs. "I told you. This place stops serving at twelve-thirty, which is any minute now. They've been raided too often. We have to go and find . . . *alternative* . . . entertainment."

"Oh." I nod, not completely sure what this alternative entertainment might be. But Caitlin is staring into space, with a look on her face that I can't quite read.

"Caitlin?" Patricia asks again, momentarily removing her mouth from where it has been nuzzling her new friend's neck.

"Yes," Caitlin says, going very still. "Find Bernie, we'll head to Al's."

"Al's!" Patricia squeals. "Oh, darling, *heaven*! It's been an age since we went there."

"Yes." Caitlin's voice is dangerously quiet. "It has." Her hands are clutching at the white tablecloth, and her knuckles turn white. Something about this decision has her shaken, but I have no idea what it is. I don't know where or what Al's is, or what to expect when we get there.

Patricia disappears, towing her young man behind her,

and Caitlin catches a passing waiter by the elbow. "A gin rickey, please," she says, and then she lingers, holding on to his arm for a little longer as he begins to pull away. "Make it two," she adds.

"Is something wrong?" I ask as soon as the waiter vanishes.

Caitlin shakes her head. "It's nothing," she replies. "I'm just thirsty." It is perhaps fortunate, then, that moments later the waiter reappears with our cocktails. I take mine and sip at it, wincing at how strong it is. Caitlin, on the other hand, lifts the glass to her mouth with a trembling hand and drinks the whole thing in one go. Then Patricia appears again, this time with Bernie in tow.

"I hear we're going to Al's?" Bernie says. "What a thrill. It's really been *too* long."

"Yes," Caitlin says, getting unsteadily to her feet. "It *has* been too long, and Lou should see it." She turns to smile brightly at me, but it seems as though her eyes aren't quite focused on my face. "You'll love it," she finishes, clasping her hands in front of her.

"I'm happy to go wherever you like," I say carefully. "What is Al's? Is it another nightclub?" There's something else going on here, but I don't know what it is. If the thought of going to this Al's place is upsetting her so much, then why has she decided we should go?

"Oh, yes," Bernie drawls. "But it's nothing like this place, I can assure you of that, my little snowdrop."

Whenever Bernie refers to me as a daisy or a snowdrop

or a buttercup, I know that it means that we are about to get up to no good. I think he quite likes the idea of shocking me, and I'm stubbornly determined not to let that happen. I pull my shoulders back. "Well, then," I say, "what are we waiting for? Let's go." Wherever Al's is, perhaps it holds the answer to what is bothering Caitlin. I just hope that whatever is there won't do any more damage.

"You heard the woman," Caitlin says now. "Let's go!" She flings her arm out, gesturing toward the door, before setting out on a slightly unsteady path in that direction.

We tumble out of the club, laughing and rowdy. A row of photographers wait outside and at the first pop of a bulb Bernie steps neatly in front of Caitlin. These men must know Caitlin, must know about Robert's deal, the one Bernie told me about, because they turn their cameras away from her and on to me. "Over here, love," one man calls. "Give us a smile!"

I stand frozen as the flashes of light explode around me, leaving stars dancing in front of my eyes. "Save your film, gentlemen," Bernie calls imperiously. "She's nobody of interest to you."

I am torn between relief at the men turning away, and the hollow feeling that comes with the words "nobody of interest." It's another painful reminder that I don't really belong here with these people. Bernie hails a cab while Patricia says goodnight to her new friend, winding herself around him like a boa constrictor going in for the kill. Caitlin leans against me, and although the night air is still quite warm, I can feel her trembling. We drag the young man from Patricia's clutches, and then the four of us pile into the back of a car, with Caitlin sitting on Bernie's lap. She is as animated as I have ever seen her, rattling on as though she can't bear to stop talking for even a second. Her cheeks are flushed, and she seems almost feverish, bouncing impatiently on Bernie's knee as the car rumbles along.

When we pull over we are in a different part of town. The others spill out of the car and stand in the street while I clamber out behind them. I take a moment to look around me. This is definitely nothing like the other places I have been with Caitlin today. The road we are on is narrow and dingy. Tall buildings line the sides, looming over us and casting threatening shadows. I notice that several windows are boarded up, and apart from the four of us there seems to be no one else around. "Are you sure we're in the right place?" I ask in a whisper, not wanting to disturb the dark stillness.

"Oh, this is the place, all right," Caitlin says, and I think her voice sounds a little grim. "Come on," she calls over her shoulder as she starts walking toward one of the closed-up-looking buildings.

When we reach it, I notice that there is a black iron staircase leading down to some sort of basement. The others charge down the steep steps and come to a halt at a green door. As usual, I am left trailing behind, looking nervously over my shoulder. I'm no longer sure that I know what is going on. This dingy street seems like an unnatural fit for Caitlin, Bernie and Patricia, who look as out of place as peacocks in all their finery, with the easy mantle of privilege draped around their shoulders. I realize with a start that tonight I am one of them as well. The gold embroidery on my dress glints in the muted glow of the streetlamp, and only I know that I don't belong in it—that I am only shamming—gold leaf, not solid gold.

Caitlin reaches up and pulls the bell beside the door, which swings open a few moments later, revealing a tall black woman in a green evening dress. She has glowing, amber eyes, and a slow smile spreads across her face.

"Well, well, well." There is wryness in her voice, something a little taunting. "If it isn't *Lady* Cardew."

"Hello, Al." Caitlin smiles up at her. "It's been a long time."

"It certainly has," Al says, and the air seems charged with something that I don't understand.

"Take pity on us, Al," Bernie cries then, staggering forward. "We poor bored creatures are looking for some entertainment."

"Is that so?" Al says, and her amazing eyes take each of us in. They come to rest, finally, on me. "Well, maybe I can help with that." She opens the door further, and stands to one side.

Bernie glides in, followed by Patricia. Caitlin and I stand on the doorstep.

"Al," Caitlin says brightly, "this is my friend Lou."

"Al and Lou." Al grins at me, and the grin scrunches up

her nose a little. I like her at once. "We sound like a couple of real gentlemen, don't we? Come on in, won't you?"

I look at Caitlin, and she nods briskly, taking a deep breath as though steeling herself for something terrible. We step through the door. There isn't a lot in the room—it is dark and dank with a couple of bits of rickety furniture. There is a small table pulled up beside a couple of chairs with a tea set on top of it. A shabby red curtain hangs against the wall in one corner. There is no sign of Bernie or Patricia, and I wonder briefly if they have simply disappeared, if this night is truly as unreal as it seems.

"Let's go, shall we?" Al says, looking at Caitlin. "You remember the way?"

Caitlin pulls back the red curtain, revealing another door, and when she opens it the sound of music drifts up from the bottom of another flight of stairs. "Come on, Lou! Down the rabbit hole!" she calls over her shoulder.

The first thing I notice is the wall of heat and sound as we descend into the room below. It is like entering an engine room, and the air is thick and damp. The heat is sweltering, but the music is the thing that stops me in my tracks. It is amazing, and something about it is familiar.

The room we are in isn't huge, but there must be over fifty people down here. This crowd is certainly more eclectic than the one we have just left. There are still a few of the moneyed types about—though they are definitely from the younger end of that crowd—but there are also a lot of people who aren't wearing Madame Carradice's finest creations or expensive jewelry. People from all walks of life are here, coming together to hear the incredible music filling the air, a diverse collage of city life, about as far away from Penlyn as it's possible to imagine. There is a blue haze of smoke and the room is dim, lit mostly by candles stuffed into the tops of old whisky bottles.

Hardly anyone is sitting in the seats that line the sides of the room, clustered around small tables. Instead they are dancing, leaning toward the music like plants toward sunlight.

I look at the stage and feel a jolt of surprise. "Why didn't you tell me . . . ," I begin, turning to look at Caitlin, but she is frozen, pale and trembling, her eyes locked on the band. Or, more accurately, on one particular member of the band. I turn back to the stage.

The man who is singing and playing the piano looks up, and catches my eye. It is Lucky. A smile of recognition touches his lips, and then his eyes move past me. Something in his face changes. Twirling around, I realize that he and Caitlin have locked eyes, and although he is still playing the piano without missing a note, his movements seem almost mechanical. It feels as if all the air has been sucked out of the room as the two of them stare and stare at each other. Suddenly, I know whose voice I overheard in the orchard that night. Then he looks away and goes back to playing as if nothing has happened.

Caitlin, on the other hand, looks as if she is about to fall down. "Let's sit," I say quickly, guiding her to one of the seats and pushing her down into it with as much gentleness as I can manage.

She slumps back, looking dazed and trembling for a moment, and I don't know what to do. Finally, she turns to me, her face pale but composed. "Well," she says matter-of-factly, "I've seen him now. That's the worst of it over."

"Lucky," I say, not bothering to pretend to be ignorant over who she is talking about. I am shocked by the revelation. I have seen enough of Caitlin's world to know that Lucky's position would be enough to keep them apart, but the color of his skin is of course the even bigger barrier. In a world so ruled by appearances, one where Caitlin obsesses over every detail of her life being approved by an audience of strangers, it would be impossible.

"His name is actually Freddy," she says softly now, "but everyone calls him Lucky. It's a silly name." She laughs without humor. "It doesn't even make any sense. He's not lucky. He can't gamble at all because his luck is so terrible, everyone knows that." She is rambling, her hands playing with the fringe on her dress.

"When did you last see each other?" I ask, puzzled. "Was it that night at the Cornwall house?"

"Yes," Caitlin says weakly. "Five weeks and four days ago." She adds after a pause, "I can probably tell you the hours too." That laugh again, dry, hollow, with nothing like the runaway glee her laughter usually contains. It makes sense now that I think about it, watching Caitlin wind herself tighter and tighter over that time.

"What happened?" I ask, but a shadow appears over the table.

"Thought you might be needing this." Al has arrived, holding a tumbler full of whisky.

"Thank you," Caitlin says gratefully, taking a long drink.

"I didn't know if you'd like anything?" Al asks, turning to me.

"I'm fine, thank you." I shake my head. She gives Caitlin another long, assessing look.

"Better bring another, Al," Caitlin says ruefully. Al hovers for a moment as if uncertain, and Caitlin scuffles in her purse, pulling out a wad of banknotes and pushing them into Al's hand. *"Please,"* she adds.

Al presses her lips together and then nods, moving on to speak to someone else who is calling her name.

Caitlin closes her eyes, but some of her color is coming back, and she is clutching that glass of whisky to her chest like it is a life belt. It is then that the music stops. I feel Caitlin stiffen beside me.

Lucky stands up to speak and the room falls silent. "We're going to take a ten-minute break," he says, and the crowd shouts out in dismay. "Don't worry, don't worry," he says, holding up his hands in surrender. "After that we'll be right back." He is smiling, charismatic; he gives nothing away. The band members begin clearing off the stage and people are slapping them on the back, pressing drinks into their hands.

Caitlin is clutching at my arm. "Oh!" she hisses. "Is he coming over? I can't look." And she has swung round to face me, her eyes turned firmly away from the stage.

"He's fiddling about with the piano," I say out of the corner of my mouth, trying to be inconspicuous as I dart glances over there.

"Oh my God," Caitlin mutters, burying her face in her glass. "Why did I come? This is torture."

"I think he's coming over," I say, and she stills.

"Are you sure?" she whispers.

"Yes, yes, he's making his way through the crowd." I can feel my own heart pounding as an unbearable tension seems to fill the air, so I can't imagine what must be going on inside Caitlin.

"Laugh!" she commands. "Laugh right now as if I'm saying something hilarious!"

I give what is possibly the worst stage laugh in the history of stage laughs and just about catch Caitlin's look of horror at my acting skills before Lucky is standing right in front of me.

"Hello again," he says, looking down at me, an easy smile on his face that reveals the dimple in his right cheek.

"Hello," I reply, and my voice croaks with nerves.

He doesn't speak to Caitlin and she doesn't speak to him. I have never heard two people ignore each other so loudly before.

"It's Louise, right?" he asks, and even though he's talking to me I feel as though I'm intruding on a private conversation. Caitlin remains frozen beside me, her eyes carefully fixed on a point on the other side of the room.

"Yes." I nod inanely, feeling like I'm stuck in a bad dream as I struggle to make small talk, to pretend there's anything normal about this situation. "Like the song," I add, injecting my voice with some false brightness.

"Like the song," Lucky echoes. "That's right, I owe you one of those, don't I?" His words remind me of the conversation we had the night of my first Cardew party. I remember thinking then that we were both of us outsiders, peeking in at that golden world. I really had no idea of the truth of that. "And what brings you to London?" he asks. The question feels heavier than it should. "I seem to remember that you didn't ever want to leave that house in Cornwall."

"Well, sometimes you have to open yourself up to new opportunities, I guess," I say with a lightness I don't feel.

"I guess so." He smiles, but the smile is tight. "Anyway, I'd better get back . . ." He gestures to the stage.

"Oh, yes," I say eagerly, feeling as though I want to push him up onto the stage myself, just to escape any more of this tense conversation. I can feel the pressure building, thrumming in the air between the three of us.

"It was nice to see you again, Louise." With that, his eyes flicker across to Caitlin, but she is looking miserably at the bottom of her glass.

Lucky makes his way back through the crowd toward the stage, where he is joined by the rest of his bandmates. They have a brief conversation, and Lucky goes to sit behind his piano. The crowd falls silent once more. Something expectant fills the air, that frisson of excitement that comes when the band members take up their instruments and throats clear, fingers hover over keys.

"OK, everyone," Lucky says, "this next one is a special song, dedicated to the lovely lady sitting right over there," and he points to where Caitlin and I sit. Her head snaps up and the band starts playing. "This is for our new friend Louise," he says. I recognize the tune as soon as the first notes fill the air, and then Lucky begins singing that song, the one about being hopelessly in love with a girl named Louise, in a deep, warm voice.

A sigh escapes from Caitlin's lips, and I think from mine as well. His voice is rich as velvet. I look over at my friend. This song might have my name on it, but it is plain that he is singing it for her.

Bernie and Patricia appear at the table then. "Phew." Bernie flops into a seat. "The band is certainly playing well tonight."

"Yes," I say, biting my bottom lip. "They're wonderful."

Bernie looks from me to Caitlin. "And they're playing your song, darling!" he says. "Why don't you and Patricia go and dance?"

"I'm not sure . . ." I trail off.

"Go, go." He waves his hand. "I'll stay and keep Caitlin company. Make sure she doesn't drink all the whisky." Here he reaches over and pours himself a large glass.

"Bernie!" Caitlin cries, only just noticing his arrival. "Here you are! Terrible man, you've been neglecting me." She sticks out her bottom lip.

"You're quite right," he says, dusting off the sleeves of his impeccable dinner jacket. "But I'm here to rectify that. I was just telling Lou that she should go and dance."

"Yes! Yes!" Caitlin exclaims, giving my shoulder a push. "Go and dance!"

I get to my feet and Patricia pulls me into the crowd. I try to focus on the music, and even though I would usually be in my element, losing myself in the crowd, I just can't seem to get into the party spirit. I close my eyes and I see Lucky's face when he looked at Caitlin.

The band plays for another thirty minutes. It is now well past two a.m. and the crowd is thinning out. By the time Patricia and I catch up with Caitlin and Bernie we are just about the only people left.

Patricia assesses the situation with a sigh. "I'll have to get him home," she says as Bernie peers groggily at the pair of us. "He's useless when he's like this. Will you be all right with Caitlin?" she asks, although the question seems a little rhetorical.

"Oh!" I exclaim. "I'm sure I can manage . . ." I trail off. I am not actually sure I can manage at all. I don't know where we are or where we are going, and Caitlin is fast asleep, so she isn't going to be much help either.

"Al will find you a taxi, don't worry," Patricia says, wrapping her fingers around Bernie's wrist and heaving him to his feet. "Come on, darling," she calls to him in a singsong voice. "Let's get you home."

"Home?" he repeats, swaying on his feet. "What a good idea. Excellent. Excellent." He sways some more.

"Yes." Patricia sighs a put-upon sigh. "It is a good idea. Let's go. I can't believe you're the one I'll be tucking up into bed tonight, you old soak."

Bernie beams at her. "Are we leaving little Lou?" he asks then, looking mournfully in my direction. "Little Lou. My little rosebud." He pulls me close to his chest. I think I could probably get drunk myself just from the fumes on his breath.

"Goodnight, Bernie," I say, patting him on the arm. "I hope you don't feel too bad in the morning. I'll see you at the party on Friday."

"Party," Bernie repeats. "Friday. Oh, the masks." A wicked smile appears on his face. "People behave so badly when they wear masks," he slurs. "Not that we need an excuse really."

Patricia tugs him along and the pair of them stumble up the stairs, calling their goodbyes over their shoulders.

When they have both disappeared I turn to survey the situation. Caitlin's eyes are still closed. And I am alone.

CHAPTER SEVENTEEN

"Caitlin," I say gently, shaking her arm.

She looks up blearily. Her red lipstick is smeared and she beams at me. "Lou!" she says. "Lou!"

"Yes, it's me." I slide into the seat across from her. "It's time to go home," I say.

"Home?" Caitlin frowns. "No!"

It is like trying to reason with the triplets. "Everyone's gone," I point out. "There's no music. It's time to go."

"No, no, no." Caitlin is shaking her head. "We'll go somewhere else," she mumbles. "Somewhere else . . ." She rests her head back on the table, unable to finish her thought.

I spot Al standing by the stage, talking to the double bass

player, and I wave helplessly. She takes pity on me and comes straight over.

"Uh-oh," she says, taking in the sight of Caitlin slumped in her seat. "When she said to bring more whisky I didn't think she meant just for her."

"Oh, Bernie helped," I say ruefully. "Patricia said you may be able to get us a taxi so that I can take her home?"

"Sure," Al says, smoothing Caitlin's hair back from her forehead. "We'll get you home safe, don't worry."

"I'll take you both home," a voice says, and I look up to see Lucky standing in front of us.

"Oh, no," I yelp, flustered. "You don't have to do that, I don't want to be any trouble . . ." I trail off.

"It looks like your friend is the one who's trouble," Lucky says, and it could have been a joke except, when his eyes fall on Caitlin, his lips are pressed into a thin line. The emphasis that he puts on the words "your friend" is almost funny. Does he really think that after this evening I don't know what's between them?

"She . . . she's not feeling very well," I say lamely, and the look in Lucky's eyes tells me not to bother.

"What'd you give her so much to drink for?" He turns to Al, anger in his voice.

Al spreads her hands in front of her. "I'm not her keeper," she says.

"I think if you could just get us a taxi, we'll get out of your way," I interrupt, focusing only on getting Caitlin home as quickly as possible.

"I told you, I'll take you," Lucky says, and without another word he stomps over and lifts Caitlin into his arms as though she weighs nothing at all. Her blond head lolls against his chest and she opens her eyes.

"Freddy?" she murmurs, and her arm curls up around his neck, before her eyes shut again.

Lucky's mouth is still pressed together in a firm line. "Let's go," he says as he carries Caitlin toward the stairs. There is nothing for me to do but grab our bags and scurry after him.

"Thank you," I mutter to Al as I pass.

"Come again," she says serenely, her eyes on Lucky's back.

Lucky strides outside to where a beaten-up silver car is parked with its hood down. It is in such bad shape that it makes Gerald look like a luxury Rolls-Royce. Lucky lifts Caitlin into the passenger seat and gives me a weak smile. "It goes OK," he says, "it just looks a mess. Are you all right in the back?"

"Yes, of course," I say, jumping in. "Thank you so much for doing this."

He doesn't say anything, just slides in behind the wheel. As he has promised the car starts without complaint and runs smoothly. It seems as if Lucky knows where he is going and I am relieved by this, as I have no idea.

I sit back in my seat, feeling fingers of cool night air ruffling my hair. After the heat and the noise of the club it is something of a relief. The roads are dark and almost deserted, and streetlamps burn with a smudgy golden light that makes the world seem as though it is in soft focus. I fight a sudden yawn. It has been a long night. And it isn't over yet, I remind myself.

Finally, I am relieved to see a road I recognize, and we pull up outside Caitlin's house. Diving in her bag, I pull out her key and trip up the stairs first, fumbling with the lock and opening the door to let Lucky carry Caitlin inside. He takes her straight upstairs and is back moments later.

"She's out cold," he says. "She'll sleep now until the morning, but she won't feel great when she wakes up." He makes it sound like this has happened before.

We stand awkwardly in the hallway.

"Won't you have a drink?" I ask, just as he says, "I should be going."

We both laugh nervously. "Please have a drink," I say in a rush. "Just a quick one?" I can't bear the sadness in his face. I am sure he needs someone to talk to. I know I do.

"OK, sure." He nods, and follows me into the sitting room. I walk over to the bar and grab two glasses.

"I don't think there is very much here," I say apologetically, "and I don't know where things are kept." I splash an inch of something clear into the glasses and hand one to him.

"Thanks," he says.

We both sit down then, across from each other, neither of us touching our drinks.

"So," I say finally. "Caitlin says you haven't seen each other for a while."

A muscle twitches in Lucky's jaw. "That's right." He nods, staring down into his drink. "Has she . . . told you about it?" he asks.

"Not really," I say, taking a sip of my drink and wishing I hadn't as it burns its way down my throat. I cough. "I think she's very upset about it, though," I say hoarsely. "She's been so *agitated* since we arrived in London."

"Well, I can't take all the credit for that." Lucky grimaces.

"Why not?" I ask.

He looks at me now, his dark eyes inscrutable. "London isn't a happy place for her," he says. "There are a lot of . . . bad memories."

"Oh," I say. "I thought it was . . ." I break off awkwardly.

"Because of me?" Lucky shakes his head. "There's a lot more wrong than that. I actually thought I was helping her with it for a while." He gives a bitter bark of laughter. "I guess I just made it all worse in the end."

I let that sink in for a moment. If Lucky isn't the source of Caitlin's unhappiness, then I don't know what is. "Still," I suggest cautiously, "it was her decision to come and see you."

"God knows why." Lucky drops his head into his hands. "We ended things almost six weeks ago," he says. "We had to, I guess; we couldn't carry on as if nothing was wrong. It all had to be a big secret, and it couldn't ever go anywhere. We . . . we loved each other, I think, but it couldn't go anywhere," he repeats sadly.

Tears prickle at the back of my eyes. I don't know what to say.

"I asked her to leave," he says suddenly, and the look he flashes me is defiant. "I asked her to leave with me that night, right before I saw you. If we just got away from this place, these people . . ." He rubs a hand across his jaw. "For all their talk of being modern, they're still ruled by their conventions and their prejudices. There's an order to be preserved and people like us don't fit into it. I don't belong with someone like Caitlin, not in their eyes." He slumps back in his seat, the indignation draining out of him. "And I guess it was like you said—why would she leave it all behind for me? You don't walk away from that life if you can help it." He places the glass carefully by his feet. "Even if it's killing you," he adds quietly.

A shiver rushes through me at this. I think about Lucky's words. "People like us," he said. He's right, I don't fit into that neat order either. Maybe I have a free pass for the summer, and of course it's much easier for me than for him—the color of my skin means I was born with a privilege I have never considered before, but in a way we're still both outsiders in the Cardews' world.

"I'm worried about her," I say now, and my voice is small.

"Well, you're right to be" is all that he says.

A heavy silence fills the room. I try to untangle everything he has said, to lay out all that I saw tonight in front of me and to make all the pieces fit. But something is wrong.

This isn't neat and tidy storytelling. Lucky and Caitlin aren't characters that I'm writing. They're messy, vital, real.

"She's burning away," Lucky says, and his voice is a confession. "She has been since her father died. Soon there won't be anything left of her. Nothing but ash and bone."

He sighs and then rubs his face with both his hands. Finally, he gets to his feet. "It was really good to meet you, Louise," he says, holding out his hand. "Take care of yourself . . . and that friend of yours." Those words again, building a wall around his heart, distancing himself from the girl he loves so much.

I slip my hand into his and we shake as though sealing a contract, which I suppose, in a way, we are. For a second his fingers squeeze mine, and the look in his eyes is enough to break my heart.

"Maybe I'll see you around sometime," he says, recovering his jaunty smile, returning that naked emotion to some hidden, secret place. With that he turns and leaves the room, whistling under his breath. As the front door opens I hear him singing softly one last time.

I sit quietly by myself for a few minutes after Lucky leaves, sifting through the conversation, and then I drag myself up to bed, emerging around midday to find an incredibly pale Caitlin sitting on the settee in an elaborately embroidered silk dressing gown.

The smile she gives me is tremulous. "Seems that we had quite the party last night," she says.

"We sure did," I reply, perching on one of the other chairs. "How are you feeling?"

She grimaces. "I've certainly felt better."

"And what about . . ." I hesitate.

"Freddy?" she says with a sigh.

I nod.

She gives me that wonky smile that doesn't quite reach her eyes again. "It's over," she says heavily, fiddling with the tie on her dressing gown. "It's silly, because it was over before." She laughs here without a drop of humor. "But I still had to go, I had to see him." She shakes her head. "I thought it might make things easier. I thought seeing him would prove that I was over it all, that I didn't still . . ." She trails off with tears in her eyes.

"Love him?" I ask quietly.

She nods, and sits in silence for a moment. "It was foolish. To go there, to see him. Nothing has changed. Nothing *can* change for us. I wish things could be different, but that's not the world we live in. It's easier in Cornwall"—she looks at me now—"to be somewhere else. But when we came back here I just couldn't resist."

"He said he asked you to leave with him," I say cautiously.

Her smile is wan. "Did he?" she murmurs. "Yes, I suppose he did. But how could I?" Her eyes turn to me and they are filled with sadness. "How could I leave the only world I know and stop being Caitlin Cardew? How could I leave Robert on his own? Think of the scandal." She sighs heavily, and then sits up a little straighter, her gaze suddenly intense. "I understand now that it can't be. I can't keep living in the past. I need to move on with my life, meet someone else, get married and settle down, maybe."

"Get married!" I exclaim, taken back. "What are you talking about? Get married to who?"

Caitlin shrugs. "Oh, I don't know. Someone suitable. Maybe someone who will take me far away so that I can start again."

"You can't do that!" I am stunned. "How could you do that when you feel the way you do about Lucky? How could you just . . ." I trail off here, horrified.

Caitlin comes to sit beside me then, clutching my hand. "You can't say anything to anyone," she says then. "You have to keep it a secret. Robert doesn't know any of this. He would hate a scandal, and I couldn't bear it either, not after everything he's done for me. Please, promise."

"Of course I promise," I say, startled by her intensity.

There is a pause then, and Caitlin sits back and closes her eyes. "He left me a note, you know?" she says suddenly. "Freddy. Last night. I found it this morning."

"What did it say?" I ask.

"It said goodbye," she says. Her eyes open and she looks at me levelly. "Now, for heaven's sake, let's go home."

CHAPTER EIGHTEEN

That was four days ago and now I am back at the farm. It is also my eighteenth birthday. I wake up to the sun streaming through the small window above my bed. As I lie under my soft white cotton sheets I watch the odd cloud roll across that little square of blue sky. *Eighteen*. How old that sounds. And how much older I feel now than I did even a week ago. Since we returned from London I haven't seen much of Caitlin, but when I have I've had a careful eye on her, watching for signs of unhappiness. Her mask is firmly back in place, and she has given nothing away, been nothing but bright and breezy. Robert has been away again, so I haven't been able to talk to him about it . . . not that I'm sure what I could say, and the others don't seem to have noticed anything amiss with her.

I know that preparations for the party are keeping her busy, and when I try to suggest she take a break she tells me in a firm voice that staying busy is what she needs at the moment. It's hard to know if the confrontation with Lucky has made her better or worse. She seems the same, but I don't know what that means. I realize that, as close as I feel to Caitlin, there's so much about her I still don't know.

The party this evening is a bright spot that we are all focusing on. I can't quite believe that it's happening at all. A party, in my honor, at the Cardew House. A party to celebrate the end of summer. Like Caitlin I am choosing to look forward to it, refusing to think about what comes afterward.

My plans for the day are exciting—a birthday lunch with my family before heading to the Cardew House for the big party tonight. I haven't been over there for the last couple of days. Caitlin has strictly forbidden it so that I don't see any of her preparations and ruin my surprise. I stretch and wiggle my toes, testing out my eighteen-year-old body.

"Happy birthday to you . . ." The sound of singing drifts up the stairs, along with giggles and eager footsteps. I sit upright, bringing my knees to my chest as the door bursts open. The triplets are first, singing noisily and climbing straight onto the bed with me, burrowing under the blankets like a basketful of eager puppies. Tom is behind them, frowning with concentration as he carries a wobbling cake alight with candles. (He is not singing because, as he later points out, he has enough to do, what with stopping the cake from burning the house down, and if I will be so old

that I need so many candles as to become a fire risk then that is my own business.) Freya next, who looks younger and more vulnerable than usual, still in her pajamas, with her arms full of presents wrapped in brown paper and red string. Finally, behind her come Pa, who is carrying a big parcel, and Midge, who is carrying the baby. Pa's voice is deep and warbling, Midge's thin and reedy, but I love hearing them sing together.

The room is small and not made for nine people, but somehow we all squeeze in, and when their song comes to an end I clap as hard as I can and blow out my candles. Tom places the cake on top of the dresser with a profound look of relief and flops into the chair. "What a family of musicians, thank you!" I say, as Freya dumps the gifts unceremoniously into my lap and joins Pa and Midge in perching on Alice's empty bed.

I open my presents—sweets from the triplets and Anthea, a book of poetry from Freya, ribbons and a prized green marble from Tom.

The present from Pa and Midge is bulky and it weighs a ton. I peel back the brown parcel paper, so slowly that Tom and Freya howl with impatience. Finally, I unwrap a hard black case, and when I pry open the shiny gold latch I reveal a beautiful, gleaming typewriter. There is a piece of paper already sticking out the top, and on it in uncompromising black ink are the words:

For the next adventure.

"Oh!" I exhale. My heart thuds in my chest. I turn to look at Pa, and his eyes are glittering.

"A serious piece of equipment for a serious writer," he says. His words feel like another kind of gift, and I luxuriate in them for a moment. I look back at the words and feel a thump of sadness, a tremor of anxiety. *The next adventure.* As far as I can see, my adventure is coming to an end. It is hard to see how returning to life as normal in Penlyn can possibly be anything but a disappointment. At least I can write, I think, and maybe this is the gift that the typewriter represents—writing is an escape, an adventure in itself. I will have to hope it is enough.

I stand then, hugging everyone I can reach. "Thank you, thank you!" I exclaim. "I love them all!" I can't resist stroking the typewriter keys, thinking about all the words I will capture with them.

"Well, I had better get back to preparing lunch," Midge says briskly. "And you had better get dressed. Your guests will be here soon."

Everyone leaves, and I hum to myself as I dress in one of the Madame Carradice creations that Caitlin bought for me in London. It is a light, clotted-cream-colored dress with violets embroidered around the neckline and hem. It makes me feel pretty.

After primping for a while, I examine my presents once more, setting the typewriter up on the dressing table where it looks enormous and—I have to admit—a little intimidating. I decide to name it Gladys, and once that decision has been made the typewriter looks a lot friendlier. "I'll see *you* later, Gladys," I call over my shoulder as I make my way downstairs. There is a lot of noise coming from the kitchen where Midge, true to her word, is baking up a feast composed of all of my favorite things. Aren't birthdays wonderful?

There's a knock at the door and Alice and Jack arrive. I run forward to greet them, but then I falter. It has been so long since I've seen Alice and so much has happened. I see her now, the shock in her eyes as she takes in the sight of me in my new dress.

"Happy birthday, little sister-in-law," Jack says, oblivious, as he crushes me to his chest.

"Don't crinkle her, Jack!" Alice exclaims, but her jollity sounds a bit forced. "Look at that dress! You're too fine for us, Lou." She shifts on the spot, and I know I'm not supposed to, but I notice the tiny movement of her hand as she tries to cover the darned bit on the sleeve of her own dress. It's an instinctive motion, I understand, because of course I know the dress is darned. I'm the one who ripped it when I borrowed it last year.

I stand awkwardly in front of her. "It was a present," I say. "You can borrow it any time," I add quickly, and it feels strange although I don't know why—Alice and I have always shared everything.

Alice makes a visible attempt to rally. "That's why you're my favorite sister," she says with a smile that makes her look more like her usual self.

"I *can* hear you, you know," Freya says from her position at the kitchen table.

"How would I know that, when you haven't even lifted your nose from your book to say hello?" Alice puts in sweetly.

"Children, children," Midge interrupts. "If you're going to bicker, then please go through to the living room."

"First"—Alice lifts her finger—"a birthday crown for the birthday girl," and she runs back outside, returning with a ring of baby's breath. She places the crown of tiny white flowers on my head, although I think her fingers are trembling a little. She's standing so near and I can smell her familiar Alice smell, and I want to hug her and laugh with her and tell her everything that's happened to me over these past few weeks, but for some reason we're being so stiff and polite with each other that I can't do any of those things.

Freya is looking at us with her head tilted to one side like a little bird. Her eyes narrow thoughtfully.

"Very nice," Midge says briskly, blissfully unaware of any awkwardness. "Now off you go, out of my way."

At that moment Aunt Cath arrives with Uncle Albie, closely followed by Aunt Irene. We spill through to the sitting room, which is decorated with streamers and paper chains, and I feel my heart lift at the sight.

Aunt Irene presents me with a set of handkerchiefs, and I swear I hear her mutter something about how I'll be needing them soon enough, before settling herself regally in the corner and sending Tom into the kitchen for a cup of strong tea. Aunt Cath and Uncle Albie are much jollier and give me a new Duke Ellington record that I insist on playing immediately. The huffing sounds issuing from Aunt Irene are just a bonus as we dance around the living room furniture.

Jack and Alice are showing Aunt Cath a new step, and Uncle Albie is twirling me around, when I notice two more guests standing in the doorway watching the festivities unfold.

It is Robert and Caitlin.

"What are you doing here?" I exclaim, and the dancing stops abruptly as everyone turns to stare.

"I invited them, of course." Midge's voice comes from behind the Cardews, and she nudges them into the room.

"Surprise!" Caitlin sings, tripping in and wrapping me in a warm hug. "Is it a good one?" She steps back to look at my face.

"Of course it is!" I say, but I'm not sure it is, really. I can feel Alice's eyes on us, and the strange atmosphere between us seems to grow even stranger. "I just didn't think I would see you until tonight," I say faintly to Caitlin.

"Well, we can't stay long," Caitlin smirks, and she wags her finger at me, "because there is still a lot to do. But I couldn't resist the thought of meeting your family."

"And I couldn't resist the thought of your mother's cooking." Robert steps forward and kisses me on the cheek, his warm, spicy cologne filling my senses. "Happy birthday." He smiles, his eyes crinkling.

"Thank you," I say, feeling suddenly shy. The room seems too small for him. He is taking up too much space, he is standing too close. My confused body feels like it's bursting into flames. *Is it hot in here?* My nerves are jangling and I take a step back from him. It must be because I haven't seen him for a while. He has gone back to being the man in the magazines, rather than the overbearing know-it-all who teases me and tries to catch me cheating at cards.

"You look . . ." He pauses for a moment, as though searching for the word. His eyes meet mine.

Beautiful, my brain screams. *He's going to tell you that you look beautiful!* Do I want to hear him say it? I'm confused, overwhelmed. I feel like when he looks at me like that he is seeing me, *really* seeing me, not as someone who blends into the background, not as someone else's shadow.

"Old," he finishes, and it's the perfect thing to say because it makes me laugh and the room seems suddenly to fill up with a bit more air. Whatever those rattling, shaky feelings were, they recede a little.

"I must be catching up with you," I manage, feeling my heart return to a more normal rhythm.

"Maybe," he replies, tipping his head to one side and looking me over. "It's all this hard living. I hear London was as debauched as always."

I wonder how much he has actually heard. I don't really want to think about that. My eyes slide over to Caitlin, who is introducing herself to everyone. She is pretty, charming, gracious. I search her face for any sign of secret, hidden anguish but I can find nothing.

"Speaking of London," I say, turning back to Robert, "why didn't you ever tell me what an artist you are?"

He clears his throat. "That was a long time ago."

"Well . . . you're quite good," I say a little awkwardly.

"Given your own artistic talent I know that is high praise," he says, and he gestures toward a smudgy and rather lopsided picture of a blackbird that hangs on the wall. I close my eyes for a second, silently cursing Midge's pride in our mediocre-at-best artistic efforts. Trust Robert to notice that kind of thing straightaway. I briefly consider denying any knowledge of the picture, but there's no lie to be told—it has my name in one corner, written in a young, round hand.

"Well, *exactly*," I say, instead, drawing myself up to my full height. "I speak from a position of great authority." I tilt my head, studying the picture. "Of course, my own work owes much to the early impressionists."

"I thought I detected the influence." He nods solemnly.

While we have been speaking, Caitlin is on a full charm offensive. I notice that Alice hangs back, watching her warily.

I decide it will be best to handle this particular introduction myself.

"Lou has told me so much about you." Caitlin's voice is at its most musical; her perfect vowels cutting through the air feel like an attack. She makes everything around her look shabby, and I don't know what Alice is going to make of her. Although they share many similarities, seeing them side by side now highlights only their contrasts. They are both so important to me, but they know me in different ways . . . it's hard to see them together for some reason; it makes me feel unsure of myself.

Alice tucks a long strand of golden hair behind her ear, a gesture that I know means she is nervous. Not that anyone else could tell by looking at her. She stands upright, tall and ravishingly beautiful in her worn dress. "Oh, really?" she says blandly. "All good, I hope?"

"Of course," I say hurriedly, realizing immediately that I sound too earnest, that I should have made a joke. My words hang limp in the air.

Caitlin is looking back and forth between us now, and a crease appears between her eyes. Alice is staring at a point on the wall somewhere to the right of me.

"Well, it's nice to meet you," Alice says now, and the words come out all in one breath as though they've been stitched together. "But I'd better go and give Midge a hand in the kitchen."

"I'll come too—" I begin, but Alice lifts a hand.

"Don't be silly, Lou," she says, and her voice is smooth, unemotional. "It's your party, you stay here with your guests."

I make a move toward her, but Alice sweeps out of the room.

"Is everything OK?" Caitlin asks, and she looks anxiously at my face. "I hope we didn't . . . I hope it's OK that we came?" She sounds uncertain.

I smile. "Of course it is." I draw my shoulders back. "It's just sister stuff. Now, the real challenge is over here." My voice dips low as I guide Caitlin over to where Aunt Irene sits. A mischievous look flickers across Caitlin's face before she pulls up a seat beside the sour-faced woman and settles in for battle.

Robert, it seems, has been commandeered by Tom, who whirls into the room, shouting that the blue car is sitting on the drive and that *somebody* owes him a ride. By the time Robert returns with a windswept and jubilant Tom, lunch is ready. And what a lunch it is. A feast of summer tarts and vegetables fresh from the garden, there is warm bread and ham and cheese, and cold roast chicken, then three different types of cake and strawberries and cream for dessert.

It is scorching hot again and we eat in the front garden, where Pa has created a long makeshift table out of some big planks of wood resting on several trestles. Mismatched bed-sheets have been thrown over the top as tablecloths, and Freya has filled milk jugs with posies of wildflowers for decoration. We sit in the long grass, looking out over the sea while bees hum sleepily from flower to flower. Pa brings the old gramophone outside, and the familiar crackle of the needle against our old records drifts through the air.

At first the conversation is awkward, and I fret over how the Cardews will fit into the scene, as if a jigsaw puzzle piece from the wrong box has crept in by mistake. Gradually, though, the talk becomes easier, and Robert and Caitlin seem to be enjoying themselves. Even Aunt Irene appears to be working hard to cover up her pleasure, but I am still worried about Alice. While everyone else chatters and laughs, Alice is mostly silent. She picks at her food, even leaving her cake untouched. It is then that I know that something must be really wrong. Finally, Caitlin gets to her feet. "I'm so sorry," she says, "I really do hate to leave, but we have to get back to the party preparations."

Robert stands as well. "Thank you so much for inviting us," he says. "And for the wonderful food."

They say their goodbyes to everyone. "Lou, we'll see you at seven," Caitlin calls as they make their way to the car. "And don't worry about bringing anything . . . we have it *all* covered."

"What a nice pair," Aunt Cath says as we watch them drive away. "No airs and graces. How lovely that you've made such good friends, Lou."

"Hmmph," Aunt Irene sniffs before I can reply. "It will all end in tears, mark my words." She shifts in her seat. "Although I will say that the newspapers seem to have exaggerated their behavior atrociously," she concedes grudgingly. "I spent quite some time talking to *Lady Cardew* and she was terribly kind about my poor Art." Out comes the handkerchief, and we all bow our heads dutifully for a moment.

"Well," Midge says brightly, breaking the silence and ignoring Aunt Irene's stormy glare. "Is everyone finished? Shall we get these things packed up inside?"

As everyone starts bustling around, Alice appears at my side and tugs on my arm. "Come with me," she says. "I have to talk to you about something."

I follow her in silence, and we wander through the garden

toward the coastal path. "Here," she says, when we are out of earshot of the others. "Sit here with me," and she pulls me down beside her on a grassy bank.

"What's all this secrecy in aid of?" I ask.

"I need to talk to you," Alice says.

"I'm glad," I breathe in a rush. "I hope you didn't mind Caitlin and Robert turning up. I didn't invite them, but they're my friends and . . ." I trail off hopelessly.

"Mmm." Alice makes a nondescript noise, and I don't know how to interpret it.

"Is everything . . . OK?" I ask. "I'm sorry I haven't seen much of you lately, I—"

Alice waves her hand and cuts me off here. "That's not what I want to talk to you about," she says, and her voice is almost wary, uncertain.

"Well?" I say after a moment. "What is it?" I aim for cheerful. "The suspense is killing me!"

"I wanted you to be the first person to know," she says. "It felt right that you should be first. I don't know how to . . ." She pauses and takes a deep breath. "Jack and I . . . we're having a baby." The words are as fragile as tissue paper, and I feel the earth shift beneath my feet.

"C-congratulations!" I stutter, in a daze.

"You look so surprised!" Alice smiles. "I was sure you would have guessed already, somehow. You always seem to notice everything. I can't keep my food down, so I didn't eat my cake, and I think I'm already showing," she rattles breathlessly as she pulls her dress tightly over her flat stomach.

"I had no idea," I say, grasping for words, for thought. "I'm just . . . I can't believe it."

Alice frowns. "Well, there's no need to say it like that," she says, and her voice holds something peppery and sharp. "It's not *that* shocking. I am married, you know, these things do happen."

"Of course they do," I say, and I squeeze her hand. "It's just so soon."

"It's not that soon," Alice snaps, pulling back her hand. "We've been married for nearly two months."

"You're right, you're right," I say, and all my words sound wrong. I'm off balance. The news of the baby changes everything. Nothing will be the same now, not for Alice. She's starting something wonderful and new, something that pulls her even further away. "I just thought you'd have more time," I finish lamely.

"More time?" Alice echoes dangerously, and I close my eyes. "More time for what exactly?"

"Nothing, nothing," I say quickly. "I didn't mean anything, I'm just surprised. But of course I'm happy; I'm so happy for you."

"More time for running around and being independent like you?" Alice says, ignoring me.

"No," I begin. "Of course not." She cuts me off.

"I have a life, Lou." Alice gets angrily to her feet. "It may not be the kind of life your fancy new friends live, but it is mine and I like it. I have a husband and we're having a baby. What exactly do you have?"

"That's not fair, Alice," I say desperately. "I didn't mean any of that, I wasn't trying to upset you. I meant more time settling in to married life, more time before things changed again."

Alice isn't listening anymore. "You act like those people are so great. Like I'm the one throwing my life away. Meanwhile you have beach parties and drink cocktails and ignore your real life completely," she storms. "It's been like this for weeks. I've hardly seen you and you're running around with *them*, pretending to be one of them, but you're not like them, Lou, no matter how much you want to be."

"I know that!" I say, and there are tears in my voice as I feel anger welling up inside me.

"Do you?" she asks, looking at me with something suspiciously like pity, and it's that that breaks me open. I feel a tear slide down my cheek. "Because you don't act like it. But what happens when they leave in a couple of weeks? Do you think they'll take you with them?"

"Of course not," I manage, and then I pull my shoulders back. "And you should be careful, you sound just like Aunt Irene."

"Well, maybe Aunt Irene is right for once!" Alice yells.

"Can you even hear yourself?" I ask. "You're defending Aunt Irene. When did you turn into such a disapproving old woman?"

"I guess it was when I married the love of my life, which you seem to think is the worst thing I could possibly have done," Alice snaps, twirling and stomping back toward the house. "I can't believe you acted like this," she calls over her shoulder. "Thanks a lot."

"You're welcome," I shout after her, like a petulant child. I flop back down onto the ground, my head buzzing. I am angry and upset, and I spend a few minutes muttering some choice words under my breath and thinking about all the witty, hurtful things I should have said to Alice.

But slowly, slowly, I begin to realize that I am not angry at her, I am angry at myself. Yes, I had been surprised, but I should have been happy for her—this is what she wants. Instead I felt the ground being tugged from underneath me, felt another part of my familiar world slipping further away, felt Alice leaving me behind. And not only that. The Cardews are leaving me behind as well. I know that my summer escape is coming to an end and I feel so lost. I was horrible to Alice. And I was selfish.

I get to my feet and hurry back to the house, calling Alice's name.

"She and Jack left about ten minutes ago," Midge shouts from the kitchen. I am about to go after them, but she calls me back into the kitchen. "They are going straight to see Jack's mother, remember?" she says.

"Oh, I'd forgotten." I sigh, slumping into a nearby chair.

"You two have a fight, did you?" Midge asks, putting dishes back in the cupboards. I get to my feet to help.

"How did you know?" I ask.

Midge chuckles. "You act like I haven't known you for eighteen years. Don't worry, you can make it up tomorrow."

"I don't know," I say. "It was pretty bad. The worst, really."

"It will be fine," Midge says calmly. "No use worrying over it tonight. Don't let it spoil your party."

"I'm not feeling in the party mood right now." I sigh again.

"After all the trouble those nice friends of yours have gone to?" Midge asks. "That's very pretty behavior."

"You're right," I say, trying to sound more cheerful.

"Of course I am." Midge comes over and hands me a plate. "Now, you've still got other guests in the house. Take some of these biscuits through and see if anyone wants one."

"Midge!" I laugh. "No one's going to have room for biscuits after all that."

"Oh, I'm sure they'll fit a couple in," she says. "Now, run along. I heard Irene complaining about the music again. Go and put that nice Mr. Jelly Roll on."

"Good idea," I say, heading through to the sitting room. If anything will cheer me up right now, it's scandalizing Aunt Irene.

CHAPTER NINETEEN

By seven o'clock I am determined to push the fight with Alice out of my mind. Midge is right, I reassure myself, we will make up, and tomorrow I'll go and apologize. For now, I just want to focus on the excitement of the party. After all, how often do things like this happen in real life? Still, I can't seem to shake the feeling, the edgy, anxious feeling that the argument has left me with. It is like a bitter taste in my mouth.

When I reach the house, with my black dress tucked carefully over my arm, Caitlin is waiting outside for me. "You're here!" she cries. "Now, I need you to put this on." She holds up a silk scarf.

"A scarf?" I say, reaching out to touch it. "Why?"

"It's a blindfold, silly!" She laughs. "You need to put it on so that I can get you upstairs without seeing any of the secret party business."

"Are you serious?" I ask, but apparently she is because she is already covering my eyes with the scarf. "Now what?" I ask after she ties it firmly in a knot and confirms that I can't see anything.

"Now I guide you to your room," she says.

This is, predictably, easier said than done. There is a lot of bumping into things and muttered curse words on my side, and a lot of stifled giggling on hers, but eventually she takes the blindfold off and I find that I am standing in my bedroom.

"Ta-da!" Caitlin sings, throwing her arms up in the air.

"Yes, seamless." I nod, rubbing my knee where I am certain a bruise is forming. "Have we missed the party yet?"

"Don't be grumpy," she pleads. "I told you I was sorry about that wall. I got my left and right confused for a second."

I roll my eyes, but she knows that I am only teasing. Now that I am in the house I can feel the harsh words I exchanged with Alice receding, like they were part of some distant bad dream. The building is working its magic on me already, and a tingle of excitement runs down my spine at the thought of all that lies ahead tonight.

"Anyway," Caitlin says, with a gleam in her eyes, "how can you possibly stay angry when there are presents to open?" And she steps neatly to one side, revealing a small pile of beautifully wrapped gifts on top of the bed.

"Caitlin!" I exclaim. "That's too much!"

"They're not all from me," she says. "They're from everyone."

There are silk stockings from Patricia, and a cloche hat from Bernie. Laurie has given me a bottle of scent that smells like bluebells in the spring, and there is even a flat, square parcel from Charlie. There is nothing particularly inspiring on the card, but I tear at the paper, revealing the record that lies inside. It is Maurice Chevalier singing "Louise." For a moment my and Caitlin's eyes meet, and I see a flicker of sadness, but it is quickly gone.

"Ooooh, *Louise,*" she hisses, jabbing me in the arm. "You know how that goes . . . all about being in love." She sings ardently, clutching at her heart and sliding from the bed in a dramatic heap.

"I'm sure he doesn't mean anything by it," I say, stroking the record with my fingertips. "Other than it's got my name as the title."

"I don't know," Caitlin says from the floor. "I think maybe tonight's the night."

"What do you mean?" I frown.

She swings around onto her knees and looks up at me. "I mean that tonight's the night something happens," she says. "You declare your undying love for each other."

"I don't know why you keep going on about me and Charlie," I grumble. It's silly that Caitlin has latched on to the idea with so much determination. I like Charlie fine, but I'm certainly not in love with him. I remember watching Alice fall in love with Jack, the way she lit up around him, the way he made her laugh, the way he looked at her. There's nothing like that between me and Charlie.

"Well, for starters, you did say he was the most handsome man you'd ever seen," Caitlin clucks. "Why not live a little? Have some fun? It's no use always waiting for him to take the reins. If he's still being so slow about it, you should just march right up and kiss him. That would do the trick." Her eyes are enormous, shining dangerously.

"I couldn't do that!" I exclaim.

"Hmm." Caitlin sniffs. "Well, I think it would be mighty effective, and this is a night you'll want to remember forever. It's a night *made* for kissing."

"What's this?" I ask, changing the subject. There is one present left—a large, white box tied with silver ribbon.

"Oooh." Caitlin jumps to her feet, and her movements lack some of her usual grace, as if she is wound tightly, carrying her tension in her limbs. "I can't *wait* to see you open this one."

I pull the card from where it is tucked beneath the ribbon. "It's from you . . . and Robert," I say. The message is simple. *Happy Birthday*, the card reads, with a "C" and an "R" at the bottom. I trace my fingers over the handwriting. It is Robert's, and it is elegant and precise, just like him.

I lift the lid from the box and gingerly pull back the layers and layers of pale pink tissue paper inside. I gasp when I catch a glimpse of pale green silk. No, I correct myself, stroking the material with trembling fingers, not pale green at all . . . *seafoam*.

I lift the dress from the box as gently as I can. It is, without a doubt, the most beautiful thing I have ever seen. It is made with the silk organza that I fell in love with at Madame Carradice's, a sleeveless gown with a dropped waist and a hemline that is slightly raised at the front. The skirt falls in soft, rippling waves, and beautiful, intricate embroidery in gold thread and tiny green and gold beads snakes across the hips and down the sides like tiny, shimmering scales. It feels light and fragile, and each stitch is absolutely minute and absolutely perfect. Attached to one shoulder is a short, removable train in the same light silk, covered in more of the exquisite feathery beading. Everything about it is ethereal, fairy-made. It looks like something from another world. I stand speechless, holding it in my hands.

"Well?" Caitlin says, breaking the silence as she dances in front of me. "What do you think?"

"What do I think?" I repeat mechanically. I look at the dress some more, my eyes catching on every detail. "It's a dream," I breathe.

"I knew you'd love it!" She claps her hands gleefully. "And you thought I was going to let you go to your own party without a new dress!"

"Oh, but, Caitlin, I love my other dress. I've only worn it once." I still can't take my eyes off the new dress in my hands.

"Pfff." Caitlin makes a dismissive noise. "It's your eighteenth birthday; of course you should have something new, something utterly beautiful." It's so easy for her, I realize, so inconceivable to think of recycling an outfit. Just another example of the difference between us, but in this instance I can't bring myself to be sad about it. I hug the dress to my chest, deciding just to be grateful.

"It's some of Madame Carradice's best work," Caitlin continues. "I have to admit that I was really quite jealous. And so unlike Robert to take such an interest! He and Madame schemed together to make it, and she must have worked around the clock—it was his idea, you see, to take the inspiration from your love of the water. He said you'd like it if it reminded you of the sea, and for once I agreed with him."

"The sea," I repeat, still dazed and still clutching the dress.

"Yes." Caitlin nods. "And, of course, once he mentioned it, Madame knew exactly what to do. It is going to suit you perfectly. There's a mask in the box as well, I think."

I lay the dress reverently on the bed and I peek into the box. Sure enough, there is a mask inside made of gold silk overlaid with gold lace. I'm overwhelmed by how perfect it is. The silk runs through my fingers like water. It really does capture that feeling of magic that hangs over the sea for me. It's truly a dress for a sea sprite. The fact that it was Robert's idea, that he could know so well what I would like, is stunning. There is an ache in my chest as I come close, dangerously close, to something I have been trying desperately to avoid.

Suddenly, the bedroom door swings open with a bang, to reveal Laurie standing there in her dressing gown, a bottle of champagne in one hand and four glasses in the other. Elodie rushes in behind her, and she kisses me warmly, wishing me a happy birthday. Just like that the moment is gone and I allow myself to be pulled into the bright, chattering world my friends bring with them.

"OK, birthday girl," Laurie drawls in that warm honey voice. "We're here to do your hair. Let's get started."

Elodie takes my hand and guides me over to the dressing table, pushing me down onto the seat. "You are going to look magnificent tonight, Lou," she says, and her voice is hypnotic. "You will be the most beautiful girl in the room."

"Not if you're there," I say honestly.

"Bah!" Elodie exclaims, scrunching up her nose. "This night is for you, Louise. Everything is here for you, for the taking. Let that sink in and you will be . . . radiant." I feel her words working on me like a spell, spreading through me as if they're making their way into my blood, firing up my whole body.

"Do you trust me?" Laurie asks, brandishing a pair of scissors as she stands behind me in the mirror.

"I take it that's a rhetorical question?" I ask, but I eye the scissors nervously. "What did you have in mind?"

"Something . . . *bold*," Elodie says, and her eyes meet mine in the mirror, daring me to say yes.

"Yes," I say.

Caitlin is pacing the room like an expectant father. "Are you sure, Laurie?" she asks.

"I'm sure," Laurie replies. She grins, lifts one of my long

curls and, *snip*, chops it above my shoulder. "No going back now," she says.

Thirty minutes later and the rest of my hair has followed suit, falling silently to the floor.

"It looks wonderful," Caitlin breathes. The reflection in the mirror shows the three of them standing behind me, their approval written on their faces.

"Very chic." Elodie nods.

"Much more modern," Laurie puts in.

I am silent, tilting my head from side to side, trying to get used to the feeling of lightness, to the ends of my hair tickling my neck. Laurie has cut it so that it falls about an inch above my shoulders at the front, slightly shorter at the back. Somehow she has managed to tame my curls so that they are smooth and glossy. My neck looks longer, my eyes bigger, my cheekbones higher. I still look like me—it is a haircut, after all, not a magic trick—but a better version of me. In the mirror I see a slow smile spread across my face.

"I think she likes it!" Caitlin says, wrapping her arm around my shoulders.

"Women spend a lot of time and money trying to get their hair to wave like that." Laurie nods. "You're lucky."

She picks up her glass of champagne and holds it up. Caitlin, Elodie and I lift our own and clink them together in a toast.

"OK," Caitlin says breathlessly, her voice taut with excitement. "Stage one is complete. Now, you need to get dressed and I'll do your face."

"I'm going to go and get ready myself," Laurie says, yawning and stretching languorously. "I think my work here is done."

"Thanks," I say, reaching out to squeeze her hand. She bends down and plants a warm kiss on my cheek.

"Happy birthday, honey," she says, and then she sashays out of the room.

Elodie follows behind her. "Remember, Lou . . . tonight, you are bold!" she calls over her shoulder. "Tonight is yours!"

There are butterflies in my stomach. I am flooded with anticipation. It feels as though something extraordinary is going to happen tonight, and the fact that this night may be one of my last here gives it a charged, reckless feeling. "You should go and get ready too," I say to Caitlin.

"Oh, it won't take me long," she says, and her hands flutter by her sides.

I give her a look, the look of someone who knows precisely how long it takes her to get ready, thanks to much experience.

"Fine, fine." She laughs brightly. "But I'll be straight back, you'll see . . . tonight is all about you."

"I already feel completely, utterly spoiled," I say honestly.

"Good." Caitlin lifts her chin, a satisfied look on her face. "Then my plan is working. See you in a minute." She slips from the room, leaving me alone.

I look at my reflection in the mirror again, and lift my hand to my hair, tugging on one of my curls and watching it fall magically back into place. What will Alice say? I can't wait to show her. Then, like a kick in the gut, I remember our fight and tears prick my eyes. I look around the room. Alice was right about one thing, I realize—all of this will soon be coming to an end.

I stand and move to the bed where my beautiful dress lies, the green silk flowing across the sheets. Taking my time, I strip off to the pale pink slip and underwear that Madame Carradice insisted on and slide the dress over my head. It fits perfectly, of course. The silk whispers against my skin, and it is so light that it feels almost indecent—as though I am wearing nothing at all. I clip the train to my left shoulder, and it spills down my back, falling almost to the floor.

Taking a deep breath, I stand in front of the mirror. It is the perfect dress for a sea sprite. It is the perfect dress for me. It ripples and shimmers when I move and the color is amazing—it brings out the tiny bit of red in my hair, and the gold in my skin. Unlike the experience of wearing the beautiful dress in London, this time I don't feel like I'm pretending to be someone else. It's ironic, I suppose, when dressing for a masquerade, but I realize that I don't need to pretend. I am someone. I notice then that there have been no shoes included with my costume, but this time I know that only bare feet will work.

And just then Caitlin bursts back through the door like a whirling dervish, true to her word for once about getting ready with great speed. She wears an incredible short navy-blue dress embroidered with large silver stars and with silver fringe around the bottom that trembles as she moves. Silver stars are pinned in her hair and silver bangles jangle on both her wrists.

"Oh my God!" she squeals, and she claps her hands together, setting the bangles ringing. "You look amazing!"

"So do you," I say, as Caitlin continues to run an approving eye over me, but the truth is she looks a little pale, a little drawn. She is certainly too thin now, and her cheeks are hollow, her shoulder blades visible beneath the blue straps on her dress. Was Lucky right? Is she burning away? I turn to face her, but her eyes show nothing but girlish delight over two beautiful dresses. I want to help her, but I don't know how.

"Are you sure you're all right?" I ask, my hand on her arm.

Caitlin says nothing, but I notice there are violet shadows under her eyes.

"We don't have to do this, you know," I say quietly. "It's a masked party. No one will miss us. We can stay up here and talk."

Caitlin's face softens. "You'd miss your own party?" she asks.

"Of course," I say firmly, although if I'm completely honest I do feel a tingle of disappointment.

"You're so sweet." Caitlin takes my hand in hers and squeezes it. "But, honestly, what I need right now is a distraction. I don't want to be sad. I want to be happy, I want to dance and to forget my troubles. Let's have a wonderful time . . . please, Lou?" She looks at me with pleading eyes.

"If that's really what you want . . . ," I say uncertainly.

"It is." Caitlin is vehement. "I promise it is."

"OK," I say, and I can't help feeling a little relieved. I know it's selfish, but if Caitlin wants to dance and be happy rather than dwell too much on the future, then who am I to judge? It's an instinct that I understand completely.

"If Charlie Miller doesn't kiss you tonight then the man is an idiot." Caitlin is gleeful as she gives me another look. "And Robert will be very pleased too, I should think."

Something in the way she says it makes my insides squirm.

"Now, sit down," she commands, "and I'll just quickly do our faces." She dusts my cheeks with something sparkling, lines my eyes with smoky makeup and paints my mouth the warm red of a ripe apple, before turning her attention to her own face. "Oh, drat," she says. "I've left my lipstick in my room, it's a darker red than this. Will you be a darling and fetch it? It's in the gold tube on my dresser."

"Of course," I say, leaving her sitting in front of the mirror, blackening her lashes.

Stepping out onto the landing I can hear the sound of the band warming up and the chatter of guests already arriving below, and my stomach flutters with anticipation. I rush down the corridor toward Caitlin's room just as someone emerges from one of the doors to the right, and I collide with a broad chest in a white shirt.

"Oof," a voice exclaims in surprise.

I take a hasty step back. It is Robert.

We stand staring at each other for a second. His face is difficult to read.

"Well, what do you think?" I ask nervously, and my voice sounds a little high. I twirl around to give him the full effect of my costume.

"I think you look"—he pauses here, and I wait for the punchline—"beautiful," he says finally. "You look beautiful." There is none of the usual teasing in his tone. There is also something in his eyes as he takes in the sight of me in my dress that makes my stomach flip over. He looks a little stunned, and I know the feeling. I feel like I'm on fire, as if he must be able to see the glow coming off me. It's almost unbearable.

"Thank you," I choke and, unable to hold his gaze any longer, I look down at my bare toes. When I look back up, whatever I thought I had seen in his eyes is gone. "And thank you so much for the dress." I smile, relaxing now. "I love it. It's the most beautiful thing I've ever owned."

"Good," he says. "I'm glad. It was all Caitlin's idea, of course." He clears his throat.

"Of course." I nod.

"I do have something else for you, actually," he says, reaching into his pocket.

"I don't need anything else," I say quickly, but then he places an empty envelope in my hand.

I turn it over and frown. On the front is an address written in his elegant handwriting. I look up at him, confused.

"It's time for you to send Lady Amelia out into the world," Robert says, and he shifts nervously from one foot to the other. "I know the editor at this magazine. I'm certain he will love it. Just like I do."

I think I've forgotten how to breathe. The envelope shakes a little in my hand.

"It's your birthday, Lou." Robert clears his throat again, looking anxiously for my response. "Time to be brave. Time for something new."

"Thank you," I manage. I realize I am blinking back tears. It is a wonderful gift. Not only the opportunity it might bring, but what it represents—his belief in me. Because I can see that written all over his face. He really thinks my writing is good enough, he believes that I can do this, and that helps me to feel brave.

I look up at him, and we still seem to be standing very close together.

He lifts one hand and softly brushes my hair. I freeze. "You cut your hair," he says quietly.

"Yes." My voice is almost a whisper. "I mean, no." I shake my head like someone waking from a dream. "Laurie cut it. Do you like it?"

He smiles down at me. "I do," he says, and he lets his hand fall, taking a step back.

I let out a long, shaky breath. It is then that I notice a red smudge on his shirt. "Oh, no!" I exclaim, pointing to it. "A casualty of our collision. I'm afraid I've ruined your shirt."

He looks down at the mark. "Never mind," he says, and unlike me he seems very calm. "I have another. I can change."

"Oh, good," I rattle. "I wouldn't want you to have to explain lipstick on your shirt to Laurie." I laugh nervously. "That could be awkward. Anyway, I'd better go; your sister asked me to fetch something for her and she'll be wondering where I am."

"Of course," he says. "I should go and change, anyway."

We both stand as though glued to the spot for another beat.

"Lou," he says, and my nerves are shredded. Whatever he is going to say, I can't stand to hear it. I am full of too many things that I know I shouldn't be feeling.

"Sorry about that," I interrupt him, darting by and toward Caitlin's room. "I'll see you later," I call over my shoulder. "At the party."

CHAPTER TWENTY

Caitlin's room looks like it is the site of a recent hurricane.
I go over to her dressing table, and find that my knees are
trembling so much that I have to sit down. The table in front
of me is littered with objects, and I stare blindly at them for
a moment before identifying the lipstick that Caitlin wants.
There are also, I notice, a cluster of glass jars—some of
which are empty—labeled "Veronal." I pick up one of the
empty pots. I have seen this before, I realize. Midge bought
some for Aunt Irene after Uncle Art died, to help her sleep.
It looks like Caitlin has used quite a lot of it. I place the jar
back carefully where I found it. By the time I return to my
room, Caitlin is ready. "What took you so long?" she asks.
"Couldn't you find it?"

"Yes," I say. "I mean, no. But then I did, here it is." I hand her the lipstick. I am not sure why, but I don't tell her about running into Robert. I also don't ask her about the Veronal. If Aunt Irene used it, it can't be anything too dangerous, can it? I look closely at my friend, searching her face, but she is intent on her own reflection.

"OK," she says, after carefully painting her lips. "Time for the finishing touches." And she reaches for my gold mask, standing behind me and wrapping it around my eyes before tying the ribbons carefully at the back of my head. It feels funny, though not uncomfortable, and when I look in the mirror I understand what everyone has been going on about when they say that masks give you permission to behave badly. Looking at the girl I see reflected back at me, with the curving red smile and beautiful dress, I feel a thrill of excitement. It is strange, but liberating . . . like a pass to the kind of boldness that Elodie encouraged.

I help Caitlin with her mask, which is the same as mine but made of silver lace, and then there is a knock at the door. I open it and find Charlie standing there.

"Hello, ladies," he says, and his eyes travel appreciatively over my costume. "You look wonderful." I feel a little zing at the compliment. It is obvious from his face that it is sincere.

"So do you," I say, and he does. He is wearing a black embroidered frock coat over a white shirt with black breeches and black shoes with silver buckles. On his head is a powdered wig. The effect is dramatic and very, very attractive.

"You look like quite the Regency buck," Caitlin says approvingly, peering over my shoulder.

"Thanks, I guess," he says, scratching at his wig. "I'm pretty glad I don't have to wear these things all the time, though."

"But where's your mask?" I ask.

"Yes," Caitlin says. "Rules are rules."

Charlie grins. "Don't worry, I've already had this from my sister. Robert has it. I think he had to change, but I'll get it from him in a minute." He turns to Caitlin. "Laurie told me to tell you that everything is ready when you are."

"OK, thank you," Caitlin says, and Charlie wanders off toward Robert's room. "Are *you* ready, birthday girl?" she asks.

"Yes," I say, taking a deep breath. "Let's go!"

We descend the stairs into another world. A gold carpet runs down the middle of the staircase, which is lined with hundreds of small white candles in glass jars. The entrance hall is decked out in twinkling lights and the ceiling has been swathed in broad strips of black and gold fabric as if we are inside an enormous marquee. The space is absolutely heaving with masked people in extravagant costumes who turn and cheer as we walk down the stairs.

"Oh my God," I hiss, grabbing Caitlin's arm. "Don't let me trip over with all these people watching."

"Shhh," she whispers. "Stop worrying and enjoy yourself. You're the guest of honor."

There is a table to one side that is heaving under the weight of expensively wrapped gifts.

"What are those?" I ask.

"They're your presents," Caitlin replies easily.

"My presents?" I echo. "What are you talking about?"

"People know it's a birthday party so they bring a present." Caitlin says. "Don't worry, it will mostly be stuff someone else gave them at their birthday party. Everything gets sent round and round in an endless circle. At *my* last birthday party, I got back three things I had gifted other people. One of them was a tiepin engraved with their initials!" I think about the gifts that I received from my family and friends, and about the thoughtfulness behind each one. This pile of "gifts" from strangers is just another performance, part of the illusion. There's nothing real about any of them.

Waiters in black tie and black domino masks are circulating with gold trays. On the trays are champagne saucers full of a pale green drink. Caitlin grabs two and hands one to me.

"What is it?" I ask.

"I can't remember," Caitlin replies, "but it's called a 'Lou.'"

"What?" I ask again.

"It's something special the bartender designed in your honor. I think it has Chartreuse and gin and some other things," she says. "It's delicious."

I take a sip. "And lethal," I gasp.

Caitlin grins. "As all good cocktails should be, darling. Now come, come." She takes me by the hand and leads me through to the sitting room, which has been completely transformed. All of the furniture is gone, and the room is done up like a real nightclub, full of small tables covered in gold tablecloths and chairs with black velvet cushions. More candles burn, and the *plinky-plink* of a piano fills the dim room with a seductive, almost sleepy feeling. This is a place for intimate conversation and slow dancing, the kind of place where scandalous things happen in smoky corners.

We walk through the room and out of the French doors that open onto the lawn. Out here the sky seems to be filled with enormous round white lanterns and twinkling lights.

"Oh, Caitlin," I breathe. "How beautiful! I don't understand. It's like magic!"

"Aren't they clever?" she says, pleased. "They're attached to very thin wires." She points overhead. "You can't see them now that it's dark."

There is a huge white-and-gold bandstand on which a seventeen-piece jazz band, all wearing masks, are setting up their instruments. It is not, I realize with a pang, Lucky's band. Not that I really expected him to come, but when everything feels this much like a dream, it seems so easy to expect a happy ending. I don't know if Caitlin is thinking the same thing, but her eyes seem to linger there too.

A dance floor of checkered white and gold stretches out in front of the bandstand, ready to welcome the growing crowd. A bar reaches along the front of the lawn, overlooking the sea, and eight bartenders stand behind it already mixing drinks for the hordes gathered there. We stop here for a moment, greeting people. I am surprised by how many people I know from various parties over the summer. When my green drink is finished I am handed another. I can't stop looking about, reminding myself that this is for me. A party like this, for me.

"There's still one last thing," Caitlin says, tugging my hand. We walk around to the walled orchard. Hundreds of candles are lit on top of the wall, and when we make our way inside I can see that long tables have been set up, stretching the whole length of the tree-lined avenues. Down the center of the tables run twisting decorations of fruit and flowers, interspersed with heavy gold candelabras. It looks like we have stumbled across a party in a fairyland forest.

"It's for a midnight feast," Caitlin explains. "People will need food to soak up the drinks." She turns to me, her voice nervous, expectant. "Well, what do you think? It's harder to tell when you're wearing a mask."

"What do I think?" I ask, dazed. "I think . . . I think it's the most magical, ridiculous, extravagant, wonderful thing I've ever seen." I shake my head. "I think you'd better pinch me because I feel like I'm in a dream."

Caitlin obligingly gives me a good pinch, proving that I am, in fact, very much awake.

"Happy birthday," she says, raising her glass. "Here's to you!"

"I'll drink to that," I say, and we both drink, the green cocktail somehow both sweet and spicy at the same time.

"I'm so glad we got the chance to throw a last, really big party before we leave," Caitlin says, slipping her arm through mine and turning to wander back toward the crowds. "And that it is for such a good reason."

Despite the balmy evening I feel a cold shiver rush through me at her words. Of course they're leaving, I tell myself sternly. The summer is ending and you know that they will leave. You have always known. I hear Alice's voice ringing in my head again: *You're not like them, Lou, no matter how much you want to be.* Pushing the words away, I drain my drink in one go, feeling a rush of light-headedness.

"Easy, darling," Caitlin says. "Those things will go straight to your head."

"And why not?" I say, enjoying the reckless feeling that sings through my body. "It's a party, isn't it? *My* party."

Caitlin's eyes shine behind her mask. "Well, when you put it that way . . . ," she says, emptying her own glass.

I laugh, delighted. If all of this is about to end, then tonight I want to believe in the fantasy. I want to be bright and young and impetuous. I am enjoying this world, in which all the sharp edges seem to have been rubbed off and I have only to think about what will make me feel good. We trip, giggling, across the lawn toward the bar. The band are set up now, and they are playing something sparkling. The lanterns tremble overhead in the light breeze that is rolling in from the sea and the sea stretches out in front of us, dark and unfathomable.

It is as if we are on a boat, I think dreamily, one of those big ships all lit up and bobbing about on the inky water, headed for who knows where.

"Daaaaaaaarlings!" I hear a familiar voice cry, and there is Bernie, descending upon us with his arms outstretched. "Happy birthday, darling. I've been looking for you everywhere," he says, kissing me on both cheeks. "What a scrum," he groans, turning his attention to Caitlin. "It's already the party of the season. Too, *too* sick-making that you have such style you can pull this together in under a week." He steps back, allowing me to admire his costume. Had it not been for his greeting I may not have been able to pick him out of the crowd. He is dressed as a matador, in a black coat with gold embroidery and a red cloak. A red domino mask gives him a rakish look.

"You're not doing too badly on the style front yourself," Caitlin says, eyeing his outfit.

"You're too kind," he says preeningly. "But how can I compete with you two beauties? And you, birthday girl." He lifts my hand and spins me around, sending my silk skirt rippling around me. "What a revelation you are. You look like a beautiful nymph."

"A sprite, actually." I giggle.

Bernie lets out a low whistle then, and I glance over my shoulder to where he is looking. Laurie is walking toward us and her costume is turning every head as she passes. She is dressed as Scheherazade, in flowing blue silk pantaloons and a blue-and-silver top that exposes her smooth, golden midriff. Bangles and scarves adorn her wrists and a jeweled headband crowns her short, dark hair. The blue mask that she is wearing does nothing to disguise her . . . no one else could wear such a costume, no one else sways in such a sultry way, and she wears an anklet covered in tiny bells that jangle as she walks toward us.

Behind her is the prettiest boy I have ever seen, and it takes me a moment to place that mischievous grin. It is Elodie, in a top hat and tails, a neat white waistcoat nipping her in at the waist. Her dark hair is coiled at the nape of her neck, and her hat sits at a rakish angle. A black mask frames her expressive eyes, and a small, thin mustache has been etched on her top lip with charcoal.

"Bernie," Laurie says, upon reaching us and dishing out lingering kisses. "You remember Elodie?"

"Of course." Bernie's eyes travel from the top of Elodie's hat to her toes with a languid show of appreciation. "You both look ravishing."

"Elodie is going to sing." Laurie gestures to the stage. "Dance with me, will you?" she asks Bernie.

"Delighted," Bernie purrs, taking her arm. As they move away I realize that Laurie is completely oblivious to the eyes that follow her every movement.

"Lou," Caitlin says, touching my arm. "I have to go and take Elodie up to the stage and check on the food for later. Will you be OK? I shouldn't be long."

"Go, go." I wave them both away. "I'm going to get another drink. I'll be fine."

I push my way through the crowd to the bar. "Champagne, please," I say to the man mixing the drinks.

"Make it two," an unfamiliar voice says. It's a man I don't know, and he seems to be wearing some kind of toga. "I like your costume," he says, running his eyes over me with a little too much interest.

"Thank you," I say politely. "I like yours too."

"My friend and I both came in togas." He shrugs. "Afraid we had to rather throw things together to get down here from London in time. Bloody middle of nowhere, eh?"

"Oh, yes," I say, gratefully accepting my drink from the bartender.

"Know the girl whose party it is, do you?" he asks, moving closer to me. "Lois?"

"No," I say flatly.

"Oh, shame." He leans in closer to me. "She's a terrific girl. I'm quite good friends with the Cardews, actually," he says.

"Is that so?" I murmur.

"Oh, yes." He leers at me. "I'm here all the time. I could introduce you later if you want?"

"That would be nice," I say, edging away from him. "Sorry, I think I see my friend over there . . . it's been lovely talking to you." I slip away through the crowd, lifting my glass of pink champagne to my lips.

Elodie is on the stage now, and her outfit seems to have given her an extra pinch of swagger. Still, she looks very small, surrounded by the band. She stands before the microphone, her fingers fluttering up to caress the stand. And then she starts to sing and the crowd goes wild. I stand as if in a trance, listening to her beautiful voice. It is incredible that such a sound can come out of such a tiny person. I find that I am on the dance floor before I even know what has happened, and I am welcomed by everyone. I make my way to the front and Elodie spots me, winking behind her mask as the music pours from her, soaring through the air like stardust. I dance for a while, how long I'm not sure, just as I am not sure who with. Each masked face swirling around me wears the same grin. Finally, I need to take a break.

I walk across the lawn, the grass soft and cool under my feet. The floor seems to be moving around a little and I bump into someone. "So sorry," I mutter. I keep on walking without really knowing where I am going. I am feeling a little light-headed. It is time to sit down, somewhere still, somewhere quiet . . . and suddenly I know where my feet are taking me.

"Hello, old friend," I call as I reach my trusty oak tree. I press my palm against the rough bark, thinking that it feels like a long time since Robert caught me hiding in these branches. It is dark and quiet here, and I lean back against the tree, closing my eyes for a moment. I am haunted then by images of Robert from that first night. Of the look in his eyes when he turned to look up at me, of the sound of his laugh, of that first taste of champagne. I remember the way I felt about him then, the way I feel now, and I am almost knocked out by a sense of longing that overwhelms me. Panic begins to rise in my chest as I draw too near to something I have been trying desperately to ignore and conflicting emotions battle inside me.

"Lou?" I hear a muffled voice behind me, and I turn to see a powdered wig and a black frock coat in the dim light. With a happy sigh I realize that it is Charlie, come to check on me, and his uncomplicated presence is a relief. He is wearing a black domino mask now, and as he walks toward me I find myself thinking about Caitlin's advice. Perhaps it *is* time I take control of the situation. Well, it is my party, and I am eighteen and the night is wonderful and soft music is playing in the background. What better time for a kiss with a handsome man? This handsome man.

I sway toward him, and the champagne coursing through my veins gives me courage. He opens his mouth, but before he can say anything I reach up with my hand and draw his face down to mine, brushing my lips softly against his.

He stands very still for a second, and I can feel the pulse racing at the base of his throat. In a dream I wind my other hand up behind his neck, and he begins kissing me back, softly at first, as though I have taken him by surprise, and then more urgently. We stumble until my back is pressed against the tree and he is pressed against me. Still, I pull him closer, closer, wrapping myself around him, wanting more of him. My fingers tug at his dark coat, and I feel his heart thumping in his chest, in time with my own. He raises one hand to my face and his fingertips brush softly against my neck, sending white flames of desire crackling through me. He trails light kisses along my jaw and I almost stop breathing. His mouth is on my mouth, his hands are on my hips, pulling me toward him, and I want more, *more*. I want everything.

It is like no kiss I have ever experienced, it is all I wanted it to be . . . and I find myself imagining it is with someone else.

As this one clear thought pushes its way into my brain, I pull away from Charlie's kiss, my breathing ragged: I am thinking about kissing Robert.

I place my hands on Charlie's chest.

"Charlie," I whisper, my voice hoarse, and I feel him stiffen and take a step back. "I can't . . ." I trail off. "I'm sorry." And with that I slip away from him and stumble back to the party as quickly as my trembling legs will take me. I almost run straight into Laurie.

"Laurie," I gasp, raising a hand to my lips.

"What have *you* been up to?" she asks, smirking as she takes in my disheveled state, my rumpled hair.

"N-nothing," I stutter.

"Oh, really?" She raises an eyebrow. "Because it looks as though someone has kissed all your lipstick clean off." She smiles, that slow feline smile. "Come on, honey, let's fix you up. Everyone's going to the orchard for Caitlin's midnight feast and you want to look your best."

Numbly, I let her guide me to the bathroom, where she fixes my smudged makeup and I try to stop thinking about how much I want to kiss the man she is going to marry. As Laurie chatters away, I am struggling simply to remain upright. It is as though a dam has burst inside me. With that one admission—that I wished I was kissing Robert—I have opened a box that I was keeping so firmly closed I had denied that it was there at all. Am I in love with Robert? Is that what this pain means, the one that feels like it is cracking me in two? Tears smart in my eyes. Over the summer we have fought and laughed and teased each other and I have loved it. The thought of not seeing him anymore is physically painful.

"Have you been having a good time?" Laurie asks, brushing powder from a golden compact across my cheeks.

I nod, but my movements are jerky.

"So, the summer is coming to a close." Laurie sighs and stretches. "Tell me, little Lou, did you find your something more?"

"W-what?" I ask, dazed.

"Your passion, your next adventure?" The warmth in her voice slices through me. My feelings for Robert are a betrayal of our friendship. I feel sick.

"No, no," I say quickly. "No passion." I try to make my voice sound as firm as possible. I have to keep a lid on this. I need to put my feelings away, locked up somewhere tight.

"Oh?" Laurie quirks an eyebrow and looks pointedly at my smudged lipstick. Before I can say anything else she begins repainting my lips with her own crimson lipstick.

"Good as new," Laurie says then, standing behind me in the mirror. She turns me around and leans forward, taking me by surprise as she plants a full, warm kiss on my mouth. "And completely kiss-proof. Now, let's go." She pulls my arm through hers and we saunter through the front door and around to the orchard. All the time my brain is running wild. Now, here is Caitlin waiting by the entrance and clearly on the lookout for me.

"Lou!" she cries. "Thank goodness, there you are. I thought you'd disappeared! Now close your eyes," she says. I know there is no use protesting so, in a daze, I do as I am told. Between them Laurie and Caitlin guide me through to the orchard. It is very quiet, but I can hear some giggling and whispering that is making me feel nervous.

"Now," Caitlin says. "Open them!"

I open my eyes and hundreds of people start singing "Happy Birthday" while several members of the band join in on horns and trumpets. I am standing at the top of one of the long tables and in front of me is an enormous, four-tiered birthday cake covered in candles. I see Charlie standing further up and though I can barely bring myself to look at him, he is singing and smiling so I think that perhaps, at least, I haven't embarrassed him too much. I find my eyes drifting from face to face, searching for Robert, but I can't see him anywhere.

"*Happy birthdayyyy toooooo youuuuuuuuuu.*" The raucous singing draws to a close and the orchard erupts into cheers.

"Happy birthday, Lou." Caitlin squeezes my shoulders. "Now, make a wish."

I blow out the candles.

CHAPTER TWENTY-ONE

The rest of the evening is a blur. I sit with Caitlin and eat birthday cake, I chat and I laugh, and I dance. And all the time, in spite of myself, I know that my traitorous eyes are searching for Robert.

Now that I have looked my feelings squarely in the face, can I go back to hiding them, even from myself? Can't I make myself want something else, someone else? Can't I make my own heart see sense? I did just kiss Charlie, after all . . . and what a kiss it was. Truly, the knee-trembling, swoon-inducing stuff of great romance novels. It was a kiss so full of promise and yearning and something else, something deeper. It was perfect. So *why* did I have to start thinking about Robert? I try to examine my feelings but they are so swirling and confused that I don't even know where to start.

Except, perhaps, with the fact that Robert is getting married to someone else. And that the person he is marrying is my friend. That small wrinkle. So why am I even thinking about kissing him? Why does the thought of being near him and spending time with him fill me with a kind of happiness so big and brilliant that I can't bear to look directly at it?

I don't know what time it is when I find myself sitting in one of the plush black chairs in the sitting room, listening to the pianist play something melancholy and nursing a glass of something alcoholic. Two o'clock? Perhaps three? I have no idea. The key, I realize, is to keep myself occupied, just enough so that I don't have to think about the trouble I am in. So that thoughts of Robert and Caitlin and Alice and the rest of my messy, unresolved life are kept to a gentle whisper, rather than a deafening roar.

I lost track of Caitlin and the others a while ago, I can't quite remember when. I know that they are around somewhere, and that I should go and find them, but for now I am feeling languid and I am enjoying the feel of the music washing over me. My mind is pleasantly empty, as if it is full of the kind of static you hear on the wireless, or the sound of champagne bubbles fizzing. Another girl is sitting at the table with me, but I have no idea who she is. She keeps calling me Cynthia, and I have accepted that it is easier just to let her do so. She is speaking now.

"The thing is," she mutters, her eyes trying to focus on mine. "The thing is, Cynthia," she tries again. I wait. "The thing is, I *told* him, you know?"

I nod. I have also discovered that it is easier to nod than to question her pronouncements.

"Knew you would," she mumbles, pulling out a cigarette case. "Want one?" she asks.

"Why not?" I say, taking the cigarette and leaning forward for her to light it. Either she is swaying around a bit, or I am, or we both are, because the operation takes some time. I inhale and choke a little. I have smoked before, but I don't really care for it. I feel light-headed and I lean back in my chair, waiting for the world to steady itself.

My new friend has gone back to muttering darkly into her glass. "I *told* him," I hear her hiss once more. It is then that I spot Caitlin. She is running in from the garden, her hair disheveled and one shoe in her hand. The other is nowhere to be seen. She is laughing. I recognize that laugh, her too-bright laugh, her high-as-a-kite laugh.

Stumbling after her is Charlie, his powdered wig askew, showing his tousled blond hair underneath. He is wearing a white domino mask. No, I frown. That is wrong. His mask is black, isn't it? I shake my head, trying to remember. He is laughing too, catching at Caitlin's arm as she dances away from him. I stand unsteadily, and begin making my way toward them. Perhaps we can dance some more, I think. It would be nice to dance.

They have disappeared through the door, into the hallway, and I follow after them, dodging through the crowd.

"Wait," I call, but my voice gets lost in the noise. They are turning down the corridor toward the library now. Caitlin has put luxurious red love seats into all the alcoves along the hallway, where various busts and artworks usually sit, and there are plenty of amorous couples making the most of them. I hurry along, trailing behind Caitlin and Charlie. I can still hear them laughing together. Finally, they come to a stop outside the library door, and instead of calling after them again, I too grind to a halt.

Caitlin is standing with her back against the door frame, and Charlie has his arm resting on the wall above her head. He leans over her until their faces are only a few inches apart. I feel my breath catch in my chest. Caitlin reaches up and runs her finger along the side of his cheek, and the space between them closes until they are kissing.

I am still frozen to the spot, unable to look away as their kiss deepens. When they finally break apart, Charlie mutters something in her ear and Caitlin giggles. Then, with a knowing look at him, she reaches one hand behind her back and opens the door. Her other hand is grabbing on to his jacket, pulling him toward her, and Charlie is kissing her again as they fall into the library. The door swings shut. My head is buzzing, my heart pounding.

What does this mean? Caitlin and Charlie. How long has this been going on? Does she know that he kissed me only a couple of hours ago? Is this something else she's been holding back from me? More secrets? And what about Lucky? What about all the love that they feel for each other? My stomach lurches as I think about Lucky's face when he left the house in London. I realize that my sense of outrage is all for him. I have no claim on Charlie, have never felt anything more than friendship for him . . . But what Lucky and Caitlin had . . . that was something real. I saw the depth of their feelings so clearly—even when both of them were in pain. How could Caitlin just turn her back on that?

"Lou?" a voice says from behind me, and I turn to find Laurie ensconced on one of the sofas. And she isn't alone. Elodie is sitting with her, her arm thrown around the back of the sofa behind Laurie's head. Her hat lies tumbled on the cushions beside them, and her long dark hair is falling from its pins. The charcoal mustache has been badly smudged and so has Laurie's lipstick. It is obvious that I am interrupting something. My heart clatters in my chest.

Laurie seems completely unperturbed by my intrusion and, judging by the sympathetic face she is making, she also saw Charlie and Caitlin disappear into the library.

"I wouldn't worry about it," she says gently, shrugging her shoulders. "They'll have forgotten all about it in the morning. These things don't often mean anything."

I stand still for a moment, considering this. I think about Caitlin and Lucky, and I think about Robert. "They mean something to me," I say quietly. I may not want exactly what my sister has, but I know that her love for Jack is real. It's honest and precious, and she values it above anything. And that's what I want. Not this game, not this refusal to care properly about anything. It's heartless. It makes people disposable. People like me.

"Don't be silly, honey, we all have our little *affaires*." She speaks in a soft, teasing voice.

"Come on," Elodie joins in, her voice coaxing. "Don't let it spoil your party." As if I am a child who hasn't got the present she was hoping for.

In the end I say nothing; I just turn and walk away.

I wander outside and stand at the front of the house, listening to the sounds of the party still filling the air. I need to be quite alone, I realize, and I slip toward the crumbling stone steps that lead down toward the beach. The moon still hangs above the water, but the sky is already beginning to lighten. Down here in the cove all is quiet and still. The only sound is the gentle rush of the sea as it ripples onto the shore; scrabbling white fingers of foam clutch at the sand before being pulled back, once more, into the inky water. I stand for a moment, looking out, and trying to calm the noise inside my mind.

I untie my mask and drop it by my side. I pull the beautiful green dress from my shoulders so that it slides down, pooling on the sand at my feet, and I step out of it, walking toward the sea in my shell-pink slip. Slowly, I wade into the water, my fingers trailing on the surface. Thanks to the alcohol I barely register the cold. Instead, the waves washing over me feel like silk ribbons being drawn across my feverish skin. I swim out a little way and then turn onto my back, spreading my arms and legs wide, just as Alice and I used to do when we were little. "We are starfish," Alice would say, as we floated side by side, and her fingers would wrap around mine, keeping us tethered together, suspended between the sea and the sky.

I stare up at the sky now as it shimmers in that moment between night and morning, and I feel small and light. My hair drifts out around my head like a halo. I concentrate only on the sound of my own breathing.

I don't know how long I float like that. It is probably only a couple of minutes, but it feels like longer. Eventually, I turn back over and swim to shore to find that there is someone waiting for me on the sand. Robert is sitting on one of the rocks, watching me. He wears a white shirt, open at the collar, and black trousers, and there is an unreadable expression on his face. I'm not sure how many of my own feelings are on display, but there are certainly a lot of them. The shock of seeing him is welcome and unwanted at the same time, and my heart aches in my chest.

I clamber out of the water, shivering as the cool air hits me and suddenly very aware that I am wearing only my underwear. Robert stands with his face turned away and his jacket held out in his hand. I slip into it gratefully, pulling the dark material tight around me, balling my hands up inside the long sleeves.

"What are you doing here?" I ask finally. Seeing him now,

after all that has happened tonight, stirs such a bewildering mix of feelings in me. I'm so conflicted, so confused. What do my feelings for Robert mean? What do I mean to him?

"I saw you come down," he says. "I wanted to make sure you didn't drown."

I smile at this, at the offhand way he says it. I find it reassuring, the normality of it. I snuggle further into his jacket, and perch on the rock he has been occupying. He sits next to me.

"Lou," he says after a moment. "There's something I need to tell you." He stops himself there, hesitating.

"Oh, really?" I say, nervously drawing circles in the sand with my toes. "There are lots of things I need to tell you."

"Are there?" he asks.

I nod. "I've had quite an eventful evening," I say. Filling the air between us with meaningless chatter seems like the only way I'm going to survive being so close to him. "I met a girl who thought I was called Cynthia."

"Ridiculous," Robert declares. "Who could ever mistake *you* for a Cynthia?"

"I heard a lot about a girl called Lois," I say. "Apparently this is her birthday party." I can't bring myself to meet his eye. "It seems that she's a local heiress who spends half the year in her family's estate in the south of France. She owns a yacht and part of a racehorse . . . though which part of the horse is a little unclear." Lois actually sounds like she would fit in perfectly, I think. She certainly doesn't sound an awful lot like me.

"She sounds dreadful," Robert says. "Just the sort of bore you would run into at a party like this."

"Oh, yes?" I say with a prickle of relief.

"Mmm." Robert nods. "I was beginning to despair of ever meeting anyone interesting again. Before we came here."

"Before you . . . came here?" I swallow nervously.

"Yes." He leans back on his elbows. "Before I met your aunt Irene. What a fascinating woman."

I smile tremulously, because the warmth in his teasing voice pierces me with such pleasure and pain that I feel like it might tear me apart.

"Lou, what's wrong?" he asks then, and his voice is tender, gentle, like I have never heard it before.

I shiver in his jacket and pull the back of my hand roughly across my eyes.

"It's nothing," I say. "I'm just . . . I'm so confused . . . and I saw something that surprised me." My voice wavers here. "Caitlin and Charlie were . . ." I trail off miserably here, because after all, this is only a tiny fragment of the story, but what more can I share with him?

"Ah." Robert exhales slowly.

"You don't sound surprised," I say quietly.

He is silent for a moment. "I am," he says, "but Charlie has made his interest known in the past . . . and Caitlin has a habit of making . . . rash decisions." He looks at me, his green eyes thoughtful. "I'm sorry if it has caused you pain, though." Then he takes a deep breath. "There's something I need to tell you," he announces for the second time.

"Oh, yes." I nod. "You did say and I interrupted you. I'm sorry, what is it?" I reach out and touch his arm apologetically.

And suddenly, just like that, something changes between us. It is as if something in the air around us shifts. We are sitting so close together, and I can feel the warmth coming from his body. I am suddenly very aware that the top of my leg is just grazing his. I can hear my heartbeat thundering in my ears. When I turn to face him his eyes are close enough for me to see the flecks of hazel in among the green. I watch my fingers reach up toward his face as though they belong to someone else. Surely this isn't my hand gently pushing back Robert's dark curls? He raises his own hand to mine, catching it there against his cheek. We sit like this for a moment, and that moment is sweet torture. I think I could kiss him now. I think he wants me to. But if I did, what would that make me? Kissing someone else's fiancé, dismissing the promise he made because it suits me. I'd be as bad as the rest of them.

I pull back. "I should go back to the house," I say, and my voice sounds hoarse.

The spell is broken. "Of course," he says, back to the polite, distant voice he uses for other people. "I'll see you back." Until this moment I hadn't realized that he has a different voice for me, but he does—a warm, teasing voice that is like a secret between us.

I go to collect my dress, which is thankfully none the worse for the adventure. I think ruefully of what Alice will have to say about leaving a bespoke couture creation in a pile on the sand, and decide that if we ever do make up I will never, ever tell her about it. Robert and I walk back to the house in silence. The sky is burning orange around the edges now, like touchpaper about to burst into flames, and the party has all but dispersed. Only a few of the more dedicated drinkers remain, slumped in corners or giggling together on the sofas. At the bottom of the stairs I turn to Robert. "Well, goodnight," I say, staring down at my feet.

"Goodnight," he replies. "And happy birthday." The words ring coldly in my ears.

I turn and stumble up the stairs, heading for my bedroom. Once I am safely inside I carefully hang up my beautiful green dress, trailing my fingers over the shimmering beads, the golden thread. It is then that I realize that I am still wearing Robert's coat. I brush the top of one of the sleeves, admiring the soft material. The front of the jacket is covered in elegant black frogging. I frown, looking at it more closely. I have seen this coat somewhere before.

I feel something dawning on me, a realization that is slowly, slowly making its way into my fuddled mind . . . This coat is just like Charlie's. I remember, very clearly indeed, the feel of this braiding beneath my fingers when we kissed. But why would Robert have Charlie's coat? The answer, of course, is that he wouldn't. I saw Charlie, wearing his coat, before I went down to the beach, and it certainly wouldn't have been at a convenient moment for Robert to ask to borrow it. This is Robert's costume, then, my brain finally concludes. Robert and Charlie have the same costume.

I freeze, a shiver running through me. With trembling hands, I reach into the jacket pockets and feel my fingers brush against a piece of soft, silky material. I can feel my pulse trapped at the base of my throat, beating insistently like the wings of a caged bird. Slowly, slowly, I pull the silk object out of my pocket and hold it in my hand. I know with absolute certainty what it will be, but the sight of it there, in front of me, still takes my breath away.

It is a black domino mask.

CHAPTER TWENTY-TWO

The next morning, I am feeling even more confused after a restless night full of dreams of masks and kisses and swirling faces with green eyes. It seems impossible to separate the dreams from the reality after such a strange evening. My stomach is in knots and my head is pounding. Robert . . . I kissed Robert last night. And that kiss is playing on an endless loop in my brain. I know that it shouldn't have happened, but now that it has, the memory of it is too searing and wonderful not to revisit. I lift a hand to my lips, remembering the feel of his mouth on mine. I think about repeating the kiss again and again, a million times more. Of curling my fingers into his dark hair, of pulling him against me.

Knowing that I have shared such a kiss with Robert

should feel like a shock, but instead it feels right in a way that scares me even more. None of this changes anything. Robert is not mine. Robert is getting married. Robert is marrying Laurie.

But what about Laurie and Elodie? What did I interrupt there? Is Laurie in love with someone else? And Robert might have kissed me but it really wasn't his fault; after all, I did literally throw myself at him. There wasn't a lot of time to protest as my lips smashed into his. I groan, waves of mortification rolling over me. *Only,* a voice in my head whispers, a wicked little voice that won't be quiet, *he didn't push you away. He didn't have to kiss you back. But he did.*

I groan again, balling my fists and slamming them ineffectually against the white bedsheets. I am just lying here going round and round in circles, much like the ceiling above my bed. There is nothing for it but to get up and face the music.

I drag myself from bed and go to the bathroom to splash my face with cold water, dismayed by the pale, drawn face looking back at me in the mirror. Eventually I manage to dress and stagger down to the dining room. Pushing the door open, I find Robert sitting at the table, alone. He gets to his feet and we stand staring at each other in silence. His eyes are careful, wary. I hold out my hand and the black mask unfurls from where I have been clutching it. His eyes meet mine and I see that he understands. That I *know.* He takes half a step forward, and his mouth opens to say something when Laurie appears behind me in a floral kimono dressing gown.

"Coffee!" she croaks, slumping into a chair. "Need coffee. Right now."

I shoot a desperate glance at Robert, stuffing the mask back into my pocket, but he has turned his attention to pouring coffee for Laurie. The pot is empty.

"Perkins," Robert calls, but the butler fails to materialize. "I'll grab it myself," Robert says quickly, taking in the air of desperation that is hanging around Laurie. He disappears from the room.

"I think I might have given you a shock last night," Laurie says now, turning to me with her eyebrows raised.

"Oh." I jump. "No . . . not really," I say awkwardly. She continues to look at me. "Well, maybe a little," I admit. "So you and Elodie are . . ." I hesitate here.

"Lovers." Laurie nods. She says it plainly, without emotion, as if she is commenting on the weather.

"I see," I say, dropping into a seat beside her.

Laurie laughs and takes my hand, squeezing it gently. "Poor Lou," she says. "I forget that anyone can find *anything* shocking these days."

"What . . . um, what about Robert?" I ask as casually as I can. "Aren't you in love with him?"

"In love with Robert?" Laurie frowns. "No more than he is with me." She says this lightly, as though it is not something terribly important. "Anyway, he doesn't mind," she says, waving her hand in the air. "Although he might tell me to be a bit more discreet than I was last night. It was those green cocktails, deadly things, had me throwing caution to the wind!"

"Robert knows that you . . . er . . ." I trail off, confused.

"That I enjoy the company of other people?" Laurie gives a throaty chuckle. "Sure he does. He and I are honest with each other. I have a great deal of respect for that man, and God knows marriages have been built on much less."

I am quiet for a moment, trying to absorb this. I knew that Laurie didn't exactly have a conventional view of marriage, but it hadn't occurred to me that she might not love him.

"Does Robert have his own . . ." I trail off again, too mortified to continue.

Laurie looks at me through narrowed eyes. "That," she says carefully, "is something you'll have to take up with him."

A feeling of intense nausea rolls over me. Perhaps this is it; perhaps this is why Robert kissed me back. Because he wanted to, because it meant so little, because who is about to be shocked by a little kissing between friends?

"I don't understand," I say, and my voice is tight as I hold back tears. "Why bother getting married at all?"

Laurie shifts a little in her seat. "That, if you don't mind me saying so, Lou, is a pretty naive question."

"Is it?" I ask weakly.

"Listen, honey." Laurie's voice is gentle now; she's still holding my hand, and it's as though she's explaining something unpleasant to a child who doesn't want to hear about it. Perhaps that's exactly what she is doing. "In the world that Robert and I live in, marriages are like business contracts," Laurie continues. "You have your wealthy American heiresses, with their fathers who have a soft spot for a title"— she gestures to herself here—"and you have your penniless British nobility, desperately trying to keep the family name going." She shrugs. "Everyone wins. It's a common story."

"Robert's marrying you because of . . . money?" I am horrified. Of all the things I thought Laurie might say, I never expected this. It seems so cold, so calculated. I can't imagine Robert making such a decision. Or can I? No. Perhaps the Robert I met at the beginning of the summer, but not the one I know now.

Laurie only laughs. "Well, I hope that's not the only reason." A smile clings to her rosy lips. "But, I guess, in the baldest terms, the answer is yes." Laurie lets go of my hand and sits back in her seat. "Neither of us wants a stuffy marriage," she continues. "He's a good man and he will make a good husband, just the kind my daddy and all his business cronies heartily approve of, but he's free to take his pleasure where he likes." She raises her arms over her head and stretches, a slow smile spreading across her face. "As am I."

I sit, digesting this, and staring at the empty teacup in front of me. I think part of me thought that if Robert and Laurie loved other people perhaps they wouldn't get married. But here it is; Laurie is telling me that they can both see other people whenever they like. What happened with Robert and me meant nothing to him. I am just another girl that he has kissed at a party. The novelty of me will wear off soon enough, and then, like Lucky, I'll be cast aside and forgotten. And the wedding will go ahead anyway, because that is just the way these things work. Marriage is a contract, and I'm naive for thinking it is anything more. For using words like "love." I feel completely adrift as I sit at that table. How can I have been so oblivious?

Robert reappears then with a silver coffee pot in his hand. He pours a cup for Laurie and she stands, kissing him on the cheek as she accepts it. I keep my eyes down, looking at the ground. I can't bear to meet Robert's eye—I don't know what I will find there.

The three of us sit in silence, a clock ticking sullenly in the background. I pour a cup of tea and warm my hands around the cup. It is another sunny day, but for some reason I can't seem to stop shivering. The silence feels thick and oppressive, and I don't know what to say to break it. I need to leave. I am going to leave.

It turns out that I don't get a chance to. At that moment Charlie bursts into the room, dragging Caitlin behind him. Charlie's handsome face is radiant; he is wearing a grin that stretches from ear to ear. The same cannot be said of Caitlin, whose face is pale and pinched. She is carefully avoiding my eye, and in other circumstances it might be funny how many of us in this small group are trying not to look at each other. Charlie, like an enthusiastic puppy, is oblivious to any tension.

"We have big news!" The words burst from him in a rush.

"Caitlin and me . . . I've finally worn her down . . . we're getting married!"

The teacup in my hand clatters back against its saucer as I almost drop it onto the table. I feel Robert and Laurie both looking at me. Caitlin's eyes are still on the floor. *Married.* That word again that means so little here. Now Caitlin is going to marry Charlie? Of all people?

"Well, that's wonderful, darlings." Laurie breaks the silence, getting to her feet. She hugs her brother and then Caitlin. "Such a surprise, but really wonderful."

Robert gets to his feet as well and shakes Charlie's hand. "Congratulations," he says quietly. His eyes meet mine and I feel a stab of pain as I see the concern there.

Plastering on a brilliant grin, I stand too. "Yes," I say, and my voice feels too loud, as though it has suddenly outgrown me. I can't bear to be complicit in this. I am acting a part in this scene and I know it's all for show. "Congratulations, Charlie. That's really . . . I'm so pleased for you. Now"—my voice is bright—"I'm sorry I can't stay to celebrate, but this seems like a family occasion. I think I'd better be going."

"I'll take you home." Robert is moving toward me, but I raise my hand.

"No, no," I say, and I can feel a dangerous wobble in my voice that I try to control. "You stay here, celebrate."

Laurie places a hand on Robert's arm. "She's right, Robert," she says. "Lou can get home just fine. She knows the way."

I flash her a grateful look, because I don't think I can

342

bear to be with Robert, with any of them any longer, and I feel tears starting in my eyes. "Of course I do," I say. "So I'll see you soon. And thanks again for the party." I turn and leave the room with as much dignity as I can muster. I walk straight out of the house and stand on the gravel driveway taking deep, shuddering breaths of the fresh air.

Hearing a crunching sound behind me, I spin around to find that Caitlin has run out after me. She looks at me and her eyes are sad.

"I'm sorry," she says softly.

"You're sorry?" I repeat, and my voice sounds like it's coming from far away.

She nods. "I am. So sorry."

"Why are you sorry?" I ask.

"Be-because I didn't tell you, and because I know you like him, and now I . . . ," she stammers.

"God, Caitlin!" I exclaim. "Don't you understand? This isn't anything to do with him. This is about you. Do *you* love Charlie?"

She stops, and her face is ashen. "I like him," she says.

"Do you love him?" I ask again, and my voice is a needle.

"You know I don't," she whispers.

"Then what are you doing?" I cry. "Why are you doing this? I don't understand *any* of this. I don't understand what's going on here. You'll be miserable, and he'll be miserable because you are."

"I'm sorry," she whispers again. "I know you're right, but I was so sad, and Charlie says that if we get married he'll

343

take me away, back to America, and I just want to leave it all behind and I just . . . I just said yes." She holds her hands in front of her as if she is surrendering. I feel myself deflate as I take in her pale face, her slight frame shaking as she begins to cry. I move forward and put my arms around her.

"I understand," I say. "But, Caitlin, what do you really want? Is it really worth this? Lying to everyone, to Charlie, to Robert? Are you going to build a marriage on a lie? You shouldn't be doing this, Caitlin. You love Lucky."

"You don't know what you're talking about." Caitlin stiffens.

"I saw you together," I say. "I saw his face. He loves you."

"Don't." Caitlin pulls away. "Don't talk about that."

"Why not?" I'm frustrated. "Someone has to. You won't talk about it, Caitlin, not to me, not to anyone. No one here talks to each other. There are so many secrets."

Her hands are curled up by her side now, and she paces, agitated. "You have no right to bring Freddy into this." She sways a little here; just saying his name seems to untether her. "You're supposed to be my friend. Those things are private."

"I am your friend," I say, shocked that she is lashing out like this. "And you can talk to me about this, you *should* talk to me about this. You can trust me."

"I can't talk to you." Caitlin's face is empty now. "I can't talk to anyone. Don't you understand? I'm Lady Caitlin Cardew. I have to do everything perfectly. I have to look perfect and I have to be bright and gay and throw the perfect party. Those are my jobs. I have to do them perfectly because otherwise none of *this* means *anything*. My father died and Robert and I are all that's left. We have to keep things going as he would want them. I cannot run away and live in some fantasy. I cannot create that kind of scandal." She is standing taller now, but her voice is hoarse with unshed tears. It hurts just to look at her. "I cannot do that to his memory," she finishes.

"Caitlin," I say, and I reach out my hand.

She shakes her head. "You think it's so easy, Lou," she says quietly. "You watch us and you write about us in your notebooks and you judge us, but we're just doing the best we can."

"Is that what you really think?" I feel a sob rising in my own throat. "I care about you, Caitlin. I care about what is happening to you. I just want you to be happy."

"I told you once," Caitlin says, "people can be unhappy anywhere. Now you know it's really true." With that she folds her arms around her waist and turns, walking back to the house.

I watch her go for a moment, and my heart is breaking. I feel small and brittle, as though a sturdy breeze could be enough to blow me away, splintered like dandelion seeds on the air. Finally, I turn and walk out onto the causeway. It is time to return to my real life.

This time, I don't look back.

CHAPTER TWENTY-THREE

After I leave the Cardew House in a daze I find my legs carrying me straight to Alice. She opens the door, clearly ready for round two of our fight, but after one look at my face she sends Jack packing instead and puts the kettle on. I fall into her arms and she holds me while I cry, terrible, hacking, red-faced tears, soothing me and stroking my hair away from my face. I tell her everything, all of it, even about leaving the dress on the beach while I swam (and there *is* a sharp intake of breath at this point), and she listens calmly, without interrupting, without judging. I tell her about Robert, about the way that he makes me feel, about the kiss, about the way that he looks at me sometimes. I tell her that I don't understand the choices he is making, that I'm scared that he may not be the person I thought. That I feel like that house is running on some secret set of rules that I don't understand.

I tell her about the way this summer swept me away into something new and exciting. I talk about my feeling of being adrift, of not knowing what I want to do. I confess to her all of my petty, jealous thoughts and how difficult I found it when she left. I tell her that I know I'm selfish, a monster, but that I don't think her life is small . . . not at all. It's my own life that feels mean and aimless and I don't know what to do about it.

At the end of all of this Alice sits quietly, sipping her tea. "Well," she says finally, "I wish you had talked to me about all of this sooner. I know it's difficult now, but I think you have to realize that something good has come out of this whole experience."

"Oh, really?" I sniffle. "And what's that?"

"You saw something, Lou," she says, leaning forward and squeezing my hand. "You saw something different this summer. Another way. You met people, you went out into the world. You didn't just watch, you didn't just follow. You were *part* of something."

"I suppose," I say, wrapping my arms tightly around my stomach as I sit in one of the battered armchairs.

"You went to London," Alice says, "and you saw all those people, living their lives. You said yourself that the world is a lot bigger than Penlyn. Why are you so intent on keeping yourself here, on shrinking down trying to fit in when you can go anywhere you want?"

"You mean leave?" I say, dazed, and I let Alice's words sink in. They feel like a balm. Could I ever be brave enough to do such a thing? To make my own way like that? To break away from everything and everyone I know?

"People move to London all the time." Alice's voice is soft.

"Not from Penlyn they don't," I point out hesitantly. "Especially not girls on their own."

"No," she says, and then that familiar dimple appears. "But there's a first time for everything."

"But what about Midge and Pa?" I ask. "What about you?"

"Lou, you have to stop worrying. You and I want different things. And that's OK. They're all good things, they're just . . . different. There's no one way to be. I'm not the mold you need to fit into. You have to live your own life, and I don't understand why you would think that I don't want that for you."

I launch myself at her, throwing myself into her chair and hugging her tightly. "I'm so sorry," I whisper. "I'm so, so sorry. I am an idiot."

"You are," she says simply. "Now stop squishing the baby."

"Oh!" I leap back, but Alice is laughing. "Hey," I say. "This is no laughing matter, that's my little niece or nephew in there."

"Niece, definitely." Alice grins.

"I don't know," I muse. "That bump looks like a boy to me."

"There *is* a bump, isn't there?" She pats her stomach. "Jack says you can't tell yet, but I think you can."

"You can definitely tell," I agree, curling back up in my chair.

Alice looks at me and clears her throat, her face earnest. "Well, now that we're friends again, can we talk about something important?" she asks solemnly, leaning forward and clasping her hands together.

I shift anxiously in my seat and nod.

"I love your hair," she says. "Do you think mine would look good like that?"

When I leave Alice's house I feel a lot better. Still sad and hurting, but full of some new sense of purpose.

I am trying hard not to think about Robert. This is made much more difficult by the fact that he is waiting for me when I arrive home.

My heart twists at the sight of him sitting on the doorstep, his elbows on his knees, his dark, curly head resting in his hands. When he looks up and sees me he jumps to his feet. He looks disheveled, much less pristine than usual.

"Hello," he says in a low voice. "I was worried about you."

"I was at Alice's," I reply, coming to a stop in front of him. "What are you doing here?"

"You always seem to be asking me that," he says with a faint smile. He rubs a hand across his jaw.

I remain silent, glued to the spot. There has been so much to take in, I feel hollow, wrung out.

"I thought we should talk," he says. "After last night."

"Right," I murmur. He's come to apologize, I realize. He's come to apologize for that kiss that meant so much to me, and to clear things up between us. I can't bear it. I can't bear to hear his careful explanation, to have him let me down gently in that same practical voice that Laurie used. I won't let him. "I'm sorry about that," I say, as lightly as I can manage.

"You're sorry?" he asks, and it sounds like a loaded question.

"Yes." The word sounds small. "It was all my fault. I didn't know it was you. If I had known, obviously I wouldn't have . . ." I lift my hand, feebly, trailing off here.

"I see." His voice is cool. "I see," he says again.

"Laurie . . . explained some things to me this morning," I exhale finally.

There is silence. "Lou," Robert says, and his voice is gentle. "I wish you would look at me."

It takes an enormous effort to lift my gaze to meet his. I feel as though my whole heart is in my eyes, as if he'll be able to see right into me, to see every single thing I feel for him.

"Come and sit down," he says, gesturing to the step that he has recently vacated. "Talk to me."

We both sit. I fiddle nervously with the hem of my dress.

"What did Laurie say to you?" Robert asks.

"She explained a bit," I say. "About your arrangement.

350

About the—um—openness." I feel my face turn red at that. "And about the money." I definitely can't look at him now.

There is a long silence, and we sit side by side. The warmth from his body is intoxicating. It's all I can do not to lean against him.

Robert lets out a long breath. "I need to tell you something," he says. "I need to explain. To help you see why this"—he waves his hand in the air as though gesturing to the whole world around us—"has happened." He puts his head in his hands again, his fingers pulling at his hair. I can't help it, I reach out and put the palm of my hand against his arm. He reaches over and puts his own hand on top of it, squeezing my fingers.

"I suppose it all starts with my father's death." Robert's voice is tight, and I can tell that the words are difficult for him. "I don't know how much you know?" He looks at me.

"Not very much," I say carefully. "An accident at the house in Derbyshire."

"Mmm." Robert makes a sound in the back of his throat. "Our father was a good man," he says. "But when he came back from the war he was . . . different."

I nod encouragingly. I have a little experience with this.

"He was sad, terribly sad. And angry." He is talking faster. "We tried to help him, but there was just nothing we could do. We weren't enough; we couldn't be what he needed. It took me a while to understand, but in a lot of ways he was still fighting. And then he was . . . lost." There is a tiny pause, and I find I am holding my breath as something big and terrible seems to fill the air. Robert steels himself for the words, and then, finally, they come. "It wasn't in Derbyshire, and it wasn't an accident. He killed himself."

"Oh, Robert." My hand is in his now, and I bring it to my cheek.

He smiles a grim sort of smile. "It's OK," he says. "Well, it's not OK, obviously. Frankly, it's the absolute opposite of OK." His voice is hollow. "Afterward, I didn't know what to do. It turned out that he had made some fairly catastrophic financial decisions, and things were left in a real mess. Suddenly I was supposed to be Lord Cardew and to find a way to manage the whole failing estate while keeping all the gory details of his death out of the wretched press, who were hovering like vultures. We struggled on for a while . . . it took about a year for me to find out the full extent of the damage. Meanwhile"—he closes his eyes here—"Caitlin was falling completely to pieces. It was worse for her, much worse than it was for me." He turns and looks me straight in the eye. "She was the one who found him, you see. In the house in London."

"Oh, God." I shudder, burying my face in my hands.

"I don't know what happened between you two this morning," he says quietly, "but you should know what she's been through. I know she should be the one to tell you, but I honestly don't think she knows how."

I nod, unable to speak.

"After that Caitlin was ill, very ill. She couldn't sleep, she hardly ate, she was anxious all the time and her behavior was erratic." My heart hurts at the vulnerability in his voice. Doesn't he see that Caitlin is still like that?

"I know what you're thinking," he says, reading my expression at once. "But she was worse, much worse than she is now. I had to have her . . . she had to stay in a hospital for a while." His voice is tight with emotion as he says this, and I feel my own heart stutter as that piece of the puzzle falls into place. I can only imagine how difficult it has been for both of them. "Afterward she seemed to be getting better, and we came to Cornwall to get away from London and all the bad memories. We had already closed the big house in town. Neither of us has been there since the . . . incident; that's why you didn't stay there when you went to London with Caitlin. But I thought in Cornwall we could have a real break from it all." He smiles ruefully. "It was our mother's favorite place, you see, but we haven't spent much time there. It's not so haunted by memories. I think it helped at first, but recently she seems to be getting worse again, and there's just nothing I can do . . ." He trails off here, and the look on his face is one of total helplessness.

I think about my friend, about all the pain she carries with her, about her brittleness. She's putting so much energy into convincing people who don't care a bit about her that she's all right, simply for the sake of appearances. She's burning herself out, just as Lucky said. Ash and bone. I want to put my head in my hands and weep.

"When I met Laurie," Robert continues in a low voice, "a practical arrangement seemed like a good option. Laurie shared some of the weight, made me feel less alone. Most of all I wanted to protect Caitlin, from scandal, from any further upset, from going without any of the things that are important to her." He pauses here. "And I care a great deal about Laurie. She and I are real friends, and I have her to thank for keeping this whole show running. Caitlin doesn't know the financial situation, and Laurie has helped me to keep it that way. I will never be able to repay her kindnesses to us both." He stops, and a silence falls over us.

There it is. The whole truth. Except it's not, I realize, because Robert doesn't know about Lucky, and Caitlin doesn't know about the money, and Robert doesn't know that Caitlin doesn't want the life that he is sacrificing himself to give her, that it is causing her more pain. What a mess.

"I think you need to talk to your sister," I say finally.

Robert's eyes register his surprise at this response.

I hold up my hand to stop him from talking. "I know why you haven't, and it's really up to you, but I think that you should. I think there are things that both of you need to say. For her, as well as for you." I stop there, because to push any further would be to spill secrets that aren't mine to share.

And I stop because I know now that this means good-bye, and I understand why. I love Laurie too, and Robert will never do anything to hurt her. I am glad about that at the same time as I am devastated by it. I think that somewhere in his confession he is telling me that he cares for me, but I see that it doesn't matter now.

I get to my feet and so does he.

"I brought you this," he says, picking up a white box that I hadn't noticed sitting on the ground beside him. "I wanted to give it to you before we leave."

"Leave?" I say, and the word is a whisper.

"Yes." He clears his throat. "Now that the engagement is about to be announced we're all going back to London to see to the arrangements. Apparently Charlie and Caitlin want to do it quickly." Even though I have always known it would end, that they would go, the sudden reality of it all leaves me breathless.

"I see," I say, and I take the box from him, tucking it under one arm.

"Goodbye, Lou," he says softly.

"Goodbye," I reply.

And then he leans forward and kisses me on the cheek. It is the briefest touch of his lips against my skin, and a drop of rain in the desert. I don't watch as he walks away. I stand perfectly still, my trembling fingers pressed to my mouth.

Sitting back down on the step, I open the box. The tears come in earnest then. Inside is my green dress carefully wrapped in tissue paper.

PART THREE

"Life starts all over again when it
gets crisp in the fall."

—F. Scott Fitzgerald, *The Great Gatsby*

CHAPTER TWENTY-FOUR

SEPTEMBER 1929

It is four weeks later and Alice is helping me to pack up my bedroom. It turns out that Uncle Albie's cousin knows someone who knows someone who is looking for a typist in London, and Mrs. Bastion's nephew's wife's friend has a room to let in a boarding house for young women. Much more importantly, the magazine that Robert encouraged me to write to has bought my story, and I will be writing monthly installments for their readers. It will barely pay enough to keep me in typewriter ribbon, but I will be a real writer, and my words will be in print. The thought is electrifying. I sent off the pages the day that the Cardews left, in Robert's envelope. It's one final gift from a summer that has changed everything.

Once word gets out that I am moving to London "like one

of them young, independent *New Women,*" everyone has an opinion. Fortunately for me, enough people enjoy running contrary to Aunt Irene that when she blows a gasket over me throwing away my virtue and good name, they rally around. I become something of a pet project for the village, and people are dropping in at all hours with strange and wonderful objects that they think I may need for the move. Mrs. Penrith has just brought over four big bags of flour because she has heard that the cost of bread in London is absolutely criminal.

"You'll never fit all of this lot in Gerald," Alice says, surveying the mountains of stuff that surround us. My room looks like we are about to stage an enormous jumble sale.

"I know." I sigh. "Still, I suppose I can leave some stuff behind . . . Freya will go mad, though, she's so excited about having our old room. She's not upset about me leaving at all."

"Well, she's the only one." Alice slings an arm around my shoulder.

"Just think how much fun we'll have when you come to visit me," I say, resting my head on her shoulder. "I might actually know where I'm going by then. I can show you around."

"As long as you know the way to all the good clothes shops we'll be fine," Alice says, moving away and grabbing another bucket, which she throws onto the "discard" pile.

"Why *do* you have so many buckets?" she asks.

"I have no idea," I say, shaking my head. "People keep bringing them over. I dread to think what they're for."

There is a knock, and Pa sticks his head around the door. "How is it going, girls?"

Of all the surprising things that have happened lately, I have to say that my parents' response to me wanting to move to London has been up there. I expected tears, hurt, anger. What I got was support.

"Of course you're going to go," Midge said placidly as I stood with my mouth hanging open.

"But . . . but . . . ," I sputtered. "Don't you want me to stay here and settle down and get married like Alice?"

Pa and Midge exchanged a look. "Why would we want you to do the same thing as Alice?" Midge asked, perplexed. "You two are as different as chalk and cheese and always have been."

"Why do you think we gave you that typewriter?" Pa said. "Time for you to go and set the world alight, our girl."

Of course I cried then. It seems the Cardew family doesn't have the monopoly on misunderstanding each other.

Now, Pa is holding out a small parcel. "This came for you, Lou." I take it, recognizing the messy handwriting on the front immediately. Alice catches the expression on my face and tugs Pa away by the elbow.

"OK, Pa," she says. "Let's go and have a look at the pile downstairs." And she leads him out of the room, so that I am alone.

I sit on the bed and stare at the parcel for several minutes, wondering at what it might contain, and then, taking a deep breath, I tear it open. Inside is a letter.

Dearest, darling Lou,

I am writing this letter to you from the most terrible dive in Paris and I could not be any happier about it. Freddy is sitting across the table from me, and he says to send you his best love, although I told him that you would happily settle for second best, after me.

My darling friend, I am more sorry than you will ever know for how we parted that morning in Cornwall. What you said to me was right, but I was too afraid to hear it. I hope that one day you will be able to forgive me. I called it off with Charlie almost immediately, and I think the poor boy knew in the end that he had had a lucky escape!

Not long after we got back to London, Robert and I had the first completely frank conversation that we have had since our father died. He told me that he had filled you in on the grisly details and, darling, I am truly relieved that you know. Not sharing it with you myself was another mistake, but it seems that I am full of those. I have got some help now, and I am trying to do better about opening up. Robert and I were keeping far too much from one another, while trying to do what was best, and it was only because of you that we were able to untangle ourselves. For that, and for so many other things, I will always be grateful.

Of course, I should have had more faith in my

brother. Freddy and I are together now, with his blessing. I think I would have gone with Freddy anyway—I hope I would have found the courage—but I have to admit that Robert's support has lifted a heavy weight from me. It was Elodie who suggested Paris, and she was quite right. Freddy's band has taken the city by storm, as you might expect. Things are so much easier for us here, and for the first time in such a long, long time I feel . . . <u>free</u>.

Robert and Laurie have called off their engagement. It happened two weeks ago, and I think they have managed to keep it out of the press so far. Robert has been so careful not to mention you that I know he has been thinking about you incessantly. Call it female intuition if you like, but I think you need to hear this: the two of you <u>belong</u> together.

We are selling the Cornwall house now. It is one of the only things I will miss, and much of that is down to you. Thank you for being there this summer; your friendship was truly a life belt that kept me from drowning. Every day I will be grateful that you climbed into our tree.

If you want to write back to me it would make me very happy, although I quite understand if you don't. I would love to hear all of your news and how you are getting on. I miss you quite terribly.

Your loving friend,
Caitlin

P.S. I know how much you loved Robert's sketches.
He left this lying around and I couldn't resist stealing
it. I think it's time it found its way to you.

I am filled with an enormous sense of relief. I am so happy for Caitlin, happy that she finally has what she wants. And I'm grateful to her for writing, for valuing a friendship that has become so important to me and for the real affection that lies behind every word. Of course I will write back to her. I will do it soon, and I will tell her about my London plans and the way I am striking out on my own. I know that she will enjoy that.

The information about Robert is harder to digest. Two weeks. His engagement ended two weeks ago. Whatever Caitlin might say to the contrary, any part of me that thought he felt the same way I did dies then. Before, I could have believed it was his engagement to Laurie that was keeping us apart, but now that is ended and he still hasn't come for me. I was wrong. It feels like dropping from a great height, the rush of blood in my ears, the furious blurring of the world around me.

Alongside the letter the parcel contains a small black notebook. I open it and freeze.

Inside are dozens of sketches drawn with a deft hand and crackling with life. They are scenes from *Lady Amelia's Revenge.* Some of the sketches have dates beside them, and I realize that the first one goes all the way back to when Robert and I first met. As the weeks go by, the sketches become more detailed, more definite. The heroine looks, I think, an awful lot like me. When I get to Lord Marvell I can't help but laugh. There is Robert at his most smirking. He has drawn himself half in shadow, but I can still tell it is him. I pore over every drawing, committing each one to memory, tracing my fingers over the bold, black lines. There is so much time and effort in these pages, so much life and humor. It is the most wonderful thing I have ever seen, and my heart aches for the man who made it.

I sit and stare at the drawings for a long time. Alice will have gone home by now, I know. I will go round in the morning and tell her what has happened. She'll be with Jack, and I don't want to disturb them. I heave myself to my feet and carry on halfheartedly with my packing, until the room is in slightly better order. I want to keep moving, to keep busy so that I don't have too much time to think about what Caitlin has written. It is early evening by the time I am done, and my limbs are tired from lugging things back and forth and up and down all the stairs. With a sigh, I kneel on my bed, pushing the window open and sticking my head out into the cooler air. The temperature has dropped in the last couple of weeks. Summer really is at an end.

I decide to take a walk and clear my head, so I stick my feet in some battered old shoes and pull on a scruffy cardigan— one of Midge's terrible creations that hasn't made it into a box. The breeze coming off the sea has a definite chill to it, and I pull the cardigan more tightly around me. I pretend to myself that I don't know where I am walking to, but I absolutely do. The tide is out, and I pick my way across the cobbled causeway toward the house, which I know now is sleeping once more.

I head for the orchard. The first of the apples will be perfectly ripe, and I help myself to the reddest, rosiest one I can find. I go around to the back lawn next, and over to the oak tree. I place my hand against the bark, closing my eyes and remembering that kiss, but also the first time I saw Robert. How he looked at me, how he dared me to stay and drink champagne. How that moment changed everything.

A deep rumble splits the air, and before I know it the heavens have opened and it is pouring with rain. I run over to the house, to the window with the broken latch. Somehow, I discover with relief, they have fixed everything else, but not this. I slip inside, shaking the rain from myself like a dog. I peel off the soggy cardigan and set about lighting a fire. The furniture is all under dust sheets again, and everything is back as it was when the house was mine alone.

But not quite. Now, I can see Laurie slinking through the door, I can see Caitlin draped over a sofa, I can see Robert at the bar, accusing me of cheating at cards. I think about the girl I was before and the girl I am now. Whatever else has happened, my life has been changed completely this summer. I have made something happen for myself, and perhaps I no longer quite belong in this house of shadows. I shiver, fumbling with the matches. Finally, the fire is burning and I begin to dry my hair, feeling the warmth spread through my frozen bones.

I am sitting in front of the fire eating my apple when I hear a loud bang. I freeze. Footsteps clip along the floor, the sound ringing through the air toward me.

I leap to my feet and move to grab my cardigan, ready to make my escape, but this time I am too slow and I have hardly moved at all when the door bursts open. There, standing right in front of me, is Robert. He is wearing an overcoat, and he is soaking wet. I watch, hypnotized, as drops of water fall from his dark hair and onto the floor.

The apple drops from my hand with a dull thud, and it rolls over to his feet, gently kissing his right shoe. He bends and picks it up, looking at it with great interest.

"What—what are you doing here?" I choke. It feels as though I've wished him into being. I can't believe he's truly standing in front of me. It must be a dream, some ghostly apparition that the house is teasing me with.

He smiles, a smile that goes right through me, and I see bright lights exploding in front of my eyes. I almost stumble forward, but just about remain upright. He's here. He's really here.

"What am *I* doing here?" he says casually, taking off his coat in neat, efficient movements and hanging it over the back of one of the dust-sheet-covered objects. He moves closer to the fire, closer to me. My heart is thundering in my chest. "It's my house," he says. "I think the question is, what are *you* doing here?"

I don't say anything, can't say anything. All words are gone. There's something in his eyes that's too good to be true; I can't let myself believe it yet. I just watch as he holds the apple out toward me. "This time, little thief, there's no getting out of it. I've caught you red-handed."

I look at him, and now I really do start to believe it. I feel a smile spreading across my face, a huge, unstoppable smile that makes me feel lit up like a Christmas tree. Trying hard to look serious, I reach out and take the apple from him, glancing down at it. "Surely you wouldn't begrudge a girl shelter from the storm," I say slowly.

He raises an eyebrow; his eyes are glittering. "I suppose not," he replies.

"Of course not," I say. "That would be completely heartless."

"Mmm," Robert agrees, "which I most certainly am not."

"Maybe not," I say, tilting my head to the side. "And what about a little sustenance? Would you deny a girl that? To keep her going?" I look up at him.

He laughs. "No, not that either."

"So I wasn't really doing anything wrong when I . . . ," I begin, and then I can't say anything else because he has pulled me into his arms and he is kissing me as if he can't stop himself. Not that I want him to. I melt into him, the taste of him, the feel of his lips against my skin. It is all I have been able to think about for these last four weeks and here it is, finally happening. Kissing Robert Cardew is as good as I remember . . . better, even, because this time there are no misunderstandings, no secrets between us. When we eventually break apart, I look up into his eyes and see so much there that my heart feels as though it might burst.

"Robert," I say finally. "What *are* you doing here?"

"Having a very nice time," he murmurs, kissing my neck in a way that turns my knees to water.

"Robert!" I gasp, and he grins, kissing my nose, but I am not to be distracted. I need to understand why he is here to be able to believe it all.

"Fine," he says. "I'll tell you the whole story." He sits on the floor in front of the fire and pulls me down next to him, his arm around my waist.

"Now, tell me," I demand. My head is reeling, and while I couldn't be much happier about my current situation, I have absolutely no idea how it has come to pass.

"I came to see you," he says simply. "I tried to stay away, but I couldn't. I drove down to Cornwall in the rain like a madman and I was headed for the farm when I saw the smoke coming from the chimney here. It wasn't hard to guess who had broken in."

"Why were you trying to stay away?" I ask, frowning.

Robert rubs his fingers across my forehead, smoothing the frown away. "Well, for starters, I was sort of under the impression that you were in love with Charlie," he says.

"What?!" I pull away to get a better look at him.

He nods. "I see now that I had that part wrong."

"Of course you had that wrong," I say. "What on earth were you thinking?"

"Well, to be fair, you did rather throw yourself at me and call me by his name," Robert says mildly.

I blush crimson. "Well, that is not really the whole story . . ."

"And when I tried to talk to you about it, you said that you had no idea it was me. A thought that, by the way, made me feel completely miserable."

"Did it?" I ask, dazed.

"Yes," he says. "And you also told me that if you had known it was me, then you definitely wouldn't have kissed me in the first place." Robert doesn't look like he enjoys remembering that bit of the conversation.

"Ah," I say. "I can see how that *could* look bad."

"How generous of you to admit," Robert says.

"But in my defense," I protest, "I did think you were going to apologize for the kiss and tell me that it was a mistake, so I just got in first."

"I see," Robert says indulgently. "Very sensible."

"I thought so at the time," I huff, needled.

"Mmm." Robert continues. "And then, you know, Caitlin was always going on about you and Charlie, and when she announced her engagement you seemed so upset . . . so you see, until about ten minutes ago I had no idea that you were pining for me."

"I wasn't *pining* for you," I exclaim, trying to recover some sense of dignity.

"Well, I was pining for you," Robert says.

"Were you?" I ask. "Really?"

"Yes." He nods. "And for much longer than you were pining for me, I think. I was planning to come here and throw myself at your feet and just hope for the best."

"So, you thought I liked Charlie . . . Is that why you didn't tell me when you and Laurie called off the engagement?" I ask, and he nods again.

"That, and another reason," he says. "You didn't correct me on the pining front that time," he points out.

"No." I smile. "I didn't." There is a pause. "I'm sorry about Laurie," I say. "I mean, I'm not really sorry, obviously." I smile up at him. "But I hope it was OK. For both of you."

"I told you she was kind," he says, his eyes holding something teasing in them. "And this one I really can't ever repay her for. You see, she knew that I'd fallen in love with someone else."

Then he kisses me again, and again, and this time we are on the floor, and this opens up all sorts of interesting possibilities that we are both keen to explore. And as Robert kisses me I feel beautiful and desirable and burning up with love for this handsome, funny, maddening man.

"Oh, Robert!" I say, at one point, breaking away from him. "I'm moving to London."

"Are you, darling?" he murmurs.

"Yes, in a couple of days," I say, screwing up my nose. "I have a job and a place to live, and I'm excited about it."

"I'm glad," he says, propping himself up on one arm.

"Are you?"

"Of course." He grins. "It's wonderful. And I don't know if you know this, but *I* actually live in London."

I bite back a smile, tracing the dip at the base of his throat with my finger. "Rrrrreally?" I drawl, lifting one eyebrow in what I hope is a perfect impression of him.

He laughs, catching my hand against his chest and lowering his mouth to mine, kissing me so sweetly that my whole body tingles. "Really," he breathes.

"Oh!" I exclaim, suddenly remembering. "What was the other reason that you didn't tell me straightaway when you called off the engagement?"

Robert lies back then, and a frown appears on his face. This time it is my turn to smooth it away.

"Ah," he says. "That."

"Yes," I say, poking him in the chest. "That. Come on, out with it."

"Well, the other thing about the engagement ending is that a lot of things in my life are changing," he says quietly. "I've worked hard to make the best of it, but there's nothing like the money needed to continue as we were. We're selling this place, of course, but that's just the start. I'm afraid I might not be quite the . . . um . . . prize I once was."

I look down at him for a moment, and then burst out laughing. I can't believe any of this is real. The giggles leave me clutching my stomach, gasping for air. "Did you really just refer to yourself as a prize?" I snort.

Robert looks a bit miffed. "Well, yes, but I—"

I dissolve into laughter again, and finally he joins me. "You are *such* a brat," he says, reaching up and tickling me so that I laugh harder, crashing into his chest. I lie there for a second, perfectly happy. How quickly everything has changed. Nothing is as I thought it was.

"Of course it is a hard pill to swallow that I'll be giving up the diamond-encrusted motorcar." I sigh.

I feel him smiling against my hair. "Yes, I can see that it would be."

"I'll have to make do, I suppose," I say, lifting myself up onto my elbow and looking down at him. "When we get to London maybe I can treat you to a nice supper." I run my finger along his jawline, marveling at his perfect face, a perfect face that I can touch and kiss as much as I like.

"That," Robert says, his eyes warm and full of laughter, "sounds like heaven. And as luck would have it, I'm headed that way myself. I'll give you a lift."

"But not *right* now," I say, smiling down at him teasingly.

He pulls me toward him. "No," he mutters against my mouth. "Not right now."

ACKNOWLEDGMENTS

This book is absolutely the book of my heart and it would not exist without the help and support of a huge team of wonderful people.

First of all, thank you to my agent and kindred spirit, Louise Lamont, who listened to my first vague, rambling description of this book and immediately knew what it was. I am so lucky to get to hang out/work with you, and every element of this book is better because of your involvement.

Thank you to the whole team at Scholastic. I have been so overwhelmed by your dedication and enthusiasm, and by how well you have loved this book and looked after me through this whole process. I have had the greatest editorial team imaginable, who are really responsible for everything good here: Gen Herr, whose belief in this book meant everything to me; Jenny Glencross, whose talent made things shine; and Sophie Cashell, who cheered me on at every opportunity.

Thank you all so much. Working on this project with you has been one of the most joyful creative experiences of my life and I have loved it.

A huge thank-you to Jamie Gregory and Yehrin Tong for creating the most beautiful cover I have ever seen. When you love something so much it is difficult to imagine anyone being able to capture that feeling for you, but you guys did that for me and I am so grateful. Thank you to the brilliant Róisín O'Shea and to Olivia Horrox for being so lovely and for taking the book on its own tour of Cornwall when I couldn't. Thank you to Pete Matthews, Jessica White and Emma Jobling, and to all of the amazing people at Scholastic who reached out just to say that they loved the book . . . I can't tell you how much that meant to me.

Thank you to the brilliant bloggers who cheered me on when I was feeling nervous at the Bloggers' Book Feast and who have been so sweet and generous in their support ever since. Special thanks to Chelley Toy and Amy McCaw who gave me so much joy on Twitter at a nerve-racking time.

Thank you to my friends and family for all their love and support. It's hard to write a brief paragraph on how much you all mean to me, but I hope that you know. Special thanks to my nan and paps, who let me steal from their lives and who gave me Cornwall. Thank you always to my mum and dad, whose love and pride borders on the embarrassing— you are my favorite people and I love you so much. And, of course, thank you to Paul. Without you, there would be no books. I love you and I like you.

LAURA WOOD is an award-winning author who lives in a cottage in the English countryside. She recently received a PhD from the University of Warwick, where she taught about nineteenth-century literature, feminism, and children's literature. When she's not traveling to far-flung places, she enjoys watching old movies and swooning over good romance novels. *A Sky Painted Gold* is her YA debut.

lauraclarewood.com